The Kitty Hawk Cowboy

An Outer Banks
of
North Carolina Novel

J. Willis Sanders

BUGGS ISLAND BOOKS

Printed in the United States of America
Cover art by BookCoverZone.com

Books by J. Willis Sanders

The Outer Banks of North Carolina Series
The Diary of Carlo Cipriani
If the Sunrise Forgets Tomorrow
Love, Jake
The One Red Brick
The Kitty Hawk Cowboy

The Hope Series
The Coincidence of Hope
The Yearning of Hope
The Gift of Hope

The Essence of Emmaline Strong

The Eliza Gray Series
The Colors of Eliza Gray
The Colors of Denver Andrews
The Colors of Tess Gray

The Clara Engelman Series
Clara's Mourning
Clara's Courtship
Clara's Choice

The Amish Holiday Series
The Forgiveness Quilt: An Amish Christmas Carol
The Easter Prayer: An Amish Easter Story
The Christmas Wedding: An Amish Christmas Story

Writing as J. D. James
Reid Stone: Hard as Stone
Reid Stone: Red Rage

Writing as W.E. Needlove
Finnigan Malone's Magic Garden
Fingernail Moon

The Kitty Hawk Cowboy

Foreword

As anyone who's read any of my Outer Banks of North Carolina novels can tell, this amazing place has left an indelible mark on my heart. From its northernmost tip above Corolla, to its southernmost tip at Ocracoke Island, not only is it filled with natural beauty, its history, as well as its inhabitants from both the past and the present, offer plenty of material for fiction.

My first experience on the Outer Banks came in the early 1970s, when my parents brought my sister and me on vacation. I was just a boy of twelve or thirteen, but there was something about this place that seeped into my soul. We surf fished, pier fished, swam and played on the beach, got sunburned, enjoyed seafood, and never tired of any of that.

Us Outer Banks lovers, especially those who have been visiting for most of our lives, understand what I mean. As I aged, married, and had my own daughter, the air of the Outer Banks, sweet with salt, always drew me back as often as I could come. Like my other Outer Banks novels, The Kitty Hawk Cowboy embraces a specific time, and I enjoyed learning about the area from 1946 on. Children walked sandy paths in live oak woods to attend Up the Road School. On Sunday mornings, families who attended the Methodist church visited the area called Down the Road. General stores served as places to get groceries, the mail, and the latest news. Hotels, motels, and restaurants were few. People worked hard, many of them in the fishing business, and, in general, life passed at a much slower pace than it does in 2025, because of the always expanding tourism.

In closing, I hope you enjoy this story. Although the main character, Seth Callahan, lived an intriguing life, sometimes in other countries, he never grew tired of his home in Kitty Hawk, and his heart never strayed from there for long. For those of us who feel the same way about the Outer Banks, we understand why.

Please note: To readers considering the AI narrated audio version of this book, be aware that AI narration isn't perfect. One issue you might notice is AI narration is unable to use different voices for different characters, so it may not be clear which character is speaking for short sections of dialogue. Another is the lack of emotion in the narrator's voice. Despite those issues, AI narration has come a long way, and is still an enjoyable way to listen to a book, especially since they usually cost the purchaser much less than human narrated books.

Regardless of whatever way you choose to enjoy this book, it's greatly appreciated.

J. Willis Sanders
2/20/2025

The
Kitty Hawk
Cowboy

Saying Goodbye

I've never thought of myself as anyone special. I worked hard, paid my taxes, and married amazingly, which is the only thing that makes me feel special. Of course, us raising four great kids helps that feeling.

Now, after my wife came home from an oncology appointment an hour ago, I'm not sure how to feel. She's been sitting at the kitchen table ever since, typing furiously on our laptop in a Word document. Her brown eyes are narrowed. She licks her lips every so often. The keys click faster and faster. She's as focused as I've ever seen, so I know better than to ask how the appointment went. Still, I'm worried like a caring husband should be, especially a husband who's love for his wife has grown through almost fifty-five years of marriage.

I make coffee to wait. When I set a steaming mug on the table for her, she points at the Word document and says, "Seth, with what we've been going through with my cancer, we knew what might happen. Instead of talking about it now, I want you to read this. You're going to need something to take your mind off of what's going to happen, and I think this has a good chance of doing that." She sips from the mug. "Use what I've written to start the rest. We'll talk about it after you've read it."

She takes the mug to the deck outside the sliding glass doors and sits in one of the patio chairs, where she can watch our amazing view of the Albemarle Sound from our home in Kitty

Hawk. Knowing I better do as she asks, I pour myself coffee and sit to read, tears welling at her first sentence.

I'm not encouraged by my doctor's expression. I don't say anything. Like us, he and I have been through a lot in the last eight months, so I know how he feels.

Again, his eyes wander to the open folder on his desk. Like you, whom I told to stay home for this appointment because I was expecting this news, he's an old curmudgeon who means well. I wouldn't care to tell a patient what I think my doctor is about to tell me either.

His chest swells with a deep breath. Unless I'm seeing things, his eyes grow wet with nervousness, apprehension, or caring. I'm pretty sure it's all three, because I've seen the same things in your eyes since my diagnosis.

My doctor's wife makes him cucumber sandwiches for lunch. A single dot of mayonnaise clings to a single gray hair on his moustache. In profile he reminds me of Augustus McCrae, from the novel *Lonesome Dove*. I dearly love a good western, and I think *Lonesome Dove* is one of the best.

My doctor sips decaf from one of those insulated mugs. I wait while he sips again. We've undergone this ritual before.

The cool air from the air conditioning vent overhead flutters the few white hairs clinging to the top of his head. He sets the cup down and licks his lips of both the brown stain of coffee and the dot of mayonnaise. I continue to wait. The news will come when he's ready. There's no need to rush.

Some people would say he's not being very professional, but I'd rather have a doctor who cares this much instead of one who's nothing but cold and clinical.

As much as I dread the coming news, I dread telling you even more. We've had an amazing life together, and I know my death will be hard to take. Our children will help you get through the funeral. They'll also keep you company after, with phone calls and visits. Regardless, life must move on, and I especially want it to move on for you. Like most people our age know, happiness is a fleeting thing, so it should be grasped when the opportunity comes along like it did for us.

I won't pretend the start of our relationship was easy. It wasn't love at first sight, or anything like that. You always say I rescued you from a lonely life, but I know better. You are my hero—somewhat of an Augustus McCrae who rode up in the saddle just when I had given up on happy endings.

My doctor sets the mug aside. He looks through the folder, likely to make sure he has all the information arranged in his mind before he tells me.

I don't mind waiting. When I was younger, I was impossibly impatient. No matter the direction of the wind, I wanted it to blow me anywhere but where I was, and I let other people influence me the same way. High school classmates claimed to be my friends. Young men on college dates claimed to care. I believed them when things were going well. Sadly, you only learn if someone is your friend when things are going wrong. Oh, sure, one guy claimed he cared, but a person who truly cares doesn't make demands. That person will stand by you through whatever comes. Their eyes will understand. Their heart will bleed for you. You'll share tears and hints of laughter. You'll hold hands. In our case, Seth, as we both know, you'll fall in love, and you'll wonder how you ever lived without this amazing person in your life.

Yes, we sound like the perfect couple. No, not at all. As we well know also, perfection in a relationship never happens. Passion grows stale. Children take time from simple pleasures, like walks on the beach and making love when the urge hits.

My doctor looks up from the folder. "I apologize for taking so long." He rubs a palm across his mouth. "You really should have your husband here. What if we make another appointment for both of you?"

I press my lips together. I start to cross my arms but don't. "If you don't mind, I'd rather get on with it."

Beneath the gray moustache, the hint of a smile forms. My

stubborn streak is well known at this oncology center. He returns to the folder, a good man fighting his emotions to be the professional he is.

Seth, I know you'll try to be strong like him. As anyone in a marriage like ours knows, you're stronger together instead of apart, and we'll be apart sooner than later.

In case this happened, I've spoken to our neighbors. They've promised to visit so you won't become a recluse. Then again, if you were to go first, that's likely what would become of me.

I never thought I would love someone this much. You never thought you would love someone this much. Miraculously, at the point in our lives when we were ready to give up on love, we found each other.

You wouldn't have given up, though. You learn from your mistakes. You try to do the right thing. You forgive and move on.

Like I already said, you're my hero. I've never met another man like you, and I never will.

My doctor looks up again. His eyes are dry. His voice doesn't quaver. He tells me the truth. He tells me what to expect. He tells me how much time I've got.

I don't ask about the pain. Thank the good Lord there are drugs for that.

If only there were drugs for you, Seth, to ease your soon to be broken heart.

I take a tissue from the box on the corner of my doctor's desk. I don't cry for myself. I cry for everyone I'll leave behind.

At the thought of what my death will do to you, Seth, I stiffen my spine, ashamed of myself. You're stronger than I've ever been. It isn't a woman or man thing. It's something in your soul, as if it's always been a sail to catch and hold the winds of our love, when I, in the beginning of our relationship, doubted it.

Yes, you'll be all right eventually, but you'll need a

distraction to ease your mourning, and I know exactly what it should be. After all, you can be quite the sweet talker when you want to be, so I know you can find the words. Yes, it'll be a struggle at first, but your story needs to be told. It's not often for a man to have so many women in his life until he finds the one he's meant to be with.

I love you so much. You're my hero in countless ways.

Most of all, you're my Kitty Hawk Cowboy.

Chapter 1

As my wife and I always said after we were married for a while, we never know the paths our lives will take. Like the sea captains of old, people do their best to chart their way. Then, when they least expect it, a storm comes along and blows them off course. Sometimes that storm is just a spring shower. Sometimes it's filled with thunder and lightning. Sometimes, like here on the Outer Banks of North Carolina, it's a nor'easter that blows and moans and gusts for days and days.

Of course, my storms had to be women, all category five hurricanes that rocked my world in various ways. Of course as well, some of those women wrecked me like the ships in the waters off the Outer Banks, in what's known as The Graveyard of the Atlantic. Of course as well again, some of those women gently blew me into the arms of a life-changing experience. Hey, that beats the heck out of being wrecked, but I've learned that taking the bad with the good is just another part of life.

My first storm was my mom. She left my dad and me in 1955, when I was nine. Although there were hints at why she left, the only thing that eventually got him back to normal was becoming a minister. He said it gave him the faith that everything would be all right no matter what. Regardless, from time to time, he still moped around our house in Kitty Hawk

Village, which is now called Kitty Hawk, on the shores of the Albemarle Sound.

My excuse for her leaving came in the form of the old western radio show *Gunsmoke.* I wanted Dad to be a cowboy and ride off on a horse to rescue Mom from whatever villain had taken her, because I couldn't believe she would leave on her own.

While there are no horses in Kitty Hawk, there were horses in Corolla back then—wild Spanish Mustangs said to have been left by either shipwrecks or failed colonization attempts in the early 16th century. Their descendants have now been fenced between Corolla and Virginia, and are often seen in the community of Carova or along the beach.

I asked Dad if we could catch one of those horses, the goal in mind of Mom swooning when he rode up to rescue her. "No," he said, his voice filled with melancholy. "Those horses are wild. They belong there and nowhere else."

That was true about those particular horses, but a person could get a horse on the mainland if they knew where to find one. Dad looked away when I told him that, possibly remembering how Mom was now somewhere on the mainland and not with us, nor would she ever be with us again.

I understand how Dad felt. At seventy-eight, I still live in our house in Kitty Hawk, where someone eventually paved the sandy path and named it Sound Landing Road. My wife died last year. Our children pursue their lives on the mainland and visit when they can. On Thanksgiving and Christmas, they bring our grandchildren and a few great-grandchildren. I'm not sure how I'll feel about those visits with my wife gone. I suppose I'll get by.

A sunset breeze springs up and flutters my thinning hair. It's July. Several Jet Ski's zoom in circles in the sound. On the pier extending from the backyard, I tilt the rocking chair back and forth a few times. In my lap, on a laptop screen, the cursor at the end of the last word I typed in a Word document waits impatiently.

Yes, when it comes to some things, I'm a procrastinator. When my wife's oncologist said her treatment options had run out, she asked me to write the story of how all the women in my life led to her, both for us and our family. She didn't fool me. Because she knew how her death would affect me, she wanted me to have something to do instead of sitting around and wondering how I can live without her.

It isn't working.

First, when you love someone as much as I loved her, and that person is dying, all you can do is wonder how life will be without that person. Second, when your family lives far away, you'll be left alone after the funeral.

Oh, I have a few good friends. One neighbor, Jack, comes over now and then when he sees me on the pier. He drops into my wife's rocking chair beside mine and hands me a beer. After a few sips, he'll look my way. "Let's see what's biting at Jennette's. How about it?"

Jack's in his mid-seventies. His wife's into pickleball and baking and keeping an immaculate house. He's into beer and fishing at Jennette's Pier and keeping her happy. He's also into trying to drag me kicking and screaming back into the world of the living.

I appreciate him. We've grown closer since my wife died. I told him about Mom leaving and about Dad refusing to search for her. "Why look for her when she left a note saying not to look for her?" he asked me when I said Dad should've looked for her.

I didn't get it when I was a kid, but sometimes you have to give up on people. It galls me to do that, but they'll only take you down with them. I've seen that happen on that TV show *Intervention,* where families try to get drug-addicted loved ones to, as Dad would say, "see the light." Some do and some don't, so the only route a family can take for a normal life is to give up on that person. It's sad, but eventually we have to move on.

Huh. That's what Jack's been trying to tell me with his offers of beer and fishing. Am I dumb or what? Regardless, I don't feel like moving on yet, if ever.

My other neighbor, a redhead named Liz, is a vivacious widow of sixty-seven, with a son in contracting and a daughter in nursing. Jack said I should ask her out because she was best friends with my wife. I said he should take a hike off the end of my pier.

The first time Liz came over, a week or so after the funeral, I was on the pier in my rocker, staring at the sound. It was the Saturday before Thanksgiving. Highway 158 was buzzing with tourists trying to capture a few precious moments on the Outer Banks.

Sitting in the other rocker, she set a bottle of wine between us on the gray boards, offered me a glass, and filled both. She sipped and I sipped. She patted my knee. I expected her to say something but she didn't. I appreciated that.

I wore a jacket. A comforter covered my lap because of the cool breeze. She wore khaki slacks and a cream colored cable-knit sweater. To our left and right, the marsh whispered its never-ending song.

We just sat and drank until the bottle was empty. Then, right out of the blue, the urge to share my first hurricane hit. I scooted the rocker around to keep from getting a crick in my neck while I faced her, and started. "My mom left my dad and me when I was nine. Did you know that?"

Liz shared a slight nod. "Jack told me. Your sweetie never mentioned her."

"Jack talks too much," I said, trying not to sound too grumpy.

"He's your friend, Seth. That's why he told me." Liz fingered a curl of red hair behind her ear. "Jack didn't elaborate. He just said she left. Can I ask why?"

I enjoyed Liz's midwestern accent, nothing like my wife's southwestern accent. Remembrances come often in sounds.

Because of my heartache, remembering my wife's voice was not a pleasant thing to do.

"She left a note," I told Liz. "She just said she was leaving and not to look for her."

Liz asked if Dad tried to find Mom, and I shook my head. "He refused," I said. "When I got older, I wondered if she left for someone else. Dad lavished her with praise for everything she did. He bought her flowers for no reason. He always took her out for anniversaries and her birthday. Looking back, I see why he became a minister. He had all the faith in the world in her and in their marriage. When she left, he lost faith in everything. He had to find faith again by finding God."

A breeze rustled the marsh once more. Liz looked away and back. "Don't take this the wrong way, Seth, but have you lost faith because she died?"

"Nope," I said, shaking my head. "Death is part of life. I just miss her as bad as Dad missed Mom."

"I've seen you out here with a laptop." Liz paused as if she were deciding to tell me something. "I tried online dating for a while," she admitted. "I gave up after I did background checks on the first three men." Liz crossed her legs. "Have you thought about dating?"

I tried not to frown and failed. "The laptop's not for that."

"Do I get to know what it's for?"

"Are you always so pushy?"

She patted my knee again. "Listen to you, acting rude when you're not rude."

Liz was right. A couple doesn't stay married for over fifty years if one of them is rude. I set my ankle on my knee and leaned back in the rocker. "She wanted me to write our story. I'm having a hard time getting started."

"Was she your first love?" Liz asked, sincerity in her voice. "You're very attractive."

I raised one eyebrow, a skill my wife admired. "Are you nearsighted and you forgot your glasses?"

"Being sweet and endearing, according to your sweetie, is attractive."

"Well, no, she wasn't my first."

Liz raised an index finger. The red polish on the manicured nail shined in the sun. She swiped her finger through the air. "Score one for me. Tell me about the first woman."

"That would be my mom," I said. "She was a great mom, so it broke my heart when she left like it did Dad's."

"I'm sorry, Seth," Liz said, her cheeks reddening. "But it's rare for a great mom to leave her husband and child when everything is fine unless there's another man." Liz recrossed her legs. "Do I get to know about your first love or not?"

"Maybe. If I write our story, that is. She didn't want me to leave anything out."

"Do you have a title yet?" Liz asked, her hazel eyes curious.

"She came up with the title," I said. "The Kitty Hawk Cowboy."

Liz snorted laughter. "That sounds like the name of a male stripper."

I frowned again, this time without trying to hide it. "You joke too much."

"You and your sweetie joked all the time. We were good friends, remember? She wanted you to enjoy life after she was gone."

I couldn't deny that. My "sweetie," as Liz was calling my wife, told me that very thing on her death bed time and time again. "I know," I told Liz. "I guess it's too soon to enjoy anything."

Liz left soon after, and I didn't blame her. Who wants to be around a grump?

The laptop cursor still waits. I slam the top down and start to throw the darn thing in the sound but don't. Since my wife wanted me to write our story, I have to honor her memory and do it. I just don't know when I can.

Time passes. The sun drops lower into the horizon.

Darkness gradually surrounds me. I could describe it a lot better if I felt like it. My wife and I used to sit out here and hold hands and marvel at the sunsets and how our lives turned out. It's not often for two people to find their way to each other like we did, but it happened.

I tilt the rocker forward and let it spill me out. My knees pop. My hips ache. I feel like taking my four-wheel drive Toyota 4-Runner up to Carova and seeing if any of the horses might come out on the beach tonight.

Who am I kidding? Carova and the horses remind me of my wife. If I drive up there and see any horses, I might end up driving into the Atlantic and drowning myself.

I shuffle through the yard and ease up the steps to the deck. My heart pounds halfway into the climb. I lose what little breath I have until I'm forced to stop and rest.

I was in good shape before my wife got sick. We walked every day. We'd have date night twice a week. She talked me into the health benefits of tossed salad and broiled seafood long ago, saying we needed to stick around for each other as long as possible. What's the point of that now? No one needs me. Our kids have their own lives and are doing great like we taught them. They know the value of identifying your dream and pursuing it. They know the value of character. They know the value of honesty. They know the value of being kind, regardless of a world where fewer and fewer people are not. During the summer, half the kids on Jet Skis gave me the finger when I waved. I guess they assumed I was trying to get them to slow down, but we know what assuming gets us.

I make it up the remaining steps without keeling over. Inside, I grab one of the beers Jack keeps bringing over. Maybe I should become an alcoholic. Then I could fall down the steps and break my neck and be done with it.

My wife loved the movie *Pretty Woman*. I cop a squat on a bar stool and set the laptop on the counter. The beer is bitter on my tongue and cold going down. After three more, I start to feel fuzzy, and my vision blurs. Then I realize I'm crying, and that's why my vision is blurring.

Outside the sliding glass doors, my wife, on our wedding day at the beach, decked out in a beautiful flowing dress in white, shakes her head to let me know she's not pleased with how I've given up. She jabs a finger at the laptop and mouths, *Get to work, cowboy, or I'll come back and haunt you.*

She called me cowboy because she said I saved her. I prefer to think she, along with the other women in my life, saved me. She and I talked about it a lot over the years and ended up with this saying: Life is full of heroes, but the best heroes save each other.

Our statement kindles a spark somewhere inside me. Then I feel it growing in my chest. It's dull but it's there, and I don't know how long it will last before my sadness drowns it in a tide of sorrow. All I know is I better start before it's gone.

I open the laptop and the Word document and raise my shaking hands to the keyboard.

Chapter 2

As they say, any good story starts at the beginning, so I guess I better start there.

I was born in 1946. You got it, I'm a baby boomer. Mom and Dad got married when he came home from fighting with the Army in Europe, and I came along ten months later. I don't remember any of that, of course. Their wedding date and my birthdate are recorded in the family Bible, clear as day.

My first memory was of seeing a horse on a beach. I must've been around four or so. Having driven jeeps in the war, Dad loved their four-wheel drive capability, so he picked up a war-surplus one for himself. All in all, since he was a fisherman, it was a good investment. His dad was also a fisherman, mostly for blue crabs and whatever fish he could catch from a flat-bottomed skiff in the Albemarle Sound. Making a living like that was hard work, but when dad brought that jeep home, things got better. He and his dad bought two dories with two trailers. Whenever fish were running off the beach, they'd haul those dories there and lay a net out in a semi-circle from the shore. Then they and whatever men they'd hired for the day would pull the net in and sort through the fish, both to take home and to sell.

Well doggone, I forgot about my first memory of seeing a horse on the beach. Like I said, I was around four or so. From the time Dad was a boy until he joined the Army, he fished and hunted waterfowl with his dad, so he knew the Outer Banks like the back of his hand. I followed in his footsteps to a degree, but I got sidetracked along the way. We'll get to that later.

Mom loved those horses. Dad said she'd go on and on about how she'd love to be as wild and free as they were. Huh, I never thought about that.. Unless I miss my guess, her wanting to be wild and free, even though she had a husband and a little boy, might've had something to do with why she left. It makes no sense for me to just think of this after so many years. I'm no psychologist, but I might've been repressing how she felt about those horses because I didn't want to believe she'd just up and leave us, like we were keeping her from being wild and free.

Oh, well, I'll set that on the shelf and come to it later if the mood strikes.

Anyway, Dad said he took Mom—her name was Lucille—to see the horses on their first date. His name was Thomas. Everyone called him Teak because he said if he ever got around to building his own fishing boat, he'd make the deck out of teak wood. Anyone who knows the ocean and ships knows teak is used in shipbuilding because it stands up to salt water so well.

So, on their first date, he took his dad's skiff to her house about a mile north of us and motored up to Corolla. This was a rare voyage, as it was almost twenty-five miles as the crow flies. Dad knew about the horses from waterfowl hunting up there. He thought they were interesting, but not as much as Mom did. The thing she enjoyed so much was when they walked over to the beach and a small herd was running in the surf. That's when the sight of them galloping, the water spraying from their hooves, their manes flaring, their tails flying, thrilled her to no end.

They said they took me when I was about a year old. Like I said, I don't remember that. Still, I like to imagine them on the beach, maybe all of us on a blanket, me sitting between them, him pointing at the horses and saying, "Look at 'em go, Seth. Ain't they kickin' up their heels?"

My first memory of the horses is just flashes of brown hides, flowing manes, and long tails as a few mares and stallions walk along the beach, leaving hoofprints in the sand where it glistens from the retreating surf. I do remember one certain mare with a white star on her forehead and how she stopped to nuzzle her long-legged foal, nickering softly. In later years, after Mom left, I remember thinking that mare would never leave her baby horse, so why did my mom leave me?

Yes, Mom leaving me burrowed into my brain like a mole crab burrows into the sand.

Other memories trickle into my mind from those sweet days so long ago, most from simple moments such as her teaching me to brush my teeth, to comb my brown cowlick down, and to tie my shoes. She loved reading, and she always re-read Charlotte Brontë's *Jane Eyre* every year, which Dad didn't understand, even to the point of adamantly sharing his opinion about it on more than one occasion. "It makes no sense," he'd say over and over. "I love Jane for overcoming her obstacles and refusing to accept charity to make a living—that's what everyone who lives on the Outer Banks has to do—but the way she goes on and on about loving Rochester makes her sound childish."

Ever the romantic, Mom's reply never failed to irk him. "Why, Thomas, wouldn't you like it if I went on and on about you like that?"

Of course, her comment irked him because he would've loved it if she'd gone on and on about loving him like Jane loved Rochester, and she never did. Now that I think about it, that's even more evidence that she left either for, or with, another man.

What a shame to have my parents reduced to characters in a standard romance novel—what some of today's readers might call a "bodice ripper"—instead of people to admire like in *Jane Eyre.*

Aside from Mom's yearly reading of *Jane Eyre* and Dad's

negative comments, they got along well from what I could see. He earned a decent living. She never wanted for anything. She kissed his cheek when he came home smelling of fish and tracking in sand. He kissed her cheek in return and asked how her day of teaching at the local school had gone.

Because of Mom teaching me the alphabet before I attended school, I got a head start on reading. Because of Dad teaching me how to add and subtract coin amounts, I got a head start on math. Because of how well they got along, they both, so I thought, taught me how to fall in love.

Ellie Tate, what a girl. With big brown eyes and brunette hair and the cutest smile I'd ever seen, she made my seven-year-old heart flutter like a moth around a porchlight whenever she walked by.

Schoolmates called her Ellie. I called her "sugar" once, like Dad always called Mom, and I got narrowed eyes and a finger waggling in my face for my trouble.

It was a gorgeous day in May. The classes, taught by two teachers, were eating lunch outside. As usual, I was sitting cross legged beneath a tree and opening my paper sack to take out either a ham or bologna sandwich or an apple or an orange. The apples weren't too hard to get, but the oranges were. Sometimes I just got two sandwiches, along with a Mason jar of water to drink.

As you might can tell, my folks were on the frugal end of the Outer Banks spectrum. In fact, to be honest, most everyone on the Outer Banks had to be frugal back then. Along with being a hard place to make a living, it was a hard place to live. Dad used to say if you lived near the sound, and your house wasn't elevated on pilings, the hurricanes would get you both coming and going. For anyone who doesn't understand what that means, it has to do with the storm surge. Imagine a hurricane's counterclockwise winds. As it nears the Outer Banks, the winds in the leading edge come from the east. If you're on the western side of the sound, the eastern winds blow the water toward you, and you get flooded. As the hurricane leaves the Outer Banks, the winds come from the west. If you're on the eastern side of the sound, the western winds blow the water toward you, and you get flooded. I've personally seen this many times over the years. It's a sight when the wind gradually blows the water away from you, leaving sand and puddles, only to know it'll eventually come back and flood your yard. Sure, since you only got flooded once, it didn't get you coming and going. I guess Dad didn't take that into account when he came up with that saying.

Doggone if I didn't get sidetracked again. Where was I? Oh, that's right. The day I called Ellie Tate "sugar."

Like I said, I was eating lunch beneath a tree like I usually did. You might wonder why I was alone. You see, I was what kids today would call a nerd. I was skinny because I was just skinny. My face and arms were pale because Mom made me wear a long-sleeved shirt and a wide-brimmed straw hat when I went out to play. She was ahead of her time because we didn't have sunscreen in those days. So along came Ellie, cute as can be in her bare feet and tattered white dress. I just looked up and said, "Hey, sugar, you want to have lunch with me?"

She stopped, turned, and leaned over to waggle her finger in my face while narrowing her eyes. "Boy, your face is as white as a flounder's belly. I'm not eating lunch with the likes of you."

This was one of those days I had an orange. Knowing how rare they were amongst families in Kitty Hawk Village, I took it from my paper sack and held it toward Ellie. "I'll share my orange with you."

Ellie's brown eyes widened. "I only get an orange at Christmas, when Daddy gets some from the mainland." She plopped down beside me in the shade. "How'd you get that orange?"

We'd never officially met, so I offered my hand. "I'm Seth Callahan. Nice to meet you."

She eyed my hand. "I already know who you is. I guess you talk so proper cause your momma is the teacher."

I forgot to write that. The kids sort of shunned me because Mom was one of our teachers. At least Ellie hadn't mentioned it in a bad way. "Well, yeah," I told her. "She taught me the alphabet already." I peeled the orange and gave Ellie half. "Watch out for the seeds."

Taking the orange, she rolled her eyes at me. "I already told you, flounder boy, this ain't my first orange."

I could see our relationship wasn't going anywhere soon unless I tried something new. I took a bite of orange and swallowed. "You sure have pretty eyes, Ellie. I bet no other boy ever told you that."

"They's just eyes. Ain't nothin' special 'bout them." She swallowed a bite of orange. "You never said how your daddy got that orange."

"Mom makes him get them when he takes fish to sell on the mainland. She says they keep me from getting scurvy."

About to take another bite of orange, Ellie stopped. "What's scurvy?"

"Mom never said what it is. It sounds bad, so I listen to her."

We finished the orange in silence. Ellie thanked me and stood, fingering her hair behind her ears. "You say your name is Seth?"

Mom didn't call on me much in class. She said it wouldn't be fair to the other kids because I was ahead of them from her and dad teaching me at home. I guessed this was why Ellie hadn't heard my name. "That's right," I said. "It's Seth."

She grinned. "Well, at least it ain't sugar." She paused as if she were thinking of something. "Tell you what, whenever you bring an orange for lunch, you can call me sugar. Whatcha think 'bout that?"

I returned her grin. "I think it's fine as frog hair, Ellie. What will you call me? I hope it's something nicer than flounder boy."

Mom came out on the school porch and said lunch was over. When she went back inside, Ellie asked where I live, and I said, "On the sound straight west, why?"

"My folk's house is that way," she said. "If you walk me home, I'll figure out what to call you before we get there."

Mom usually stayed after class to grade papers and such, and I was glad. For the first time in my life, I'd get to walk a girl home, and I looked forward to it.

For our walk, Ellie and I agreed to meet under the same tree after school. I hoped Mom wouldn't say anything about seeing me talking to Ellie, and I wouldn't say anything about our walk to her. She might tell Dad, and he might tease me. I was also worried about what the other kids would think, but only a little bit. When the cutest girl in class wants you to walk her home, you can put up with a lot of stuff, including the chance of being teased.

Inside, Mom wrote on the chalkboard while everyone put their lunch bags away and slid into their desks. A few fingers pointed at me, followed by snickering laughs. Mom whirled around. "That's enough, unless someone wants a note sent home to their parents."

One kid stopped pointing and laughing a little too late, and I was sure Mom saw him pointing at me. Two rows to my right, without any readable expression, Ellie looked from Mom to me and back to Mom again. Unless I missed my guess, not only would Mom talk to me after class, Ellie would walk home without me.

I raise my fingertips from the laptop. My neck and back aches from being stooped over. Suppertime has come and gone, evidenced by my view through the sliding glass doors of darkness falling over the Albemarle Sound. On the mainland, across that wide expanse of water, lights flicker like lightning bugs in the yard on a summer night.

The number of things we file away in our memories is amazing. I haven't thought about Ellie in years. It's nice to bring back nostalgia's sweet embrace after so much time.

I save the Word document and put the laptop to sleep. At the frig, I ponder supper, eventually deciding on a bologna sandwich and an orange in honor of my first childhood crush.

I know. You expected me to say Ellie was my first love. Absolutely not. Because of all the women in my life, I learned the hard way about what love is, and it isn't something as simple as a crush, no matter what age we are.

My wife and I have great children. We raised them to trust our shared life experiences and taught them to come to us with questions about anything, especially about affairs of the heart.

That doesn't mean we weren't firm with them about various issues. Some people like to say parents should be their kid's friends. No, the most important thing a parent will ever do in life is to be a parent to their kids instead of claiming to be their friend. Saying you're their friend makes them think you'll give them a pass on important issues like friends sometimes do. True friends tell it like it is. That's how my wife and I raised our kids, and that's a large part of why they turned out so well. Like any kid, though, they had their growing pains. One thing about growing pains is how — if you're able to look back on them as experiences, which is what my wife and I did when we were young — you'll learn from them.

Sorry about that. Although age can bring wisdom, it doesn't give me the wisdom to know people sometimes don't like an old guy getting on his soapbox. In my defense, there's only one reason any parent does that, and it's the same reason my wife and I gave our kids the benefit of our experiences — because we care.

I wash the salty bologna down with a bottle of water. My wife told me bologna was bad for me, but I splurge on the rare occasion. The orange is sweet and citrusy and smells great. I don't know if citrusy is a word, but it works.

I take the bottle of water to the pier and sit in my rocker. Solar LED lights along the edge allowed my wife and I to cherish our many evenings out here. Although I've enjoyed writing the first two chapters of our story—what she demanded was my story—I feel a bit overwhelmed by the time and memories it'll take to finish it.

Even with the sun hidden behind the horizon, the July heat conspires with the humidity and the soft lapping of wavelets in the marsh to make me sleepy. I doze now and then, waking to the realization that I should go to bed so I'll be rested enough to continue writing in the morning.

I still have my teeth, thank goodness. After I take a quick shower and brush and floss, I pull the air conditioned sheets up to my chin, whisper goodnight and I love you to my sweetheart, and turn the lamp off.

As darkness engulfs the room, I feel good about the start to our story. I just hope it'll go this well tomorrow. If there's one thing I've learned over the years, you can never guess what a new day will bring.

Chapter 3

That day after school, I was amazed when Mom didn't keep me after class to talk about Ellie. I was also amazed to find Ellie waiting for me beneath the tree. To keep the other kids from seeing us leave together, I waited on the porch until they were gone. When I got to Ellie, her arms were crossed. "I seen you watching them other kids leavin'. Why you so bashful?"

I scuffed the toe of my shoe in the sand. "Well, to be honest, I don't want them to tease me about you."

She grabbed my hand and pulled me toward the path heading west. "I don't know if you're worth an orange or not."

This was the first time I'd held a girl's hand. Mine was warm and sweaty. Hers was cool and dry. Oaks and pines and thick brush lined the path, which curved back and forth like a water moccasin. I was so choked up, I didn't know what to say. Then again, at seven-years-old, kids are just kids, and they just want someone to like them. At least that was how I felt.

Before I knew it, Ellie was stopping at a narrower path going north, toward the community of Otila. "All right then, I live yonder. Do I get a kiss goodbye?"

Astounded at her suggestion, I took a step backward. "Why should I do that?"

"Ain't I your girl? You done give me half an orange and called me sugar. Now you done walked me home. I reckon all that's gotta mean something."

"We're just getting to know each other, Ellie. That's all."

Ellie licked her lips. "I seen some older kids kissin'. Ain't that what we s'posed to do?"

I grabbed her hand and gave it a firm shake. "That'll do until we get older."

She released my hand. "Well, I reckon I'll see you tomorrow. Don't forget to bring another orange."

Watching Ellie's thin body fade in the shade of the limbs hanging over the narrow path, I knew I should tell her today's orange was the last one, but I just couldn't do it.

On the way home, I started thinking about girls in general. Then I realized I didn't know enough about them to have an opinion. Then I realized Ellie was more interested in oranges than me. Then I wondered if all girls were that tricky. I'd have to talk to Dad about it when he got home.

Before I got there, I passed the Austin Cemetery. Last year, on the first day of first grade, when Mom took me with her to school, those gray stones spooked me something awful. As many times as we had passed them on the way to the general store, where the post office also was, they shouldn't have done that. I guess it was because of how they looked in the morning, with the rows of headstones casting long, eerie shadows like they were going to snatch a body from the sand. This time, though, I just gave them a quick glance, but I also gave them a passing thought.

Since we lived toward the southern side of Kitty Hawk Village, in the area commonly known as "Down the Road," we attended the Methodist church, while most folks to the north, in the area known as "Up the Road," attended the Baptist church. In various conversations at the general store, I'd heard old timers discussing the pros and cons of both religious doctrines and how they pertained to what happened to us when we die. No matter how hard my boyhood brain tried to make sense of those discussions, the idea of dying gave me the chills. Some of those men said we waited in our graves until

Resurrection Day. Others said we'd go straight to Heaven when we breathed our final breath. I preferred to go straight to Heaven. After seeing enough rotting fish on the beach, or on the shores of the sound, I could easily imagine what a person would look like when they rose from the grave, and I didn't like that idea one bit.

Compared to the 2024 version of my house, the 1953 version was small. Not much more than a fishing cabin, it included two bedrooms, a parlor with a ratty sofa and an easy chair, and several oil lamps for light. In the kitchen, we ate from an oak table with four ladderback chairs. Mom cooked on a wood cookstove and kept our perishable food in an icebox. Out back, we kept a cow for milk in a small barn, chickens for meat and eggs in a henhouse, and an outhouse for what came after eating. I despised that stinky, black hole every time I sat on it.

I much prefer the 2024 version of my house, which doesn't resemble the old one at all. Over the years, Dad and I added more rooms and the deck. I've mentioned the modern kitchen and living room. Although I now enjoy electricity, indoor plumbing, and grocery stores, I'm not too fond of how the area has grown from tourism. Still, if not for that, I wouldn't have met my wife, so I can't knock it too much.

When I got home after walking with Ellie that day, I drank a glass of milk from the icebox and settled down at the table with my homework. Like I said, Mom and Dad gave me a head start on spelling and math, so I finished pretty quick. Mom came about thirty minutes later. One of my chores, along with milking the cow, gathering eggs, and keeping our drinking pail filled with water from the well, was to bring wood in for the cookstove after Dad chopped it. Seeing some was needed for whatever Mom was going to cook for supper, I brought an armload inside and set it in the box by the stove.

She started the fire, spooned lard into a black, cast-iron pan, and floured chicken pieces from the one Dad killed the day before, so Mom could soak it overnight in the icebox.

When the chicken sizzled nicely, tempting me with its delicious aroma, she faced me. "Is there something you'd like to tell me, Seth?"

I pretended not to hear her question. "That chicken sure smells good. Do you need any more wood?"

"I don't recommend it, Son."

"I like it crispy. That means you'll need more wood." Yes, I figured her comment was about Ellie and me, but I intended to lead that conversation astray.

"I suppose you think I mean you and Ellie," Mom continued. "What I mean is marriage in general, especially out here where life is so hard." She showed me her palms. "I'm a teacher. That means I shouldn't have callouses from chopping wood when your dad comes home late from fishing."

I couldn't handle an ax yet, and I didn't like it when Mom complained about Dad getting home late. He worked hard to earn us a living, and she knew it. He often told her about his dreams of a larger house and more children, both to love and to help with the chores. When he did, she always snapped back, forgetting how he'd just said he would love more children. "Parents shouldn't have children for chores, Thomas. That's wrong."

"I know that, Luce, but it can't be helped. That's just the way it is on the Outer Banks."

Mom didn't like Dad cutting her name in two to make it "Luce," and he'd rather she call him "Tom," short and sweet. With her preference for proper names, "Teak" was out of the question.

This scene happened once a month or so. By the time Mom's complaint about children not being meant for chores was answered by Dad's, "That's just the way it is on the Outer Banks," she would let it go. Even my childhood self could tell both were firm in their ideals, and nothing would change them.

Mom swept a tendril of brown hair behind her ear. Sweat beaded on her forehead, a result of the warm May day and the heat from the cookstove. "I'm serious, Son. If you want a decent life, you need to attend college. And if you want a wife who'll love you, you'll move away from here. It's difficult to love a man when life is so hard."

This was the first time Mom said this to me, and it shocked me to my core. "Do you mean you don't love Dad? He's good to us. He works hard to take care of us." Tears stung my eyes. I'd heard tales of divorce and sad children in our small community, and now that rooster might come home to roost at my house.

Mom ignored my tears, which shocked me even more. In the past, if I'd scrape a knee or get a sandspur in a foot, she never failed to comfort me and say everything would be all right. Now, though, her stony expression seemed to say her son's feelings didn't matter to her at all.

The lard popped, and I smelled the hint of burning chicken. Mom turned the pieces, closed the damper on the stove, and faced me. "Yes, your dad works hard to take care of us. I appreciate that."

That didn't make me feel any better. "It still sounds like you don't love him," I said, wiping tears. "I'm just seven. I shouldn't be worried about stuff like this."

Mom handed me a large pot. "Fill that with water from the well. I'm going to make extra mashed potatoes."

I stared at the pot. For someone who didn't think children should do chores, she'd dismissed me and my feelings exactly like that was all I was good for.

In the front yard, as I pumped the handle to fill the pot, I heard the puttering of Dad's skiff approaching our pier. Grandpa and grandma, worn out from their years of working like my own parents were now working, had moved to Manteo, where Grandpa had opened a general store. Sure, the irony wasn't lost on my seven-year-old self, but for Mom to think she couldn't love Dad because of where they lived broke my heart. More than one family out here was happy and thriving, and she should remember that.

I took the water inside and ran to the pier in time to catch the rope Dad tossed me. "Good catch, Seth. You're a natural." He raised a stringer of fish. "Had a good day." His nostrils flared. "I smell chicken cooking. While your mom is fixing supper, we'll clean these flounder and trout and get 'em in the icebox."

We did so on the pier, Dad's filleting knife flashing in orange light of the setting sun. I saved the insides in a bucket, baited our crab pot with them, and returned it to the water.

At the well, Dad drew a bucket of water. Rinsing the fillets, he looked up at me. "Why're your eyes red, Son?"

The last thing I wanted was to mention mine and Mom's conversation. "I think I got some sand in one."

"But they're both red. Is something wrong?"

I leaned my behind against the weathered planks of the well. "Do you think I'm too young to have a girlfriend?"

"What's that got to do with why your eyes are red?"

"I got sand in both, okay? What about a girlfriend?"

Dad put the fish in a pan we kept at the well for the purpose. "A girlfriend already?"

I nodded. "Ellie Tate. Do you know her folks? I've never seen her at our church. I guess they go to the Baptist church up the road."

"That'd be Allen and Sue. They're older than your mom and me. They've got four kids. Ellie's their youngest. Allen said she surprised them."

"What's that mean?" I asked, truly curious as to how a kid could surprise their parents in whatever way Dad had meant.

He grinned. "I'll explain it when you get older. Does Ellie like you?"

"She said I could call her sugar whenever I share an orange with her. I walked her home today." Remembering what Mom said about marrying and living here, I decided to carefully broach the subject. "Mom said living here makes it hard to be happy."

Dad wiped his hands on his coveralls and raked a hand through his dark hair. "She tells me that before we go to sleep at least once a week, but never in the morning. It's common to feel that way at the end of a long day. I tell her she needs to be grateful instead of complaining. The grass might seem greener on the other side, but that isn't always so. I've heard men and women at the general store talk about leaving to start a different life on the mainland." Dad looped his arm around my shoulders. "Son, if there's a lesson we need in life, it's how happiness comes from the inside, not the outside. The more material things it takes to make a person think they're happy, the more they're fooling themselves about what happiness is." He squeezed my shoulders. "That's a fact you can take to the bank."

Although Dad's opinion about happiness seemed like a good way to live, it was a shame it hadn't rubbed off on Mom. The differences in their ideals felt like a hurricane about to smash into the Outer Banks, and I didn't know how to stop it from happening.

Looking back, I suppose her ideals might've come from her wealthy parents in Elizabeth City. Dad admired them because his father-in-law, William Mitchell, and his mother-in-law, Mary, started a seafood restaurant that was hailed for miles around. This was well before tourists started visiting the Outer Banks in large numbers, so there were few restaurants here.

Once in a while, after Dad made a great catch, either with his skiff in the sound or with the dories in the ocean and a few hired hands, I'd board the skiff when he took his in-laws the fish. Grandpa Mitchell never failed to welcome him with a smile and a pat on his back. Grandma Mitchell never failed to ask how Mom was getting along out on that "forsaken strip of sand." I could hear Dad's hurt feelings in his hesitant answer and see them in his downturned eyes. "Luce is fine like always, Mrs. Mitchell."

Grandma never failed to frown at Dad's name for Mom. "I distinctly remember naming my daughter Lucille, Thomas. Why do you chop it off like that?"

By this time, Dad would be twisting his beat up old cap in his hands. "If you don't mind, ma'am, I prefer Tom. I was never one for putting on airs."

Grandpa eyed Grandma. "Now, now, let's be civil, Mary. Lucille chose Tom and Tom chose Lucille." He patted my head. "Isn't that right, Seth?"

What could I do but nod?

In the kitchen, mashing potatoes at the table beside the cookstove, Mom didn't turn around. "How was the fishing?"

Dad showed her the pan. "Got some nice trout and flounder." He took a roll of money from his pocket and showed it to her. "I like it when my customers are grateful for everything I do for them." He kissed the back of her head. "Like I appreciate everything you do for Seth and me. I hope you know that."

Mom said nothing. Dad's expectant smile fell to a frown. He put the pan in the icebox and faced Mom's back again. "Can I do something to help, Luce?"

Mom still refused to face him. "You can save that money for Seth's college fund. That's how you can help both of us."

Her statement was like a nor'easter roaring through our little home. All I could gather from it was she was only concerned about us, and she didn't give a hoot about Dad.

Standing behind her, he blinked several times, until a single tear tracked down his tanned cheek and quivered on the dark stubble of his whiskered chin. The sight of him so vulnerable weakened my knees. She might as well have stabbed him through the heart with a butcher knife.

When I look back on the moments that led to her leaving, it makes me wonder how I didn't remember them until I started writing this chapter. Maybe the pain Mom inflicted on Dad made me hide it away. If that's not the reason, I can't think of another one.

Supper came and went as silently as the graves in the Austin Cemetery. Dad and I picked at our food. Mom actually had the audacity to eat on the end of the pier, swinging her bare feet off its edge like the happiest schoolgirl you'd ever seen, satisfied from letting Dad know she didn't care for him in any way whatsoever. I'd always idolized her. I'd also listened to the Methodist minister when he preached about not hating anyone. Regardless, at that moment, I hated Mom for how she'd hurt Dad, because I loved him dearly.

After supper, Mom washed the dishes silently. Dad offered to dry them, but she remained silent. I usually dried them. I'd rather break every single one of them.

I went to my room, washed off in a basin, then brushed my teeth and went to bed. Their voices didn't murmur through the wall separating our bedrooms like they usually did. Sometime in the night, I woke to visit the outhouse. On the way to the door, I saw Dad on the sofa. His eyes followed me, but I said nothing. I'd rather let him think I thought he was asleep than for him to know his and Mom's marriage had taken such a terrible turn.

The next morning, after I milked the cow and gathered eggs, Mom cooked breakfast like nothing had changed. Dad usually ate leftovers from supper so he could leave in the skiff before dawn, or trailer the dories to the beach behind the jeep. This morning he stayed, saying he wanted to do some things around the house. Mom started to fill our plates. Dad said he could help. Mom started to eat. Dad asked how her students were doing, asked if he could carry her books this morning, asked if he could carry them back this afternoon. Mom's brusque "No" at the end of every question was like a punch to his gut, visible in how his face sagged further and further with each "No."

I ate breakfast as fast as I could, told Dad bye, and hurried along the path to school. I knew I shouldn't hold a grudge against Mom, but the last thing I wanted was to walk with her. When a parent does another parent wrong, it cuts a child to the bone.

The mile walk took no time. Mom entered the classroom a short time later. Other kids soon trickled in, and I was glad. It would keep her from talking to me about either Dad or Ellie, and I didn't want to hear anything she had to say. Like I said, she'd cut me to the bone.

When lunch came, I went to my tree and waited for Ellie. She came out on the porch a few minutes later and headed my way. I smiled, not even caring what kids saw us together. Then it dawned on me—she wouldn't have wanted a kiss yesterday if she only wanted my oranges. In the shade beneath the huge oak, she sat cross-legged beside me. "Hey there, sugar pie."

I sure liked her extreme southern accent. "Hey there, sugar pie" sounded like "Hey they-uh, shoo-guh pie."

"Hi, Ellie," I said. "You sure look mighty pretty today."

She took a sandwich from her paper sack, potted meat from what I could see oozing from the sides. "Do you really think so, or are you just bein' nice?"

"I really think so," I said, bobbing my head. "I took a bite of my ham sandwich and washed it down with water. Since she wanted the truth about something, so did I, but I wanted to tiptoe around it instead of just blurting it out. "I'm sorry, but we're out of oranges. I hope you don't mind."

To my shock, she drew her bony fist back to sock my shoulder and grinned instead. "I'm just messin' with you. I got to thinkin' 'bout it last night, and I like how nice you are. Momma and Daddy are nice to each other. It only makes sense to be like that when you love one another."

Although Ellie's news eased my worry about Mom and Dad, it made me wish she would be nice to him again. I finished my sandwich and cut my apple in half with an old pocket knife Dad had given me. "You want to share my apple, Ellie?"

From a jar like mine, she washed down the last bite of her sandwich with what resembled lemonade. "Why, I sure do, sugar pie."

Today was like yesterday, warm for May, a nice breeze rustling the oak leaves over our heads. Some boys across the yard were on their knees in the sand, playing marbles. A group of girls by the porch were watching them, grinning and whispering now and then. Groups of older boys and girls, from the third grade up, were scattered around, some eating, some talking.

Everything was going as usual until Mom came out onto the porch and eyed me while shaking her head. Sure, I was only seven, but that didn't mean that knife wasn't cutting into the bone even deeper.

She stopped shaking her head and said lunch was over. I told Ellie I'd see her later, and she said she looked forward to it.

The rest of the day, whenever Mom faced the class, I could feel her eyes on me. Whatever had made her stop loving Dad had got hold of her like a crab gets hold of a chicken neck, and it sure wasn't going to let her go. No doubt about it, life was hard on the Outer Banks, but I hoped she'd see the light and realize loving us was worth the effort.

For one thing, she and Dad had married in their late twenties, after meeting at a dance in Elizabeth City. He'd sometimes talk about that night whenever we worked on his old jeep. "See this here engine," he'd say. "It's the heart of this old jeep, and it can't run without it. That's how I feel about your mom. She's my heart, and everything I do is for her and you."

For another thing, Dad wasn't what I'd call handsome. In the war, a Nazi had broken his nose with the butt of a rifle before a buddy could stick him with a bayonet. Thank the Lord for that miracle. Not only would I have lost my Dad, I wouldn't even have been born.

For the last thing, even though he made what most folks in Kitty Hawk Village would consider a decent living, he'd rather save money than waste it on things we didn't need. He'd bought gold wedding bands for him and Mom. He wore his constantly. Mom complained he'd scratch it in his rough work. The funny thing, though, was she never wore hers at all. I guess that's another one of those warning signs I missed.

When Mom ended class for the day, she did so by the door instead of from her desk. When I tried to bolt by her, she grabbed my arm. "I need you to help carry some papers home, Seth."

Outside on the porch, Ellie's smile turned into a frown. I jerked my arm loose from Mom's hand. "Dad offered to help. That's what you get for ignoring him."

She pointed toward her desk. "You wait there. I'll tell Ellie you can't walk her home today."

I wasn't going to have any part of that. After rushing out the door, I took Ellie by the hand and led her toward the path as fast as we could go.

As soon as we got out of sight of the school, Ellie pulled me to a stop. "What's wrong, Seth? We coulda helped your momma carry her papers."

I'd hoped she hadn't heard what Mom said. Now I had to lie about it. "You didn't hear her when she pointed at her desk. She said to go ahead because it wasn't that many papers anyway."

"Oh. I guess that's ok then."

We walked along, glancing at each other from time to time. The afternoon was warm enough to draw the mosquitos from the black-water lagoons scattered in the woods, evidenced by their buzzing in my ears. "Doggone skeeters," Ellie said, squashing one on her arm and leaving a bloody spot. I squashed my share too, until we got away from the water and they let us alone.

At the path to Ellie's house, she pecked my cheek. "You sho

is a sweet boy, sugar pie. That's why them skeeters was after us so bad. Tomorrow's Saturday, you wanna go fishin? Daddy's got cane poles we can use."

I checked my memory. The jeep was running well, so Dad wouldn't need my help with that. He'd said something about checking the paint on his duck decoys. If he asked me about it, I knew he'd understand about me fishing with Ellie. Mom, on the other hand, might throw a fit. I returned Ellie's peck. "What time?"

"I figured I'd make us some meat loaf samitches. Momma's makin' it for supper tonight."

"Wow, that sounds good," I said, my mouth practically watering. "Meat loaf is one of my favorites."

"All right then," Ellie said. "See you 'round lunch time. Just walk north along the sound a little ways. It ain't far."

I watched her walk down her path again. Being friends was fine, but Ellie and I might make a finer husband and wife one day. We were like fried fish and hush puppies—the perfect match.

Now I needed to meet her parents and see what kind of folks they were. I sure hoped they were happier than Mom was with Dad.

Chapter 4

I should've known my good mood wouldn't last. In fact, because I was so excited about going fishing with Ellie the next day, I forgot about Mom trying to stop me from walking her home after school.

At home, Dad was hoeing our garden spot near the chicken coop. He said when Grandpa built the house, he'd cut down some trees to make room, and those years and years of fallen leaves before then had mixed with the sand to make it rich and easy to work. I left my books and lunch bag inside, and joined him to ask if he needed any help.

He wiped sweat from his forehead with the back of his hand. "No, Son, I'm about ready to call it a day." He tilted his head to one side, looking up the path toward school. "I guess your mom is grading papers."

I wasn't sure if I should ask Dad about fishing with Ellie. Although I was only seven, parents back then let kids run and romp and play on Saturdays. All they asked was for them to come home at mealtimes and to not get hurt. Then again, Mom and Dad did want to know if I was going to be out of hollering distance.

I plucked a blade of grass from the yard and tried to whistle with it between my thumbs. All I got was a shrill squeak, which made Dad's shoulders bounce with a silent laugh. "You're getting there. Just keep practicing."

I dropped the grass. "Dad, Ellie asked me to go fishing with her tomorrow. She's bringing something for lunch. Can I go?"

"As long as you do your chores and your homework." He rubbed the back of his neck. "All this garden work put a crick in my neck." He stopped rubbing. "I see your mom coming down the path. She sure is stepping high. I hope she's in a better mood than last night."

That's when I remembered how Mom tried to stop me from walking Ellie home.

Mom went in the house with her satchel of papers. She hurried back outside and broke a switch off a bush as she passed the henhouse. "Seth Callahan, I'm tired of you disobeying me. You're getting a whipping."

Dad held up his hand. "Hold on there, Luce. What's he done to deserve a whipping?"

"I wanted him to help me carry my papers home, and he ran off with that—" Mom's mouth clamped shut before she told the truth of the matter.

Dad lowered his hand. "Ran off with that what? Were you about to say something unchristian about little Ellie? Seth hasn't done anything wrong. You're mad at how your life has turned out, and you want to take it out on him and me." He pointed at the switch. "Maybe you should use that on yourself, Luce. You could use a lesson or three."

Mom's face turned as red as a boiled blue crab.

"Well?" Dad demanded. "Are you gonna start appreciating your blessings or not? If not, you might as well go on home to your folks. Heck fire, I'll take you myself and tell them how you were about to call sweet little Ellie some kind of childish names, exactly like a child at that."

Mom threw down the switch and whirled to go in the house. The hem of her blue dress flapped around her legs. Her blonde hair shined in the sun. I looked up at Dad. "I'm sorry for causing a fuss."

He patted my head. "It's not your fault, Son. I suppose it's been building for a while. I just wish I'd known it before it got this bad. Let that be a lesson. Always tell the people you care about how you feel about things. Then you can avoid troubles like this and have a happy marriage."

"Do you still think I can go fishing with Ellie?"

"Darn tootin'." He handed me the hoe. "Get yourself a tin can out of the trash and head to that pile of old chicken manure we use in the garden. I bet there's enough worms in there to catch a mess of fish for you and Miss Ellie tomorrow."

I took the offered hoe. "Mom sure won't like it."

He gave my shoulder a little push. "Go on now, get those worms. I'll talk to your mom while you do, and make sure she knows to leave you alone about Ellie."

Like I said, I was seven then. Two years later, not long after my ninth birthday, Mom left us.

The whole thing made me cry like a baby because I thought it was my fault. Dad had to constantly remind me that it wasn't, and it gradually sunk in. Regardless, he was a sad sight for several months, and her note that said for him to not look for her didn't help at all. That's what love will do for you when the person you give your heart to stomps all over it.

I asked Dad if he would mail Mom's folks to let them know she was gone. He said he'd tell them the next time we took a load of fish to Grandpa Mitchell, as it was only right to tell him and Grandma that Mom had left in person. When we did Monday afternoon, a sly little smile curled the corners of Grandma's mouth. I took it as meaning she and Mom had planned the whole thing. They probably did it with letters, especially since Mom made sure to get the mail on the days before she left.

Unlike Grandma's apparent glee at the news, Grandpa shook his head mournfully when he went out to the skiff to check the fish. "I'm sorry, Tom. I'm sure Lucille's mother helped her, but she won't say how. I hope she'll come to her senses one day and come home. You're a fine, hardworking man, and Seth is a fine grandson. I'll keep you both in my prayers." He turned to leave but faced Dad again. "Mary won't like it, but this mess doesn't affect me buying fish from you. Bring it when you can. I'll make sure you get top dollar."

Dad shook his hand. "I sure appreciate it, sir."

"Me too, Grandpa," I chimed in. "Next time you visit, we'll look for shells on the beach."

Grandpa tousled my hair. "I'm mighty busy feeding folks their seafood, Seth. You take care. Maybe I'll see you before too long."

That night at home, Dad took to reading the Bible like a man on a mission. Of course, his mission was to pray Mom back into our lives.

All that summer, Ellie and I were still like fried fish and hush puppies. If you saw one of us, you saw the other. Her folks were as fine as any I'd ever met—her brothers and sisters too. They even invited Dad and me to supper once a month or so. This started the trend of us attending the Baptist church one Sunday and the Methodist church the next. Word had gotten out about Mom. No matter where we went, people always said they were praying for us.

Six months later, Dad said he was going to be a minister, but he would still fish during the week. Both churches took up an offering to help with his schooling. That's when the trouble started.

On Manteo, Grandma and Grandpa Callahan took the news of Mom leaving us hard. Grandma suggested we live with them for a while. Grandpa suggested Dad become a minister at the Baptist church in Manteo. Dad refused both suggestions. He didn't say why, but I thought he wanted to stay at home in case Mom came back before he left for school. Grandpa's general store was doing well. Whenever we visited, he always sent us on our way with a bottle of grape pop each and a two bags of peanuts.

As far as which church to be a minister of, there were no

openings. Besides, the schooling it took to be a minister was expensive, and the offerings from both churches wouldn't begin to cover it. I was glad. If Dad went away to school, I'd have to stay in Manteo with Grandpa and Grandma Callahan, and I didn't want to be away from Ellie.

Nine-years-old going on ten may not seem like much in the romance department, but it's a lot in the best friend department. When Ellie and I weren't in school or doing chores, we were either fishing, wading the sound, or walking the beach. We'd talk about this or that, hold hands on summer nights in the moonlight, and do our homework together.

The new teacher, a Miss Englebright, tortured us with long division, learning the multiplication tables, and endless dates in history. We didn't mind much because it gave us an excuse to spend time together to learn all that stuff.

Then, in the summer of 1956, a few weeks after I turned ten, Dad said he'd saved enough money to go to school to be a minister. I admired him for choosing such an honorable profession, but I thought earning your way in itself was honorable. When I told him that at supper, right after he said he would be going to school that fall, he gave me a warm smile. "Why, Son, anything we do to earn our way is honorable. That's why I want to preach, to teach folks how the Bible calls us to earn our bread by the sweat of our brow, along with how living a Christian life leads to a grateful life. You know how important being grateful is, don't you?"

I nodded. "I know, but I'd be more grateful if I didn't have to leave Ellie. She's about the only friend I got."

Dad spooned butterbeans. "That's because she's the only person your age you spend time with."

"That's because the boys at school don't want anything to do with me," I said, and swallowed the lemonade I'd made for supper. "I don't mind. Ellie has stuck with me no matter what. She doesn't care if I get a cold or nothing like that. She still wants to be with me."

Dad grinned. "Amen to that. It's like those old timers at the general store say, 'When your pockets are full, you got more friends than you can count. But when your pockets are empty, only your true friends stick by you.'"

Those old timers sure knew what they were talking about. I took a bite of a fried chicken leg Dad had learned how to make. "If you go to school, can I use the skiff to visit Ellie on the weekends?"

"Sure you can," Dad said, sharing an understanding smile. "I'll be back in the summer. You can see her then, too." He patted my shoulder. "I'll sure miss you, Son. Be good for your grandma and grandpa."

That night I snuck out of bed, got dressed, and ran to tell Ellie. We'd been getting together like this all summer, tapping on each other's bedroom window after our folks had gone to sleep.

I'd been warning Ellie about Dad going to school, plus how he'd mentioned talking to me about it today. As soon as I tapped her window, she raised it and climbed out. We knew to be quiet until we wouldn't wake anyone, so we ran down the moonlit path to the sound.

Ellie, wearing a hand-me-down pair of her older brother's dungarees and a yellowed white T-shirt, plopped to the sand. "I just knowed this day was comin'. Is they anyway we can stop it?"

I sat beside her. "Dad's going to let me use the skiff. That way I can visit you on the weekends."

"Not on Sunday," Ellie said, hanging her head. "That's church day."

I hadn't thought of that. "Well, we'll have all day Saturday, and Dad said he'll be home in the summer."

Ellie put her arm around my waist and leaned her head on my shoulder. "You is my best friend in the whole wide world, Seth. Please don't go."

Her sad voice tugged at my heart. I sure didn't want to go,

but what else could I do?

The first Saturday in September, Dad packed his cardboard suitcase, put on his best church clothes, which were a pair of black pants and a blue, button-up shirt, and caught the bus over the wooden bridge from Kitty Hawk to the mainland. School in Manteo started the next week. I'd be in the fifth grade, and I didn't know what to expect from the kids there.

After Dad left, I drove the jeep back home. Kids were doing all kinds of grown-up things back then, but that might be because the Outer Banks was so isolated.

In my room, I packed my own suitcase. Grandma had fretted about me taking the skiff to Manteo on my own. Grandpa told her I was grown enough and responsible enough to do as I pleased. I made that deal with Dad because I wanted to tell Ellie goodbye.

I locked the door. At the end of the pier, I put my suitcase in the skiff. Dad had asked Mr. Tate to feed the chickens and the cow, saying to take the eggs and milk in trade, and Mr. Tate said he was glad to help.

Ellie and I agreed to meet for one last lunch together at our favorite beach on the sound. I motored there and found her on a quilt in the shade of a live oak, with its crooked limbs reaching out low to the ground.

Wearing cut-off dungarees for shorts and an old blue T-shirt—no shoes, of course—I anchored the skiff and waded ashore.

Taller and not so thin, her brown eyes smiling, Ellie ran to meet me. "Wowwee, look at you," I said. "Is that a new dress? You sure look nice in yellow."

"Cindy let me borrow it." Ellie turned a circle, her little toes kicking up sand. "I'll be so purty one day, you'll ask me to marry you."

"I don't know," I said, using my best teasing tone. "Cindy caught my eye the last time Dad and me ate with y'all."

Ellie poked my stomach. "Phooey on you, sugar pie. You

just like her cause she's fifteen and looks more like an hourglass than a stick like I do."

Despite our teasing, a sudden burst of melancholy filled my chest. To not let Ellie see how I felt, I suggested we eat.

As we did, I took note of how she was growing up. Her hair, once brown and stringy, was getting thick and wavy. Her lips, once thin and shapeless, were now fuller and resembling a bow. She'd told me I was getting handsome, but I didn't know about that. Since I'd stopped wearing that dumb straw hat and long-sleeved shirt after Mom left, my wiry frame was tanned. I knew I had muscles from chores, which now included chopping wood, as well as all my running around on the beach. Mom used to cut my hair in a crew cut. I never liked it much. It now grew to cover my ears, dark and curling before dad took a pair of scissors to it. At least I didn't have his crooked nose, so maybe that helped.

Ellie gave me a second sandwich from a basket. "I'm glad Momma made meat loaf. I wanted our last day to be special."

Staring at her, I took the sandwich. "You say it's our last day like we'll never see each other again. I already told you I'll come back every Saturday."

"Cindy says it isn't good for a girl to stick to one boy. She says it's best to play the field."

I could see that for teenagers, who were looking for a good match in a husband or a wife, but not for best friends. I told Ellie that very thing, adding how Cindy should mind her own business. Besides, Ellie had been the one who'd just made the remark about me asking her to marry me. None of it made sense. Still, I wanted to make the best of the day, so I thanked her for the sandwich and took a bite.

The September day was perfect, not too warm, not too cool. A blue sky filled the horizon. Out on the sound, shimmering with sunlight, a pair of men in a skiff pulled crab pots. A breeze from the north brought the faint aroma of a dead fish, but not too much to bother my appetite for Mrs. Tate's delicious meatloaf.

Done eating, Ellie stretched out on the quilt, folding her arm under her head for a pillow. I was tempted to tickle her sandy toes but didn't. Although I'd enjoyed the meatloaf, what she'd said about this being our last day together was bothering me again.

I washed the last bite of sandwich down with water from a Mason jar, capped it and returned it to the basket. Ellie patted my back. "Lay on down beside me, sugar pie. I'm sorry my talk about this being our last day made you sad."

I lay on my side and propped my head up with my hand so I could face her. Grinning, she touched my nose with a fingertip, a habit from us spending so much time together. I touched hers back. Maybe I'd taken what she'd said about this being our last day together the wrong way.

We relaxed like that for a while, simply looking at each other. I wished I didn't have to leave. Ellie was my best friend, and I'd miss her worse than anything. Each and every Saturday couldn't come quick enough, and I hoped she felt the same way.

Between the nice breeze and the lapping of the sound against the shore, the next thing I knew, our eyes were closing and opening, closing and opening. The sun was on its way down, but I didn't care. I still had plenty of time to get to Manteo before dark. Half-asleep, I woke up when my head slid out of my hand. Ellie blinked her eyes open. "I reckon you better go, Seth. It's gettin' late."

I helped her fold the quilt, thanked her for lunch, and hugged her goodbye, saying I'd see her next Saturday morning, soon as I finished my chores at my grandparents' house.

One good thing about living with them was Grandpa was going to pay me to put stock up in the store, and that money would help pay for gas for the jeep and the skiff. The pay wouldn't be much, just a quarter a week, which sort of aggravated me. The jeep was almost out of gas, and I wanted to take Ellie to see the wild horses at Corolla. At a quarter a week, plus buying oil to mix for the skiff's old outboard motor, it'd take a while to save enough to make that drive up there and back. Heck, since taking the skiff back and forth to see Ellie every Saturday was my priority, I might be a durn teenager before we could get to Corolla.

I carried the anchor out to the skiff, got in, and waved bye to Ellie. "Have a good week at school. I'll see you Saturday, soon as I can."

She returned the wave. "All right then, sugar pie. Don't go gettin' sweet on any of them girls in that Manteo school."

I jerked the pull rope on the outboard, and it puttered to life. Blue smoke bubbled up from the water, where the exhaust came from what Dad called the "lower unit," where the propeller was. I sat on the hard wooden seat and twisted the throttle. The bow rose, slicing the water, and I was on my way, leaving Ellie behind for a whole week, the longest time we'd been apart since we'd met in the second grade.

The first day of fifth grade in Manteo went as expected. Sure, I tried being nice by holding the door for the girls and smiling as the teacher, Mrs. Rosemont, introduced me. The thing was, as soon as she said I was from Kitty Hawk Village, I knew the whole class would think I was nothing but a beach bum that smelled like dead fish, and that's how they looked at me after cutting their eyes at each other. Whenever Mrs. Rosemont asked questions, I kept my hand down even though I knew the answers. I just stayed to myself and did what I was told. That way I figured I'd keep out of trouble. Then Grandma and Grandpa wouldn't have any excuses to keep me from taking the skiff to see Ellie.

At lunch, I found me a tree. No one came over. No one asked, "How're you? Why're you eating alone? Wanna eat with me?" I didn't care. I had me a fine friend in little Miss Ellie Tate, so those kids could take a long walk off a short pier as far as I was concerned.

I stop typing on my laptop and get up from the dining room table to stretch and smile. It's funny how I've started writing like my ten-year-old self used to talk.

How about that? After being miserable for so long after my wife died, I actually think something is funny. She really knew what she was talking about, having me write this story to help ease the pain of losing her.

I fill a glass at the faucet and go to the sliding glass doors to sip. August has replaced July. The sun is glaring down from the midday sky. Jet skiers zoom by. In the distance, I can just make out the blue dot of a parasail tethered to a boat. Entrepreneurs sure came up with a lot of different ways to earn a living out here on the Outer Banks over the years.

From time to time, I picture my life without Ellie in it. When you connect with someone like she and I did, it's a treasure to remember. If we're blessed, we have a childhood friend like her, someone you can trust to listen when you're down. It's just a shame when you lose them.

I swallow the last of the water, pour two fingers of bourbon in the glass, and return to the laptop. The next chapter is both good and bad, and the bourbon might smooth the edges of the bad.

Chapter 5

My first school year in Manteo passed slowly. Dad sent a letter every week, asking how I was doing in class and if Ellie and her family were well. He also asked how I liked working in Grandpa's store. I liked it fine and told him so. Still, I liked it better on Saturday mornings, when I ran down to Grandpa's pier and took the skiff to Kitty Hawk to see Ellie.

When Dad came home for the summer, things took a turn for the worse. The Tate family's milk cow died, and when Dad said he and I needed our cow's milk in the summer, Mr. Tate seemed a bit put off. "I got four growing young'uns and me and the wife," he said. "Is there any way you can share the milk?" Dad allowed him half, but Mr. Tate wasn't happy with that. Then Dad mentioned how we'd be eating our eggs instead of Mr. Tate taking them, and that didn't set well either. "Well, Tom, since you said I could have them, I was selling some for cash money, and it sure came in handy." Dad said he was sorry. Mr. Tate had more chickens than us. If he needed more eggs to sell, he could buy more hens.

We left Mr. Tate scratching his head and Mrs. Tate with her arms crossed. At home, Dad said he felt bad about it, but the Tates knew the deal when they agreed to it.

The next time I saw Ellie, she didn't have much to say, likely from hearing her folks complain about Dad's decision. I understood how they felt. As far as people went in Kitty Hawk, they were amongst the poorest. Still, the churches helped when they could, so that kept them clothed and fed.

One day, though, Dad sat me down on our pier for a talk. "Son, I hate to tell you this because I don't want you to think badly of Mr. Tate, but a large part of his problem with money is his drinking. He's a fine man otherwise, both to his wife and to his children. It's sad to hear, but he spends a fair amount of money on hard liquor, bought from bootleggers."

This was a shock to me. Like Dad said, Mr. Tate always treated his family fine, at least from what I saw.

"Don't tell Ellie we know about it," Dad continued. "I don't want her to feel bad about it. Just let things go on between you like always."

I could do that, but I didn't understand how liquor could have such a hold on someone as to make them spend their hard-earned money on it. "Why doesn't he give up drinking, Dad? Isn't his family worth it?"

Dad took a deep breath. "He was in the war like me. That might have something to do with it. Some men can't handle the sights we saw and some can. I hope you never have to figure out which one you can do."

At the time, I hoped the same doggone thing. Little did I know, I'd eventually change my mind, and because of losing a young woman who meant a lot to me. Regardless of all that, Dad had been injured, both with a broken nose and a bullet wound to his leg. Although neither one was serious, I asked Dad if Mr. Tate had been injured, and that was why he drank.

I asked him that very thing one time. All he would say is he saw some terrible things that gave him nightmares. "As bad as that is," Dad added, "if he keeps up his drinking habit, it might ruin his liver."

I knew what that meant. More than one local man had returned from the Great War in 1918 to fall victim to alcoholism.

I told Dad I wouldn't say anything to Ellie. What I didn't

say was how she hadn't been herself since he spoke to Mr. Tate about the milk and eggs.

That fall, when Dad went back to minister school, Ellie seemed herself again, probably because Mr. Tate had more milk for his family and eggs to sell for liquor. I hated that part of it, especially because his memories of the war were likely the cause.

I'm happy to say, though, that the next few years passed without incident. Dad finished school in 1960, when I turned fourteen. Ellie and I remained fine friends. We fished and waded the sound and ran the beaches whenever we could. The thing was, we were growing up before our very eyes, evidenced by how she would look at me sometimes, with pouty lips like she wanted me to kiss her. To be honest, I didn't have those feelings for her. I suppose it was because we were best friends for so long.

During this time, Dad filled in at the Methodist church whenever he was needed. I liked his preaching style, calmer and cooler than fire and brimstone, like the Baptist preacher sometimes preached. Because more tourists were visiting the area, Grandpa Mitchell started a restaurant nearby. Between his demand for more fish and Dad's preaching money, plus how electricity came to Kitty Hawk a while back, we could afford to get indoor plumbing, a refrigerator, and a gas stove. Even though Dad took the old wood cookstove out, he put it in the woods in the backyard. I didn't ask why. He probably did it to remember Mom.

I loved the modernization of our old house. Turning a faucet for a drink of water was the cat's meow, the same as not having to drive that old jeep to the general store for ice for the old icebox or to chop wood for the cookstove.

One thing I didn't care for was helping Dad fish, which he enlisted me to do when school was out, plus on weekends. Not only was it hard, stinky work, I didn't get to see Ellie much.

Things went this way until Dad got the notion to visit what

he called The Holy Land, otherwise known as Israel. I was glad. Ellie and I could spend more time together, and I could get away from those stinky fish. It was wrong to complain. Those fish and Dad's preaching had earned us a decent-sized nest egg in the bank.

He was scheduled to leave in the summer of 1963. I was seventeen and would turn eighteen while he was gone, which would be for two weeks.

With me not seeing Ellie much, I'd been hearing about her dating. I tried not to care but didn't do a good job of it. I wanted her to be happy, but I'd heard enough talk at the general store to know boys might date a girl for no other reason than to do things they shouldn't do with them.

The week before Dad left for Israel, he said I was going with him. That ruined the time I planned to spend with Ellie. With that news aggravating me, I went to tell her about it and to say goodbye for two weeks. We walked down to the sound and sat at the same place where we had our first picnic.

After I told her about the trip, she shoved her toes in the sand and looked out over the water. "Is your daddy crazy? We've been hearing on the radio how some of those folks over there want to start a war to take back their land from the Jews."

Dad had mentioned this, but we wouldn't be visiting those areas. "Dad knows about all that," I told Ellie. "It'll be fine."

"Well, if you say so." Ellie stared at the sound again before facing me. "I need to tell you something. I won't be here when you get back."

"What do you mean?" I asked, trying and failing to keep panic out of my voice.

"We're moving in with Momma's folks in Raleigh. Daddy's doctor says his liver won't last much longer. With Cindy and the rest married, it'll just be me and Momma and Daddy. That's why Momma's folks got room for us."

The realization that this would be the last time I saw Ellie pressed my heart down to the size of a pearl. Mom had left, and now Ellie would leave. Not only that, Grandma Callahan in Manteo was having heart palpitations, and Grandpa Mitchell was retiring to let his boys run both restaurants. The circle of people I cared about was shrinking, and I didn't know what to do about it.

Before I knew what was happening, Ellie had pushed me down to sit astride me, her brown eyes gazing into mine. "I want to be with you at least once before you leave, Seth. Can't you do that for me?"

I wasn't sure what she meant. Then, when she kissed me hard and started taking her shirt off, I knew what she meant. I rolled from beneath her and got up. "We can't do that, Ellie. That's how people have to get married."

Tears rolled down her cheeks. "All this time I thought you loved me, durn you. We'll never see each other again, and you won't do that one thing for me." She sat up, raised her knees to her chest, and rested her chin on them. "I don't know what to think about anything anymore."

I sat by her. "I do love you, but not that way."

"Is it because I'm skinny? I can't help that."

"No, Ellie. I always thought you were the prettiest girl in school."

"You're just sayin' that to be nice, Seth."

"What if I kiss you goodbye to prove it?"

Ellie wiped tears. "That ain't enough."

I rubbed a circle between her shoulder blades. "It's enough when someone really cares about you like I do. Don't you know that?"

Ellie said nothing. I got up to my knees and tipped her face toward mine. Right then and there, I found out what it felt like to want a girl like Ellie, when she wanted me to want her. Despite what could happen, I kissed her, and our seventeen-year-old hormones went wild. No, thank goodness, we didn't do everything she wanted, but only because I pulled away from her and snatched my clothes on. "We can't, Ellie. I want to, but we're too young to have a baby."

Lying there on the sand in her bra and panties, her gorgeous brunette hair scattered over her shoulders, she looked up at me. "Momma and Daddy got married at eighteen."

"I'm not ready to get married," I pleaded. "I don't even know what I want to do with my life yet." The memory of why Mom left came back. "The last thing I want is to make my wife and family live a hard life in Kitty Hawk. Dad's doing well as a minister, but he still has to fish to earn a decent living."

Ellie got up and put her clothes on. "And because of what I wanted, you think I'm too sorry a person to be a minister's wife."

"You don't understand," I said, disappointed that she'd confused my words. "I don't want to be a minister or a fisherman. I just haven't figured it out yet. Don't you want to be something besides a minister's or a fisherman's wife?"

Using her fingers to comb sand out of her hair, Ellie glared at me. "It's a good thing I'll never see you again. You make as much sense as Daddy killin' his own liver." She whirled and stomped away, leaving me as dumbfounded as I'd ever been. Not only that, she'd left me with the knowledge of what it felt like to want to be with a woman, and I almost regretted not seeing what it would be like with her. If I ever got the chance again, it might be too much to take.

I brushed sand off my clothes and went home. What a mess I'd made of things. On top of that, I had to go with Dad to this whole other country I knew nothing about. Did the people there speak English? Would we have a translator if they didn't? What kind of food did they eat? Would it be something I'd like? By the time I got home, I was ready to tell Dad to go by himself while I stayed here and fished. You got it. I'd rather smell dead fish than leave everything I knew in Kitty Hawk, which made no sense after what I'd asked Ellie about living in such a hard place.

Before Dad and I left, he made me get a proper haircut

instead of him taking scissors to my curly locks. It was ok, not bristly like the crew cuts Mom used to give me, not so long it hung over my ears and down to the collar of my shirt in back. When the barber brushed hair from my neck, he chuckled. "Teak, your boy is two-toned. He's tanned everywhere except the back of his neck and his ears."

Dad returned the chuckle. "His forehead too."

"Go on and make fun," I told them. "I was hoping to date a girl from over there in Israel. Now they'll look at me like I'm a freak."

Dad paid the barber and hustled me outside. "We were just teasing you, Son. You're a good looking young man, just like I was at your age. Once we get settled in Israel, I bet you'll have to fight the girls off with a stick."

The following Saturday, Dad got Grandpa Mitchell to take us to Raleigh, both to buy some nice clothes and to drop us off at the airport. There we said our goodbyes, and there, feeling like a salt water nobody out of my element, I goggled at my first jet airplane. Dad caught me staring. Then I remembered he saw stuff like this in the war.

We checked our luggage and boarded the plane. With all those dressy folks there, smelling of perfume and after shave, I was glad I'd taken a bath the night before.

All wearing the same blue skirts, white blouses, and little blue hats, pretty ladies Dad called stewardesses patrolled the aisles like female soldiers, telling us what to do in an emergency and how to buckle our seatbelts. Before long, those jet engines whined up to shriek like a hurricane, and all I could do was to grip the armrests so hard that I thought my fingernails would stick into them. Still, that was nothing compared to when the plane tilted back and left the ground. As it did, my stomach flipped, and I hoped I wouldn't need a bag to get sick in.

The plane eventually leveled, and the engines gradually quieted. Dad patted my hand. "See? Nothing to it."

I pulled my hands up from the armrests. "Tell my fingers that. They're curled like claws because I was scared half to death."

Stewardesses started pushing little carts around, asking if we'd like something to drink. Dad and I took an ice-cold bottle of Coke and a bag of peanuts each. A few swallows later, we dumped the peanuts into the bottles and crunched them after a short soak, one of our favorite treats back home.

It's funny how those details of the flights to and from Israel are all I remember. I guess the nostalgia of Coke and peanuts and the fear of my first time flying stuck with me while little else about the flights did.

I sure remembered the lights of Tel Aviv. We'd left Raleigh in the morning, so that sight didn't stick with me like the lights of Tel Aviv did. Maybe it was because they resembled the stars on a clear night in Kitty Hawk, something I've always treasured.

With our passports checked and our luggage in hand, we went outside, in the overhead lights of the airport entrance and exit to wait for taxi. After a while I faced Dad. "Why aren't you trying to get a taxi? Isn't one supposed to take us to a hotel?"

From my left came the sound of a motorcycle engine, similar to our skiff's outboard. Expecting a motorcycle to zoom by, I was surprised to see a small, red, four-door car stop in front of us. The thing wasn't much bigger than the jeep back home. Unlike the jeep's black tires, this car had white wall tires, and the headlights reminded me of a bug-eyed bullfrog's eyes.

"This is our ride," Dad said. "We're staying with this man's family. Our minister back home got me in touch with him."

The man climbed out and rounded the trunk to meet us. "Welcome, welcome, Mr. Callahan. I'm so glad to finally meet you after getting to know you through the mail."

They shook hands before Dad gestured to me. "This is Seth. Seth, this is Mr. Levin. He's going to be our tour guide."

We shook hands. "Ah, you're a handsome young man," Mr.

Levin said.

Unless I missed my guess, because of his dark hair graying at the temples and the deep crow's feet in the corners of his eyes, he was around sixty or so. I flushed warmly at him saying I was handsome. No one except Dad and Grandma Callahan ever said that, and I hadn't really believed them.

I thanked him as he opened the trunk. "If you don't mind," he told Dad, "would you please handle your luggage? My back has been bothering me. My doctor doesn't want me to strain it."

Dad said he didn't mind at all. With the luggage secure and us in the back seat of the cramped little car, we left the airport on my first big adventure in another country.

I leaned back in the seat to rest. Along with the long, tiresome day, I was a bit disappointed to hear Mr. Levin was our tour guide. Dad said they sometimes were young women, and that would be a good way to get my mind off of Ellie leaving Kitty Hawk. Oh well, like Grandpa Callahan liked to say, "You never know what kind of fish your bait's gonna catch."

Chapter 6

To be honest, as Mr. Levin drove, I didn't like the narrow streets and square houses made of concrete, both flashing by in the light of the car's headlights. Give me the wide-open views of the Albemarle Sound and the Atlantic Ocean anytime.

Dad leaned close to my ear. "Yes, Son, I can see it in your eyes. I miss Kitty Hawk already myself. There's no place like home."

Illuminated by the dashboard's light, Mr. Levin's dark eyes peered at us in the rear-view mirror. "Tom, have you told Seth about our conflicts with the Arabs?"

"Just enough to let him know we'll be safe with you," Dad said.

"What's it about?" I asked Mr. Levin, hoping to verify what Ellie told me.

"As you know, Seth, being the son of a minister, we Jews have lived here since biblical times. After the Holocaust in Germany, many of us left Europe to come here. My wife and I lost our parents in Poland, but we managed to escape. Unfortunately, the Arabs don't care for us returning to our homeland."

I'd learned about the Holocaust in school. How the Nazis could be so cruel was beyond me. On top of that, after escaping from the horror of over six-million Jews dying in concentration camps, they weren't welcome in their own homeland, which the United Nations said they should have.

"Are there any attacks now?" Dad asked.

Mr. Levin slowed his car and took a right, down a narrower street. "I'm sure the Arabs are thinking of something," he said. "Yassar Arafat is stirring things up with his anti-Jewish rhetoric. Some say he won't rest long before he talks his people into striking us again with their despicable guerrilla tactics."

"What kind of tactics?" I asked.

"Bombing the innocent," Mr. Levin said, frustration in his voice. "To them, every Jewish man, woman, and child is the enemy. I pray for peace, but people who hate like they do have no interest in peace."

"How are your daughters?" Dad asked, likely to change the subject. "Alma and Lia, right?"

"Yes, that is correct," Mr. Levin said. "Lia just turned fourteen. Unfortunately, unlike her sister, she's getting interested in boys."

I was curious about Alma. Maybe she was too young to be interested in boys.

"I believe Alma just graduated from college," Dad said.

"Yes, yes," Mr. Levin said. "She did well enough in high school to start college early. She's much more the bookworm than Lia is."

Interested in the subject because I didn't know what I wanted to do with my life, I asked Mr. Levin what Alma's plans were.

"She hasn't decided yet," he said. "She loves history and knows my tours as well as I do. She may return to college to be a history professor." Mr. Levin turned onto a wider street, drove a few more blocks, and parked in front of a two-story concrete house. I liked this one, covered in white stucco with a red tile roof, better than the gray ones. Several trees grew around it. Climbing out of the cramped back seat, I asked Mr. Levin what they were, and he said they were olive trees. To one side of the house was a smaller but similar house. When I asked about it, he said it was a rental. No one lived there now, the renter having left last month, and he and his wife wanted to remodel it before they leased it again. All in all I liked their home. It was on a hill. If I looked to the east hard enough, over the multitude of rooftops in Tel Aviv, I could make out the reflection of the moon in the Mediterranean Sea.

Mr. Levin opened the trunk and jerked Dad's huge suitcase out. "Oh no, " he said, his face twisting in agony. He set the suitcase down and stayed leaning over, pressing his hands against his lower back. "What a putz I am, forgetting about my back."

Dad took his elbow. "Can I help you inside?"

"No, no, it's too bad to walk. Tell Rachel to bring my wheelchair."

I assumed Rachel was Mr. Levin's wife. At the door, Dad knocked. A light beside it came on, and it opened to reveal a young woman with a dark complexion that equaled my tan. Seeing Mr. Levin leaning over with his hands on his back, she ran out to him. "Oh, no, Abba, I see you hurt your back again. Can you walk?"

"No, Alma dear, it's worse than the last time. Get my wheelchair."

So this was Alma, the oldest daughter. She caught my attention but I couldn't say why. Maybe it was her huge, dark eyes behind a pair of eyeglasses shaped like those one of my teachers wore, the frames made of tortoiseshell and shaped like a cat's eyes. Then again, her thick hair, black and tied in a ponytail, could be it, or maybe it was her strong nose that gave her profile a striking appearance. In one way, she did look like a bookworm. In another she didn't. She wore a white, long-sleeved blouse with a stiff collar, a blue skirt just past her knees, and a simple pair of cloth shoes, the soles flat. She was average in height and size, somewhat reminding me of Mom.

Dad stacked our suitcases behind Mr. Levin. "Can you sit until Alma gets your wheelchair? That might help the pain."

Wincing, Mr. Levin sat and waved Alma away. "Get my chair. I need my pain pills and my bed."

As Alma hurried away, Mr. Levin faced me. "Young man, my wife and I don't care for formalities. You and your father will be living with us for two weeks. Please, call me Morris and my wife Rachel."

I said I would. The door to the house opened again, and out came an older, thinner version of Alma. With dark hair streaked with gray, this must be Morris's wife. Behind her came a younger version of Alma, but with dark, curly hair and no glasses. Behind them, Alma rolled a wheel chair toward us. "I'm coming, Abba."

"Seth," Rachel said, "please put your strong, young arms to work and help me put this old man into this wheeled chariot of his." She frowned at Morris. "You tried to pick up that big suitcase, didn't you? No matter how careful I tell you to be until your back is better, you won't listen."

Alma and Lia steadied the wheelchair. I took one of Morris's arms while Rachel took the other. Despite his grunts of pain, we managed to ease him down. I closed the trunk, and Dad and I followed everyone with our suitcases. I didn't say anything to him, but with our tour guide hurt, I wondered if we had come all this way for nothing.

Inside, Lia closed the door. She started to roll Morris down a hall, but he told her to turn the chair toward us. "Welcome to our home. Although I am sorry for what happened, I am glad you are here. If my back is not better tomorrow, Alma will be your tour guide."

Alma's eyes flashed toward Dad and I before returning to Morris. "But, Abba, you asked me to clean the rental house and paint the rooms."

Dad tilted his head toward me. "Seth can help when we're not out and about, if your parents don't mind."

Rachel shared a soft smile with her eldest daughter. "A fine idea. I feel as if I know our guests from the letters Morris shared with me."

"Good," Lia said. "Now someone can help paint besides me."

"I'd rather you not help," Alma said to her sister. "The last time we painted your room, you spent more time talking about boys than painting."

"You can paint when our guests are gone," Morris said. Show them their rooms and offer refreshment from their journey. They've come a long way." He faced Rachel. "Please get me into my bed and bring my pills."

Lia went through a doorway and came back with a glass of water and a pill bottle. "I'll put them on your nightstand, Abba."

Rachel rolled Morris down a hall, Lia behind her. Alma waved us through the living room and toward a hall. We followed until she opened two doors beside each other. "Seth, the first door is your room. Mr. Callahan, the other room is yours. Seth, your room is my room, and Lia's room is your abba's room. She's going to sleep on the sofa. I'm going to sleep in the rental house."

"We're sorry to put you out," Dad said.

Narrowing her eyes, Alma blinked at him. "We'll sleep inside. You're not putting us out."

"It's an American thing," I said. "Putting you out means to cause problems."

"It's no problem. I like being by myself. If you had a sister, you'd understand. When you're ready, come to the room where I got the water, and I'll have you a little *nosh*."

She left, and Dad grinned at me. "In case you didn't know it, *nosh* means snack."

"Thanks for clearing that up, Dad. I guess I get to call you abba while we're here."

"They're a nice family, Son. What do you think of Alma? We'll be spending a lot of time with her if Morris's back doesn't get better. Maybe she'll get your mind off of Ellie while we're here." He picked up his suitcase. "Let's put these away and see what our *nosh* is so we can get to bed. I'm tired."

I turned a light switch on by the door and went inside. The head of Alma's bed sat near the far wall. To the left, two bookcases were filled. To the right, a hair brush sat on a dresser with a mirror. She must've taken her things to the rental and had forgotten the brush. On the wall over the head of the bed hung a framed photograph of Albert Einstein. Below it, written in ink on a sheet of paper, was a quote: *Love is Light*.

With a quote like that, maybe Alma wasn't the bookworm Morris thought she was. I'd have to ask her what the quote meant. Maybe I could use it to get a girlfriend when I got back home.

Dad stuck his head in the door. "You ready?"

I said I was, and followed him down the hall and into the kitchen, where Alma was setting a tray on a table. "Please sit," she said, returning to a counter for two glasses and a pitcher. "This is lemonade with mint. On the tray is pastrami and latkes and rye. I hope you enjoy it."

I had no idea what this food was. Alma must've caught my puzzled expression. She pointed at each in turn. "Pastrami is cooked beef mixed with spices. The latkes are made from potatoes and fried in a pan. The rye is a type of bread." She went to the refrigerator and returned with a jar. "A sandwich with pastrami, rye, and mustard is delicious."

Dad thanked her for her hospitality, bowed his head to say grace, and raised it to start making a sandwich. Always trusting of a potato, I tried one of the latkes. "Wow, Dad, you gotta try one of these."

About to bite his sandwich, he stopped. "I will if you let me try this first."

Alma poured lemonade. "Let me check on Abba. I'll be right back."

I compared the watch Dad gave me for my fifteenth birthday, something I rarely wore at home, to a clock over the sink. "Sheesh, Dad, it's 12:30 here."

Swallowing lemonade, he lowered the glass. "Thanks for reminding me. I need to set my watch too."

Alma came back. "Ima and Abba said to tell you goodnight, and Lia has gone to bed. Do you need anything before I go to the rental?"

"We were just changing our watches to match your time," I said. "What time should we get up?"

"Since we stayed up late to welcome you, we're getting up at nine."

"Thank you for the snack," Dad said. "We'll clean up when we finish."

"Oh, no, please don't. I'll come back before I go to sleep and do that."

I enjoyed Alma's accent, but I couldn't think of what it was similar too. Her voice had a musical quality to it, rich and smooth. Not that I wanted Morris to be in pain, but I'd rather she be mine and Dad's tour guide until he got better.

As she went to the rental, I could see her through the window in the door, illuminated by moonlight.

"I see you looking," Dad said. "Alma's helping you forget about Ellie already."

Ignoring his teasing, I took another bite of my delicious pastrami on rye. I wouldn't say Alma made me forget about Ellie, but her courteous demeanor and sweet disposition was a nice change from Ellie's Kitty Hawk Village ways, not to mention my own.

"Well?" Dad asked. "Aren't you going to answer me?"

I grabbed one of his latkes. "I don't know, Dad. I do know if she cooked our *nosh,* she's got a lot going for her."

"I hear you. Just don't go falling in love with her, or any other girls around her. They sure are easy on the eyes."

Dad's suggestion made sense. It would be pretty dumb to start a relationship with a girl half way around the doggone world.

We finished eating. Dad stood and stretched. "Man, am I ready for bed. I guess Alma will take care of this stuff soon."

I poured a few more swallows of lemonade in my glass. "You go ahead. I'll hit the old hay after I drink this."

As Dad's bedroom door closed, Alma came in. "Oh, you're still eating. I was hoping you could help me with something."

I downed the lemonade and stood. "Sure, what's up?"

Alma looked at the ceiling. "The ceiling is up. Why do you ask?"

"That's just how some of us Americans ask what someone wants."

"Oh." She grabbed my hand and pulled me out the door, across the yard, and inside the rental house. She must've been getting ready for bed. Her hair was down and her blouse was unbuttoned enough to reveal the curve of brown skin. Still clutching my hand, she pointed toward a corner. "Do you see it? I can't sleep in here with a rat."

I held in a laugh. "I'd say that's more of a mouse than a rat." A few feet away from the mouse, a paperback made me almost laugh for real. "I see you missed it with your book."

She took off one shoe, crept forward with it raised, and threw it at the mouse. The shoe hit the wall above the mouse, which scared it toward us. Shrieking, Alma jumped onto me, wrapping her arms around my neck and her legs around my waist. I opened the door and herded the mouse outside with my feet. "Okay, you can get down now."

She let go and landed on her feet, leaving the sweet smell of some kind of perfume hanging between us. With her hair all over, her dark eyes wide, and her chest rising and falling from all the excitement, I thought she was the prettiest girl I'd ever seen.

She buttoned her collar and smoothed her dress. "Thank you. I don't normally get so flustered."

I got her shoe and came back to offer it to her. "You might need this tomorrow for our tour. You know, if your Dad's back is still bothering him."

She took the shoe. "Thank you, you can go now. We really should get some sleep."

I nodded. "Sure. If you need any more help with your varmints, just holler."

One the way out, I closed the door behind me, wondering if she knew what a varmint was. While I brushed my teeth, I heard someone in the kitchen, likely Alma cleaning up after Dad and me.

Sitting on the bed to take my shoes off, I saw her hairbrush on the dresser. The way her hair was all over the place after she jumped me, she needed it. I took it to the rental, noting the clean kitchen as I passed through. The rental door was near the right corner. Before I knocked, I noticed a light coming from a window on that side of the house. Curious, I leaned around the corner and almost dropped the brush.

Wearing a thin nightgown, Alma was standing just inside the window, her elbows on the sill. I said she was pretty before. Now she was gorgeous. Then again, it was probably my male hormones doing backflips, because of how the outline of her body was visible in the bright moonlight that shone through the thin material of her nightgown.

All I could do was grit my teeth. Alma stirred the same feelings Ellie did when we were half naked. No, those feelings were stirring more than that now. Alma was a beautiful, exotic woman, not some skinny gal from Kitty Hawk.

Yeah, the moment I thought that, I knew it was wrong to compare Ellie and Alma by their physical appearance. Like Dad had been trying to teach me since Mom had left, it takes a lot more than looks to make a happy marriage. Looks eventually fade. Then you're left with all the important things, like love, friendship, and what you have in common.

I knocked on the door. "I brought your hairbrush. I'll leave it on the steps. See you in the morning."

Safely in bed, and despite knowing I shouldn't think of how

much I was attracted to Alma, I closed my eyes. With any luck, I wouldn't dream about her like I sometimes dreamt about Ellie when we were half naked. Besides, I needed to be a gentleman around Alma for the next two weeks, not some idiot with his hormones doing backflips.

Chapter 7

I woke to the smell of coffee. Man, I've always loved coffee, and a hot cup would clear the cobwebs of sleep from my brain. I also was looking forward to ham, sausage, or bacon, but Dad, to educate me for our trip, said Jewish people didn't eat pork for religious reasons. He did say they drank wine. I tasted some Grandpa Callahan made and thought it was pretty good. Maybe I'd get the chance to try some here.

I dressed, combed my hair, and found Alma in the kitchen at the stove. She wore a yellow, long-sleeved blouse buttoned to her throat and a green skirt past her knees. Dad had also told me that Jewish women were modest with their clothes. This morning, unlike last night, Alma wore her hair down, except with the addition of a green scarf tied beneath her hair at the nape of her neck. I thought the triangle of green cloth covering her hair from the forehead back set her eyes off perfectly.

I joined her at the stove. "Can I help with anything?"

"That would be nice," she said, glancing at me. "Ima is tending to Abba. He had a difficult night. Lia, with her lazy self, is still asleep."

"Good morning," Dad said from behind us. "Did you say Morris had a bad night?"

Using a spatula, Alma moved several sizzling latkes from a pan to a plate. "He's still in pain. Ima's going to take him to the doctor." She nodded toward a coffee pot on the stove. "Seth, can you fill our cups while I make scrambled eggs? It will only take a moment."

"Sure," I said, taking the pot to the table. "Your family speaks English really well. In Kitty Hawk, some folks' southern accents are so thick, you can hardly understand them."

Dad chuckled. "You should hear some Ocracoke brogue, Son. That's what I call thick."

"The schools here teach English," Alma said. "Ima and Abba make sure Lia and I use it often." She cracked several eggs into a bowl and stirred them with a fork. "Abba said Kitty Hawk is on the ocean. I like going to the beach here." She poured the eggs into a pan and eased them around with the spatula until they were done, then added them to the plate with the latkes and took it to the table. "Seth, there's a plate of bagels keeping warm in the oven. Can you get them, please?"

I didn't know what bagels were. There was only one plate in the oven, so I took it to the table after filling the cups. Alma got a bowl from the refrigerator, brought it to the table and sat. She closed her eyes and bowed her head. "*Barukh ata Adonai Eloheinu melekh ha'olam shehakol niyah bidvaro.*"

When she stopped, I opened my eyes and raised my head. "Do you mind if I ask what you said?"

"Not at all. I said, 'Blessed are You, Lord our God, Ruler of the universe, at whose word all came to be.' It's the blessing we use when we have a variety of foods. We have blessings for bread, fruit, vegetables, and grains." She spooned eggs onto her plate. "Oh, and even one for wine and grape juice."

"What about coffee?" Dad asked after taking a sip. "As good as this is, it deserves one."

"Not that I know of," Alma said, passing me the plate of eggs and latkes. "Have you eaten bagels with cream cheese, Seth?"

"I sure haven't," I said. "I wouldn't know a bagel from my big toe."

Smiling at my joke, Alma offered me something from the

plate I'd brought from the oven. It resembled a doughnut cut in half. "This is a bagel," she said. "That's cream cheese in the bowl you brought from the refrigerator. Spread it on the bagel and try it."

I'd never seen white cheese before, let alone cheese in a bowl. Using my knife, I spread some on a bagel and took a crunchy, chewy bite. I didn't know what to expect from the cream cheese. It sort of reminded me of buttermilk, but it didn't taste as strong. I gave Alma a thumbs up. "I like it. Have you ever tried buttermilk?"

She made a face. "I tried it once. I didn't care for it."

Dad drank coffee. "With your dad's back problems, I guess you'll be our tour guide."

"That's right," Alma said, lowering the coffee cup she was about to drink from. After sipping, she licked her lips. "We talked about it this morning. In your letters, you said you wanted to visit Jerusalem's holy sites, but we're not comfortable going there. The news has been talking more about Yassar Arafat's Fatah political party and the possibility of guerilla attacks. I'm sorry you came all the way here expecting to see the holy sites and can't. Still, we have museums and sites in Tel Aviv."

"To be honest," Dad said, "I made alternate plans in case this happened. My minister said I should visit St. Peter's church, and, like you say, any museums in the area." Dad winked at me. "This boy of mine could do with some culture."

I grinned at Alma. "Tell Dad about the culture we had last night. If I remember right, it was about two inches long and furry."

"I don't care what you say," Alma said, her dark brows knitting together. "It was a rat."

Trying not to laugh, I faced Dad. "Before I went to bed, our tour guide asked me to get a mouse out of the rental. My ears rang all night from her screaming. How did you not hear that?"

"That's what that was?" Dad's eyes crinkled with humor. "I

thought it was a jet plane flying too low."

Alma's lips pressed into a tight line. "I see you American men stick together like our Jewish men do." She drank coffee. "I suggest we finish eating so we can start your tour."

These days, in 2024, it's easy enough to visit Israel on the internet, so I won't go into too much detail about our trip. For me, having turned eighteen while I was there, and being a young guy who loved the outdoors and the ocean, the detail I enjoyed the most was the time Alma and I spent on the beach.

During our tours, Dad sometimes wandered around on his own. I think he did that to allow Alma and I some time alone to help me get over losing Ellie. I'd never told him how I thought of Ellie as a friend instead of a girlfriend. He probably assumed we were more than friends, but he never said. Regardless, he must've thought I wouldn't get romantically involved with Alma because we lived so far apart.

To put it bluntly, he thought wrong.

Along with my initial attraction to her, I admired her intelligence even more. She was worldly, but in a humble sort of way. Although she could talk hours and hours about the history of Israel, including its conflict with the Arabs, she had the maturity and the perspective to see the point of view of both sides.

After a week of tours, when Morris and Rachel had gotten to know me pretty well, she told Alma we should visit the beach. Lia, of course, wanted to go, but Rachel said she needed her to help with Morris, and not to ask anymore.

On a sunny Saturday, late in the afternoon, Alma packed some food and drove the little car through the streets of Tel Aviv, eventually parking near the Mediterranean Sea. During some of our private talks about the beach, she said she could only wade because she wasn't allowed to wear a swimsuit. I said I didn't mind, as I spent enough time in the water at Kitty Hawk.

Carrying the basket with our food, I let her lead me across

the bright sands. We'd parked in a secluded area, so no one was around. Wondering if this was a special place of hers, I asked about it.

"I like to come here to get away from everyone and everything," she answered, glancing at me.

I assumed she meant getting away from all the conflict. I didn't say so to keep from ruining what felt like our first date.

Carrying a blanked for us to sit on, she hugged it tight. "You've told me a lot about Kitty Hawk. Do you have a girlfriend there?"

The question surprised me. Then again, she'd never mentioned having any boyfriends, or even dating. "Well, I never felt comfortable around girls except one," I said. "I thought we were best friends, but she felt more than that."

Alma spread the blanket on the sand, not far from the ocean waves lapping on the beach. "Will you be more than friends when you go home?"

"Her family moved away." When I said that, it made my heart hurt. Maybe I hadn't felt like a boyfriend to Ellie because I hadn't tried—and I mean *really* tried. We had practically everything in common, and she never complained about living hard in Kitty Hawk like Mom had.

Alma took our food from the basket. "I've never felt comfortable around boys. I went out with a few in college, but they never asked me out again. I don't say this to criticize them, but I think they were intimidated by my intelligence." She took waxed paper off a rye and pastrami sandwich and gave it to me. "You never act like that when we're talking. Does it bother you?"

"Not at all. I admire anyone who's smart. It beats being dumb."

Reaching into the basket, she shared a slight grin. "Good." She took out a bottle of wine. "I think you're very handsome. I especially like your brown eyes. They have the tiniest bit of green in them, like the sea."

My cheeks grew hot. "You're the only person to ever tell me that."

Alma laughed. "I see you're embarrassed." She uncorked the wine, filled two glasses, and kissed my cheek. "I think that's sweet. Would you like to say our blessing?"

She'd been teaching me the various blessings, so I didn't mind. "Which one should I say?"

She raised the glass. "This is the first time we've had wine. You can say that one."

"Do you mind if I say the English version?" I asked. "The other one ties my tongue in knots."

"Of course I don't mind, Seth. I'll say my version. Then you can say yours."

Bowing my head, I closed my eyes. "Blessed are You, Lord our God, Ruler of the universe, who creates the fruit of the vine."

Alma's warm hand enclosed mine. *"Barukh ata Adonai Eloheinu melekh ha'olam borei p'ri hagafen."*

We opened our eyes and stared at each other. Alma took off her glasses and gave me a quick kiss to my lips instead of to my cheek. I can't say why, but unlike Ellie's kisses that one time, Alma's one kiss jolted me all the way from the top of my head to the tips of my toes.

She put her glasses back on and started eating. What I thought was going to be a romantic supper by the Mediterranean Sea faded with the coming sunset.

More wine followed. I began to feel woozy. The horizon glowed red as the sun touched the distant waves. Alma put everything away and lay on the blanket. I did the same, not knowing what to expect. After a few minutes, I stretched my right arm out. As if she'd always belonged there, she curled into my side with her head on my shoulder.

I'd never felt so calm and relaxed. My senses were filled, from the press of her hand on my chest, to the warmth of her head on my shoulder, to the sweet smell of her perfume, to the silky softness of her hair against my cheek.

Then my calm turned to a mix of fear and anticipation.

Alma unbuttoned my shirt halfway down my chest and started kissing me there. What can a guy do except shut the heck up and let it happen.

"Oh, Seth, I've never felt this way before," she murmured. "I wish you didn't have to leave."

I rolled away from her and sat up. "Believe me, I didn't get up because I didn't like what you were doing. I just don't want to rush things."

Alma rubbed my thigh. "I know our situation is impossible, but I can't help how I feel. Is it bad of me to want you like I do?"

"I … well, I wouldn't say it's bad."

She took the scarf off and shook her hair out. It spilled along her shoulders and framed her face like a thundercloud, making me lick my lips. To say she looked amazing lying there would be the understatement of my life. She was stunning in every way, and no single word could describe her.

I took her hand in mine and raised the palm to my lips for a kiss. "It's not bad, Alma. I want you too, but I want to be in love before I do that." I shrugged. "I guess most guys don't care, but I do."

She sat up and hugged me, following up with a quick kiss. "That makes you all the sweeter, Seth. I've never been with a boy that way. I don't know if I ever will because you're the first one to make me feel like this. The idea of marriage has never appealed to me, especially not if love isn't involved. With the way I intimidate boys, none will ever love me like I need them to for marriage, much less to sleep with one." She tousled my hair. "Since we share those same ideals, you've never slept with a girl, yes?"

"Not a one," I said. "I know what you mean about finding someone to love that much. If I ever get married, I'd be surprised." I didn't say the rest, which was how, if I could stay here, I was sure I'd fall in love with an amazing young woman from Tel Aviv. In fact, I felt like I was doing that now.

We spent the rest of our date lying on the blanket like before, with her in the curve of my arm. Before it got too dark, Alma took a candle holder with a glass globe, lit the candle, and set the holder in the sand beside us.

In the flickering yellow light, we raised our fingers to point out and name the constellations. Now and again she'd kiss my cheek. Now and again she'd trace her fingertips across my chest. Now and again I'd kiss her forehead and tell her how much I was enjoying our time together.

Between the sound of the waves washing ashore, the soft breeze caressing our skin, and the smell of salt air I was so familiar with, it was one of the best nights of my life. Before Dad and I left, Alma and I spent many more nights like this. Here, in each other's arms, we were two people trying to understand where love's pull was taking us, all while knowing I'd leave soon, and we'd never, ever, see each other again.

On that particular night, when we got back to her house, Dad and Rachel were in the living room. It was past eleven, so Morris and Lia were asleep. Alma took the basket to the kitchen and returned to the living room. Noting Dad's and Rachel's eyes darting at each other, I said I was going to bed. Alma said the same thing, but Rachel stopped her with a raised palm. "I need to talk to you about something."

Dad faced me. "Come on, Son, let's go to bed."

I didn't care for his firm tone. "Go ahead and brush your teeth. I'll do mine after you."

"Already done. Let's give Alma and her mom some privacy."

I hurried down the hall. Dad's big feet clomped along behind me. Before I could close the bathroom door, he grabbed my arm and pulled me to his room. With the door closed, he sat on the bed. "I'm sure you know what this is about."

I crossed my arms. Dad and I had never argued about

anything, but this was — no doubt about it — going to be the first time. "Durned if I know," I said. "Tell me what you're talking about so I'll know too."

He rubbed his chin. "There's no need to get your back up, Son. All the times we've had serious talks, they were because I care, and that'll never change. I'm your father. I'm trying to keep you from getting hurt. Rachel feels the same way about Alma. That's what good parents do."

I uncrossed my arms and hooked my thumbs into my pants pockets. "Good parents trust their kids, Dad. Sure, Alma and I like each other. Still, we know we live too far apart for it to be anything permanent."

"Neither one of you is dumb, Son. Rachel and I know that."

"What does Morris say about it?"

"She hasn't mentioned it to him. He's got enough to worry about with his back."

"What's she telling Alma?"

Dad raked a hand through his hair. "Well, since you're eighteen, and since Alma's over eighteen, it's not like we can force you to stop going out alone. I'm a minister, so you know how I feel about certain subjects."

I knew what *that* meant. "Right, like the subject of sex before marriage."

"Exactly, and Rachel has the same ideals." Dad paused, obviously trying to get his thoughts together before continuing on such a touchy subject. "Look, Son, I know what it's like to have the feelings you're having for Alma. Unfortunately, those feelings almost always override logic. Sure, she's an attractive young woman and you're a handsome young guy. It's only natural for one thing to lead to another. As I've tried to teach you because of how your mom left us, physical intimacy should only happen between a committed couple in a committed marriage. Anything less cheapens the bond between a man and a woman. Do you understand?"

For all of my life, except for when Dad was preaching, he'd

been a man of few words. This was the longest speech he'd ever given me in one conversation, which meant he couldn't be more serious. "I get it, okay? If you and Alma's mom are worried about that one thing, we'll make sure it doesn't happen. Like you said, we're not dumb."

Dad stood from the bed. "That's all I needed to know. We're not forbidding you from going out, like we could anyway. We just don't want—"

Shaking my head, I raised my hand to stop him. "Okay, okay, I get it. You don't have to worry anymore."

He patted my shoulder. "Good. If you don't mind me asking, do you think much of Ellie now? You two sure seemed sweet on each other. I've always thought she'd make the perfect wife for a fellow living in Kitty Hawk."

I remembered how I'd told myself I'd never really tried to be a boyfriend to Ellie. Now, though, she was far away in Raleigh, so I told Dad that.

He yawned. "Raleigh's not that far from Kitty Hawk. You should take the jeep there when we get back. You never know until you try."

To me, the only thing I wanted to try was being with Alma. Of course, if I told Dad that, he'd start in on me again. I told him I'd consider seeing Ellie and went to bed, wondering how the talk between Alma and her mom had gone. Sure, I'd find out soon, but soon isn't quick enough when you're falling in love with somebody.

Chapter 8

The next morning, although I expected Alma's mom to act strange around me at breakfast, she didn't. Maybe it was because Morris rolled into the kitchen in his wheel chair to eat with us. Maybe it was because Lia was there. Maybe I was assuming she was mad at me when she wasn't. I took it as a good sign. Like Dad had said, they couldn't force us to stay away from the beach, or away from each other.

Now, sixty-one years in the future, in 2024, I'm glad Dad and I went to Israel. Despite the pain to come before he and I left, our trip, as well as my knowing Alma, led me to where I am today. You see, like Mom and Ellie, Alma is one of those category five hurricanes that blew my life toward a different path. Sure, it was a path filled with pain and confusion, but the love we experienced, as well as everything that came from it, was worth it.

The final days of our week passed entirely too fast. Dad regretted not visiting Jerusalem and said maybe we would come again.

We never did.

We were leaving on a Saturday. Wednesday afternoon, like we'd been doing since our first date, Alma packed us something to eat and drove us to the beach.

Unlike our first date, when it was warm and sunny, it was overcast and much cooler. The Mediterranean Sea's usual aquamarine waves were gray like the sky, and I had the distinct feeling that something bad was going to happen.

The first time Alma and I came here after our parents talked to us about our relationship, we discussed it. Unlike mine and Dad's somewhat reasonable conversation, Alma's conversation with her mom hadn't gone so well. She confessed to caring about me deeply, even saying she might leave with us for Kitty Hawk. Her mom, of course, said that was just immaturity talking. At least the talk had ended without any yelling, or without Alma's mom threatening to tell her dad.

Like our first afternoon here, we held each other. There was nothing intimate about it, though. I knew she needed to be comforted, and I was happy to do it.

On Wednesday, we ate on the blanket like always. Alma was quiet. I figured she had something on her mind and would tell me when she was ready.

By the time night started to fall, the clouds were breaking, and stars were peeking out. Alma lit the candle and set the holder in the sand. I lay down on the blanket so she could cuddle her head into my shoulder as I held her tight.

With my eyes closed, I listened to her breathing. Sometimes she'd drift off to sleep. This wasn't one of those times.

"I've been wondering something," she whispered. "You've never mentioned your mother."

If there was one subject I didn't want to share with Alma, it was that one. Still, as much as I cared about her, she deserved an answer, so I told her how Mom left Dad and me when I was nine.

Alma sat up and took my hand. "I'm so sorry, Seth. It must've been terrible for you both."

The sympathy in her voice said she might've thought Mom had died. "If you think she died, she didn't. Her and Dad had argued about how she didn't like our life in Kitty Hawk. It was a hard place to make a living back then, but it's better now."

Alma's mouth fell open. "Didn't she know all that when she

agreed to marry him?"

"She did. Her folks live in Elizabeth City. We didn't have electricity or running water like they did. She never said, but I don't think she liked the outdoors like Dad and I do either. In the long run, I guess she cared more about her old home than her home in Kitty Hawk."

"I don't understand," Alma said, blinking at me. "She now lives with her parents?"

"No, Dad thinks she preferred some place similar to Elizabeth City. Someplace she was used to, if you know what I mean."

Alma lowered her head. "I suppose …"

The way she trailed off twisted my insides like a waterspout had spun through me. "Hey," I said, lifting her chin with my fingertips. "That doesn't mean we can't be happy wherever we are. I love Kitty Hawk, but I could get used to anywhere as long as you're with me."

Alma said nothing. After a while, she said we should go, and I knew I was losing her.

Thursday and Friday were the last tour days. Alma's voice carried a distant tone, cold as the rare Outer Banks blizzard. By this time, Morris could get around with a cane, and he insisted on taking Dad and I out to supper. Sitting across from me, Alma wouldn't even look my way. Dad and her mom had to be glad. I'd be gone soon, and things would go back to normal. Morris and Lia did ask why we were quiet. I said I was looking forward to going home. Alma said she was trying to decide about more college and becoming a history professor.

Before Dad and I went to bed, he came to my room and closed the door. "Son, I admit I wanted your feelings for Alma to be more like friends, but are you two mad at each other?"

Sitting on the bed, about to take my shoes off, I shook my head. "I told her why Mom left. She changed after that." Taking a huge sigh, I ran a hand through my hair. "You know, maybe you're right about Ellie. We have a lot more in common than Alma and me. If I married Ellie, we would be happy in Kitty Hawk. I doubt if I could be happy in Israel, and I'm pretty sure Alma wouldn't want to leave her family to move halfway around the world on a whim. After all, we've only known each other two weeks, and I've known Ellie my whole life."

Sitting beside me, Dad patted my shoulder. "You're a smart fellow, Son, a lot smarter than me when I was your age."

I didn't agree. For one thing, I didn't know what I was going to do for a living. For another, although I might drive to Raleigh to see Ellie, I wasn't about to propose until we both had a plan for our lives together. The last thing I wanted was for her to leave me because I couldn't provide for her and a family, and that would drive us apart quicker than a hard living in Kitty Hawk.

Dad told me goodnight and left. I undressed and pulled the covers to my chin. After my prayers, which included a special one for Alma's happiness, I turned the lamp off.

As darkness engulfed the room, something tapped the window beside the bed. I turned the lamp on and got up. Outside, Alma motioned for me to raise the window. When I did, she stepped closer. "Come to the rental," she whispered, and hurried away.

I got dressed, tiptoed through the quiet house, and eased the kitchen door closed. Regardless of what Alma wanted, I was glad we were going to talk. The last thing we needed was to never see each other again without a sincere goodbye.

Waiting at the rental door, she opened it. As soon as she closed it behind me, she led me to the kitchen table, where an opened bottle of wine and two filled glasses were waiting. With her hair down, she sat across from me and reached over to take my hand. "I'm sorry for how I've been acting lately. The last thing I want is for you to leave without knowing how I feel about you." She took a sip of wine. "I realize our lives are very different. I realize we would never be happy away from our families and our homes. That doesn't mean I don't care about you." She squeezed my hand. "What I'm trying to say is I love you, Seth, and I want you to spend our last night together with me."

Confused, I asked what she meant. Instead of answering, she drank wine. Not knowing what to do, I did the same thing. She took off her glasses, and I fell into the depths of her dark eyes. Now I knew what she meant, and I wasn't about to let this chance get away.

She must've known I was ready. She took my hand and led me up a set of stairs to a bedroom. On the nightstand burned the same candle we used at the beach. The covers were turned back. The only other light was moonlight spilling through the window.

We came together with a gentle kiss. Buttons were unbuttoned. Clothes fell to the floor. In bed she rolled me over. Dark hair fell across my face and chest. My hands roamed her back as I pulled her to me.

Soon, I knew what it was like to be with a woman, and she knew what it was like to be with a man. We slept and woke to discover those sensations twice more before she woke me and said I should go. She put on the same nightgown she wore the night I saw her in the window. I put my clothes on. At the door, we hugged and kissed and said we loved each other. As the door closed behind me, she burst into sobs that tear at my heart even now, sixty-one years later.

Although the memory of that night hasn't faded, the day after has. The only thing I can recall is how much I missed her, how much I wanted her to be happy, and how much she would always mean to me for a multitude of reasons.

On the laptop keys, my fingertips falter.

Oh, yes, I remember how my sobs, once I got home where I could run off to be alone at the sound, were as heart wrenching as hers.

It took me a while to stop hurting, but the wound never fully healed. Because of that, I didn't go see Ellie right away.

When your heart has been cut that deeply, the next person you hope to love will always — even if you think they won't — see the blood.

Dad let me alone about things. He never said, but he couldn't help seeing how sad I was. For one thing, I needed to make up my mind about a profession. For another, no jobs on Kitty Hawk thrilled me enough to think of them as a lifelong calling. In the meantime, I worked with Grandpa Callahan at his general store in Manteo. He and Grandma had married when they were twenty-five. Mom and Dad had married when Dad was twenty-eight and Mom was twenty-six. All this meant Grandpa was getting on in years, so the best solution for me to get Alma off my mind, and to give the full-time store business a try, was to help him.

I won't say I did or didn't like it. Meeting new people was okay. Ordering and stocking goods was okay. What wasn't okay is how Grandpa played the radio all day because of the buildup of American troops in Vietnam. He'd even bought a tiny black and white TV for him and Grandma at home. She said she despised the thing. He said it was important to know the world's events. Dad agreed, worry in his eyes whenever he looked at me as the news played. People were talking about the prospect of full-scale war, which meant the possibility of a military draft.

1963 passed without seeing Ellie. I considered writing her, but I didn't know her grandparents' address, and she hadn't seen fit to write me either. Sad to say, Alma and I hadn't thought about trading addresses. Sure, she could've asked Morris for my address, and I could've asked Dad for hers. I suppose, though, somewhere deep down in our souls, we knew there was no need to torture each other with letters.

On Sundays after church and lunch, I'd either walk along the beach or the sound. Every few weeks I'd end up at the place on the sound where Ellie and I had almost made love. At seventeen, I knew we were too young for the possibility of children. At eighteen going on nineteen, I knew it was time to see if she wanted to give me a chance at a serious relationship instead of one based on youthful desire.

Dad was now a full-time minister at the Methodist church. He still fished, and Grandpa Mitchell's restaurants took the catch without fail. Monetarily, things were looking up. Even though I stayed with Grandpa and Grandma Callahan while I worked in the store, Dad decided to add on to the Kitty Hawk house. When I asked why, he said he hoped I'd marry one day, and he wanted to leave the house to me for my family.

This conversation happened after church one spring Sunday in 1964. Getting feeble, Grandpa Callahan didn't drive anymore, so he gave me his 1960 Ford pickup. I liked the red color but didn't like how the two-wheel drive wouldn't take me on the beach at Corolla to see the horses. It was definitely more comfortable than Dad's old World War II surplus jeep, but that thing refused to get stuck in either wet or dry or soft sand as long as I lowered the air in the tires.

Anyway, I now drove the Ford home on Sundays for church and to visit Dad. From Nags Head northward, tourism was on the rise, resulting in more attention to the paved roads, more hotels, and more restaurants. It was nothing like it is now, but things were definitely changing.

On this particular day, Dad and I had eaten lunch and were sitting on our new deck, level with the house on its stilted supports. More boats were on the sound than it used to be, some fishing, some crabbing, some for pleasure.

Dad cleared his throat. He didn't care much for the new women's bathing suit styles. What once were one-piece suits with a fringe of cloth half way to the knees had transformed to two-piece suits that revealed firm stomachs, plenty of cleavage, and long, tanned legs from the top of the thigh down.

I punched his shoulder. "Come on, old man. Time to get modern."

He rubbed his shoulder. "I don't mind women showing all

that skin as much as I mind them using birth control pills. God decides when to form a baby in the womb, not some pill."

Of course, he was referring to when the pill came out in 1960. He also preached about how it would lead to more sexual promiscuity. Although that might be true, since it was only available to married women, I thought it would lead to more babies being born to families who planned for them. When I mentioned that the first time, he begrudgingly agreed. There was more talk in the news about the right to abortion, and he thought killing babies in the womb was the work of the devil.

I hadn't given it much thought. I'd rather do that if I ever met a woman who'd had an abortion and could tell me why.

Another pleasure boat roared by. One of the women's dark hair and thin frame reminded me of Ellie and Alma at the same time. I faced Dad. "I wonder how Alma and her folks are doing. Do you ever hear from Morris?" As soon as I asked that, I realized I could write her because Dad had their address. Talk about dumb. Either that or our last night together had emptied my mind of everything besides us making love three times.

Dad's head turned as he watched the boat go by. "Did you say something?"

I started to tease him about watching those pretty young ladies but didn't. "I asked if you ever heard from Alma and her family in the mail."

"Not a word," he said, still watching the boat. He finally faced me. "I keep them in my prayers, though. I was watching TV the other night, and the Arab rhetoric against the Jews is heating up again."

Influenced by Grandpa Callahan, Dad had finally gotten a TV last Christmas, surprising me. Sure, he was old fashioned in some ways, but he didn't let it override his belief that being informed about the world was a good idea.

"Do you have Morris's address?" I asked. "I'd like to see how they're doing."

Grinning, he cut his eyes at me. "Tell the truth. You want to see how Alma's doing."

I shrugged. "Is anything wrong with that?"

Dad paused. "Well, there wouldn't be if I hadn't lost Morris's address."

Right then and there, I took that as a sign to take the Ford to Elizabeth City to see Ellie. I didn't much care for the general store business, but I'd put up with it for Ellie's sake.

"What are you thinking?" Dad asked. "I hope it isn't to fly to Tel Aviv to propose to Alma."

I stood from the old ladder-back chair and turned around. "I look pretty good in my church clothes. I got a haircut the other day." I sniffed an underarm. "I don't stink."

"And all that means what?" Dad asked, raising an eyebrow.

I took the Ford's keys from my pocket and jingled them in his face. "Guess who's driving to Elizabeth City to see Ellie?"

Dad shook his head. "Not without her address, you can't." He snapped his fingers. "You got a letter from Ellie Thursday." He stood. "It's on my dresser."

He soon returned with the envelope. I sat and opened it, curious as to why Ellie had finally written me after so long. After the first few sentences, and seeing there was only one short paragraph, I stopped reading. Just when I was about to finally get my life on track, another category five hurricane had ruined it.

Balling the letter up, I kept squeezing it. Blood rushed to my face, heating it like the worst sunburn I'd ever had.

"What is it?" Dad asked. "You don't look happy at all."

"Ellie got married two months ago, Dad. That's what I get for waiting." I slammed my fist with the letter in it into my other palm. "I lost Ellie when she moved from Kitty Hawk. I lost Alma when we came back home. Now I've lost Ellie to some other guy. My life cannot get any worse."

Before Dad could say anything, I took off toward the pier, running as fast as I ever had in my life. At the end, I ripped the letter to shreds and threw it into the water. Then I pulled off all my clothes except my boxer shorts and dove into the sound.

Behind me, Dad's Sunday shoes clomped on the pier. "Seth!" he yelled. "Please come back so we can talk about it! You're still young, Son! You've got plenty of time to meet someone!"

I didn't want to hear another word. Diving beneath the surface, I held my breath and kept swimming. Maybe I'd drown and be done with it. Anything was better than having my heart broken over and over again.

Chapter 9

A fellow can't stay in the water for the rest of his life, but I sure tried. Dad gave up hollering and went inside when I waved him away, so I swam on in.

I found him waiting on the sofa, having changed into his fishing clothes. In my wet boxers, I'd walked from the pier with my church clothes in my arms, hair dripping. Minutes later I came from my room in my fishing clothes too. "Sorry about that," I told him. "Life just gets to be too much sometimes."

"Been there, done that," he said. "Your mom turned my proposal down three times before she finally gave in." He gave me a look I couldn't figure out. "She sure put me through the ringer when she left, but I'm glad we had you." He stood. "Let's take the jeep up to Corolla to see the horses. On the way back, we'll stop at one of those new seafood restaurants for supper."

I winked. "Only if you're buying, and only if I can get a steak. As much seafood as we catch and eat, I need a break sometimes."

Dad laughed. "You and me both, Son. You and me both."

Since it was about two o'clock, the return drive might happen at night, so we agreed to throw our jackets in the back seat of the jeep. Dad and I replaced the engine and transmission a few months ago, and it ran like new. Back in 1964, Highway 12 North wasn't as busy as it is today, so we got to Corolla and onto the beach a little before three. Dad eased us along at a steady speed to keep the tires from bogging down in the sand. Out over the Atlantic, a line of pelicans, their wings still, swept up the waves, along the crests, and down again. Just as it seemed they'd touch the water, the lead pelican would flap a few times, followed by the rest, one by one in sequence. By the time one line of them faded to the north, another would pass by. A person could almost get hypnotized watching them.

Dad pointed up the beach. "There's a herd yonder. Looks like a stallion and his harem and a few yearlings."

I shaded my eyes. Sure enough, Dad's eagle eyes were accurate like always.

He steered us in a circle and parked about fifty yards from them. Eyeing us, the stallion pawed the sand and snorted. He sure was something. His black hide was so glossy that it actually reflected the sun. One of the mares whinnied. The stallion trotted to her, nipping at her flanks.

Dad chuckled. "Too bad a fellow can't do that to keep his ladies in line."

I said nothing. With the heartache my ladies had been giving me, they were more likely to kick me in the head.

The herd moved on.

Blinking as if he had an idea, Dad faced me. "With all those tourists taking an interest in the Outer Banks now, I wonder what they'd pay a fellow to drive them out here to see the horses? Anytime some come to church, they're always asking about them."

I rubbed the jeep's dash. "This thing is too small for a business like that. You'd want to bring more people at once to maximize the profits."

"Not a bad idea," Dad said, nodding. "If you ever get tired of the general store business, maybe you can give it a try." He cranked the jeep. "I don't know about you, but I'm ready for that steak."

To the west, the sun glowed like an orange ball sinking into the sound. The sight always settled my mind except for this time. With Ellie married and Alma gone out of my life for good, I wanted to find a woman to love me like I loved Kitty Hawk. If she did that, she would love Kitty Hawk like I did, and we'd have a fine life together.

Fifteen minutes later, darkness swallowed the road, and we chased the jeep's headlights along the blacktop until Dad parked at a restaurant. Since it was spring, it wasn't too crowded. After we were seated, a waitress took our orders.

As she left, Dad nodded toward her. "I've been thinking, Son. If I were you, I'd steer clear of women for a while. You act like you've got no time to start that part of your life when you do. Give the good Lord a chance. The right girl will come along one day when you least expect it. As far as right now, I think you should try dating just for dating's sake. Have a little fun. Get to know more than one girl and see how it goes."

I was sitting with my elbows on the table and my chin in my hands. "Didn't you just say I should steer clear of women for a while?"

"I meant for you to steer clear of them with the thought of marriage. You're a good looking guy like me," he continued with a grin. "Sow some wild oats, but not so wild you become a dad. Like I said, just enjoy getting to know them. Then, when the right one comes along, your experience will help you figure it out."

I started to say his experience didn't help with Mom, but that would hurt his feelings. "I'll think about it. Right now I just want to enjoy that steak when it gets out here."

For a while we just sat there, me trying to get a grip on losing Ellie, Dad with that look he got when he was thinking about Mom.

A few more people drifted in. Some were couples. Some were single. Some were families. The aroma of seafood frying and beef searing came from the kitchen, making my mouth water. I sipped sweet tea with lemon to ease my hunger, but it didn't help.

The waitress brought some hushpuppies. "One of our cooks is out. I thought you guys might like these until your steaks are ready."

Dad thanked her. As she turned to leave, I called her back. "Could I get a beer? Whatever you have on draft is fine."

As she left, Dad eyed me. "I didn't know you drink."

"We drank wine with Alma's family," I reminded him. "You didn't mind then."

As Dad finished saying he drank with them to be sociable, the waitress brought the beer in an icy mug. "There you go. Your steaks will be out in a minute."

I took a long, cold swallow. Ellie had brought us two of her dad's beers once. I didn't care for it then, but this one sure hit the spot.

Dad's chin shifted to one side. "You're enjoying that too much. Is it because of losing Ellie?"

I tipped the mug toward him. "I'll let you know after the next one."

When the waitress returned, she brought two plates with two sizzling rib-eyes, along with baked potatoes and plenty of butter and sour cream. I ordered another draft, and she brought it right back, smiling at me. Dad was busy cutting steak, so he didn't see the folded note—or the wink—she gave me. I glanced at the note in my lap. It said she planned to have a migraine when we were done eating, and she wanted me to drive her home. A complete stranger had never come on to me like that. To be honest, I kind of liked it. Not only that, I liked how her blue jeans hugged her behind, how her blue eyes sparkled, and how her tanned cleavage reminded me of Alma's olive-toned skin. She was also a blonde, and I'd never known a blonde. Trying to decide what to do, I shoved the note in my pocket and turned my attention toward my meal.

For one thing, I didn't know how I'd get home. For another,

if I spent the night with her, which was probably what she had in mind in this time of college kids and the news talking about the so-called sexual revolution, Dad would have something to say about it when I got home. For the last thing, my eighteen-going-on-nineteen-year-old attitude, especially after losing Alma a few months ago, was getting to where it didn't care what Dad thought.

Sure, at seventy-eight I can look back at my youth and wish I'd made better choices. In 1968, at fifty-years-old, Dad was no dummy, and his experience and wisdom were worth listening to. At the time, being an idiot teenager, I didn't know any better. My wife and I went through the same thing with our own kids. Lucky for us, they listened a lot better than we listened to our own parents.

As Dad and I ate, he started talking about Mom. Over the years I'd asked him why he hadn't remarried. His answer, because he was still legally married to Mom, sounded like an excuse. Plenty of single church ladies paid him plenty of attention, and I knew he liked it by how he smiled at them. All in all, I think he thought Mom was his soulmate even though she wasn't, or she would've never left us like she had. Maybe he was in denial about that, or maybe not. Sometimes we don't see what's standing right in front of us until it's gone, like when I found out Ellie had gotten married.

Dad was really feeling nostalgic about Mom. I'd heard it all before, except this time he had to wipe his eyes with his napkin a few times. When his third refill of tea was gone, he left for the bathroom. The waitress must've noticed because here she came, smiling from ear to ear. "Did my note make an impression, baby doll?"

"Sure," I said, failing to look into her blue eyes because she was leaning over to give me a peek at her cleavage. "I'm up for it."

"That's exactly what I hoped you say," she purred. "I'll be by my car when you come out, holding my head."

I started to ask how I should handle Dad, but he was on the way back from the restroom. "We're almost done," I whispered. "Bring our check. I'll see you outside."

Sitting in his chair, Dad watched her leave. "I think you've got an admirer. Have you asked her out yet?"

I drank the last swallow of my third beer. "I'm thinking about it."

The waitress—she hadn't even told us her name—came back with the check. "What a night," she groaned. "On top of my aching feet, I've got a migraine."

"That's too bad," Dad said, giving her the cash. "Maybe you'll feel better in the morning."

She glanced my way. "I'm sure I will, sir." She paused. "Hey, I forgot to tell y'all my name in case y'all come back. It's Diane. My friends call me Di." She folded the cash. "I'll be right back with your change. Then I'm taking my fanny home."

Diane's southern accent was a southern as southern gets. I could imagine all kinds of intimate inuendo drawled into my ear while I drove her home.

Di returned with Dad's change, and he gave her the tip. "I hope you feel better Diane. Goodnight."

She thanked him, hustled outside with her purse strap over her shoulder, and we went to the jeep. By her car near the corner of the restaurant, Di pressed her fingertips to her temples. Dad, being a nice guy, walked over. "I've heard about migraines. Do you have a friend you can call to take you home?"

Di lowered her fingertips. "My roommate is waitressing at another restaurant. I hate to ask," she said, taking the keys to her Volkswagen Beetle from her purse and giving them to me, "but could you drive me home?"

"Sure thing," I said, taking the keys.

"My son's a fine driver," Dad said. "I'll follow you two."

On the way to the passenger door, Di stopped. "Why's that?"

"To take my son home. That's why."

Di looked at me. I looked at Di. Our eyes must've said it all: *Boy, are we dumb.*

I grabbed dad's arm and pulled him away a few steps. "Look, Dad, she doesn't have a migraine."

In the parking lot lights, I could see his eyes widen. "Do you mean she wants you to spend the night?"

"Hey, you're the one who said I should sow some wild oats. If it makes you feel any better, I won't do anything you wouldn't do."

Dad's jaw tightened. "In my younger days or my older days?"

I laughed out loud. "You're funny when you want to be."

"I'm not trying to be funny, Son. I'm trying to give you some good advice. Anyone who'll invite another person home for the night after just meeting them is not someone who has your best interests at heart."

Behind me, the Beetle's door clicked open. "Can we go before I get sick?"

Dad tilted his head to look around me. "Just a moment, Diane." He leaned toward me and whispered, "If you sleep together, just sleep, okay? Can you do that for me? The last thing you want is to have a baby with some woman you just met."

"Hey," I said, patting his back, "I'm not as dumb as I look."

A low growl rumbled in Dad's throat. "Fine. In case you didn't remember, today's Saturday. If you're not home in time for church, you're cooking lunch."

As he walked to the jeep, I grinned. A night with Di just might be worth me cooking lunch tomorrow.

When I turned the ignition, the Beetle sputtered to life. "Where to, Di?"

She rubbed my thigh. "What's your name, baby doll?"

"Seth."

"I like that, it's sexy. Leave the parking lot and take a right."

I did as Di asked, then followed her directions to a cedar shingled cottage on the sound side, tucked away down a long drive in an oak thicket. She pulled me up the steps and into the living room, asked if I wanted a beer, and said to wait on the sofa while she got two.

In the ash tray on the coffee table, a few cigarettes meant Di smoked. Two things about them puzzled me. One was neither she nor the Beetle nor the house smelled like cigarette smoke. Two was the cigarettes were rolled by hand, like Grandpa Callahan smoked.

Diane returned with the beers and snuggled up beside me. After a few swallows, she took some rolling papers and a little pouch of tobacco from her purse and rolled a cigarette. As she lit it, I didn't recognize the smell of tobacco. Maybe it was some brand Grandpa had never tried. She drew in a lungful, held it for a second, breathed it out and offered me the cigarette. Not wanting to be rude, I followed her lead.

We finished our beers and she brought four more. We finished the cigarette and smoked one more. The next thing I knew, not only was bright sunshine beaming through a window to wake me up, I was in a bed beside a naked Di, sprawled face down on top of the blanket. Raising the blanket, I saw I was naked too. Since we were on opposite sides of the blanket, maybe we'd passed out from the beers before anything happened. I dropped my head to the pillow and rubbed my eyes. "What the heck have I gotten myself into?" I moaned.

The bedroom door opened. A redhead wearing a robe came in. "What'd you say?"

Blinking furiously, I gawked at the open robe, which revealed no clothes whatsoever. "Who are you?"

"I'm Mindy, Di's roommate. We met when I got home last night." She opened the robe wider and gave her hips a little shimmy. "We sure had us a party, you sexy thing. I ain't had that much fun since the pigs ate my little brother."

Di rolled over and glared at Mindy. "You and that hick humor. Make us some breakfast. It's the least we can do for Seth after he showed us such a good time."

Mindy left and came back to throw my clothes on the bed. "You better get dressed before Di and me attack you again."

Di untangled her long legs and lay down beside me, draping one leg over mine. "Don't mind her. You laughed yourself to sleep. We undressed you and put you in bed."

My mouth fell open. "Do you mean you and me, or she and me, or all of us didn't do what I think we did?"

"Afraid not." Di slid her hand beneath the blanket. "But we can after breakfast." Ignoring my nakedness, I rolled out of bed and threw my clothes on. "Suit yourself," Di said. "Maybe you'll change your mind after breakfast. Mindy's a great cook. Every time I try to cook eggs-over-easy, they turn out hard."

I glanced at my watch. Church was in three hours. Hey, I could do worse things than have breakfast with these two gals. It's not like I'd ever gotten to know any young women besides Ellie and Alma anyway, and the experience might do me good.

I asked for the bathroom. Di pointed. "Out the door and to the left. Don't leave the seat up. I hate a wet behind."

The delicious sounds and aromas of sizzling country ham and coffee percolating accompanied me down the hall. Combined with eggs-over-easy, grits, and red-eye gravy, if all that was on the menu, talk about a meal.

Behind the bathroom's closed door, I finished at the toilet and flushed, then lowered the seat for the ladies and zipped my zipper. After washing my hands, a red-eyed me stared back from the mirror. I wasn't much of a drinker. Those three beers at the restaurant, plus the three I drank here, must've knocked me for a loop.

Yes, I eventually figured out those cigarettes were what, as Di had said, made me laugh myself to sleep. Fair warning: that wasn't the last time I smoked marijuana in my story. At least I'd know what it was next time.

I washed my face, and, using my finger, brushed my teeth with a dab of toothpaste from a tube on the sink to get the taste of stale beer out of my mouth. Then I used Di's hairbrush, evidenced by the blonde hairs in the bristles, to make me look human again. Satisfied with the results of my make-do morning routine, I found the ladies standing by the stove, sipping coffee. Both now wore tied robes. Both looked me up and down in a way I didn't necessarily mind.

"You sure are looking good," Mindy said.

"Not last night," Di said. "He was a mess."

I made myself at home by pouring a cup of coffee. "I appreciate you ladies taking care of me last night."

Mindy eyed Di. "He thinks we took care of him. Dragging him to the bed was nothing compared to what we wanted to do."

"Oh, poo," Di said. "He's just one of those fisherboys who's still wet behind the ears. I bet he's never been with one woman, let alone two at the same time."

"I guess you're right," Mindy said, adding eggs from a pan to a plate. "We'll feed him and take him home to his folks." She took the plate of eggs to a table, where it joined a plate of country ham, a bowl of grits, and a stack of buttered toast. There was no red-eye gravy, but I doubted if I'd get that lucky.

Mindy had piled her red hair on top of her head and secured it with a few bobby pins. That and her green eyes really appealed to me. Of course, how she looked when she opened the robe and gave her hips a little shimmy was helping things along.

On the other hand, Di was smoking another one of those strange cigarettes and blowing the smoke in my face, which didn't appeal to me at all.

Mindy waved the smoke away. "Cut that out. I can't taste my food for all that smoke."

Di took another drag, blew the smoke to one side, and faced me. "Little miss goody two shoes might take a couple of puffs and that's it."

"That's because I get high on life," Mindy said, screwing her face into a frown at Di. "Turn the TV on while we eat. I want to see the latest news on Vietnam."

Dad and I mostly watched the weather the night before we went fishing, so we didn't know much about America's involvement in South Vietnam's war with North Vietnam. At the general stores, both in Kitty Hawk and at Grandpa's store in Manteo, customers talked about the possibility of a military draft. I'd do my duty if called, but I wasn't thrilled about doing it in some little country halfway around the world that didn't seem to have much of anything to do with America. No, Dad and I, other than voting and watching the local news on occasion, didn't keep up with politics much. We didn't even know John F. Kennedy had been shot in Texas last year until a week after it happened. I guess we should've done better. A citizen who doesn't care enough about his own country to know what's happening in it isn't much of a citizen.

While we enjoyed Mindy's excellent cooking, the Sunday morning news filled us in about Vietnam, not the least of which was how the number of US troops there, identified as "advisers," was growing.

The news ended. Mindy cut the TV off and returned to her chair. "Well, fisherboy, are you going to wait to get drafted, or are you going to join so you can have your pick?"

Di swallowed coffee. "I'd join the Navy. Who wants to fight in the jungle?"

Mindy patted my hand. "Di and I are nurses. We quit our jobs and came here for a month for a little vacation before we join the Navy."

"That's not how it is," Di blurted. "Your uncle got you that job at his restaurant and I came along for the ride." She faced me. "Mindy's uncle didn't pay the rent for this cottage. That's why we're working on our vacation."

I faced Mindy. "Your uncle owns a restaurant. Does that

mean you live around here? I live in Kitty Hawk."

"I live in Manteo. Small world, huh?"

"It sure is," I said, nodding. "When I'm not fishing with my dad, I help my grandpa at his store in Manteo. It's been there a long time, but it's kind of off the beaten path, not too far from the sound."

Mindy took a bite of eggs. "Mom and I do our shopping in town." She drank coffee. "So, what do you think about the Navy?"

Chewing ham, I couldn't answer. I hadn't given Vietnam much thought. With a draft looming, it might be a good idea.

Chapter 10

When we were done eating, Di, sipping coffee, gave me a glance. After swallowing, she faced Mindy. "I think you should take Seth home. I'm gonna flop back in bed." She stood and yawned. "Besides, I think he's more your type than mine."

I wasn't sure what Di meant. I'd been looking at Mindy more than Di while we ate, so maybe that was it.

Mindy stood. "Let me get dressed." On the way to the hall, she looked over her shoulder at me and winked.

While I waited, I studied the cigarette butts in the ash tray on the coffee table. I thought we'd smoked two, but there were four butts there.

Wearing snug blue jeans, a white T-shirt, and sandals, Mindy returned with a purse over her shoulder. She'd added a bit of eyeliner and some pink lipstick. Opening the door, she waived me out. "Let's hit the road, Seth. I'd like to find out where you live."

Who knew what that comment meant. In her red Ford Mustang, we left the driveway and turned onto Highway 12 South. Between the directions I gave her, she kept glancing at me, this strange little smirk on her face. When I asked why, she patted my leg. "Unless I miss my guess, you've never been with a woman, right?"

Talk about an unexpected question. "I was with you and Di last night. I guess that counts for something."

"You're funny. I saw your red cheeks when I opened my robe. I've never seen someone so embarrassed." She patted my leg again. "Don't worry about it. I think you're sweet. I've never dated a sweet guy." She laughed. "I see that puzzled look. No, we haven't dated. I'd like to before Di and me join the Navy. What do you think?"

I told her to take the next right. "Sure, why not. What do you like to do?"

"Well," she said, as the sound came into view, "what if you take me for a ride in that skiff at the end of your pier?" She parked and took a pen and paper from her purse, scribbled on it and gave it to me. "That's the number at the cottage. Call me before the weekend. We'll plan something."

I took the paper and got out. Before I closed the door, I leaned down to look at her. "Thanks for the ride. See you later."

I closed the door and watched the Mustang leave, wondering if Mindy would change my life like Ellie and Alma had.

I showered and dressed. Dad had already left for church, where he taught one of the Sunday school classes. With the note on my nightstand, I found myself looking forward to taking Mindy on a boat ride. The question my hormones kept asking, which I couldn't seem to control, was how skimpy a swimsuit she'd wear.

I still had thirty minutes before church, so I turned on the TV for the heck of it. Although no news was showing, it still made me think about Vietnam. I admired Di and Mindy for joining the Navy. During breakfast, they'd said they'd probably be on hospital ships. From the stories from some of the local men who'd fought in the Korean War, I didn't envy those two ladies for the wounds they'd be seeing, anything from missing limbs to mental issues, what people now call PTSD.

I checked my watch and turned the TV off. In the Ford pickup, I drove to church, thinking about Alma and her family.

Vietnam had been monopolizing the TV and radio news, so I wondered what was going on between the Arabs and the Jews.

I took a seat on the back pew with ten minutes to spare. Dad walked back and sat by me. "I'd almost given up on you. How did the oat sowing go?"

"Believe it or not," I said, using my most sincere tone of voice, "not a single oat was sown last night."

"Please," he said, disbelief in his voice. "I didn't just fall off the fish truck."

With my fingertip, I crossed my heart. "Honest, Dad, nothing happened but a good night's sleep and a great breakfast."

"Di must be a good cook," Dad said. Like me, he enjoyed a great breakfast.

"Her friend Mindy is," I said. "She brought me home."

It was Dad's turn to raise an eyebrow. "Wait a minute, Seth. Are you saying you spent the night with two women? Is that supposed to be what some of today's young people are calling the 'sexual revolution?'"

"Not for me, Dad. Mindy and me hit it off. We're going out on the skiff Saturday."

Dad patted my shoulder. "Good deal. It'll be hard to sow any oats on a skiff in the daylight—wild or otherwise." He stood. "See you at home after the sermon."

Congregation members filed in and sat. Some were families. Some were single men and women. Some were elderly folks. All were dressed neatly, hair combed or brushed.

I checked my watch. It was almost eleven, so that should be everyone. Yawning from my strange experience last night, not only from those funny cigarettes, but from seeing two women treat public nudity like it was the most natural thing in the world, I was shocked when Mindy, fresh as a daisy in a yellow dress that set off her red hair, came in and sat beside me. "Hey there, sweetie pie. Imagine meeting you here."

"I leaned close and whispered, "My dad's the minister here.

I come all the time and have never seen you. What's up?"

Mindy pulled the hem of the dress to her knees. "Can't a girl come to church if she wants to?"

I tapped her leg with a fingertip. "That's a lot of modesty after last night."

She twisted her lips to one side. "I was in a mood last night. Haven't you ever been in a mood? Besides, you didn't seem to mind ogling me while we were eating."

Up front, Dad cleared his throat and welcomed everyone. His eyes lingered on Mindy and me before he went on.

When the choir leader led the first hymn, Mindy stood and sang with a clear, feminine voice. When the offering plate came around, she dropped a five-dollar bill in. When Dad said which Bible verse he'd be reading from, she took a Bible from the holder on the back of the pew ahead of us and opened it. Obviously, I didn't know Mindy like I thought I knew Mindy.

During the sermon, she brought her lips near my ear. "Do you believe in love at first sight?" she whispered.

Taken aback, I gawked at her. "Not really. I think a couple should be best friends first."

"Oh, poo, you take all the fun out of it. Ever since Di and I undressed you and put you to bed, I've been dying to kiss you. You're just about the handsomest fisherboy I've met on the Outer Banks, and I've met a lot of them."

Mindy had showered, evidenced by the floral aroma of shampoo drifting from her hair. Her blue eyes were bright, her pink lips were pouty, and her cheeks were rosy. Truth be told, I wanted to kiss her too.

Forty minutes later, Dad finished speaking. When the altar call hymn started, I nudged Mindy toward the end of the pew. "I want to take you to lunch. I'll bring you back for your car after."

Outside, bright sunlight greeted us. I hustled Mindy past the oaks surrounding the church, toward the jeep parked near the road. She hopped in and let her hair down, which she'd piled on top of her head like this morning. "I like the wind in my hair, sweetie pie."

I turned the key. The jeep puttered to life. Minutes later we were on Highway 12 South. Mindy poked my arm. "If you pull over, we can have that kiss."

I smiled at her. In the romance department, she was a breath of fresh air, open and intriguing. The next block up, I took a left toward beach road, turned onto it, and took a right. We passed several older cottages to our left, with cedar siding, storm shutters for the windows tilted upward to let the summer sun in, and huge wrap-around porches. At the end of the row of cottages, I turned right to park at a rundown diner with a sign over the door that simply said EATS.

"Classy," Mindy said, reaching over to place a palm to my cheek. "Do you take all your girlfriends here?"

"You're the first one," I said honestly.

"Good," she said, leaning closer. "That means I'm special." We kissed long and firm until Mindy came up for air. "Oh, my," she said, fanning her face. "That was worth the wait."

I climbed from the jeep and hurried around it to open her door. Smiling sweetly, she remarked on my manners, and allowed me to take her hand and lead her inside.

We sat across from each other in a booth covered in red vinyl. I smelled coffee. Mindy said she sure could use a cup. A waitress brought menus and took our orders of coffee with sugar and cream.

"She didn't know you," Mindy said. "The way you drove here, I thought you were a regular."

"I've never been here," I said, opening the menu. "I stopped at the first place I saw because I was ready for that kiss."

Mindy took a compact from her purse and touched up her lipstick, returned the compact to the purse and put it beside her in the booth. "Okay, Seth, let's get something straight. Di's the loose one. She'll sleep with any guy she thinks might be a catch. Me, I'm a good girl, but you make me want to change that. We'll take it slow until I leave for the Navy. If I decide to sleep with you, we'll take precautions then."

By "precautions," I assumed she meant condoms. I'd heard guys talking about them at Grandpas general store, saying they needed to stop by the drug store before a date. I agreed to Mindy's suggestion. After sleeping with Alma, I could imagine how it might be with Mindy. The question was would we fall in love like Alma and I had before we slept together. After all, that's what I preferred.

It's funny how priorities can change. Before Alma, I thought it was best to be married before making love. Maybe our experience changed that, maybe not. Or maybe the fact that Mindy could be on a hospital ship soon had changed it. Regardless of what it was, I wasn't sure if I cared about being in love with Mindy before we slept together or not. The older I got, the shorter life seemed, and I wanted to grab it with both hands and never let go.

"You're quiet," Mindy said. "Is it because I said I might sleep with you? If that's why, I'm glad. I'm looking forward to it as much as you are."

The waitress returned with our coffee and took our orders of pancakes and sausage. Mindy added cream and sugar to her cup, stirred it in and sipped, and reached across the table to take my hand. "Are you surprised about what I said about sleeping together? Most of the girls in nursing school slept with their steady boyfriends. I dated but didn't have a steady boyfriend. I wanted to feel special about a guy before I slept with him. You're the only one to make me feel like that, and I'm not sure why." She sipped coffee. "Have you ever slept with a girl?"

What a question. If I answered honestly concerning Alma, Mindy might end our relationship before it got started. I always felt bad about lying, but I didn't see a way out of one. I sipped coffee to fortify my nerves, not only for lying about Alma, but for betraying how I still loved her. I told Mindy I hadn't slept with anyone, adding that I guessed it was weird for a guy my age.

"It's weird because you came home with Di last night," she said. "She came on to you at the restaurant, right? You thought you were going to get lucky, right?"

I nodded. "I guess. I apologize if it makes me look like a jerk."

"It makes you a man. At least you're honest about it, so don't apologize." Mindy's eyes focused over my shoulder. She moved her cup aside, and the waitress sat our breakfast on the table, along with syrup and butter.

After a few buttery bites of pancake, I brought up the subject of Vietnam. "Do you really think there'll be a draft? That's pretty serious for a little country like Vietnam."

Mindy smirked. "Mark my words, Lyndon Johnson will announce an escalation any day now. I have mixed feelings about it. I don't like communism spreading, but I hate to see America get more involved."

I tended to agree but didn't say so. Mindy was concentrating on her meal, and I decided to do the same. Sipping coffee, I was sure Dad was wondering where I was. I'd get grilled when I got home, but that was okay. I felt good about a possible relationship with Mindy. It was great that she was a local like Ellie. It was also great that she wanted to serve America by joining the Navy as a nurse. Dad, a veteran of World War II, would approve.

Mindy nibbled a piece of sausage. "I thought you'd be sitting with your Mom at church. Was she in the front?"

Not ready for that question, I gave Mindy a quick version of Mom and Dad's story, including how he became a minister.

"No wonder you're so sweet," Mindy said. "It hurt you for your mom to leave, and your dad's a minister. Di said I was a goody two shoes, but I've got nothing on you." Mindy paused for more sausage. "Do you think your dad will like me? He might know my uncle."

I asked her uncle's name, but it didn't ring any bells. The waitress offered more coffee. After we said no, I asked for the check. In the jeep, as I started it, Mindy kissed my cheek. "Thanks for breakfast, sweetie pie. Do you have to work at your grandpa's store tomorrow?"

"Afraid so, why?"

"I thought we could take your jeep down to Oregon Inlet and look for shells."

I looked behind us for any cars coming into the parking lot. "Is this afternoon ok?"

"I can't. I have to go in at the restaurant at four."

I put the jeep into first gear and left the diner. Mindy's disappointed tone sure seemed to say she liked me. At church, I parked beside her Mustang and faced her. "I'll be pretty busy all week. What if we look for shells Saturday morning instead of going out on the skiff? I'll close the store early. It's not doing much business anyway because of more stores opening in Manteo."

She placed a palm to my cheek and pulled me close. "That's a great idea, sweetie pie." She kissed me soundly. "I'll meet you here at nine." She got out of the jeep, climbed into the Mustang and drove away, blowing me a kiss and making me grin. Then my grin fell. It was time to go home and face Dad's questions, as I was sure he saw Mindy and me together at church this morning.

When I got home, he was on the living room sofa with the Raleigh paper. Since we didn't take the paper, he must've picked up a copy at one of the convenience stores popping up in the area. Whatever he was reading had his full attention. He didn't even stop reading until the screened door slammed behind me. "The prodigal returns. Who was that redhead I saw you leave with after church? Was she one of those two women you spent the night with?"

"It just so happens," I said, using my most confident tone of voice, "that she was. It also just so happens that she's a nice, local girl, so you can stop your worrying."

He tapped the paper with a fingertip. "I'm more worried about this. North Vietnam fired on some of our ships in the Gulf of Tonkin. I wouldn't be surprised if President Johnson uses this to escalate America's presence in South Vietnam." He went back to reading, eyes narrowed, crow's feet deepening.

For myself, I didn't blame him one bit. Right when I met someone interesting, the world was falling apart.

I sat beside him on the sofa. "If you were me, would you join the service before you were drafted? If you did, you could choose the branch of the military instead of it being chosen for you."

"I'd do exactly that," Dad said, glancing away from the paper. "Loving the ocean like I do, I'd join the Navy." He stopped reading to study me. "Does that answer your question? It'd be better than trudging through those jungles over there. At least you can see your enemy coming from a ship." He folded the paper. "I'm sorry about giving you a hard time about that redhead. You say she's a local girl?"

I told Dad about Mindy's uncle owning the restaurant. I'm sure I'd find out more soon, such as who her parents and siblings were. When I mentioned how she and Di were going to join the Navy, he nodded. "They sound like patriotic young ladies. I broke one of the verses straight out of the King James Bible last night—'judge not that ye be not judged.'"

When I said Mindy and I were going shelling at Oregon Inlet next Saturday, he raked a hand through his hair. "I haven't had time to tell you this. Your grandpa called me last night. With all the new businesses opening in Manteo, he's decided to close the store. He said to tell you he's sorry about letting you go. If it were me, I'd enjoy my time with your young lady until she leaves. You can always fish more with me. People still love their seafood."

What a heck of a twenty-four hours I'd had. I'd lost Ellie to another man, met someone who might take her place, been fired, and was now being forced to consider joining the Navy.

Dad reopened the paper. "All this talk about war makes me wonder how Morris and his family are doing."

I'd been wondering the same thing. That time Dad said he'd lost Morris's address, I hadn't thought about something. Now I was. "Dad?"

He continued reading. "What, Son?"

"You said you'd lost Morris's address, right?"

"That's right."

"Did you tell me that so I wouldn't write Alma?"

Sighing deeply, Dad lowered the paper. "Son, I appreciate the fact that you and Alma formed some kind of relationship while we were there. Regardless, she's in Israel and you're here, so it's time to let her go."

"But—"

"There are no buts," Dad interrupted. "Think about this— Morris probably still has my address. That means Alma could write you and hasn't. That also means she realizes that whatever you and her had has run its course, and it's time for you to do the same thing."

I noticed Dad hadn't answered my question about losing Morris's address. Then I noticed he was right about Alma not writing me. Maybe Dad had lied about losing the address, maybe not. The main thing was Alma could've written me and hadn't, and that hurt.

Dad dropped the paper to the sofa. "I'm sorry to be the bearer of bad news. I've been hoping you'd see it on your own. The world is in turmoil. I'm not about to return to Israel. You've got to decide what to do before a draft starts. All that means you'll never see Alma again."

I said nothing. For a man who believed in biblical miracles, his negativity concerning the miracle of Alma and I ever having anything to do with each other again was off the charts.

Little did we know, my faith in that miracle would eventually prove itself.

Chapter 11

Until the following Saturday, when Mindy and I went shelling, I let Dad's words about Alma sink in. All in all he was right. Alma was out of my life for good. It was time to concentrate on my present, and I intended to do that by enjoying my time with Mindy before she left for the Navy.

Unfortunately, I didn't find out when she was leaving until the subject came up on our second date, the following Saturday. We were out on the skiff, watching the sunset over the sound. I was sitting on the bench seat. She was sitting in my lap, and had pulled my hands around her waist to press them to her stomach.

When the shimmering, red globe of the sun touched the horizon, she settled back against my chest. "Do you think you'll ever move away from Kitty Hawk?"

Extremely conscious of the bikini Mindy wore, plus how, since I was wearing cut-off jeans shorts and no shirt, I could feel so much of her body pressed to mine, I hesitated. The last time I felt like this was when Alma and I made love, and I was hoping Mindy might suggest we do the same thing soon.

She squeezed my hands. "Well, do you ever think you'll move away from Kitty Hawk?"

"I like it here too much to move. What about you?"

"It depends on what I see of the world in the Navy." She raised one of my hands to kiss its knuckles. "It also depends on if I have someone to come back to when my enlistment is up."

That sounded like a marriage proposal, so I let it go. Like Dad would say, a few dates aren't enough to even talk about marriage, much less to actually consider it.

Mindy pressed my hands to her stomach. "How many kids do you want? I'd like at least six."

Being an only child, I didn't know about that. Six seemed like a lot.

Mindy kissed my knuckles again. "I shouldn't be talking about this stuff with the world as crazy as it is." She left my lap to sit on the other seat across from me. "I've been a little dishonest with you. Di and I have already joined the Navy. We're leaving for our training tomorrow morning. When we took our vacation, we agreed to act as if we had more time. That way we could have fun without thinking about it. Are you mad? I hope not. I really like you, and I hope we can date again when I get back."

Mindy's admission left me with mixed feelings. Dad had been right about Alma, so I needed to forget about her. I was attracted to Mindy and she was attracted to me, and mutual attraction was a reasonable start to a relationship. Like her, I wanted a family one day. As far as the number of kids, we could compromise. The final thing that kept my anger away was Mindy's sincerity about our future together.

I told her I wasn't mad. She sat in my lap facing me. Kisses followed, growing deeper and longer. Other things followed that I won't mention, but I could tell she wanted me and I was sure she could tell I wanted her.

Twilight surrounded us. The waves of the Albemarle gently rocked the skiff. Mindy's shoulder blades beneath my hands felt great. The curve of her behind in my lap felt great. The growing heat between us felt great. A soft moan escaped Mindy's lips. I thought it was a sign for us to make love, so I started to untie her bikini top.

Nope, I was wrong about that.

Without the least bit of warning, she jumped up. "No, Seth, I'm not ready to do that. I know I said we could, but I'd rather wait." She sat across from me again. "Please don't be upset, ok?"

Despite my body's confusion, which was kind of uncomfortable in my shorts, I smiled to let Mindy know I understood. "I'm not upset. I respect you for wanting to wait." I smiled again. "It'll make it that much better when it finally happens."

"No doubt about it," Mindy said, humor in her voice. "Di says it's just about the best feeling she's ever had."

With darkness falling, I turned the skiff's running lights on. We'd planned to take a blanket to shore and watch the stars. Instead, we spread it in the bottom of the skiff and relaxed there, wrapped in each other's arms. Lucky for us, several hard rains had lessened the fish smell in the wood. Sure, it was still there, just weaker. Mindy not complaining about it made me appreciate her even more.

Off in the distance, a boat motor whined. Someone was probably heading in with their catch of fish or blue crabs. Minutes later, the waves from that boat lapped against the skiff.

It seemed I'd found a woman to fill this particular void in my life. Now, after Grandpa had closed the store, I needed to find a job to fill that particular void, especially if Mindy and I eventually married and started a family. Fishing was fine, and a dedicated worker could make a decent living, but I didn't care to do that the rest of my life. Whatever job I chose, though, I wanted it to be outdoors, where I could smell the salt air, feel the wind in my hair, and enjoy all the views of nature. What that job would be, who knew. Maybe, like with Mindy, it would fall into my lap one day.

As the darkness deepened, Mindy told me about her family. Her dad sold insurance. Her mom stayed home. There were three kids—two boys and one girl—and Mindy was the youngest. One brother, anticipating the draft, had left for Canada. The other brother, a sergeant in the Marines, considered him a coward. Although their parents wanted their boys to stay alive, it bothered them that one son ran off to Canada instead of doing his duty.

I said Dad and I had talked about me joining the Navy, plus how he thought it was a good idea if it were him. Of course, Mindy said this meant he thought it was a good idea for me.

We kissed until things got heated again. We didn't go all the way, but we went far enough to know we should call it a night.

At the Mustang, we kissed again. During our last hug, Mindy pulled away and started wiping tears, visible in the light coming from the open door of the car. When her emotions were under control, she kissed my cheek. "See how much I like you? I've never cried over a guy before. Stay safe if you join the Navy. You never know what they'll make you do."

I didn't think much about her comment at the time. Ships were huge things with all kinds of ways to get hurt. Dad said during his trip across the Atlantic in World War II, on a troop transport that had seen better days, rumors about German U-boats made him wonder if he was going to the war or if the war was coming to him.

Mindy got in the Mustang. I leaned in the open window and kissed her once more. We'd talked about trading addresses. She wouldn't know hers until she finally got stationed, and I'd be in the same situation if I joined the Navy. We didn't know the solution to that problem, so we parted by saying we'd get together after the war by whatever way we could.

The next day during breakfast, I told Dad about Mindy leaving. Peppering scrambled eggs, he raised his eyes to me. "So that's why you've been quiet. You can't get a break, can you?"

"Not really," I said, about to drink coffee. "My life is pretty messed up."

"You're only nineteen, Son. It'll work out. Do you feel up to handling one of the dories today? We've got to keep the Outer Banks tourists in seafood, you know."

I admired Dad's work ethic. Between being a full-time minister and a full-time fisherman, not only did the physical activity keep him in good shape, he earned a good living, evidenced by the total I saw in his savings account passbook one day. He'd also sold the lots on either side of us, and rental houses were going up. Still, there was enough room between the lots to feel like we had our own place. Neither one of us cared for how some of the local rentals were being built, where you could look right into each other's windows.

Getting my mind back on track, I considered his question about fishing. No doubt about it, I had some life choices to make. Stay here and fish until the draft dragged me off to fight in the jungles of Vietnam, or join the Navy and continue to enjoy my views of an ocean, even if it was a different one than the Atlantic.

Dad tapped the table with his fingertips. "Dad to Seth, Dad to Seth. Can you help me fish or not?"

I forked eggs. "It depends on where a Navy recruitment center is. It's time I started controlling my life instead of letting it control me."

With that comment, Dad said there had to be one in Norfolk, Virginia, which took about an hour and a half to drive there. With the nice clothes on that I'd worn to Israel, no one would think I was a saltwater hick from Kitty Hawk who was as clueless as clueless gets. Now to get to Norfolk and find the place.

Roughly two and a half hours later—later because I was forced to ask directions three times and had gotten lost twice— I was signing the enlistment papers at an official United States Navy recruitment center. Regardless of my trip to Israel and my first time falling in love, I was still a saltwater hick from Kitty Hawk who was as clueless as clueless gets. Maybe joining the Navy and seeing more of the world would help with that.

Boy, was I wrong.

To start with, the Navy tests you to see what you're good at. After spending years fishing with Dad, my balance in a boat was great. No matter how it moved, I could keep my head still. When the Navy discovered that, they thought I might be a good sniper. This boggled my mind. "How can I shoot something or someone from a ship at sea?" I asked the guy to my right in our quarters at boot camp.

"You don't," Frank said. "They take you up the Mekong Delta in a patrol boat and drop you off in the jungle. Then you slither in the mud and crap until you get close enough to your target to take him out. Then you hightail it back to the river, all the while hoping the patrol boat is there to pick you up."

Frank was short for Franklin. He was from Norfolk and had joined the Navy to keep from being drafted into the Army. His dad used to take him into the Dismal Swamp to trap beavers. Sometimes they had to wade through black water with green slime floating on top. When they got back from running a trap line, they took turns using a cigarette to burn leaches off each other's backs.

I asked Frank how he knew all that about Navy snipers.

"It just figures," he said, scratching his blonde crew cut as he sat on his bunk, pausing from shining his boots. "They wouldn't mention Navy snipers if that isn't what they make them do." Obviously, Frank had a wild imagination, but you never know until you know.

Not wanting to take any chances when I tried out for sniper school, I made sure to do nothing but kick up dust around the target, 500 yards away.

I received more testing. I answered more questions. I passed all the physical fitness tests without a hitch. I tied knots even the Navy didn't know and outswam everyone. In the end, they kept coming back to how good I could keep my balance in a boat, which I took to mean they'd assign me to a job on a ship.

Long story short, my job was a mixed blessing. They

assigned Frank and me to a patrol boat. The patrol boat—not a blessing—would patrol the Mekong Delta. The job—sort of a blessing because I wouldn't have to crawl through the jungle in the mud—would be to man the .50 caliber machine gun mounted up front. The Navy, in its infinite wisdom, thought if I could raise dust around a target 500 yards away, I could easily hit a target in a river at that distance, or longer.

Very little about my job on the Mekong Delta was a blessing.

We spent the days inspecting local boats called sampans for weapons and explosives. The looks those folks gave us could kill. Here they were, trying to get from point A to point B, and we're pulling up beside them and hopping aboard to go through their stuff.

Standing at the .50 cal, I got the worst looks. To be honest, I didn't blame them. If someone pulled me and Dad over in the skiff with a huge machine gun ready to blow us out of the water, I wouldn't like it either.

On occasion we were hit with sniper fire. No one ever heard the actual firing of the gun. All you heard was the *thunk* of a bullet hitting the fiberglass hull above that muddy water. Lucky for us, the snipers were so far away, most of the bullets did little to no damage. Sometimes it was just one *thunk*. Other times it was too many to count. When that happened, I'd blast the jungle until the plinking stopped. If I killed anyone, I didn't know. The only thing that mattered was for them to stop shooting at us.

At the end of a patrol, when the crew got a chance to take it easy, everyone but Frank and me went hunting prostitutes in Can Tho. We'd buy a couple of six packs of beer and stay near the boat. We didn't do this to be antisocial. We did this because Frank had introduced me to the pleasures of marijuana, which is when I realized that's what I'd mistaken for cigarettes that night with Di.

By this time, two members of the crew had been hit by sniper fire, meaning two sets of parents back home had to bury their sons. The marijuana helped knock the edge off the grief, as well as the fear. Anyone who says they're not afraid in a patrol boat in the Mekong Delta is a liar.

Dad wrote once a month. I always said things were fine. There was no danger here. I had it made. I expected him to question those responses but he didn't. For a parent with a son or a daughter in war, ignorance can be your best friend.

The following year, in the summer of 1966, Frank went home for surgery to rebuild his right bicep muscle, hit by a sniper as we were cruising toward Can Tho. The strange thing about it was how it happened. I was monkeying around while he was taking my picture. I had my cap on sideways, acting like a saltwater hick. At the moment he said to be still and stop acting a fool, my cap went flying, along with about half of his bicep muscle. After we got him to the medics, I checked my cap. The bullet had left a hole in the brim. If I'd been leaning over just three more inches, I'd be in a body bag.

I didn't make friends with his replacement. Why do that when he might die the next minute?

Regardless of all that stuff, and if you chose to look at it like I'm about to tell you, there wasn't much difference between the Mekong Delta and the Albemarle Sound. The thing is, to see the similarities, you had to close your eyes and open your mind.

Despite what happened to Frank, the best time to do this was at the end of the day, when the scalding sun hung just above the jungle as we were heading back to base. I liked the low rumble of the patrol boat's engines. I liked the lapping of that dirt-brown water against the hull. I liked the smell of the air, kind of like the air back home after a thunderstorm had passed over.

Sure, I liked all that stuff because it reminded me of Kitty Hawk, but I liked it a lot better after I closed my eyes, because only then could I go back home for real.

I stop typing. The day has come and gone. I should eat

supper but I'm not hungry. Outside the sliding glass doors, beyond the black waters of the Albemarle, far, far in the distance, pinpoints of light mark the North Carolina mainland.

What happened next is sometimes a blur. A Purple Heart was involved. A lot of pain was involved. A lot of mental anguish was involved. Eventually there'd be heartache, but it's too soon to write about that.

I stand and stretch the kinks from my back and neck. The clock on the microwave says it's 7:30. Out on the deck, hoping for a breath of fresh air, I get a whiff of beef cooking on someone's grill. Keys in hand, I lock the doors and climb into my pickup. My appetite has returned. It says to drive to the nearest restaurant and to put something in my seventy-eight-year-old stomach before I keel over, so I do.

Chapter 12

At the restaurant, waiting for my order of a rare rib-eye steak, baked potato, and tossed salad, I start with a draft beer and fried calamari. My wife would not be happy with my artery-clogging combo, nor would she be happy with how I chug the beer and ask for more. When the meal comes, I feel misty and relaxed enough to enjoy it without guilt. The steak is juicy and tender. The potato is covered with butter and sour cream. The salad is crunchy, with hints of olive oil and balsamic vinegar. As I finish, the waitress asks if I'd like dessert. Instead, I ask for the bill, pay it, and find a booth in the bar.

I have another beer. This leads to shots of Jack Daniels. Keeping my mind blank, I pretend I don't know why I'm drinking like this, but earlier, when I finished typing that last chapter, my memory slapped me around and said, "Hey, are you gonna skip that hurricane of a woman in Can Tho? How can you forget her when she affected your life bigtime? More importantly, how can you forget her little girl?"

My memory's right.

I switch to coffee. Two hours later, when the waitress says it's time to close, I'm sober enough to walk to my pickup without staggering.

On the way home, the urge to relieve myself of all that beer, whiskey, and coffee forces me into the empty parking lot of another restaurant. As I start splattering onto the asphalt, a police car pulls in beside my pickup. I can't stop, so I turn away when the officer rolls his window down.

"Are you all right, sir?" he asks.

I finish and zip. "I'm fine, officer. When you gotta go, you gotta go, you know?"

His door clicks open. He unfolds his tall frame from the car. "Can I ask what you've been drinking?"

The hint of my misty feeling tells me I might not pass a sobriety test. The last thing I want is to get arrested for a DUI, because the next thing I want is to write the next chapter. Still, my character demands honesty, so I admit to drinking while I ate supper.

In the glare of the parking lot security light, the officer's youthful expression goes from relaxed to concerned. "Are you a local or a tourist?"

"I'm a local. Lived here all my life."

"You say it's been two hours since your last drink?"

"Yes, sir," I say, and cover a steak-flavored burp.

He points at a white line in the parking lot. "Walk that line for me. Heal to toe, heal to toe."

I do so with no problem. "There you go, sir. Anything else?"

The officer rubs his chin. "How far do you live from here?"

I lean my behind against my pickup. "Three miles north."

"Is anyone at home to come and get you?"

I want to heave the heaviest sigh I've ever heaved. I know what he sees. I'm six-one, a hundred and ninety pounds. I've got a bit of a paunch, but my shoulders are still wide and upright. My hair is white but still fairly thick, coming to a widow's peak in the center of my forehead. Of course, he doesn't see the real me, the guy who misses his wife and whose memories are now getting too touchy to relive, though I have to relive one of them in my next chapter, followed by the rest.

"No one's at home, sir. I lost my wife recently, and our kids live on the mainland." I show him my palms. "I walked that line, okay? I just want to get home and go to bed."

The officer studies me. "I'd like to do the same thing, but you worry me. I've seen too many drunk drivers kill themselves, or other drivers. I can't take that chance."

Anger heats my cheeks. I passed his stupid walking test, and he hasn't mentioned a breathalyzer test, which would end all this BS right away. "Give me a breathalyzer test. I've had enough of this."

"Let's try this first," he says, his voice going from reasonable to stern. "Stand with your arms out to the sides. Then, one at a time, touch the tip of your index finger to the tip of your nose."

I do as he says. The left fingertip to my nose isn't a problem. The right, like I knew it would be, is a problem. "Look," I say, "I was injured in Vietnam, and I don't have the mobility in my left shoulder that I used to. Like I already said, a breathalyzer test will clear this up if you just give me one."

The officer finally gives me the stupid breathalyzer test and eyes the results. "You're barely over the limit, but that's still over the limit. Turn around and put your hands behind your back. You're under arrest for driving while intoxicated."

I don't turn around. "Hold on. My neighbor can come and get me."

"It's too late for that now," the officers says, placing his hand on his sidearm. "Turn around now."

"No, sir. You're supposed to identify yourself with your name and you haven't. You're supposed to ask for my driver's license, my registration, and my proof of insurance, and you haven't. I'll make sure your superiors know all that."

He hesitates, and I take the opening. "You're about the right age. If your dad served in Vietnam, how about showing a fellow serviceman a little respect and taking me home? I promise I'll go straight to bed and won't come back for my pickup until tomorrow."

Sure, I should've been a good boy. If I had, I wouldn't be at home the next morning, my daughter glaring at me after baling me out. At least she dropped me off at my pickup so I could drive it home. I wasn't about to pay for a tow truck on top of whatever fines I'd get for my arrest.

Sitting at the bar in the kitchen, she shakes her head. "I know you're having a hard time getting over Mom's death, but drunk driving? Really, Dad?"

"Good morning to you too," I say, because we haven't said it yet. My mouth tastes like sea weed is growing in it. My back aches from that swaybacked cot in my jail cell. My eyes feel like someone kicked sand in them. I point at the coffee maker. "Want some?"

My oldest daughter is almost sixty, heading into what my wife and I used to jokingly call decrepitude when it happened to us. Her dark hair is turning gray at her temples. Her dark eyes smolder like her mom's eyes. I see her in her constantly. They both love coffee, so I go ahead with the maker.

She picks up one of two pill bottles on the bar. "Are you taking your heart medicine? This bottle is full."

"Yes, Mom," I say without too much sarcasm. "Check the date. I just refilled it."

She picks up the other bottle. "I see you just refilled your cholesterol medicine too. Good job."

Her doctor's tone is what I get for sending her to medical school. "I'm seventy-eight, young lady. Regardless of those pills, I won't live forever."

She cuts her eyes at me. "I'm long past being a young lady, and you know it." She gets french vanilla creamer from the fridge and takes it to the bar. My wife loved french vanilla creamer. I guess I keep it in the fridge to pretend she's still here.

Coffee dribbles into the carafe, filling the kitchen with its aroma. I fill two mugs and take them to the bar. After sitting on the stool across from her, I add creamer and shove the container toward her. This was our ritual for a week after my wife died. We both knew I needed company until I stopped roaming the house looking for her ghost.

I sip. She sips. I ask if she wants breakfast. She says no. She sips. I sip. I hear the muffled whine of a Jet Ski through the sliding glass doors. She looks that way, likely recalling memories of her and her siblings growing up here. It was a wonderful place for my wife and I to raise our family, filled with boat rides, fishing, walks along the sound and the beach, visits to lighthouses and historical sites like the Whalehead Club in Corolla and the British Cemetery on Ocracoke Island. We'd all sit on the deck and ponder the iconic Lost Colony, or where the original herd of Spanish horses in Corolla came from, or how much more commercial development the Outer Banks can stand.

Well, the pondering about commercial development came mostly from me. My nostalgia longs for fewer paved roads, walks to school along sandy paths, and watching the sound without seeing any kind of vessel for an hour or more.

"Dad?"

I recognize the concern in my daughter's voice. "Yes?"

"Mom told me she asked you to write your story. Have you started yet?"

"I have."

"Is it helping?"

"It was until I remembered something from Vietnam." I share a soft smile. "It has pros and cons. After that, mostly pros because of you."

"Okay, I remember now," she says, and sips coffee. "How we react to love is sometimes strange, isn't it?"

Smiling, I nod. "In this case, strange but wonderful."

We talk about the pros of that part of my story and leave the cons behind. Both won't be apparent until I get further along with my writing, but I'm now looking forward to it.

Over more coffee, I promise not to drink too much again, just a beer once in a while and to never drive after. She says I should go fishing with Jack, or ask Liz out to lunch. I say I might, that I feel more like doing those things because I'm enjoying writing my story. She kisses my cheek, reminds me to take my pills, and says goodbye.

In many ways she's a miracle. The most important way is simply because she exists. The second most important way is because if not for her and her mom, I might've ended up married to the wrong women, then divorced, lonely, and childless.

In short, life has a way of working out, but we've got to make the right choices when they come along, especially when those choices concern love.

Noting the time on the microwave, I know my attorney has just stepped into his office. I call and tell him about my DUI, including how the officer behaved during it, including not reading me my Miranda rights, which I hadn't thought about last night, or not allowing me to call anyone until morning, plus how the breathalyzer test was barely above the legal driving limit. My attorney says it's getting harder and harder to hire people with the necessary qualities to make a good deputy, that most were exemplary but this one obviously wasn't. I say I understand how serious the issue is, but I'd never done anything like that and won't again. He says he'll discuss it with the prosecutor this morning and see what can be done.

Feeling like breakfast and a nap because of my less than stellar overnight stay in jail, I take a carton of eggs from the frig. As I start cracking two to scramble, my attorney calls. He says the sheriff apologized because of the deputy's actions, especially the one of using a breathalyzer that was overdue to be calibrated, and to consider the charges dropped. I thank my attorney, say I know better than to drive if I were drunk to start with, and end the call.

Hoping the young deputy was learning a lesson from the sheriff right about now, I finish making my breakfast and go out on the deck to eat.

To my left, beneath the patio umbrella shading the table

where I sit, the sight of my wife's empty chair doesn't hurt so much this morning. Because of the stuff I could fix around the house, she always said I was a smart cookie. Maybe so, but she sure knew what she was doing when she made me promise to write our story.

A Jet Ski zooms by. Out on the sound, high in the sky behind a para-sail boat, a tourist gets an amazing view.

Although the scrambled eggs, whole wheat toast and coffee is just what I need, I have to take bites and sips between yawns. One particular yawn, the one I'm having now, makes me squeeze my eyes shut and shake my head.

Footsteps swish in the grass to my left. Still yawning, I can't stop to see whose shoes are thudding up the steps to the deck. "Did we have a late night out?"

As I recognize Liz's voice , I manage to open my eyes. "You could say that."

She nods toward the chair. "Do you mind if I sit?"

I say to go ahead, that there's coffee inside if she'd like some. She says she just finished breakfast and sits, adding to not let her interrupt my eating. I take eggs and toast, chew and chase the combo down with coffee. Liz looks at me like she's studying a butterfly on one of her butterfly bushes. About to eat more eggs. I lower the fork. "What's wrong?"

"Jack and I are worried about you," she says, sincerity in her voice. "Except for last night, wherever you went, you've been cooped up inside your house for almost two weeks."

I spread my hands over the patio table. "As you can see, I'm out now."

Liz huffs a hard breath. "You know what I mean, Seth. Don't get smart with me." She crosses her arms. "Who is she?"

Liz must've seen my daughter's car. I try to hold in a grin. "You must've seen my date last night, and now you come over here jealous."

"All I saw is a car and her when she got out. She looks too young for you."

"How could you tell when all you saw is her back?"

"That's not the point."

Liz saw my daughter at the funeral. She didn't recognize her because she's cut her hair and has a new car. I need to finish eating and take a nap so I can write some more. I continue eating, intending to let my nosy but caring neighbor stew for a while. After swallowing eggs, I jab my thumb over my shoulder, toward the door. "The offer of coffee still stands. You'll have to drink it fast, though. I need a nap after my rowdy night out with my date." I wink. "Would you believe I can still perform without those little blue pills? Not bad for a man my age."

My joking has the desired effect. Liz's eyes narrow. Then she storms down the steps and to her house. Even though it's about fifty yards away, I hear the door slam. Yeah, I feel a bit guilty, but I've got to get some rest so I can write with a clear head. Maybe I'll make it up to Liz by inviting her to lunch sometimes, like my daughter suggested.

Done with breakfast, I wash my dishes and the pan. Because I drink decaf, and because I got so little sleep last night, the two hour nap I planned turns into a three hour nap.

It's a little past noon. Walking to the kitchen, I hear the whine of more Jet Skis. The tourists are at it again.

Still full from breakfast, I settle down at the kitchen table with my laptop and tap the keys to bring Can Tho and two special people back to life.

Chapter 13

I think writing about mine and Frank's sniper incident brought back the memory of Trang and her daughter, Minh.

I met them about a month after Frank went home. The rest of the crew, as usual, were headed to bars for booze and prostitutes. Like I used to do with Frank, I preferred to hang out near the boat and relax with a joint and a six pack.

On this particular day, the gray sky was spitting rain, so I stayed under the canopy over the middle of the boat. The sun was trying to break through, and I wanted it to. If anything is constant in Vietnam, it's the rain. For me, like in Kitty Hawk, sunshine was a tonic, even more so than beer and a joint.

Well, just when I was about to cuss a blue streak because of the rain, out pops the sun, splitting those clouds like a knife through a flounder fillet. Not long after that, along comes a Vietnamese woman and a little girl down the dirt path from town. I hadn't seen them before. Kids would sometimes come down to the docks and beg. Sure, maybe men and women came, but I hadn't seen any.

Anyway, the first thing I noticed about the little girl was she must have an American dad. Her hair was dark brown instead of black, curly instead of straight. Her complexion was lighter also, not deep brown like most Vietnamese. She must've been about three or four. When she saw me, she came running to the boat with her little hand out. Both her and the woman were thin, so I gave them a couple of cans of pork 'n beans and one of my two folding openers. The girl gave the woman the cans. Then she took my opener and gave it to the woman, nodding. This was another hint of her having an American dad. Those openers are tricky to use if you haven't been taught. Since she nodded, she must've at least seen one being used by her American dad.

Wearing a loose fitting black shirt with matching pants, the woman approached me. The little girl wore the same type of shirt and pants, but they were way too big for her. With dark circles under their eyes, the cuffs of their pants ragged and torn, both without shoes, their feet dirty, both people looked worn out from the war. Despite that, the woman nodded and thanked me in accented English. I showed her my palm and said to stay. She nodded again. I found two more cans of pork 'n beans, gave them to her, and patted my chest. "I'm Seth. What's your name?"

She nodded. "I am Trang. My daughter is Minh."

I assumed Minh's dad had taught her English, but she still spoke with the high pitched tone most Vietnamese used.

We continued talking, with me carefully delving into her situation. She seemed open to sharing it, so I went further.

She met Minh's dad four years ago. I was surprised because there weren't many American soldiers here back then. Trang said they met when she was walking along the river, and Minh was the result a year later.

While we talked, it was obvious how much she loved her daughter, giving her affectionate glances, sometimes fingering a curl of hair from her eyes. Sadly, as the conversation shifted, Trang's dark eyes lowered. Minh's dad had been killed not long after she was born, and it broke my heart to hear it.

It was bad enough for Trang to lose the man she spoke about with such tenderness, but for this sweet child to lose her dad reached inside me on a deeper level. Considering the reason, I was sure it was because of Mom. After all, I knew how it felt to lose a parent at a young age. No, Mom hadn't died, but to me it felt worse than death because she'd chosen to leave us. At least Minh would remember her dad as someone who loved her instead of someone who'd abandoned her, unlike me.

Right then and there I decided to help Trang and Minh in whatever way I could. The one thing I couldn't do, like I'd done with Alma, was to get emotionally attached to them. It had gutted me to leave Alma, and I didn't care to feel that pain again.

Trang and Minh lived in what amounted to a shack, a short walk from the river. When it rained, Trang built a small fire on the dirt floor to boil rice or cook fish, which smoked up the place enough to burn my eyes and make me cough. When it didn't rain, she built the fire outside.

As far as relatives, her parents were long dead, and her siblings had scattered to other cities and towns, either to marry or to look for work. With North Vietnam's communist regime more determined than ever to conquer South Vietnam, who knew what would happen to this small family as the war progressed.

I brought Trang whatever food I could scrounge, sometimes more pork 'n beans, sometimes a full C-ration meal, which was canned meat, bread, and a fruit. Yeah, it was as appetizing as it sounds, but she always thanked me profusely.

After about a month of this, I could see affection in her eyes. That could not happen. I still visited for a while, mostly to see Minh. I'd tell her stories about Kitty Hawk, fishing the sound and the ocean, the sunrises and the sunsets. She seemed hypnotized by the notion of a place that wasn't surrounded by a jungle, so thick you could hardly walk through it unless there was a path, much less see through it.

I was staying later and later. The guys on the patrol boat were giving me a hard time about it, saying I'd fallen for a local. I knew I hadn't, but the last night I visited Trang and

Minh, after Minh had fallen asleep during one of my stories. Trang asked me to sleep with her. Part of me understood her request. Not only had she loved Minh's dad, she needed comfort in the middle of the insanity called the Vietnam War. After my experiences with Ellie, Alma, and Mindy, taking comfort in Trang's arms might do me some good, but I couldn't risk our feelings growing beyond what they were now.

I got up, gathered my gear, and left without a word, knowing I'd never return. Even now, decades later, I wonder about them on occasion. Then I tell myself to stop. Being in the middle of a war made my empathy for them too intense for my own good, and I didn't want them to get attached to me when I could die like Minh's dad had died.

Anyone reading this might see a loophole in this part of my story, like the possibility of Trang and Minh coming to the boat to see me. That was true, but fate had other plans.

The next day, as the crew was patrolling a few miles upriver, they were also ragging me again about Trang and Minh, saying I had fallen in love with a local and her kid. They were partly right. I had fallen in love with Minh because it broke my heart that she didn't have a dad. Maybe it was how she looked at me while I told her stories about Kitty Hawk. Maybe it was how cute she was. Maybe it was how she'd crawl into my lap when she got sleepy, and I'd rock her back and forth while humming to her, feeling like her dad myself. I've thought about it a lot over the years, and I think it's just another aspect of how Mom's leaving affected me. If there was one thing I couldn't stand, it was the thought of a precious child without both parents. I'm not knocking a single-parent family, but that one parent has got to be exemplary, like Dad.

Another thing about being a parent bothered me too. In 1964, talk about abortion rights was heating up across America even more than in the past. Since the birth control pill and condoms were available, I didn't understand the controversy. Still, since I couldn't get pregnant, I didn't think I should stick my nose into someone else's business. Still again, my experience of losing Mom and getting to know Minh gave me plenty of second thoughts about a woman who wanted to abort her baby for no other reason than not wanting it. Regardless of all my angst concerning the subject, I hoped I'd never meet a woman who'd done that, because I didn't know for sure how'd I'd feel about it. Yes, I hoped I'd be open minded, but we never know how we'll feel about something until we experience it.

Anyway, the crew was ragging me pretty good as I manned the .50 cal, scanning the jungle. They were good natured about it, so I wasn't taking it to heart, but I still wished they'd shut up so I could concentrate on staying alive. After all, we were in the middle of a freaking war in Vietnam.

Sometimes all it takes is one thing to change your life. Sometimes it takes lots of things. In my case, it was a combination of the two. Up until this point, lots of things had affected my life, like Mom leaving, becoming friends with Ellie, her wanting to be more than friends when we got older, falling in love with Alma and learning how it felt to make love, Ellie getting married, and finally, meeting Mindy and making plans with her to get together when we were discharged from the Navy. At this particular point in time, on this particular patrol boat cruising along the Hau River in the Mekong Delta, the single thing that changed my life was a bullet.

Finally tired enough of the crew ragging me, I'd turned to tell them to knock it off, when what felt like a giant fist punched me in the back of my left shoulder, knocking me to the deck. The thing is, a giant fist slugging the back of your shoulder doesn't spray blood across the faces of your crewmates when it hits you, nor would it go all the way through you to drill a hole into the head of the man right in front of you.

Micky hit the throttle. As the engine roared and the bow rose, Alvin grabbed our medical bag and tended to my screaming self. Tommy gaped at Mike, our dead crewmate, and crossed himself. As far as our dead crewmate, I don't recall his name because he'd only been with us two days.

We made it to base in forty minutes. Alvin had cut my shirt off and bandaged my shoulder, all the while saying I'd gotten a million dollar wound and how I'd be going back home. The triage doctor said the same thing. "You need reconstructive surgery on that shoulder if you want to use it again. A chopper's gonna get you to a hospital ship as soon as we get an IV hooked up." After that, he shot me up with what I guessed was morphine, and I drifted off into the land of blurred faces and my own slurring voice as I asked when I'd get home.

I could tell you about the chopper ride. I could tell you about the surgery on the ship. I could tell you how it never crossed my mind to ask if a nurse called Mindy was there. I could tell you about the hell I went through during rehab. Sure, I could tell you all about that, but I won't. The most important thing was when I was honorably discharged from the Navy and I called Dad to come to Norfolk to pick me up.

On the way home, he kept looking at me. We'd been mailing each other every two or three weeks, so he knew about my shoulder. I guess he was wondering if I had any other wounds, like mental wounds. Neither of us knew it yet, but I did.

In my room, when I finally got out of my uniform, I fell to my bed and took in the scent of nostalgia in my pillow. Sure, the pillowcase just smelled of fresh air from hanging on the line outside, but nothing, not a single thing, could beat that smell for telling me I wasn't going to get shot at in Vietnam.

My surgeon did a decent job on my shoulder. My therapist did a great job of strengthening it. Like I'd done with Frank in Vietnam, my brain longed for a joint to relax while my tongue longed for an ice cold beer to knock the edge off my memories of war.

The following month went to pieces. Yeah, some words other than "pieces" came to mind, but I'd said plenty of them in Vietnam. With Dad being a minister, and me hoping to get my life back on track, I'd rather dump those words in the garbage bin of my brain and lock them away.

I scratch my head. I got home in late 1965. I think it was around the first of November because Dad had a huge turkey in the freezer to cook and take to Grandpa and Grandma Callahan's for Thanksgiving. Sadly, Grandma passed the second week in November, and no one, especially Grandpa, felt like celebrating the holiday.

For about a week after I got home, church members stopped by to see how I was doing. Since I'd been wounded, the men shook my hand and thanked me for my service. The woman shook their heads mournfully. The boys wanted to see my Purple Heart. The girls asked if it hurt to be shot. Two teenage girls, arriving on their own, wanted to know how it felt to be a baby killer. I wanted to ask them how it felt to judge something they knew absolutely nothing about, other than from what they were hearing from their ignorant college friends. Dad politely asked them to leave, adding that they couldn't believe everything they saw on TV. With a beer can in my hand, I followed them out to the deck. Unclenching my teeth as they descended the steps, I then told them to tell their draft-dodging boyfriends to kiss where the sun don't shine. Sure, I could've said a lot worse, but I didn't out of respect for Dad.

On Thanksgiving morning, I woke like a sail without the wind—no energy, no nothing. Dad clanked pots and pans in the kitchen. Since I missed last Thanksgiving, he intended to make this one special by making all my favorites. Not to criticize Mom, but he was quite the cook, taking it up as something of a hobby after she left. I still wished he'd consider finding someone. For men as fine as him, life can be lonely without someone special to share it with.

I should've gotten up to help cook, but thoughts of Mindy kept me lying in the warmth of my bed. Without the threat of being wounded aboard a hospital ship, she'd stay in the Navy for the full four-year enlistment, and our relationship would be on hold. I was only nineteen, but spending time with Minh made me want to be a dad. Unfortunately, I needed a steady income to support a family, and I hadn't decided on how to do that yet.

Footfalls came to my door. Dad's knuckles tapped. "If you're up, I could use some help in the kitchen."

I said I'd be there in a minute. Then I sat up on the side of the bed and blinked to clear the haze from my eyes. That's what drinking a six-pack before bed will do for you. Lucky for me, Dad hadn't seen me sneak it to my room after I'd bought it at one of the convenience stores popping up in Kitty Hawk, which served the increasing numbers of tourists.

Having a serious case of bad breath from not brushing my teeth before I fell asleep, I shuffled to the bathroom in my boxers and squeezed toothpaste onto the brush. Bloodshot eyes stared back from the mirror over the sink. Several days of beard growth darkened my chin and jaw. The surgery scar from the front of my shoulder to the back resembled a miniature train track climbing a mountain of skin. Before I joined the Navy, Dad kept my hair trimmed nice and neat. Now it stuck this way and that, as if I'd spent the night out in a hurricane.

His knuckles rapped the door. "Get a move on, Son. There's someone here to see you."

His voice wasn't what I'd call excited. I'd driven over to Manteo to see Grandpa Callahan a few days after I got home, so the visitor shouldn't be him. It was probably one of the men from church, here to thank me for my service.

I washed my face, combed my hair, and swiped some deodorant under my arms. After I dressed in jeans, a white T-shirt, and sneakers, I went to the kitchen, pulling to a hard stop as I entered. At the table with a cup of coffee, Mindy raised her green eyes to me. "Hey there, stranger. I heard you made it back from Nam in one piece."

As I started to answer, someone knocked on one of the sliding glass doors to the deck. "I heard the same thing," Ellie's muffled voice said. "If you let me in, I'll give you a welcome home hug."

Chapter 14

At the counter beside the sink, peeling potatoes to boil for potato salad, Dad jabbed the knife toward the doors. "Where's your manners? Let Ellie in." I hurried over and slid one of the doors open. He gave her a wave. "Nice to see you, Ellie."

Ellie immediately hugged my neck, then held me at arm's length to study me from head to toe. "Well," she said, using her familiar southern twang, "it looks like you still got all your parts." She faced Dad. "I'm sorry for interrupting your Thanksgiving, Mr. Callahan."

Tall and slender, with thick brunette hair trimmed to barely touch her shoulders, Ellie wore red lipstick and a little mascara. She was a far cry from the skinny gal who'd left Kitty Hawk a few years ago. She'd filled out a little also, and the green, pleated skirt and white turtleneck sweater accented her figure to a T.

I closed the door. Wondering if Mindy was jealous, I decided to do like Barney Fife on the *Andy Griffith Show* and nip it in the bud. "Sit and have some coffee, Ellie. I'd like to hear how married life is treating you."

Mindy's eyes, which had been darting back and forth between Ellie and I, stopped on me. "I don't think you told me about Ellie. Is she an old school friend, or something like that?"

"That's right, an old friend," Ellie said, sitting. Dad offered coffee and she declined. "I just wanted to stop by and say hi."

I took the chair beside her. "Where are you and your husband living? Do you have any kids?"

"I hope not," Mindy said, making me curious because she didn't say why. I started to ask but didn't. We'd talk later, and I'd make a point to ask after we caught up.

Ellie patted my arm. "Would you believe we're moving back into my folk's old house and fixing it up? Jeff—he's my husband—just got a job managing a hotel. We have a baby boy. He's six-months old and as cute as can be."

Seeing Ellie's smile and hearing the joy in her voice, I was happy she'd found someone. Plus, since she'd just closed that chapter of my life, I could concentrate on opening a new one with Mindy.

Dad sat the pot of peeled potatoes on the stove. "It's good to hear good news, Ellie." He glanced at me. "And we'll be neighbor's again."

"I'm glad," Ellie said. "Jeff's busy a lot, so it'll be nice to have someone to visit."

Mindy cut her eyes toward me but said nothing. Even though Ellie was married with a baby, she must still be jealous. Then again, the war created insecurity in a lot of people, so that might be it.

Dad sat across from Ellie. "How're your folks?"

"Daddy passed away last year. Momma's doing fine. She got a job as a secretary."

I hated how Dad and I were ignoring Mindy, who'd been watching everyone while ignoring her coffee. I touched the cup. "Can I warm that up for you?"

"I didn't get your name," Ellie said to Mindy. She faced me. "Did you go and get married, Seth Callahan?"

"We're not married," Mindy said flatly. "We met before I left for the Navy as a nurse. I was hoping we could talk," she said to me. "After all, it's been over a year since we saw each other."

Mindy's flat tone was getting tense, and I didn't blame her.

I wanted to talk to her as much as she wanted to talk to me.

Ellie stood. "Well, I better get back home and start on our turkey. It's good to see you, Seth."

Always the gentleman, Dad opened the door for her. "Thanks for stopping by, Ellie. Bring that boy of yours when you can. I'd like to know what it feels like to hold someone's grandchild, even if he isn't my own."

Dad closed the door behind her, checked the potatoes, and sat by Mindy. "Other than seeing you with Seth in church that time, I don't know you except from what he's told me. How did being a nurse on a hospital ship go?"

Mindy pushed the coffee cup away. "I wish I'd never joined the Navy. That's how bad it was."

"How did you hear I'd gotten out?" I asked.

"Your grandpa knows my dad. He mentioned it."

"Are you on leave?"

She left the chair and went to one of the windows facing the sound. "I love your view. I don't have to worry about any helicopters bringing more wounded and dying men to tend to."

Dad and I looked at each other. From how Mindy had ignored my question, plus from her sad tone, we could tell the war had affected her.

She turned. "I better get home and help Mom cook. I'm glad you made it home, Seth. A lot of guys can't say that. Nice to meet you, Mr. Callahan."

After Dad returned the sentiment, I followed Mindy out to the deck, where she stopped at the steps. "I guess you can tell the war is bothering me. I don't even know what you did over there. Were you in the Army?"

"I joined the Navy almost as soon as you left. I thought I'd be on a ship. Wouldn't you know they'd put me on a doggone patrol boat in the Mekong Delta?" I pointed at my shoulder. "That's how a sniper got me." I paused, wondering how Mindy was home now, long before her enlistment was up. She hadn't said, and I didn't know whether to ask or not.

Mindy came closer, studying my eyes. "I'm sure you're wondering why I'm home." She went to a deck railing and leaned against it. "I was wounded too, by stress. I just couldn't take the sight of those wounded guys screaming for their moms and dads." Shaking her head, she crossed her arms. "I could never have children. Why do that when they'll just go off to war?"

The comment, of course, wasn't logical. Every kid doesn't grow up and go to war. Mindy's time in the Navy must've affected her terribly to make her think such things. I wanted to change the subject but didn't know how. I wondered if she'd heard from Di, but her being in the Navy would be the same thing.

Mindy uncrossed her arms. "Do you have any weed? I use it sometimes to knock the edge off. Know what I mean?"

A lot of guys used weed in Vietnam, so she likely assumed I did. That time with her and Di, Di said Mindy didn't like it. As I knew, the sights and sounds of war sometimes make a person turn to drugs and alcohol. Although I'd been wanting a joint, the craving had lessened. Too bad I couldn't say that about beer.

"I don't have any weed," I said. "I smoked it with a buddy in country, but I've given it up."

Mindy blew out a soft breath. "If Di weren't still in the Navy, I bet I could get some from her." She faced the sound. "Remember when we took your skiff out on one of our dates? We sure were innocent. Now I feel like I've aged a hundred years." She faced me again. "Do you still want to date and see how it goes?"

Uncertainty about the war's effect on Mindy, especially with her need for marijuana and the lack of interest in having kids, made me consider the question. I could be overreacting. After all, it was just dating, and I hadn't met anyone since I'd gotten home.

A gust of wind blew from the sound, swirling Mindy's red hair about her face. The skiff clunked hollowly against the pier, possibly a sign to tell me to give her a chance like she was giving me a chance. I shared an easy smile with her. "Sure, we can date and see how it goes. Have you found a job since you got home?"

The wind blew again, this time steadily. Mindy fingered her hair out of her eyes and held it in place. "Dad wants me to go to work with him selling insurance. The pay's okay, so I might. How about you?"

I wasn't proud of sitting on my butt since I'd come home. It was time to earn a paycheck, and I could fish with Dad until I found something I'd rather do. "I've been taking it easy since I got back. Dad will let me fish with him. The pay's not bad, but it's hard work."

Mindy's eyebrows arched critically. "I hope you don't want to fish for the rest of your life." Her eyebrows relaxed. "I shouldn't have said that. You'd be earning a paycheck, so I shouldn't criticize fishing."

"Good," I said, hoping I didn't sound as bothered about her comment as I felt. I was proud of Dad for making a living anyway he could, and I would do whatever I could to make a living like him, even if it was fishing. Besides, anything beats being a bum. "Hey," I said, attempting a soothing tone, "you're not criticizing fishing. I agree, I don't want to do it the rest of my life. I just haven't found my calling, if you know what I mean."

The wind calmed. Lowering her hands from her hair, Mindy shared a soft smile. "You were always so sweet, Seth." She took my hand. "Walk me to my car."

I let her lead me to the front of the house, where her red Mustang sat. At the door, she turned around and hugged me. "Are you sure about dating again? I'd really like to pick back up where we left off."

I didn't pull away. Instead, I enjoyed the feel of her body

pressed to mine, the sweet aroma of her shampoo, the silky softness of her hair against my cheek. Sure, we'd hugged when we dated before, but maybe I was enjoying this particular hug because of how long we'd been apart. The only thing that compared to the feel of her in my arms was the feel of Alma in my arms as we made love. The reminder made me wonder how she and her family were doing. I hadn't read or heard any news about the Arab's attacking Israel lately, so there was no telling how they were.

Mindy broke our hug to look into my eyes. "The way you hugged me says we should go out soon."

I nodded. "Sure. When's a good time?"

"Is Saturday around five okay? I like to help Mom clean the house and wash clothes in the morning since she and Dad are letting me stay there. Dad has a pontoon boat we can take out on the sound. It's even got a grill in front. We can cook something for supper."

I couldn't think of a better date. "Sound like a plan. I'll grab some steaks and beer."

"And I'll make tossed salads," Mindy said, excitement in her voice. "Too bad we don't have any weed. It'd be great to watch the stars come out with a buzz on." She pecked my cheek, told me the address, and opened the car door. "See you at five."

Waving as she drove away, I looked forward to our date, buzz or not. It wasn't like I wouldn't get a buzz after a few beers.

When I entered the kitchen again, Dad, at the counter peeling boiled eggs for the potato salad, looked over his shoulder at me. "Mindy seems like a nice girl. Did you ask her why she doesn't want kids?"

From time to time he'd mentioned wanting grandkids, but it wasn't like him to bring it up so pointedly. I poured coffee for myself and sat at the table. "I think the war affected her. You were in World War II. You can understand why."

Dad looked over his shoulder again. "Not from my perspective. Seeing all that death made me want to start a family with your Mom. I wanted to teach my kids to be peacemakers instead of warmakers like Hitler, Mussolini, and Hirohito. Now the communists are doing the same thing, trying to spread their tyrannical ideology all over the world."

I let him peel a few more eggs before I said anything. It also gave the red on the back of his neck time to fade. He didn't talk about his time in Europe during the war much, but he definitely had strong feelings about how it started.

I sipped coffee. "Like I said, I think the war affected Mindy about whether to have kids or not."

"Don't you want a family?" Dad asked, not looking back at me. "If you do, it's not a good idea to see someone who feels so strongly about the subject."

I had second thoughts about Mindy too, but we were just going to date. I told Dad the same thing, except for the part about having second thoughts. He replied like he always did when we disagreed on a subject, with a grunt.

I finished the coffee. Hoping to smooth over our disagreement, I got out Mom's stuffing recipe and started gathering the ingredients Dad had bought. While I chopped celery, I recalled how mine and Mindy's date on her Dad's pontoon boat might be cold because it was the end of November. It didn't matter. I was sure we could stay warm by cuddling beneath a blanket when the stars came out.

Dad had already put the turkey in the oven, evidenced by the aroma of browning skin making my mouth water. He always bought a huge one for leftovers. A few days ago, I asked if Grandpa Callahan wanted to join us since Grandma had passed, and he said Grandpa wasn't feeling up to it.

Three hours later, Dad took the turkey from the oven and covered it with foil. I took the pan of stuffing from the frig and put it in the oven. The other side dishes — potato salad, deviled eggs, and green beans — were ready. Dessert was pumpkin pie.

I didn't mention it being from Mom's recipe. Dad tried his best to make the holiday's special, but I was sure her absence still hurt him.

When we finally sat at the table, he looked at me. "I hope you know how thankful I am to have you home from the war. With my own mother gone, and with my dad growing old, you'll be the only family I have close by soon."

I knew what Dad meant. His brothers and sisters had scattered to several states, some married, some not, all seeking their own lives. They visited when they could, and came for Grandma's funeral. Other than that, or the occasional phone call, we rarely heard from them.

I shared a sincere smile with Dad. "I'm glad I made it back myself."

He patted my hand. "Let's say the blessing." He bowed his head. "Dear Lord, I don't have the words to express how grateful I am for everything you provide. Seth and I have everything we need and some of what we want. Concerning material things, that's all a person should need to be satisfied in life. For myself, I hope Seth can find his path in the world, both with a way to earn his living that makes him happy and with a good woman to share his life. Also, Lord, please comfort our young men and women in the military. Give them the strength and courage to do their duty. And when they come home, please ease the burdens on their minds, placed there by things they might be experiencing. Unlike the people criticizing them, have their families comfort and support them in their time of need. If they do, maybe those young men and women won't turn to alcohol or drugs, because that will only destroy them in the long run. Please bless this food for the nourishment of our bodies, amen."

Opening his eyes and raising his head, Dad glanced at me as if to say, Son, I know about the beer, and I imagine you might've smoked marijuana in Vietnam. Like I just said, alcohol and drugs will only destroy you in the long run. Please stop using them if you are.

I knew his unsaid words were right. In Vietnam, I'd heard stories of alcoholism and drug addiction. For many combat personnel, if the enemy didn't kill them, beer, whiskey, and heroin did. As far as beer, I enjoyed the taste more than the hazy feeling I got from it, so I wasn't an alcoholic. Still, my cravings concerned me, so I needed to get a handle on them before they got a handle on me. That included trying to get Mindy to stop smoking marijuana. I wanted a woman to get high by loving me, not high by being addicted to drugs or alcohol, or even both.

Dad and I were about halfway through the meal when he finally broached the subject.

"When I was in Europe during the war, men dealt with the things they experienced in different ways. Some got mad and wanted to kill the entire German Army. Some read us their letters from home. Some prayed, which is what I did, and some turned to alcohol abuse. I say abuse because the first chance they got after a battle, they drank themselves blind."

Dad paused to add extra gravy to his stuffing. "When we liberated Paris, it was something else. Women kissed us. Children patted our legs. Men offered us food and wine. The drinkers drank it by the gallon, and I wondered how their livers could stand it. I also wondered if they'd take the habit back home with them, and how it would affect their lives."

Dad forked stuffing and looked me in the eye. "I saw your beer cans in the kitchen trash can. Six in one night makes me wonder if you brought your habit back home and how it will affect your life."

He ate the stuffing. "An occasional drink is one thing, but alcoholism is another." Studying me, he placed a firm hand on my shoulder. "I love you, Son. I want the best for you. If you need to talk about the war to ease your stress, I'm always here for you. The answer isn't in a can of beer. The answer is talking to someone who's experienced what you have, and I have."

In 2024, it seems we're in a shortage of good dads. Kids are dying from fentanyl overdoses at record rates. They're taking advice, much of it bad, from people other than their parents. Sports stars, movie stars, singers, and other kids don't have the monopoly on good advice. If you have good parents, that's who you should listen to because, like my dad, they love you and want the best for you.

Dad was still studying me. Since I was young, the rebellious part of me wanted to shrug his hand off my shoulder and tell him to mind his own business. Instead, the part of me that he raised to be a good person nodded slowly. "I was just thinking the same thing, Dad. Like father like son, huh?"

He squeezed my shoulder. "Hey, I'm not perfect by any means. Being a Christian allows me to see how not being perfect is an opportunity for growth instead of something to beat myself up over. When we stop becoming better people, not only do we hurt those who love us, we hurt ourselves."

He returned to his meal. "I won't say anything else about Mindy unless you want to discuss her. Just remember, you two should be best friends before you consider marriage. I was too young to know that when I married your mom, and I sometimes wonder if that's part of the reason why it didn't work out. Best friends talk about anything and everything. If we had talked more about what we wanted in life before we got married, we would've known if we were a good match or not. As you know, we were not."

The melancholy tone in his voice kept me from saying anything. Over the years, I'd tried to forgive Mom for leaving us, but I hadn't. The least she could've done was to divorce him. Then he might feel like he could move on and meet someone else.

As we continued eating, the conversation made me consider the women in my life so far. Ellie had been a great friend until she tried to force herself on me, an example of young people not making adult decisions. Now she was married and happy, and I was happy for her.

Alma … now she was another story. I'd thought about her off and on since I'd left Israel. I thought I loved her back then, but I wasn't sure now. Like Dad had said about best friends, we were definitely headed that way, so we might've made a great marriage. One thing for sure, I'd never forget our last night together, or how we made love, not only for the first time to each other, but for our first times to anyone. Yep, Alma would always hold a special place in my heart, both for what we had and for what might've been if we hadn't lived half a world apart.

As far as Mindy, her insistence on smoking marijuana bothered me, and I didn't care for her lack of interest in having kids, either. She could change her mind, though, and the only way I'd see if she could was to get to know her better.

Chapter 15

Like Mindy and I had planned, we took her Dad's pontoon boat out the following Saturday. When I parked at her parents' house at five, expecting her to come out and take me around back to the pier and the pontoon boat, she opened the door and waved me inside. Three vehicles, including her Mustang, were parked in the driveway, so I guessed she wanted me to meet her parents. Although she'd met Dad, I really wasn't ready to do the parent thing. After all, we were just dating, and I wanted to know Mindy a lot better before we got serious.

I climbed from the pickup and raised a grocery bag. "I've got the steaks and you've got the salads. We need to get going before it gets too dark." Actually, the sun was already settling above the horizon, visible beyond the pontoon boat. I should've thought about that when we made our plans.

She waved again. "The boat's got plenty of lights. Come in and meet my parents before we go."

Feeling like I was choking on a piece of steak, I followed her inside, down a hall, and to the right, where an archway opened to a sunroom with a view of the sound. When I'd parked outside, I'd noted the gorgeous two-story house, the manicured lawn, and the huge oaks. I'd never thought about it, but insurance in Dare County must sell pretty well, especially along the beach with all the hotels and restaurants being built.

Mindy's parents stood from a wicker sofa. He wore tan slacks and a collared shirt in blue. She wore a yellow skirt and a white sweater. Both were fit. Both had all their hair. She was quite striking like Mindy, with a heart shaped face and full lips. He reminded me of a lumberjack, all big and brawny.

"Afternoon, Seth" he said, his voice gruff. "I've been trying to talk Mindy into inviting you to supper here instead of on the boat." He introduced himself as Allen and his wife as Renee.

She nodded. "I understand you served in Vietnam like Mindy," she said as they sat.

Mindy sat on a wicker love seat across from them. I sat beside her. "Yes, ma'am. I served on a patrol boat in the Mekong Delta."

"I understand you were wounded." Allen said.

I touched my shoulder. "Yes, sir, right here. The surgery and rehabilitation took a while. It's still weak but getting better."

The conversation ebbed. Allen's eyes went from my beat up tennis shoes, to my faded jeans, to the frayed ball cap on my head. "Mindy hasn't mentioned what you do."

I glanced at Mindy and returned to Allen. "I'm not doing anything right now. I fished with my dad before I enlisted. I'll probably start doing that again when my shoulder can handle the work."

Allen rubbed his nose as if he smelled dead fish on me, which I knew he did not. Renee's nose twitched. "Does fishing earn enough to afford a wife and a home?"

Mindy blew a hard breath. "My old fashioned parents think a woman's place is in the home."

"It's not that," Renee said. "You enjoyed nursing before you enlisted. You never talk about it now. We spent a lot of money on your degree. Why not put it to use again?" Her eyes darted to me and back to Mindy. "If you hope to have a decent home, you'll need the income."

The derision in her voice caught me off guard. Mindy

seemed pretty down to earth, but her parents obviously thought I was lower than a mole crab digging itself into the sand.

Mindy stood. "The food I packed is on the boat. We should go."

Trying to show my polite side, I told her parents it was nice to meet them. Then I followed Mindy out the door of the sunroom and to the pier. She got in the boat, took the bag from me, and told me to take the ropes off the cleats. I did so, pushed the boat off, and jumped in. She put the bag in a cooler and sat behind the wheel. Before I got settled beside her, she cranked the outboard motor and hit the throttle. The motor roared. The bow rose. Wind whipped her hair around her face.

She looked at me. "I didn't know they were going to harass you like that."

I could barely hear her above the roar of the outboard, but I heard enough. "They're your parents. They want the best for you. They don't think that's me."

Mindy eased back on the throttle until the bow leveled off. As we continued on at about half speed, she glanced at me. "I haven't told you my age. I'm twenty-five. Mom's been bugging me about grandkids."

"What about your dad?"

"I told you about him wanting me to go into the insurance business. I might, but I've been thinking about going back to school to be a doctor." Her lips were pink with lipstick. She pursed them at me. "But that doesn't mean we can't play doctor before then."

I said nothing. For someone who didn't want kids, Mindy didn't seem to mind having sex, especially before marriage and without saying how we'd avoid pregnancy. I'd wait until she went further into the subject. I wanted kids, but both parents should want them, not one.

Another thought about her and sex — one I didn't care for — popped into my mind. With the release of the birth control pill, people were having different attitudes about sex, regardless of the pills only being available to married women. After I enlisted in the Navy, some of the classes were about sexually transmitted diseases, and how condoms should always be used because the pill didn't prevent the transfer of any of those diseases. As far as the idea that had popped into my mind, it was about Mindy wanting to play doctor. If that meant full-blown sex, had she been having sex with any of the men on the hospital ship? If so, I hoped they were using condoms. The last thing I wanted was some disease.

To be clear, I didn't like thinking about that stuff. Sure, I'd considered having sex with Di on the night we met, but meeting Trang and Minh had changed my mind about casual sex. As I'd learned from losing Mom, a child needs both a mom and a dad. Instead of just one perspective, two can give a child an even outlook on a variety of subjects. Mom was great until she left. She read to me, kissed my scraped knees, hugged me often, and told me how special I was. Yeah, dads can do that. In my experience, though, moms are more likely to provide that particular type of love.

On the other hand, Dad, through teaching me how to work on the jeep, how to fish, and how to remodel the house, gave me the confidence to tackle those types of jobs, and I got a lot of satisfaction when that work turned out like we'd planned.

The roar of the outboard motor quieted. The water slapping against the aluminum pontoons gradually stopped. Mindy dropped anchor and turned on a floodlight attached to the cover above us. "The charcoal and lighter fluid is in the compartment beneath the seat in the back. If you get the grill going, I'll cut up tomatoes for our salads. I hate soggy salads."

A few minutes later, the charcoal flames were coloring the aluminum rails around the front of the pontoon boat orange. Mindy set the salads and two beers on a small table by the back seat. I joined her, and we ate while the coals burned down to glowing embers.

Being November, our breaths made little puffs of white in the air. We both wore coats and weren't shivering, so we could deal with the cold.

Just when I was wondering why we weren't talking, Mindy pointed toward the sky. "You missed it. I saw a meteor."

"Mom called them shooting stars," I said, wishing I had seen it.

About to drink beer, she lowered the can. "That's right. You told me how she left you and your dad before you left for Vietnam. I forgot."

I spread the charcoal and set the steaks on the grate. The beef sizzled, sending up its delicious aroma. I returned to the seat. It was time to broach another subject.

"Before you left, you said you wanted me to know how you felt about me. You and the other nurses were on a ship with a bunch of men. If you had a relationship with any of them, I understand."

Looking at the stars, Mindy stopped to face me again. "I heard stories of guys seeing prostitutes in some of the cities. I wondered if they did that for the sex, or to ease the stress of combat."

I hated to ask the same question again. She'd either dodged it or was afraid to answer. If I admitted something, maybe she'd be honest with me. I told her about Trang and Minh, more so about how much time I spent with Minh in my lap while I told her stories about Kitty Hawk. To give Mindy time to think about it, I turned the steaks.

She followed and leaned against the railing. "What about Trang? I assume you slept with her."

"She wanted to," I said. "I didn't because it pissed me off to think of how some guy had gotten her pregnant when he knew he wasn't going to stay with her."

Mindy swallowed beer. "Did you have feelings for her?"

"Only as a person," I said, remembering the suffering of Minh and Trang. "Before I met her," I continued, "I couldn't put myself in her situation. She and her daughter live in a shack. They barely have enough to eat. If they're still alive, they're in the middle of a war that's getting worse by the day. They're human beings. In the middle of all that hell, even though they live on what's basically a starvation diet, they hunger for love more than food."

Mindy looked away and back. If I didn't know any better, it upset her to believe I was sympathetic toward any Vietnamese, what too many military personnel called "gooks." Maybe I was wrong to assume that. Since she'd come home due to the stress of caring for injured guys, it wasn't fair to judge her without knowing what she'd gone through.

She looked toward the west. On the horizon, house lights pinpricked the mainland of North Carolina. Safe and sound in their homes, how many of those people knew anything about war? When I'd gotten off the plane in Norfolk with some other guys, protesters were calling us baby killers and worse. As far as I was concerned, they could take a flying leap off a short pier. They hadn't been to Vietnam. They hadn't fought and bled and died for this country. They hadn't seen what we'd seen, or wondered where the next bullet would come from, or who it would kill.

I plated the steaks, wrapped them in foil, and took them to the table. Mindy's footsteps followed me, thudding softly on the boat's deck.

We ate silently. Like in Vietnam, when I needed to concentrate on something aboard the patrol boat besides the possibility of a sniper's bullet taking my head off, I set aside the subject of Trang and Minh so I could enjoy the meal.

The steak was juicy. The rest of the salad was crisp. The beer went down bitter and cold. It's hard to beat a meal like that when you're having it outside with a view of the stars while the sound of tiny wavelets everywhere serenades you.

Mindy ate half her steak and snuggled against me. "I didn't answer you. I had a relationship with a surgeon aboard the ship. He admitted to being married. We both admitted to needing someone to get our minds off the wounded and dying men. I hope you're not mad."

I was curious more than mad. I finished the last bite of steak and washed it down with beer before answering. "Well, we never said anything about waiting for each other. For the record, I didn't sleep with Trang, or anyone else." Next came the curious part. "What happened with the surgeon?"

The light shining down from the cover shone on a single tear sliding down her cheek. "I guess I wasn't comforting him very well. He jumped overboard after leaving a suicide note for his wife." Mindy wiped the tear away. "I didn't love him, but I cared about him. I'd had enough of death, I suppose. When they told me what he'd done, I started screaming and cussing and couldn't stop. One of the doctors talked me down. We had a few discussions in his office. He recommended to our commanding officer that I go home."

Mindy put all the stuff on the table away, got a blanket she'd brought aboard, and returned to my side to spread it over our laps. Sighing heavily, she snuggled against me again, this time slipping her hand around my waist. "Thanks for coming out here with me. I haven't been this relaxed in a long time."

Pulling her close, I understood how she felt. Two people who've experienced war share a bond, and that bond made me forget how she liked marijuana and didn't want kids.

When I got home that night and went to bed, I finally thought of those things. They had been a million miles away, as unimportant as a bit of cattail fluff floating on a breeze. After we kissed goodnight on her pier, we planned to see each other again.

As I dozed off and on, I thought about Mindy's relationship with that married surgeon, which disproved my concern about her possibly have a sexually transmitted disease. After all, since she freely admitted that relationship, she would've admitted another. This made me realize something else. The safest couple to have sex should be a doctor and a nurse, so they, to avoid pregnancy and any issues with his wife, would've used some type of birth control. I wasn't a prude back then and I'm not now, but there's something to admire when people think of the consequences of their actions.

Mindy and I dated every Saturday night through December. I joined her and her parents for Christmas Eve. It was a chore, but I poured on the politeness in hopes of charming them and her siblings. When Allen and Renee learned Dad was a minister, they immediately approved and then asked why he was still fishing for a living. I explained how hard a worker he was, and that helped raise their opinion of both of us.

Dad invited Mindy over for Christmas night, after she had supper at home. She poured on the charm, too, kissing his cheek and telling him how handsome he looked in a sport coat. We drank hot chocolate, sang Silent Night, and opened presents. I gave Mindy a slender gold necklace with a starfish charm on it, which she loved. She gave me a book about the wild Spanish horses in Corolla, which reminded me of how long it had been since I took the jeep up there. After I mentioned that, I promised to take her in the spring, when it had warmed up enough to go with the top down.

Dad surprised us by inviting an attractive widow from church, saying they'd been studying the Bible together. Mindy and I grinned at each other. Helen, with stylish brunette hair and a dimpled smile, likely was trying to talk Dad into studying something else.

Around ten, Mindy stood with her purse. "I had a great time, Mr. Callahan. Thank you for inviting me."

Smiling, Dad waggled a finger at her. "It's Tom, Mindy, and don't you forget it. You come back anytime, all right?"

Mindy faced Helen. "Nice to meet you. I hope you and Tom enjoy your studies."

Sitting beside Dad on the sofa, Helen patted his hand on his knee. "Oh, we will." She smiled at Dad. "I never knew learning the Bible could be so stimulating."

Taking that as my cue to walk Mindy to her car, we hurried out the sliding glass doors. At the bottom of the steps, she pulled me to a stop and pointed toward the sky above the sound. "Isn't that beautiful? I don't think I've ever seen so many stars."

I agreed, and said I was glad she liked the necklace. She took my hand and led me to the Mustang, where she asked me to get in out of the cold. As soon as I closed the door, she wrapped her arms around my neck for several kisses, moaning the entire time. When I got a chance to come up for air, I laughed. "I thought you'd like your necklace, but not this much."

She cranked the Mustang. "Would your dad miss you if we went somewhere? I know we haven't talked about it, but I want to make love to you."

"No, Mindy, we haven't talked about it. I thought you might need more time after what happened to that surgeon."

Mindy climbed into my lap. "Please, Seth, I'm on the pill. Don't you want me?"

For a second I was curious if she lied to get the pills like Martha did, but not curious enough to ask. I couldn't see her well in the dark, but I could smell her perfume and feel the solid weight of her in my lap. Remembering how it felt to make love to Alma, I started to unbutton Mindy's blouse but stopped. "Yeah, I want you, but not in a car."

She returned to her seat. "We can rent a hotel room. How about it?"

Glad for an out, I told her Dad would miss me if I stayed away that long.

Those perfect lips pouted. "Well, we'll just have to make plans for our next date, won't we?"

Although I was tempted, Dad's advice about being best friends with a woman before marriage, which I also took to mean before sex, made me ask a dumb question. "What would you say if I want to wait until I'm married?"

Mindy snorted laughter. "Listen to you, the preacher's boy."

I crossed my arms. "That's not a good answer for someone you're supposed to care about enough to make love."

"I'm sorry," she said, raising her palm to my cheek. "I hurt your feelings."

"It's not that," I said. "Well, I guess it is, sort of. Can I help it if I have old fashioned values?"

"You didn't have them when you started unbuttoning my blouse." Illuminated by the dashboard lights, her mouth fell open. "You're a virgin, aren't you?"

"Yes," I lied, remembering Alma.

Mindy killed the engine. "It makes sense now. All those times we made out, I was waiting for you to go further, and you never did." She offered me her left hand. "We could always trade in my necklace for an engagement ring. Would that be close enough for making love?"

Frustration creased my forehead. "No, it wouldn't. I think a couple should be best friends before they get married. We've only dated a few times before the war and after, and that isn't enough time to get to know each other, much less to get married."

Mindy rolled her eyes. "Now I know how you charmed Mom and Dad. You're just as old fashioned as they are." She sighed. "Okay, okay, you win. We'll wait until we're married. That doesn't mean we can't make out until then." She climbed into my lap and kissed me soundly. "Starting now."

Chapter 16

I'd be lying if I said I didn't enjoy all of our making out. Well, except for the frustration of knowing where it should lead when it didn't. Still, whenever Mindy and I realized we should stop before we couldn't, it gave us the chance to get to know each other better by talking about other subjects. Unfortunately, as ridiculous as it sounds, I'd forgotten how she'd admitted to not wanting kids. The things a half-naked woman will purge from a guy's mind must number into the billions.

This went on through the winter and spring, and I was beginning to feel like we were best friends. Mindy called each night and told me how her day had gone with selling insurance, and I told her how my day of fishing had gone. We'd even begun saying "I love you" at the end of those conversations. Dad must've forgotten about Mindy's lack of interest in having kids also, because he often said he'd never seen me happier.

Ellie, though, knew better. We sometimes saw each other walking by the sound. A wave would turn into a statement about the weather. A statement about the weather would turn into a question about the red Mustang and Mindy. A question about the red Mustang and Mindy would turn into me spilling my guts about our relationship. During one of those conversations, just after Easter, Ellie placed her son, J.J. for Jeff

Jr., in my lap. "How does that chunky boy feel, Seth?"

I sniffed J.J.'s hair, sweet with baby shampoo. "He feels like he eats a lot."

Ellie slapped my arm. We were sitting cross-legged in the sand. I couldn't slap back because I didn't want J.J. to fall out of my lap. "You're forgetting how well I know you, Seth Callahan. I've seen the way you look at my boy. You want a family of your own, don't you?"

J.J. grabbed my index finger. Without meaning to, I must've told Ellie about Mindy not wanting a family, but I couldn't remember when.

"Stop stalling," Ellie said. "You don't want to marry a girl who doesn't want kids. She'll end up leaving you like your momma did."

I narrowed my eyes at her. "You've only got J.J. How do you know having a family is so great?"

She took J.J. back into her lap and kissed his head. "Because Jeff and I love our boy more than life itself, that's how."

Our talk led to my decision to ask Mindy if she could reconsider having a family. The problem was I didn't know how to handle it if she was still against it. Not only did we get along great, she never mentioned smoking marijuana again, and I was beginning to think of her as someone I could spend the rest of my life with.

Along with all of that, I'd be another year older later this year. Sure, I wasn't old, but I wanted a few years with just Mindy and I alone before the kids started coming. If there's one thing I've learned about my problems, it was to get Dad's opinion on them, and that's what led to the following conversation.

It was in May, after a long day of pulling nets on the beach. The catch had been great, so sorting the keepers had taken well into the morning, not to mention paying the help and taking everything to the seafood market, which was now simpler than taking everything to any number of restaurants.

Done with all that work, and with a pocket full of cash, Dad drove home in his pickup while I followed in the jeep, the dories trailered behind me.

After taking turns showering the fish smell away, we met in the kitchen for bacon, lettuce, and tomato sandwiches and coffee. I dreaded asking him about Mindy, but I went ahead.

In the middle of a bite of the BLT, his eyes darted at me. He quickly chewed and swallowed, chasing it with coffee. "Doggone, Son, I completely forgot about Mindy not wanting kids. You two get along great. Maybe that's why I forgot." He paused. One bushy eyebrow raised. "Why are you asking me this now? Are you thinking about proposing?"

Dad was great at getting to the point, so I answered to the point. "Well, like you said, we get along great."

"Sure, but are you two best friends? We've talked about that before."

I sipped coffee. "I think so. We talk about anything."

"Except you haven't talked about having kids," Dad said sternly. "If you had, you wouldn't be asking my opinion about it now. That's a sign you two should wait, you know." Dad started to take another bite of his BLT but stopped. "Do you think you could be happy without a family? When Ellie brings J.J. over, I see how you like playing with him."

Dad was right. J.J. was almost a year old. I liked tickling his fat little feet and playing peek-a-boo with him. I didn't even mind him slobbering on my shirt when I held him. It was worth feeling his silky hair against my cheek and smelling the aroma of baby shampoo. He was learning to walk, and he'd wobble back and forth between Ellie and me like a little drunk, which made me grin big enough to hurt my cheeks.

Yep, Dad was right. I couldn't imagine not having a family. A girl like Minh and a boy like J.J. would be great. A pang of melancholy hit me. To make my pretend family even better, a mom like Alma would be perfect, but I'd never see her again.

"Son," Dad said, waving his hand in front of my face.

"What's going on in that head of yours?"

My memory of Alma faded. "I was thinking about Alma. I wonder how she and her family are doing?"

"I wonder about them too," Dad said. "I haven't seen much in the news lately about the conflict between Israel and the Arabs. I hope that means they're all right."

My memories of Alma returned. I missed her, but I missed her less than I had because of Mindy. Life moves on, so I needed to move on with it.

Dad and I finished eating. He washed our dishes while I dried. After handing me a coffee cup, he snapped his fingers. "I forgot about you and Mindy. Will you ask her about kids soon?"

I took the cup. "I don't know. I hate to mess things up."

Placing another cup in the sink, Dad stared at me. "I thought I taught you better. Honesty never messes anything up. If you want kids and she doesn't, it'll eventually become an issue, and you two might end up like your mom and me. Do you want that?"

I shook my head. "No."

"Good. Then you know what you need to do."

Although we finished the dishes in silence, Dad kept glancing at me. Even when I didn't see it, I could feel it. He was right, but I didn't know how to ask Mindy about it. We were going out Saturday, so I guessed I'd try then.

We've all done it. We put something off and put something off. Before we know it, so much time has passed that you stop thinking about it. In my case, unless Dad reminded me to ask Mindy about having a family, which he stopped doing six months later when I blurted for him to mind his own business, time had passed in the blink of the proverbial eye.

How can that happen, right?

You can get in a rut. You work, eat, and sleep. On the weekends, you see your significant other. You have fun. No one else catches your eye. Neither of you talk about marriage.

If things are going well, and they were, the subjects you know you should talk about get lost in the shuffle of life.

Anyway, in the spring of 1969, I was twenty-two-years old. It had been a little over four years since I'd seen Alma, and on the morning before the night I was going to ask Mindy to marry me, something would happen to make the entire issue a moot point.

It was a sunny Saturday morning. Dad and I were sitting on the deck, where I was congratulating him on becoming the new minister of the Methodist church in Manteo. The position came with three pros and no cons. Grandpa Callahan was getting even more feeble, so Dad was going to stay with him. The position paid well, so he was going to hire someone to help me fish. Since I was going to ask Mindy to marry me, we could live here, in the childhood home I loved so much because of the endless view of the Albemarle Sound.

With things going so well, I was about to suggest I take Dad out to lunch, when our heads turned at the sound of a car door closing at the front of the house.

Dad and I looked at each other. "Were you expecting Mindy?" he asked.

"No," I said. "Were you expecting Helen?"

The answer rounded the deck. Walking with a cane, his hair all gray, his other hand holding the hand of a dark-haired little girl of maybe three or four, Morris Levin, having traveled all the way from Israel for who knew what, stopped to look up at us. "Thank goodness, I found you at last. Can you please help me up the steps?"

He and the girl made an interesting pair. Morris wore dark slacks, a blue sweater, and brown loafers. A black kippah covered the crown of his head. The girl wore a simple yellow dress to her knees, which set off her olive skin. Leather flats and white socks covered her feet and ankles, while a black beret was perched atop her head. Brown eyes lighter than Alma's studied me. "Hello," she said sweetly. "I'm Talia."

Dad and I hurried down the steps. Talia went up while we helped Morris, each taking an arm. If Dad's mind was whirling like mine, we had a million questions to ask. We got Morris settled in a chair and offered him something to drink. Instead of answering the question, he asked Talia to stand beside him.

"This is my granddaughter," he said, looking at us as if we should know why he was here, the hint of a smile on his wide mouth.

Dad glanced at me and returned to Morris. "Did Alma get married after we left?"

I knew Lia, Alma's younger sister, couldn't have had Talia. Since Alma had found happiness, I was glad for her.

Morris cleared his throat. "Some ice water would be nice."

When I stood to get the water, Morris shook his head. "Tom, can you get the water and take Talia inside? I need to speak with Seth."

I sat. Dad stood. "I'll get your water, but I need to know why you're here. Whatever it is, it sounds serious."

Morris looked up at him. "It doesn't get any more serious, Tom. The welfare of my granddaughter is at stake." He looked at me. "Are you married, Seth? If you are, your wife should hear this."

Like a winter nor'easter roaring into the Outer Banks, confusion roared into my brain. "Well, no, but ..."

"Are you married or not?" Morris demanded, his voice firm. "This is important."

"He's not married," Dad said.

"I have a girlfriend," I said.

"Is it serious?" Morris asked.

"We've been dating for a good while," I said.

"Are you engaged?"

"No."

"Are you thinking of asking her?"

Dreading my answer because I hadn't told Dad, I said, "Yes, I'm thinking about asking her."

Morris heaved a huge breath. "Call her. Get her. Whatever. She needs to be here."

Dad got the water and hurried back. Morris thanked him and drank. Talia took the glass and emptied it. She gave Dad the glass, then came to me and studied my face. "Ima told me all about you. Do you still fish?"

I nodded toward the sound, where sunlight shimmered on the calm surface. "I fish out there and in the ocean."

"I love the beach. Ima took me there a lot. Will you take me soon?"

Dad's mouth fell open. "Morris, is Talia who I think she is?"

Morris nodded. "That's why I need to talk to Seth alone. I suppose he can tell his girlfriend later."

Even more confused, I looked from Dad to Morris and back again. "What are you talking about, Dad?"

Saying nothing, Dad, his face pale, took Talia by the hand and led her into the house. "Let's watch TV. It's Saturday morning. We have lots of cartoons on Saturday mornings." He shut the sliding glass doors.

Morris took another huge breath. "Seth, I'm sorry to tell you this, but Alma and Lia and their mother were killed in an Arab terrorist attack last year. They were shopping when a bomb went off. Lia and Rachel were killed instantly. Alma lingered in the hospital for a few days."

My lips—the same lips that had loved kissing Alma—parted. "I don't …" A cold wave of confusion, this time tinted with anger, washed over me, the same as what I'd felt at Trang and Minh's pitiful existence. They would never live through the Vietnam War like Alma, Lia, and their mother—and countless other Israelis—would never live through such an insane conflict.

During my reflection of this tragic news, my head had lowered on its own. I raised it to face Morris. "I'm so sorry, Morris. I know you loved your family dearly."

He shared the soft smile of a father and grandfather to a

friend of his family. "They are at peace now, Seth. Of that I am certain."

His sentiment brought tears to my eyes. I paused to get my churning emotions under control. "I appreciate you coming all this way to tell us, but you could've written."

"I have more to tell you, Seth." Morris hesitated. "Much more. First, Alma did not marry. Second, Talia was born almost nine months to the day after you and your father left us in Israel. Must I explain what that means?"

In my teen years, Dad often said wisdom comes with age and experience. My answer to Morris's nine month comment proved Dad was right. Either that or I was in denial of what his math meant. "I'm not sure. Do you mean Alma met someone after I left?"

One of the sliding glass doors opened. Dad closed it and stomped across the deck. "Talia's watching Bugs Bunny. I've been listening by the doors." He faced me full on. "Son, I thought you were smarter than that. Since Alma had Talia nine months after we left, that means you're her father." Dad turned toward Morris. "I knew they liked each other, but I didn't know how much. What did Alma say about it?"

"Nothing until she started having morning sickness." Morris sat up straighter to stretch his back. "Rachel and I sat her down and asked if she were pregnant. Of course we were upset when she admitted it. No decent parent wants a complication like that for a child. Then we decided to make the best of it. Unlike doctors who perform abortions illegally, we don't believe in killing an unborn child out of convenience. Each and every baby is a gift from God Himself."

"I feel the same way," Dad said. He paused. "Morris, I'm so sorry about you losing your family. Was Talia with you while they went shopping?"

"She was. I love spending time with her. She's as bright a child as I've known. She loves to be read to in bed. Alma told her all about Seth and Kitty Hawk, and she promised to visit one day." Morris blinked. A tear rolled down his wrinkled cheek. "Seth, she said you two were in love. Any parent understands how difficult young love is, especially the physical part of it." He looked at Dad. "I'm sure you agree, Tom? You were young once. You know what I mean."

Dad nodded. "I do. Emotion takes over and you do things you know you shouldn't." He faced me. "Are you ready to meet your daughter?" Before I could answer, he whirled toward Morris. "You didn't come all the way here to tell us about Talia and your family, did you?"

"I'm afraid not." Morris stretched his back again. "I have cancer. The doctors give me a few months." He reached over to touch my hand. "You and your father will be Talia's only family soon. I've come to leave her here, where she belongs."

I remembered how Morris lost his family in Nazi Germany. Not only was I a dad, I was about to become one full time. A warm feeling filled my chest. Yes, I always knew I wanted a family of my own. The question was if Mindy would accept Talia after I proposed.

"I see you thinking," Dad said. "You're worried about Mindy."

"What's there to worry about?" Morris asked. "If she loves Seth, she should love Talia."

"I'll worry about that later," I said. "How can Talia stay in America when she was born in Israel?"

"It helped when Alma put your name on the birth certificate. Before she died, she asked for an attorney. She signed a statement saying you're Talia's father. She also added for you to take legal custody of her if I could no longer care for her. I've taken the papers to the American Embassy in Israel, including my doctor's opinion of how long I have. They issued the Visa last week, and the paperwork is in the rental car. I'm not sure of everything you should do here. If it were me, I'd take everything to an attorney."

Morris had certainly taken care of things. I could hardly

believe it. One minute I was just some guy in Kitty Hawk. The next I was a dad. I nodded toward the house. "Talia knows I'm her dad, right?"

Morris smiled. "She does. I told her I'd have to explain everything to you before you two could officially meet." Morris paused, concern in his eyes. "You might wonder why Alma didn't write you about Talia. She and her mother and I spoke about it, and we didn't think it was fair to disrupt your life. I hope you can forgive us for that."

"I understand," Dad said. "As far as we live apart, it was a difficult situation."

I also understood. If the proverbial shoe was on the other foot, Dad and I would likely feel the same.

"Are you ready to meet her?" Morris asked me. "She's been ready ever since Alma told her about you."

"How old is she?"

"Three. She'll be four in August." Morris fingered a tear from one eye. "It will be the first birthday of hers I'll miss. It can't be helped, though. I'll be gone by then, and she'll be with her father and grandfather. After getting to know you both, I'm sure she'll be in good hands."

Like windblown sand filling a hole on the beach, thought after thought filled my brain with fatherly concern, the first being that Talia needed a room. Nope, Dad was going to live with Grandpa Callahan, so she could have his room. I assumed Morris had brought her clothes, and any luggage was still in his rental car, along with her favorite toys.

I had so much to learn about being a dad, such as Talia's favorite foods and her favorite books I could read to her. I swallowed hard. Could she bathe herself? Was she potty trained? Could she brush her teeth? Were there any foods she didn't like?

Instead of agonizing over these things, I asked Morris, sighing with relief as he answered me. She could bathe herself, but she needed help washing, toweling, and brushing her thick hair. She was potty trained perfectly. She could brush her teeth, but she liked doing it with someone while humming a little tune she'd made up. She liked any food except gefilte fish, which Dad and I had tried in Israel. We didn't like it either. It reminded us of fish jelly, and we were used to our fish either broiled, grilled, or fried.

"She's as sweet as she can be," Morris said, working himself up from the chair with the help of his cane. "Let's go inside so you can meet her properly."

Dad opened the sliding glass doors. Inside, after going through the kitchen, I stopped to watch and listen to Talia giggling at a Bugs Bunny cartoon. She was sitting cross-legged on the rug in front of the TV, hand over her mouth, eyes crinkling, dark hair framing her heart-shaped face, a silver clasp holding her bangs out of her brown eyes just below the beret perched atop her head. I pressed my hand to my chest. I was a dad, and even though I'd just found out, I loved her already.

To my left, Morris nudged me forward. "Go on," he whispered. "It'll be all right."

Talia must've heard him. She whirled toward us and lowered her hand from her mouth. "Did you tell him, Saba?"

Recalling how "saba" is the Jewish word for grandpa, and how "abba" is the Jewish word for father, I went to Talia and knelt beside her. "I'm sorry about your mom, but I'm glad you're here."

"I'm glad too, Abba. Can we —" Her eyes filled with tears. "I wish Ima was here. We could be a family, and all go to the beach together." She got to her feet. "Everyone went away. Now Saba is going away." She wrapped her arms around my neck. "You won't ever go away, will you?"

I rubbed a small circle on her back, from one sharp little shoulder blade to the other. Silky hair pressed to my cheek. Little girl smell, clean from a recent bath, filled my senses. She was thin but sturdy, like me when I was a little boy.

I pulled away to palm her cheek. "No, sweetheart, I won't ever go away."

She raised her hand to my cheek. "Ima used to call me that. She said the word for abba in America is daddy. Can I call you that?"

Dad came over. "You can call him whatever you'd like, Talia."

She faced Dad. "And you're my saba. Can I call you grandpa? Ima said I could."

Dad patted her shoulder. "I'd like that very much."

"Ima told me my grandma here is gone. Will she ever come back?"

"We talked about that," Morris said, shuffling to the sofa.

"I know," Talia said. "I just thought she might."

"I'm afraid not," Dad said. "I do have a lady friend who would love to meet you. Her name is Helen."

The mention of Helen made me think of Dad's church members. I had no idea what they'd think of me having a child out of wedlock. Dad and I would have to discuss it later. I'd hate for him to lose his new job In Manteo before he even started it.

Morris groaned as he stretched his back again. "Seth, there are two suitcases and a large envelope in the back seat of the car. Can you get them for me? They're Talia's things and the paperwork I told you about."

As I left to walk across the deck, I felt a mix of happiness and dread. The sun was shining on the sound, gulls were winging overhead, and the day couldn't be more beautiful. Unfortunately, I wasn't sure how Mindy would react to the news of Talia. She'd seemed to mellow with time, never mentioning marijuana or having sex, so maybe she had mellowed about the idea of having a family. Hey, I could always hope.

After closing the car door, I stuck the thick manilla envelope under my arm and hefted the two huge suitcases. Until Dad moved in with Grandpa Callahan, I didn't know where I could keep Talia's clothes or where she could sleep. We had added more rooms, but we hadn't furnished them. Right now they held spare parts for the jeep, some of Mom's old clothes, a sewing machine operated with a foot pedal, cased shotguns for duck and goose hunting, rod and reels for fishing, hunting clothes and waders, and a few crab pots we used at the pier.

That's what can happen when there's no woman in a home to keep her guys straight. It can become a man cave. Well, the hunting clothes and waders hung in an old wardrobe, so maybe I could take that stuff out and hang Talia's clothes in it for the time being. As far as where she could sleep, I puzzled, maybe the sofa, or a pallet by my bed, or …?

That's right, I reminded myself. There's a folding cot with a mattress in with that other stuff. I can air it out and let Talia use it in my room until Dad and I can clean up all our junk.

In the living room again, I caught my breath from climbing the steps while Talia opened the suitcases on the sofa beside Morris. "See, Daddy? Saba bought me new clothes for the beach. I've got blue jeans and T-shirts and tennis shoes." She raised a pink dress with puffed sleeves and a stiff collar to her chest. "Do I have to wear this here? Dresses are okay, but I like blue jeans."

"That's nice for church," Dad said. He faced Morris. "I see she's wearing the beret for a head covering. Did Alma want her raised Jewish, or did she mind if she attends church here?"

"She never said." Morris paused, eyes narrowed as if in thought. "Talia is an American now. As long as she's raised with good values and honors God, that's what's important."

I was glad Dad had raised the subject of church. We respected Morris and his family's faith. Since Morris also respected us in the same way, there would be no problems. Then again, Dad and I would have to deal with the fallout of me having a child out of wedlock, both from our church and our neighbors. People could be strange about the subject, acting as if they'd never made a mistake. Like Dad had always told me, the most important thing about making a mistake is learning to not make it again.

Morris raised his hands toward Talia. "Come give me a hug. It's time for me to go."

Dad nodded toward the kitchen. "Let's give them some privacy, Son."

I followed Dad to the kitchen, and to the sliding glass doors, where we'd be out of sight of Morris and Talia while they said their last goodbyes.

Dad had taught me perspective as I grew up. "Son," he said many times, "the best way to consider another person's point of view is to actually do it. Many people say they do but they don't." Dad would then quote what people call "The Golden Rule." Although it came from the Bible, he preferred the modern translation: "Do unto others as you would have them do unto you." When he spoke to kids in church about it, he'd simply say, "Boys and girls, treat each other like you want to be treated. If you do that, you'll get along fine."

Using this advice, I knew what Talia and Morris were going through. Along with that, her sobs clarified their feelings to the point of making me cry. They loved each other dearly, and the fact that they would never see each other again was as intense as if I were telling my own dad goodbye for the last time, which we all know we'll have to do one day.

Talia's sobs quieted. A red-eyed Morris brought her to the kitchen, where she looked up at me. "Saba says I'll see him in Heaven again one day."

"That's right," Morris said, softly smiling at her. "And we'll also see the rest of our loved ones." He knelt for what I knew to be their last kiss and hug, then placed her hand in mine. "God bless you, Seth." He shook Dad's hand. "God bless you, Tom. In this pitiful world of ours, where so many people prefer to think about themselves instead of each other, it's rare to find two people like you."

While we helped Morris down the steps, Talia followed behind us. As he drove away, she waved and cried, "Bye, Saba! Tell everyone in Heaven I said hello!" But as soon as the car turned out of sight, she buried her face against my waist and sobbed terribly.

Dad blinked, and I knew his emotions were getting the best of him. I picked Talia up, and we all returned to the living room to unpack her belongings.

As we did, I thought about my life so far. Even now, as I type these words, I think about my life and all of those category five women I've known.

First there was Mom. My first memories of her are good. Then she left us, so what can I say other than her leaving probably influenced my desire for a family, especially a stable and loving family.

Next came Ellie. She had grown into a fine young woman who'd married a fine young man. Had I not been an idiot, that young man might've been me.

Then there was Alma. Had I not left her in Israel, who knows how her fate might've changed. We could be married right now, loving each other as well as loving Talia.

After Alma came Di, soon to be replaced by Mindy. I had a feeling Mindy wouldn't take the news of Talia too well, but I could always hope.

Now there was Talia, my sixth category five hurricane, and I already loved her more than life itself.

If things went bad with Mindy, who would be my next category five hurricane? I had no idea then, but I do now, as I type this over fifty years later.

As they say, life goes on, and concerning my experience with category five hurricanes, my life would go on in ways I could never have imagined.

Chapter 17

Let's see, I started writing in July, or was it June? I check the date on the Word document file. Yep, July it is. I suppose my age is catching up with me. Not only is my body wearing out—you know, because I need heart and cholesterol medicine—I guess my brain is wearing out. Yesterday I went to the bathroom to make coffee. This morning I went the kitchen to use the bathroom. I realized both when I stopped in those rooms and cursed under my breath. Entering physical decrepitude is one thing. Entering mental decrepitude is something entirely different. Oh, well, maybe it happened because my mind is so focused on my writing.

Huh, here's something else I forgot. I turned seventy-nine in October. Did my kids and grandkids send any cards? I get up from the sofa, where my laptop is on the coffee table, and shuffle to the kitchen. My hips and knees ache from my hours of sitting while writing. On the fridge, several cards are secured to the white surface with magnets glued to sea shells, gifts from my grandkids for this very purpose.

In one way, I despise my fading memory. Like with my birthday, these cards, and going to the wrong rooms, recent recollections play tricks on me. In another way, I'm glad my long-term memories return, like the warmth of a kiss from long ago. If not, I wouldn't be able to finish my book.

But will I finish it before I join my wife? I think so, and since

I'm confident enough to believe that, I decide to take the day off and ask Liz if she'd like to join me for lunch.

Then again, I better apologize for making her think I was dating someone when she mistook my daughter for another woman. Boy, did she storm back home with her panties in a wad. My wife would've never done that. She would've just gotten me back when I least expected it, like with waking me up by sticking my hand in a bowl of cold water and making me run to the bathroom. She sure was a card, and that was one of the many things I loved about her. Before the kids came along, she woke me up in other ways, but a gentleman doesn't share the intimate details of his love life with anyone except his soul mate.

The microwave clock reads 11:30. I went straight to the laptop without breakfast. Wearing pajama bottoms and a T-shirt, I use my cell to call Liz.

After three rings she answers. "Is your girlfriend with you?"

"Naw," I say, chuckling. "I'm on the phone with her."

"Then who was that woman?"

"That was Talia. You just didn't recognize her."

"Does she have a different car than the one she and her family came in at the funeral?"

"Yes, ma'am, she sure does. Anyway, I'd like to apologize for teasing you by taking you out to lunch."

Liz pauses. "Where would we go? There's not much open for lunch this time of year."

I wonder what she means. Instead of asking, I check the date on my phone and almost drop the phone. It says it's February. I thought it was October. Like I mentioned earlier, I guess I've been concentrating on writing too much. Still, to let November and December slip by without remembering if my kids and grandkids came for Thanksgiving and Christmas makes no sense.

I shrug my shoulders and return to Liz. No doubt about it, I need a day off. "Do you have any suggestions?"

"Something light," she says. "I like to watch my figure."

I hold in a laugh. "I like to watch your figure with my binoculars. That red string bikini with the thong made my eyes cross."

"I hear you, you old fool. Your purple Speedos did the same to me. Enough of your nonsense. Do you want seafood or something else?"

"Anything, Liz, anything at all. It's too early to drink, though, so you won't be able to take advantage of me."

She snorts laughter. "I'm glad you're in a good mood. Let me touch up my makeup. Meet me at my car when I beep the horn."

In the bathroom, I shave, swipe deodorant, comb my hair, and hurry to the sliding glass doors, only to stop. What an idiot. I can't go out to lunch in my PJs, T-shirt, and slippers.

Dressed in slacks and a golf shirt, I sit on the bed to don socks and loafers. Liz beeps the horn. With my wallet in my pocket, I git while the gittin' is good, like the cowboys in those old radio westerns used to say.

As I head down the steps from the deck to the yard, a gust of icy wind off the sound tells me I should've worn a jacket. No matter. I'll be okay once Liz gets the car heater going.

Standing beside the open driver's door of her silver Lexus, wearing a snug pair of jeans and a cream colored turtle-neck sweater, she fingers hair from her eyes. "Will you get your old behind in the car before I freeze out here?"

I hustle to the passenger side and climb in. "That's what you get for not wearing a jacket, you old grump." I pat her hand on the console. "You look like a doggone teenager in those jeans. I look like exactly what I am, an old fart."

She shares a grin. "But a distinguished old fart." She starts the car and drives to the stop sign at the 158 bypass road. "Left or right?"

"Surprise me, old girl, surprise me."

"Look," Liz says as she takes a right, "I'm not Katharine

Hepburn, you're not Humphrey Bogart, and we're not in the *African Queen.*"

"One of my favorite movies," I say.

"Mine too," Liz says. "How do you feel about sushi?"

I stick my tongue out. "I'm not crazy about raw fish. Can I get it broiled or fried, and without soy sauce and rice?"

"Have you ever tried it?"

"I handled enough raw fish in my life."

"Do you like raw oysters?"

"Now you're talking," I say, giving Liz a wink. "Raw oysters are the ocean's answer to Viagra."

She cuts her mascaraed eyes at me. "Forget what I said about you being distinguished. You remind me of Burgess Meredith on *Grumpy Old Men,* when he was chasing that poor woman around the grocery store."

"That was *Grumpier Old Men,*" I say, and pause for a chuckle. "Two classics if there ever were any."

Thirty minutes later we're sitting at Goombays Grill and Raw Bar, slurping down oysters and chasing them with beer. Typical for the off season, the crowd is light.

I set down a shell and wipe juice from my chin. "Thanks for coming. I'm celebrating finishing a chapter of my book."

About to slurp an oyster, Liz lowers the shell. "I've been wondering how it was going. It sounds like you got over your writer's block."

"I did." I drink beer. "The chapter's about how Talia came to America."

"Came to …" As Liz trails off, her perfectly plucked eyebrows arch. "What do you mean by that?"

I wonder how Liz will react. There's only one way to find out, so I go ahead. "Dad and I went to Israel in 1964. I wasn't much more than a kid. Anyway, I met someone, and nature took its course."

After I tell Liz about Morris's visit, she leans back in the chair, as flabbergasted as anyone I've ever seen. "And you didn't even hesitate to take Talia in. If that had happened in this day and time, any other man would've been on Jerry Springer, asking for a DNA test."

"As you well know," I say with a sly grin, "I'm not any other man." I slurp an oyster. "Aside from sounding like the old fart I am, a lot of guys these days would rather shirk responsibility than accept it. If not, Jerry Springer would've never had his TV show."

Frowning, Liz shakes her head. "You mean the ones where some woman is trying to find the father to her baby. That doesn't say much for the responsibility of the woman either." Liz sips beer and picks up another shell. "How many girlfriends dumped you when they found out? It takes a special person to love another person's child."

I pause to try a little horseradish on the next oyster. It's kind of like swallowing one of those aromatic cough drops, except it's large and slick. Still, it's pretty darned good. I drink beer and wipe my lips with a napkin.

How much should I tell Liz about Mindy? I might as well share enough of it to practice writing it later. Our glasses need refills, but the dozen oysters are gone. I ask Liz if she has time for coffee.

She winks. "My place or yours?"

I enjoy her teasing. It's one of the things that keeps a marriage interesting. I return the wink. "Your place, but just for coffee. Yes, I know your wink meant you were teasing me."

She waves the waitress over and hands her enough money for the meal and a tip. As the waitress leaves, I protest. Liz says to hush and be grateful, and to get in her car.

After the drive, Liz leads me inside her house. When the original neighbors lived here, they had juniper siding on the walls and ceilings. It's still there, but it's now aged to a golden glow. The oak floors are dinged and scratched from many a footstep. I like it. I also like the shining paste wax finish, the leather upholstery on the sofa and love seat, and the nautically themed lamps and paintings on the walls. She says to sit. Minutes later, she brings two mugs steaming with the delicious aroma of coffee. Sitting beside me after kicking her flats off, she tucks her feet beneath her. I sip. She sips. The coffee is smooth enough to enjoy black.

"Okay," Liz says, after sipping again, "tell me how many girlfriends kicked you to the curb when they found out you were a dad."

"All of them," I say, "until I met my one and only."

"How many is that?"

"Let's start with one. After her, you might not want to know about any more." I sip more coffee and swallow, both because it's great and to ready myself to tell what happened with Mindy.

Leaving out the sordid details of how I found myself naked in Di's bed, I gloss over how I met Mindy, plus our few dates before she left for the Navy. Liz listens intently, sipping now and then, nodding now and then. I add my time in the Navy, how Mindy and I started dating later, and briefly include Morris bringing Talia to me. By that time I need more coffee.

Liz fills two more mugs and returns to the sofa. "For a baby boomer born in 1946, you've had an interesting life. Not everyone can say they visited Israel, fell in love with a young woman there, fathered her child, and went off to war in Vietnam."

I take the mug from her. "Well, like I said about Minh and Trang and being wounded, it wasn't all good."

Liz sips coffee. "Go ahead. I want to hear what happened when you told your girlfriend about Talia, especially after her comment about not wanting children."

"Yeah, I should've stopped seeing her after that. Live and learn, you know?"

"Oh, I know. The more I lived with my first husband, the more I knew I was going to divorce his cheating self."

Liz's antagonistic tone makes me grin. "Okay, here we go. I

was seriously considering asking Mindy to marry me. I'd thought about her comment about kids, but I was going to bring it up again to see if she might change her mind. Since that was the case, Talia's arrival brought it to a head. A few nights after Morris brought her, Mindy and I went out to supper. After, like we usually did, we parked on a secluded path outside of Manteo to watch the moon rise over the sound."

Liz rubs my knee. "Oh, how romantic. Maybe you can take me there some time."

I glare at her and push her hand away. "Do you want to hear what happened or not?"

Liz pinches her right thumb and index finger together and zips her lips. "I'm shutting up."

Doubting her, I go on regardless. "As you can imagine, my hopes were up but not too much. We kissed a while and fooled around a while. Before things got too heated, I stopped and faced her. Using my most serious voice, I said, "Remember that time you said you didn't want any kids? Do you still feel like that?"

Likely sensing an end to our kissing, Mindy buttoned her blouse. "That's a loaded question that deserves a bullet. No, I don't want kids. I told you why, remember?"

"I remember, but every child born won't go to war."

Mindy shot me a look. "I don' t care what you say. I'm not having kids."

I decided on a different tactic. "Have you ever been around kids, or even a baby? You might change your mind then."

Beaming through the windshield of my pickup, moonlight illuminated Mindy's disgusted frown. "Let's get this straight once and for all. I don't want kids."

"But—"

"No, Seth," Mindy said, her voice rising. "Let this go before it's too late."

I cocked my head to one side. "What do you mean by that?"

"If you love me, you'll let it go."

"If you love me, you'll be honest."

"That's not good," Liz says. "Honesty isn't always the best policy."

"Don't I know it," I say.

Liz sips coffee. "What happened next?"

"How do you feel about abortion?" I ask warily.

"I'm on the fence about it. It shouldn't be used as birth control, but if it's to save a woman's life, I can see that."

"I agree," I say, nodding. "I also would hate to force a woman to have a baby from rape."

"That isn't the baby's fault," Liz says firmly. "Besides, the baby can be adopted and given a new start on life." Liz pauses to eye me. "Why all the questions about abortion?"

"One more question. Do you think a man has any rights when it comes to a pregnancy? Like with Alma, what if she'd aborted Talia without telling me? Didn't I have a right to know I was going to lose my child? More importantly, didn't I have a right to take my child if Alma hadn't wanted her?"

Liz taps a red-painted fingernail to her lips. "If I were a potential father, I'd want to have that choice. Why do you ask?"

"Because Mindy said she took advantage of me on the night I met her and Di, and she got pregnant from it."

"Oh, no, Seth. You mean …"

"You guessed it, Liz. She aborted my child without telling me. She said a surgeon on her ship did it for her. Then she had an affair with him, and he aborted his own child."

Liz's mouth falls open. "An affair? You mean he was married?"

"He sure was. He ended up jumping off the ship to drown himself. Mindy said it was because of the stress of war. I think it was because of the guilt of killing his own child."

We pause for coffee, and I continue. "When I learned there was such a thing as abortion, I didn't think I deserved to have an opinion about it. Then, when Mindy told me she'd aborted our baby—a baby who would've been a son or a daughter I would've loved as much as I loved Talia—not only did I think I deserved to have an opinion about it, I thought anyone with the least bit of compassion would think I deserved to have an opinion about it. Mindy didn't regret keeping it from me, so I knew it was over between us. I told her about Alma and Talia. She got out of my pickup without so much as a goodbye and took off up the moonlit path toward Manteo. As far as I was concerned, Talia was my hero. If not for her, and if not for Alma choosing to have her, I would've ended up in a bad marriage exactly like Dad. Now you know why I asked about a father having any rights to choose if he wants his child when the woman doesn't. Because of Mindy, I lost a child I'll never know and love. It breaks my heart to think about it."

Liz rubs my shoulder. "You're such a dear man, Seth Callahan. No wonder you miss your wife so much."

I'm glad Liz didn't say I was a perfect man. Because of my opinion about abortion, in that I didn't think about the consequences of Alma and I making love on our last night together, I'd considered myself a hypocrite for many years. "But you both were just kids," someone might say to defend us. While that may be so, we were old enough to think, except we didn't think at all. "But now you have Talia," that someone might add. Regardless, that doesn't change the fact that Alma and I didn't think before we acted.

Still, I can't call Talia a mistake. What would've been a mistake was if Alma had aborted my dear daughter. Thank God she didn't. If she had, there's no telling how my life would've turned out.

Liz and I finish our coffee in silence. Beyond the double windows of her sliding glass doors that lead to a deck, the sun lowers toward the North Carolina mainland, its light transforming a low line of clouds into a red ribbon settling into the horizon. I can't begin to count the number of similar sunsets my wife and I watched over the years, and the sight makes me wonder how long it will be before I join her.

At times I'm ready to go. At times I'm not. I want to finish our story. I want to watch my youngest grandkids grow up. I want to spend more time with Jack fishing. I even want to get to know Liz better. It won't be about romance, though. I could never love another woman like I loved—and still love—my wife.

Liz asks if I'd like some supper. She says she makes a great homemade chicken soup. Rising from the sofa, I say maybe another time, and thank her for lunch and the coffee. She takes my hand and walks me down her steps. When we reach my lawn, she pulls me to a stop and kisses my cheek. "You better be glad we didn't meet before you got married, or I'd have hooked you like a flounder."

I touch my cheek, where her lips leave their lingering warmth. "And have you miss out on your divorce? Perish the thought."

We share a laugh, comment on the stars filling the sky, and I go up my steps. Inside, I glance at the laptop, and I realize that all I have to do to write the chapter about telling Mindy about Talia is to put down everything that happened today, including what I told Liz.

I consider turning on the lamp to write. Instead, I microwave some canned tomato soup and make a grilled cheese. When I'm done eating and taking my pills, I'll shower, get ready for bed, and turn in early.

After all, I've got more writing to do, and I need my wits about me to remember all the details of what's to come.

Chapter 18

Despite having broken up with Mindy in May, that summer was amazing. Talia and I were getting to know each other. Dad had started his new preaching job in Manteo, and had moved in with Grandad. Ellie kept Talia while I fished, and they were becoming great friends. Talia loved playing with J.J. She even pretended to read to him. Dad drove over from Manteo every chance he got. If he had nothing planned the next day, he'd stay the night and read to Talia in bed, dark eyes wide with wonder. No doubt about it, she'd captured our hearts like Alma had captured mine. Unfortunately, our blessings hadn't come without a trial or two.

The first trial was when we introduced Talia to the congregation of the local methodist church, before Dad left for the church in Manteo.

It was a gorgeous Sunday morning, the first in June, with a deep blue sky and warm weather. The pews were filled with men, women, and children who, Dad and I hoped, would be as grateful for our blessing of Talia as we were. After Dad welcomed everyone, and after the first hymn, he asked Talia and I to join him in the pulpit. To say the congregation's eyes were darting and their lips were whispering would be an understatement. It had been two weeks since Talia had come, and a few church members had seen us three together at the local grocery and the post office, no doubt setting off a string of rumors.

Dad and I were dressed in dark suits. I wore a burgundy tie. Dad wore a blue one. Talia wore a pink dress with a white collar. The hem ended just below her somewhat knobby knees. I'd brushed her black hair and set the beret on her head at a somewhat jaunty but cute angle. Between Dad and I, as we three faced the congregation, she took hold of our hands and smiled broadly. Thankfully, most of the congregation melted, evidenced by returning sincere smiles of their own.

Dad nodded at me. We'd hoped Talia would make our work easier, and it had so far. The rest was up to me.

Regardless, I faced the congregation with a pain in my throat, as if a fishbone was stuck there. Clearing it, I went on. "Good morning. If anyone here doesn't know it, I'm Pastor Callahan's son, Seth."

A few people nodded. Just as I was about to continue, Talia let go of my hand and patted my arm. "He's my daddy, too." She finished with another broad smile.

On the left side of the church, in the second pew, a woman frowned. "A daughter without a marriage is what I heard," she mumbled.

"A daughter conceived in love," Dad said firmly. "When Seth and I went to Israel, he fell in love, and Talia is the result. We only found out about her recently because her mother passed on. We consider Talia a blessing, and we hope all of you will agree."

The pain in my throat eased. "I'm not proud of what happened in Israel," I said as firmly as Dad, "but I'm proud to have learned from it. As Christians, we know learning from our pasts and moving forward is what matters, not living in the past and doing the same things."

In the pews, about midway back on the right side, a man's gruff voice said, "Still doesn't make it right."

I was prepared for this. I took a palm-sized rock from my suit coat pocket and held it high. "Who here has never sinned?"

No one answered. "Speak up if you're out there," I said louder. "If you've never sinned, come up here and take this stone and hit me with it. I'm not perfect and never claimed to be, but I've learned from my past. My goal now is to be the best Dad to my daughter I can be."

The man grumbled something I couldn't understand. The woman who'd complained earlier lowered her head.

In the second row of pews to the right, Ellie stood. "We've all heard stories of bad parents. I've known Seth all my life. If there's anything I'm sure of, he'll be a fine parent, and I couldn't be prouder of him."

Beside her, Jeff stood, a plump J.J. in his arms. Jeff faced the congregation. "I'd say Ellie's comment deserves an amen. How about it, everyone?"

I was watching the congregation carefully. For a count of three, no one said or did anything. Then every mouth I could see opened to share a resounding, "Amen!"

Talia looked up at me. "What does it mean, Daddy?"

I scooped her into my arms and kissed her cheek. "It means all these folks are mighty fine folks."

She and I returned to the pew. After Dad's sermon, we three waited at the back door to wish everyone a nice Sunday. When the woman who hadn't welcomed Talia started by, she stopped in her tracks to look at Talia, at Dad, and then at me. As if someone had turned on a faucet, tears filled her eyes. "Please forgive me, Seth. I'm a bitter old woman with a sour heart. I'm going straight home to read my Bible."

When the man who hadn't welcomed Talia approached us, he stopped to take my hand. "I'm a fool, Seth. Any man who takes on the responsibility of being a father is a good man in my book." He patted Talia's head. "Little lady, welcome to the neighborhood, and to our church."

Behind the man, Ellie and her family stopped. "Well, I'd say that worked out purty good," she said.

I smiled at her southern accent. "With your help, you mean.

"Now," I continued, "what's the chance you could watch Talia for me while I go to work fishing?"

"We were just talking about that," Jeff said. He elbowed my ribs. "Since Kitty Hawk fisherman make so much money, I've been telling Ellie she should start babysitting."

"Oh, stop your teasing," Ellie said to Jeff. "You bring your sweetie over anytime, Seth. She'll keep me and J.J. company while Jeff's working."

As Ellie and her family went down the steps, Dad's special lady friend, Helen, stopped before us and knelt by Talia. "Your grandpa has told me so much about you, sweetheart. Welcome to the neighborhood."

"Thank you," Talia said, smiling at Helen. She faced Dad. "Is she your girlfriend, Grandpa?"

Dad and I grinned at each other. Helen lightly slapped his arm. "Phooey on you men, acting so silly." She faced Talia again. "Your grandpa and I are special friends. That means we can be special friends too, all right?"

Of course, Talia nodded happily.

So that was our first trial concerning my new daughter. The second one was when Dad started his job at the church in Manteo. The scenario was similar, except Mindy's folks walked out when Talia and I joined Dad in the pulpit. As the double doors banged shut behind them, I wondered how they would've felt about never having the chance to love two precious grandchildren—one conceived when Mindy took advantage of me when I was unknowingly stoned on weed, the other conceived in an affair with a married man aboard a hospital ship.

Still, what he and Mindy did was their responsibility. The only thing I could do was to pray she'd learned from her mistakes and no more innocent lives would be taken. As far as him, what can you do for a dead person except to pray for them too, as well as the family he'd left behind?

Three weeks into June, Dad and I took Talia to the county

offices with the papers Morris had given us. Although the clerk's legalese twisted us in knots, the bottom line was Talia would be a legal citizen when all the checks into her background were done, including a call to Morris, whose phone number was on the papers.

Come July, the Atlantic had warmed enough for shelling and wading in the surf. I bought Talia a once-piece swimsuit, a toy shovel, and an assortment of buckets for making a sand castle. She loved digging a moat around it and filling it with the largest bucket she could lug back from the foamy water.

When she tired of that, she'd run around with her arms out, saying she was flying like a sea gull while giving a pretty good approximation of their screeching. She also loved chasing the backward-kneed sandpipers when a flock would wheel and land in the shimmering sand before us, wet from the retreating surf.

One Saturday morning during breakfast, Dad suggested we take the old jeep up to Corolla, and drive out on the beach to show Talia the wild horses. "Horses?" she asked. "I've never seen a horse."

She drank milk and lowered the glass, revealing a milk moustache. I gave her a napkin from the holder. "That's right, horses."

"Some folks call them Spanish Mustangs," Dad said, pausing from his pancakes. "Theory has it that they came from Spain."

Raising a fork with a triangle of pancake on it, Talia stopped as it approached her open mouth. "That's silly, Grandpa. Horses can't swim across an ocean."

Part of our bedtime reading had been about the Outer Banks and its geography, including how the Spanish came here before the iconic Lost Colony was lost. Talia soaked everything up like a little sponge, verifying Morris's claim about her intelligence. Was I a proud dad? You're doggone right I was.

Dad explained about the Spanish horses, exciting Talia. We

planned our visit and finished breakfast, packed soft drinks and sandwiches for lunch in a cooler, and climbed into the jeep for the forty-mile drive.

In the late-sixties, Outer Banks tourism hadn't grown to the degree it has in 2024. Highway 158, which paralleled what the locals called Beach Road, was still two lanes. Hotels and restaurants were being built, but there was still plenty of land without businesses, with plenty of those crooked live oak trees and brush to hide white-tailed deer, raccoons, possums, and other wildlife.

When Highway 158 curved toward the west and the Wright Memorial Bridge, we took a right on Highway 12. Fifteen minutes later we passed through the town of Duck. Now, in 2024, especially in the summer, enough tourists visit there to bottleneck traffic running both north and south. When Talia came, we were able to cruise straight through, enjoying intermittent views of the Currituck Sound through maritime forests to our left. Just beyond Duck was a World War II bombing range, now protected by No Trespassing signs.

After another twenty miles, we started catching glimpses of the top of the red brick Currituck Lighthouse, where its black painted metal walkway once welcomed the keepers who maintained it. The height scared Talia. She couldn't imagine climbing the spiral stairs and standing on that narrow walkway. As we passed it, she pointed and asked about the yellow building to the left, now known as the Whalehead Club. I told her a man and his wife built it long ago as a place to vacation, calling it Corolla Island because it stood on a raised island of sand. She nodded and said it didn't look very cozy, like her home now. Satisfied, she faced forward again, and asked how long before we would see the Spanish horses. I told her to keep looking ahead because it might happen anytime.

"But we're not on the beach yet, Daddy. You said we had to be on the beach."

Dad laughed. "She got you there, Son."

"They live everywhere up here," I said to Talia. "I like seeing them run on the beach instead of grazing between the houses."

Talia's fine eyebrows scrunched together. "All the houses I see have sand in the yards. Do the horses eat sand?"

"Well," I said, realizing my sweet daughter had gotten me again, "some yards have grass and some don't, okay?"

She grinned at me, melting my heart. "I know, Daddy. I'm just teasing."

The jeep slowed. Dad took a right toward the beach. "Hold on, you two. Someone has left some ruts." He gunned the engine and bounced us over the ruts until we reached smooth sand.

As anyone who frequents the Outer Banks knows, the wind can shift from one minute to the next. Today's wind blew from the northeast. A bit cooler than normal, it brought us the smell of the Atlantic, briny and sweet to ocean lovers like Dad and me.

Up ahead, maybe half a dozen four-wheel drive vehicles were backed up near the surf. Most were pickups with the tailgates down. One was a Chevrolet Suburban painted baby blue. Folks today would call it an SUV because of its enclosed rear, which could hold two bench seats and up to six passengers, eight if you counted the two who could sit on the bench seat up front, beside the driver.

On the beach, where the sand sloped toward the waves, people were either casting bottom rigs or watching the tips of fishing rods in holders stuck into the sand. Since it was Saturday, kids built sand castles or tossed beach balls while their parents kept an eye on them.

Giggling, Talia pointed at a flock of sanderlings scurrying back and forth above the surf, their pencil thin beaks probing the wet sand for a meal. "I love those funny birds," she said. "Can we stop? I want to chase them."

"We're here to see horses," Dad said. "We can see

sanderlings any old time."

"Please, Grandpa, just for a little while."

In the short time Talia had been with Dad and I, I guess we'd spoiled her, evidenced by her pleading tone that we usually gave in to. "Be patient," I told her. "I think you'll like the horses more than chasing the sanderlings."

"Really? Can I ride one?"

Dad chuckled. "You just had to open that can of worms, didn't you, Seth?"

"I didn't say anything about riding them, Dad."

"You didn't have to. You used to take things a step farther like that when you were Talia's age."

Up ahead, maybe a hundred yards away, several horses ran down from the dunes and continued toward the ocean. Talia had been watching the beach, probably for more sanderlings. I pointed. "Do you see what I see?"

"Oh, Daddy, is that little one a baby horse?"

"We call them foals," Dad said. "That one's probably a few weeks old."

I pointed again. "I see two more. How many is that?"

Talia raised her fingers. "One plus two is … I forget."

I touched the tip of her index finger. "One. What's next?"

"It's three, Daddy. I was just teasing you." She faced the horses again. "That's too many for me to count. How many is it?"

"I'd say eight," Dad said, slowing the jeep and stopping as the herd neared us.

In the lead, a black stallion with a star in the center of his forehead stopped. Not caring for the human intruders on his beach, he stomped the sand, shook his head, and whinnied a warning. The rest of the herd gathered behind him to study us while the foals continued toward the surf, their hooves kicking up sand.

Talia's gaze followed them. "You're right, Daddy. I like them better than those birds."

After one last whinny, the stallion led the herd to the surf. Two mares rolled in the sand on their backs. Two more waded into the waves. A stallion a bit smaller than the black one approached him. The black one wheeled and kicked at him. Luckily for the smaller stallion, the hooves missed, but only by a hair. Sensing he better fight another day, he trotted away.

The foals chased each other, twisting sideways while lowering their heads and kicking sand in the air. The rest of the herd still standing watched their progeny. Now unconcerned about protecting his mares, the black stallion dropped to the sand for a roll on his back.

"Why do they roll in the sand like that?" Talia asked.

Dad and I knew the horses rolled to scratch an itch, to get rid of fleas, and just for the pleasure of it. I decided to tease my sweet daughter like she'd been teasing me. "The sand cleans their manes. I can scrub your head in the sand and see if it works."

Crossing her arms, Talia pursed her lips at me. "You're fibbing, Daddy. Why do they do it?" Dad told her why, which satisfied her.

A short time later, the stallion led the herd back to the security of the live oak trees and scrub brush behind the dunes.

I was sitting in the back of the jeep with Talia. Dad turned to face me. "Remember that time we came up here, when I said with all those tourists taking an interest in the Outer Banks now, I wonder what they'd pay a fellow to drive them out here to see the horses?"

I remembered all right. It was the day I met Di at the restaurant and Mindy later, when I drove Di home after she pretended to have a headache. As much as I hated to think about it, it was also the night Mindy had taken advantage of me in my stoned state, becoming pregnant with our child. To imagine my son or daughter dead disturbed me to my core. As I'd learned with Talia, a child was a precious blessing to be loved and cherished. Yes, a man would never know how it felt to be pregnant with an unwanted child, but that didn't mean a man who would love a child as much as I loved Talia had no rights concerning that child.

Dad shook my arm. "Well, what do you think?"

Returning from my thoughts, I blinked. "Think about what? Oh, how much someone would pay to see the horses. I don't know. Whatever the amount, I wouldn't want to gouge anyone just because I could."

Dad smiled broadly. "I raised you well, Son. You're always considerate of other folks."

I appreciated Dad's comment. "Would fifty dollars for adults and twenty-five for kids be too much?" I asked. "I'd have to buy a Suburban, and I'm sure they're expensive. Then there's the cost of gas and upkeep, plus my time driving up here. Like with selling fish, I want to be fair to my customers like I want to be fair to myself."

Talia pulled my sleeve. "Can we get out, Daddy? I want to look for shells."

We climbed out of the jeep. While Talia looked for shells along the tideline, Dad and I continued our conversation. The more we talked about my new business venture, the more it seemed like it was going to happen. The only problem was a downpayment for buying a Suburban. Dad said I should get a new one instead of a used one, because the salt air in our area would rust the bodies out in no time. Since that was the case, I'd need to make enough money to replace them when they started looking like the many rusty fishing vehicles that locals drove up and down the beach. Like our jeep, which would need to be retired before it became unsafe to drive, many local vehicles were spiderwebbed with rust around the fenders. The only reason the jeep had lasted so long was because I rinsed it off with the water hose every time I got home from pulling the dories.

I raked my fingers through my hair. "Do we have a rich relative who'll lend me the doggone downpayment for a new

Suburban? I guess I need to come up with a logo to paint on the side, too."

Dad stepped away from the jeep and turned around to point at it. "I can see it now, on the side of a brand new Suburban—a cowboy hat flanked by two horses with the words 'The Kitty Hawk Cowboy' below them. Add how you'll take people to see the world famous wild Spanish mustangs of Corolla, plus your name and phone number, you'll be good to go."

"Yeah, right, " I said, trying not to sound too critical. "You forgot how I'm supposed to pay for all that."

Dad slipped his arm around my shoulders. "It just so happens I know a guy who's saved for a rainy day just like today."

I looked into the blue sky. "In case you haven't noticed, there's not a cloud anywhere."

Dad turned around and leaned against the jeep. "Oh, ye of little faith, Seth. As a partner in our little venture, I'll loan you the money."

I leaned against the jeep beside him and cut my eyes at him. "Okay, Mr. Money Bags, has Helen been paying you to be her beck and call guy since she transferred her membership from your old church to your new one?"

"Not at all, not at all. We just enjoy each other's company." Dad winked. "You know, as friends and companions."

"That's not what that lipstick on your collar said when you stopped by to read to Talia the other night," I said, elbowing him in the ribs.

"Never you mind that," Dad said, his voice firm but playful. "I didn't work my behind off all those years of fishing to not save any money. Besides, I know fishing isn't something you want to do the rest of your life, so I'm willing to help out with your new position as the Kitty Hawk cowboy."

Watching Talia brush the sand off a huge oyster shell, then raising it before her squinting eyes, I was struck with a sense of overwhelming gratitude for having a dad as great as mine.

Then, like an icy wave from the Atlantic, an overwhelming sense of sadness washed over me. In a few years, Mom would be gone for twenty years, and Dad refused to hear any talk of divorcing her so he could remarry. As Helen's lipstick suggested, they got along well, so it broke my heart to think of him without someone to love full time instead of just when they saw each other.

This thought led to another one that concerned me.

I'd fallen in love with Alma, only to lose her after two weeks. I doubted if I'd loved Mindy because our breakup hadn't bothered me as much as I thought it would. Ellie was happily married, and no other women in the area had caught my eye. Did this mean Talia and I were destined to live the rest of our lives without a great woman to love? Back then like now, in 2024, I firmly believe a family does its best when it has two great parents in it. What it would take for that to happen for Talia and me, I had no idea whatsoever.

To end my disheartening thoughts, I helped my dear daughter look for shells. Dad joined us, and we three strolled the sand, only pausing when a shell caught someone's eye.

My life, or rather, my dream, was falling into place. I was a father, and I loved the responsibility of it as much as I loved Talia. Like Dad becoming a minister, I was going to become a cowboy of sorts, taking people to see the horses I loved so well. The only thing left, if it was possible, was for a love of a different kind to enter my heart, the same as when Alma's love had entered my heart.

Talia ran ahead to chase a flock of sanderlings, dark hair streaming behind her. Dad must've sensed my sadness. A moment later, he stopped smiling at Talia and turned to face me, as serious an expression on his face as I'd ever seen. "I guess you miss Mindy, but if you had married her before Talia came, the result would've been the same as my marriage to your mom." He rested his hand on my shoulder. "Be patient, Son. You've got a good heart. When you least expect it, a woman with a heart like yours will come along, and you'll have all the love you can handle."

I squatted to pick up a broken oyster shell and stood. "I don't know, Dad. I feel like an oyster without a pearl in it."

Dad chuckled. "Talia's your pearl, Son. What you mean is you feel like an oyster without a heart."

Trying to ease my melancholy again, I offered a sad smile. "Do oysters have hearts? I never thought about it before."

"To be honest," Dad said, "all I know about oysters is they taste great."

Still chasing the birds, Talia squealed happily, taking our attention until Dad faced me again. "Someone will come along, okay. You've got to have faith."

We continued along the beach. At the moment, my faith felt faithless. Still, I needed to be more positive, and what better way to do that than to look forward to my new job as the Kitty Hawk Cowboy.

Chapter 19

Dad was right about Talia. As summer passed, whenever my mood darkened because I was lonely for a special woman in my life, my little pearl of joy never failed to brighten my days.

One way she brightened my days was when we visited Grandpa Callahan. A few days after Morris left, I visited Grandpa to explain about Talia. Sitting on a ladderback chair at the kitchen table with a cup of coffee, he raised his hazy eyes to me. "You mean I have a granddaughter I didn't even know about? And all the way from Israel?"

"You sure do," I said, glad to hear the joy in his voice.

A slow smile spread across his wrinkled face. "I don't recall you getting married, Seth. When did that happen?"

I wondered about his smile. I would've thought he'd be upset at missing my wedding.

Grinning big enough to bare his false teeth, Grandpa reached across the table with his gnarled hand and tousled my hair. "Don't you worry about it. Tom told me everything." He sipped coffee. "I imagine you thought I'd be upset about your relationship with that young lady in Israel, but I'm not. Like I've always said, youth is for the young and experience comes with age. As long as you don't keep doing the wrong thing, you're learning from it, and that's what matters the most."

Dad hadn't mentioned telling Grandpa about Talia. Maybe he thought the news would go better coming from him. I didn't mind. At the time, I'd stopped by in preparation for telling everyone at the church in Manteo, and I didn't want it to be a shock to Grandpa. Since it was over and done, the only thing left to do was to introduce Talia to Grandpa, unless Dad had already done that too. When I told Grandpa this, he chuckled. "I've already met that cutey pie. Me and Tom thought we'd let you sweat about it for a while. That's why he hasn't told you."

I shook my head at Grandpa. "You could've told me before I started running my mouth just now."

"Oh, no, not at all. I wanted to see if you'd be man enough to tell me yourself, and you are." He sipped more coffee. "Tom also tells me you're not sure if you'll find the right woman one day. You're a good boy, so try not to worry about it. A good woman will recognize how you chose to take care of Talia without a second thought, and she'll appreciate that."

I appreciated Dad and Grandpa. Without solid male role models like them in my life, I might've ended up with someone like Mindy, and that would've been a mess from the word go.

My conversation with Grandpa led to our visits with him. Nearing eighty, he shuffled around his home and front porch with a walker. His mind was still sharp, though, and he loved telling Talia stories about taking me fishing when I was her age, how the various hurricanes and nor'easters, such as the 1962 Ash Wednesday Storm, devastated the area, or how the group of English people who eventually became known as the Lost Colony inexplicably disappeared from Roanoke Island. Of course he included Native Americans in the story, and Talia always asked endless questions about them and Virginia Dare, the first English child born in what would eventually become America.

Looking back, the modern story of the Lost Colony would've been more interesting to her. Archaeological digs in the towns of Frisco and Buxton, both on Hatteras Island, strongly suggest the Native Americans there, known then as the Croatoans, took the colonists in to keep them from dying of hunger. Other historical evidence, such as a written account of the gray-eyed Native Americans there wearing English clothing, suggests the colonists permanently assimilated with the Croatoans. Pretty cool, huh?

On our visits to Grandpa's, as the afternoons darkened to evening, and when the whippoorwills sent out their plaintive calls, we sometimes turned the crank on his old ice cream freezer. I'd add ice while Talia added rock salt, always asking how much longer before the ice cream was ready. Then, as mine and Dad's arms were about to give out, Grandpa would declare the ice cream ready. He'd then work the dasher out of the frozen mass and offer it to Talia. With a grin of delight, she'd start licking it clean of either strawberry, chocolate, or vanilla ice cream.

Another way she brightened a particular day happened on the first Saturday in August. As dawn yellowed my window, Talia crawled into bed with me and patted my face. Blinking in confusion, I woke enough to recognize her soft hand on my cheek and her dark eyes watching me. "I'm up, I'm up," I said. "I guess you're ready for breakfast."

"No, Daddy. I'm ready for something else."

I rubbed the sleep from my eyes. "Well, I don't know what it is unless you tell me."

She covered a girlish giggle. "It's a secret. You have to guess." She took a length of her long, dark hair and tickled my nose with the ends. "And I'm going to tickle your nose until you guess."

Enjoying the sweet smell of baby shampoo, I grinned. "Are you ready for sand in your swimsuit? That happened last weekend, and you didn't like it one bit."

Talia's dark eyebrows scrunched together. "That big wave did it. I like the little ones better."

I was tempted to laugh at this memory. Talia had been sitting at the edge of the surf, when the remains of a larger than average wave rushed in to cover her with foam up to her waist.

With her hands pressing into the sand behind her to stop the wave from knocking her over, she squealed about "that mean old wave." When it subsided and she could stand, she spread her legs and squealed even louder, "Daddy! That mean old wave got sand in my butt!"

I couldn't help laughing, especially when she waggled her little finger at me and told me to stop. It was hard not to laugh, though, because the sand made her swimsuit look like a full diaper. I picked her up and waded to the calmer water over a sandbar. There I opened the legs of her swimsuit and swished her around until the sand was gone.

What a cherished memory, just one of who knows how many she shared with me over the years.

Frowning because I'd mentioned her sandy swimsuit, Talia poked my chest. "You behave, Daddy. Can you guess my secret or not?"

I sat up against the bed's headboard and rubbed my chin. "Let me think. What kind of secret would my little sandy drawers have?"

Talia poked me again, this time harder. "It was my swimsuit, not my drawers."

I couldn't help but grin at her serious expression. "You're right, you're right."

She crossed her arms. "Well, can you guess or not?"

I sniffed the air. "Have you cooked breakfast? I don't smell anything."

"You won't let me cook," she huffed.

"That's right," I said, holding in a grin. "I forgot."

"Here's a hint," Talia said. Raising a hand, she folded her thumb into her palm. "How many fingers is that?"

I touched each fingertip and counted. "One, two, three, five. That's five fingers, right?"

Talia giggled. "You're just being silly, Daddy. It's four, like you taught me.

An overwhelming urge to hug my daughter brought tears

to my eyes, only to be replaced by an overwhelming surge of sadness. If Mindy had wanted kids, she would've had our son or daughter instead of having an abortion. If so, we might've been happily married by now. Then, instead of having one sweet child to hug, we'd have two. How anyone could destroy such an innocent life with so much potential for love escaped me, and the evidence of all that potential for love was sitting in my bed beside me, waiting patiently for me to ask again about her secret.

"Yes, I'm just being silly," I said, fingering the hint of tears from the corners of my eyes. Her hand was in her lap. I raised it and touched each fingertip again. "One, two, three, four. Is that right?"

"That's right," she chirped. "Now, what does my hint mean about my secret?"

As we like to say in the south, "My momma didn't raise no fools," so I knew exactly what her secret was. I pulled her to my chest and hugged her tight. "I think a certain little girl turns four today. Is that your secret?"

She hugged me back and sat up, dark eyes bright with happiness. "You knew it all the time. You were just teasing."

"I wouldn't tease you if I didn't love you so much. What can I make for your birthday breakfast?"

"Cereal's fast. Then I can open my present."

I poked her tummy. "Did you forget that we're going to grandpa's house for your birthday?"

Talia's expression fell. "Because he can't come up all our steps with his walker. Yes, I remember."

Wearing pajama bottoms because she might come to my room while I slept, I climbed out of bed and waved toward the door. "Go get dressed like a big girl. Close the door behind you so I can get dressed too."

"Okay, Daddy." Behind the closed door, Talia's little feet pattered to her room. Before she came along, I would've never thought I'd love a child as much as I did her. The only thing that would make it better would be to have a wife and family. Then this old house would be filled with love from the sand beneath it to the sky above it.

Dressed in cut-off blue jean shorts and an old white T-shirt, I found Talia in the kitchen, dressed similarly with clothes I'd bought at a thrift shop. Filling two bowls with cereal at the table, she asked me to cut a banana for us. After doing that and adding it to the cereal, I added milk to the bowls and got the coffee percolator going on the stove.

As we ate, the sky over the sound, visible through the sliding glass doors, brightened. About a quarter mile out, on the steel gray water dotted with whitecaps, two men were pulling crab pots into a skiff. Kitty Hawk was waking, and I loved everything about this amazing place.

The day went as planned. I took Talia to the beach, where she didn't sit near the foamy surf for fear of another wave filling her swimsuit with sand. Instead, she played in the water's edge, running toward the waves and back like a single sanderling, squealing each time the surf gurgled around her ankles.

Tourists strolled by, most wearing swimsuits. A few young women and a few young families caught my eye. I caught the eyes of some of the young women, evidenced by their slight smiles at me. I imagine some wondered who the handsome man was. If so, I'm sure some of them would've talked to me if I tried, at least until they discovered I was a single dad. I didn't blame anyone for thinking that. To take on the responsibility of loving someone else's child can be a challenging task. I doubted if I'd ever find a woman like that. Like many men, many women weren't attracted to ready-made families.

When we grew hungry, we returned home for hot dogs and a stroll along the sound. At the shore below Ellie's house, we met Ellie, Jeff, and J.J., sitting on a quilt by the water having a picnic. The sight both gladdened and saddened me. This was what I wanted, a family to love and cherish like Jeff loved and cherished Ellie and their son, who was sitting in Ellie's lap with a cookie in his plump hand. Jeff wore jeans and a T-shirt with paint stains from some recent remodeling. Ellie wore a yellow sundress and looked fresh as a flower. J.J. wore a blue jumper. All were barefoot. All smiled at Talia and I. Jeff waved us over. "Would you like some lunch? We've got tomato sandwiches and potato chips."

"We just had hot dogs, thank you," Talia said sweetly.

Ellie looked up at me. "She's always so polite, Seth. That's the sign of a good dad."

"I'm sure that's from your influence, too," I said warmly. Like Alma, Ellie was one of my regrets. Had she been this mature when we were teenagers, we might be together now.

J.J. reached for Talia. Ellie had been telling me how close they'd gotten while she'd been keeping her.

Talia helped J.J. up. "Can we walk by the water, Ellie? We won't go far." Ellie said they could, and off they went, hand in hand, leaving two sets of footprints in the sand.

I sat on the quilt. Jeff swallowed a bite of sandwich. His eyes darted between me and Ellie, as if he had something on his mind. Ellie rolled her eyes at him. "What's going on, you two?" I asked.

Ellie gave her head a little shake. "Jeff wants to set you up with a blind date."

I didn't know what to think about this. To mask my surprise, I laughed. "Is she a relative?"

Jeff smirked at Ellie. "You already told him, didn't you?"

"No, sir," she said, indignation in her voice. Ellie faced me. "She's Jeff's sister. She's— Well, how do I say this kindly?"

"She's not very attractive," Jeff said. "She's nice, though."

I wished Talia and I had said hi and continued on our walk. I'd never been on a blind date and didn't want to start now. Along with that, if the date went bad, Jeff might think it was my fault. I liked Jeff and didn't want to take that chance. "Do we have anything in common?" I asked, trying to be reasonable about it.

About to bite a chip, Jeff lowered it. "You're both single. That's a start."

"Anything else?"

"She's a she and you're a he. That's a plus."

"She's independent," Ellie said.

"What exactly does that mean?" I asked.

"She owns her own home. She's a chemistry professor."

It was my turn to dart my eyes between Jeff and Ellie. "A chemistry professor? How old is she?"

"Only thirty-five," Jeff said.

"I'm sorry," I said firmly. "I'd rather date someone around my own age. Ten years is too much."

"I told you," Ellie told Jeff. "Quit trying to marry off your old maid sister to our friends."

"It's just a blind date," Jeff said. "It's no big deal."

I was tempted to get up and continue walking with Talia, but I felt bad for any woman who hadn't found someone to love at thirty-five. "You say she's a chemistry professor? That means she doesn't live around here."

"She's coming for vacation next week," Jeff said. "She teaches in Raleigh." Jeff took his wallet from his back pocket and opened it to show me a photograph. "Here she is. Her name is Martha."

Martha's dark, shoulder-length hair framed her face. She wore horn-rimmed glasses and a serious glare. Neither thin nor plump, she was standing on a beach in a skimpy bikini. I couldn't get a good look at her face because of the glasses, but I wouldn't have said she wasn't attractive. I hadn't dated anyone since Mindy. What would be the harm? Besides, I wasn't going to leave Kitty Hawk, and she wouldn't leave her job in Raleigh. Just in case, I had one more question for Jeff and Ellie, who were eyeing me expectantly. "Does she like kids? Dating anyone who doesn't like kids is a deal breaker."

"Because of Mindy," Ellie said. "Yes, as a matter of fact, Martha loves kids."

"Then why isn't she married?" I asked. "She looks fine to me, so what's going on with her?"

"Nothing," Jeff said. "At least that I know of."

I didn't like his doubtful tone. "You don't sound so sure of yourself, Jeff."

"She's not a fan of the war in Vietnam," Ellie said.

"I'm not a fan either," I said. "I get why we're there, but I hate how so many people are dying." I paused, hoping I wouldn't regret this. "You know my work schedule, Ellie. Set the date up and let me know when." I got up to continue my walk with Talia. "Oh, and you'll keep Talia that night for free, right?"

"Glad to do it," Jeff said. "Just show my sister a good time."

Talia was bringing J.J. back. After she sat him down on the quilt, we said our goodbyes and left for our stroll along the sound.

Despite the growth in the area, with motels, restaurants, and cottages popping up along the beach, Kitty Hawk in August of 1967 could still be lazy and quiet. Once in a while a fishing skiff or a ski boat cruised by in the sound, the motor humming along. In the distance, maybe halfway to the mainland, the tiny white triangle of a sailboat shimmered in the hazy horizon.

Adding to the serene surroundings, Talia's hand—small, soft, and warm in mine—comforted me. She kept looking up at me, though, as if she sensed my worry about being alone for the rest of my life. "Daddy?"

I looked down into her dark eyes that reminded me so much of Alma. "What, sweetie?"

"I miss Mommy. Will you ever find another mommy for me?"

Like a sandspur piercing the sole of my foot as a boy, my daughter's plaintive tone pierced my heart. "Well," I said, pausing to get my thoughts straight, "that's a hard thing to do."

"Why? J.J. has a mommy."

"Ellie's J.J.'s mommy because she fell in love with J.J.'s daddy first." I gently squeezed Talia's hand. "Like I fell in love with your mommy first." Her eyebrows, dark and fine, formed a V. I'd seen this expression of deep thought before. This time I was pretty sure I knew what it meant. "You're wondering if I can fall in love with another lady who can be your mommy. She would have to be very special, you know."

Yes, Daddy. Special enough to love both of us very, very much."

I didn't know Talia had been thinking about this subject so much. The age difference between Martha and I wouldn't be so bad if she were nice. Our upcoming date, whenever and wherever that would be, would be a hint.

Chapter 20

At certain times in our lives, we have to cut to the chase. Shoving a fishing hook through your fingertip and snipping the barb so you can pull the rest out is one of those times. In this case, it was my date with Martha.

Did I say "cut to the chase?" I sure did, and the word chase describes exactly what happened on our date.

Talia and I returned home from our walk to a ringing telephone. We thought it was Dad calling about her birthday party at Grandpa Callahan's later. We were wrong.

"Hello?" I said into the handset as I took a seat on the sofa.

"This is Jeff. Martha's looking forward to the date. She'll pick you up in her car Monday night."

"That's the day after tomorrow," I said, as confusion arched one of my eyebrows. "When's she coming from Raleigh?" I also wondered what was wrong with us going out in my pickup but didn't ask.

"She's coming tomorrow," Jeff said. "Monday's okay, right? Talia can stay with us while you two are at the Nags Head Casino. Martha loves that place. She goes there every time she visits."

I knew about the Nags Head Casino. Built in 1932 across from Jockey's Ridge, the tallest sand dunes on the east coast, the huge dance hall could accommodate over a thousand customers at a time. Over the years, on its polished hardwood dance floor upstairs, where couples were required to dance without shoes, they could enjoy a night filled with music from performers like Louis Armstrong, Artie Shaw, and Duke Ellington, to name a few. The casino also sported pool tables, pinball machines, duck pin bowling, and a snack bar that served ice-cold beer. It sounds like I've been there but I haven't. Some of my fishing buddies told me about it. I've never been much on crowds and loud music. I'd also heard that the beer could make jealous hotheads—both women and men—start fights, and I wanted no part of that.

Jeff's revelation about Martha loving the casino puzzled me. How had a single woman in her mid-thirties—a chemistry professor at that—come to love such a place?

I didn't ask Jeff that question either. I wanted to, but I decided on a different tactic. "Dancing at the Nags Head Casino. I'd rather go out to eat, or take a walk on the beach. You know, just to get to know each other without a big crowd and loud music."

Coming through the phone, Jeff's steady breathing faltered. "Look, Seth, if you don't want to take her out, just say so."

I didn't care for his defensive tone, especially when I'd never heard it before. "It's not that, Jeff. I've heard the casino isn't a good place to get to know someone."

"Because of the crowd and loud music," Jeff said, his tone critical. "She works hard. She just wants a good time. Is that so hard to understand?"

As hard as I worked fishing, I understood. Regardless, I preferred to sit on the deck and watch the sunset after a hard day of fishing. Nothing rested my mind and body better than that. "All right," I said, trying not to huff the words out. "What time will she pick me up?"

"Eight sharp."

"What about supper? We could still do that."

"She doesn't like to dance on a full stomach. Thanks."

Before I could say goodbye, Jeff hung up. Beside me on the

sofa, Talia's confusion was clear in her squinting eyes. "Daddy, what's a 'sino."

"Cuh-sino. It's a place in Nags Head where people dance."

"Can I go with you and Martha?"

"It's for grownups."

"Why's that?"

I rubbed the wrinkles erupting across my forehead. I loved being a dad, except for complicated questions like that. "It just is, okay?"

"Okay, as long as I can stay with Ellie and play with J.J." Talia scurried to her room, likely to find some toys to take Monday night.

At my closet, hoping to find something decent to wear on my date, I clattered racks back and forth. Since Martha was so intent on dancing, I'd better look nice trying to do it. Sunday slacks and an Oxford shirt would do. I'd recently had a haircut, so that would do. In front of my door mirror, I raised my hands to an imaginary dance partner, taking her right hand in my left and placing my right hand on her waist. After a few shuffling steps, I was satisfied. My sense of rhythm was decent, so that would also do. Little did I know, Martha wouldn't test my sense of rhythm on our date as much as she would test my sense of decency.

Talia's birthday party at Grandpa Callahan's went well. Dad even updated me on the paint job for the Chevrolet Suburban, saying it would be ready in time to take tourists out on Labor Day weekend. Unfolding a sheet of paper from his pocket, he grinned. "Since you've been busy fishing, I put an ad in the local papers a week ago. The phone has been ringing off the hook."

"Sure has," Grandpa said from his chair at the table, where we'd been eating ice cream and birthday cake. He faced Dad. "How's Seth gonna take all those folks to see the horses?"

"Can I go?" Talia asked. "I can tell the people about the horses while you drive."

"This is work," I told her. "I'll have to concentrate on not getting stuck in the sand."

"That's why you need me, Daddy."

"That's not a bad idea," Dad said, spooning more ice cream into his bowl. "The folks might like to hear the history of the horses."

"Then I can go?" Talia asked, her voice plaintive.

"No, honey," Dad said. "Your daddy will be gone all day."

"Okay. I'd rather play with J.J."

Glad that problem was solved, I faced Dad. "How many people called?"

"Enough to pay for that customized Suburban in a month."

"How many is that?"

Dad glanced at the sheet of paper on the table. "Two hundred and thirty-six. If you start at eight in the morning, you can take each group of eight out and back in about an hour. With breaks for lunch and gas, you should be able to make five or six trips a day. Multiply that by eight by fifty dollars a person, you've made 2400 dollars, and that's just in one day. Of course, taxes will lower that amount, but it's still a lot of money for a day's work."

The amount astounded me. The best part about it was that I could easily afford college for Talia. The next best part was I could take care of a wife and family if either ever came along, as unlikely as that seemed.

"If you make that kind of money," Grandpa said, "maybe you can hire someone to talk about the horses."

His idea wasn't a bad one. I'd lose one tourist and fifty dollars, but having a tour guide of sorts might draw more customers. I'd ask around when I got the chance. Right now I had to concentrate on my date with Martha Monday night, as nervous as I was about it.

It turned out that I had a right to be nervous. Despite that, our date started out well enough when she picked me up at 7:45, in a Chevrolet Corvette painted a shiny red. I liked the rumbling engine. I liked the sporty appearance. I even liked Martha's matching lipstick and nail polish as she waved at me to climb in.

After closing the door, I offered her my hand. "Nice to meet you, Martha."

"You too, Seth." She took a compact from her purse and powdered her nose. While I watched her, I realized her beach photo didn't do her justice. With high cheekbones, shiny brunette hair falling in waves across her shoulders and full cleavage, supported by a snug, white sweater, she caught my eye immediately, even with the horn-rimmed glasses. The red mini-skirt, revealing shapely legs, didn't hurt matters any. "If you don't mind me saying so," I said, "Jeff didn't tell me you were so gorgeous."

Martha snapped the compact closed and dropped it into her purse. "Brothers aren't supposed to think stuff like that about their sisters." She eyed my hand still waiting to be shook. "I see you're a gentleman. My experience with gentlemen isn't good." A garish smile split her face. "Your expression is priceless. I always tease first dates as a way to break the ice." She shoved the Corvette into first gear and revved the engine. "Let's boogie. I'm ready to dance."

The acceleration pressed me into the seat. Martha grinned, like speed gave her a high. At the stop sign, she looked left, right and hit the accelerator again. The rear tires squealed. The back of the Corvette fishtailed. I checked the side mirror for a police car. Well, honestly, I hoped for a police car before she got us both killed.

"Are you nervous?" she asked. "Nervous is good. I make all my dates nervous. When they finally release it, it's like a nuclear bomb going off."

Yes, I was nervous. Yes, I was pretty sure I knew what she meant about a nuclear bomb going off. Licking her lips, she looked my way. "You're hot."

"I'm okay. Why do you say that?"

Her lips twisted into a sideways smirk. "Unless I miss my guess, you're not very worldly. Maybe I can change that before I'm done with you."

I grew more nervous. The way she studied me made me feel like a piece of meat, with her being the hungry lioness. Now I knew how women felt when men looked at them like that. Not cool.

She patted my knee, adding a firm squeeze. "How's it hanging? If you know a place to park, the dance can wait."

Like I've already said, I didn't care for crowds and loud music. The sun was setting over the sound. Although Martha was tall and full-bodied, I could handle her if she tried anything. Watching the sunset would give me time to find out if her personality so far was real or a bluff. Some guys were like that, so she could be like that. As we passed the Wright Memorial, where Wilbur and Orville made history by flying the first motorized airplane on December 17, 1903, I pointed to a road to the right. "That leads to the sound. We can watch the sunset."

Martha clicked the turn signal. "You're a romantic. I like that. It's been a while since someone romanced me."

She pulled into the road. I wanted privacy for our talk, so I suggested a sandy path overhung with tree limbs a quarter mile later that should continue to the sound, adding to take it slow because deer were common in Outer Banks woods. Up ahead, as the sound came into view, the path ended at a place where people had been launching boats over the years. Martha parked and said we should get out. I met her at the front of the Corvette, and asked if she liked the view. She said nothing, so I tried something else. "What made you want to teach chemistry?"

She ran her fingers through my hair. "Let's go skinny dipping. You know you want to see me naked."

I pulled away from her. "You know we just met, right?"

She returned to the car and came back with her purse. After

opening it enough to look inside, she closed it and dropped it to the Corvette's hood. "Just checking."

I cut my eyes at the purse. "Just checking what?"

"Just checking to see if I took my pill today. You can't be too careful, you know."

Jeff hadn't mentioned Martha being sick. "I'm sorry you don't feel well. We can leave if you want."

Those red-painted fingernails rose to my shirt buttons and started undoing them. "My pills are birth-control pills. I borrowed a friend's wedding ring to get a doctor to prescribe them. As soon as they're legalized for single women, we can do whatever we want whenever we want without worrying about getting pregnant. That's what I call a real sexual revolution, Seth baby." Martha finished my buttons and peeled off her sweater to reveal a lace bra bulging with cleavage. Looking back, I guess I was so dumbfounded at what was happening that I let her unbutton my shirt.

She turned around and pressed her bottom against me, I guess to tease me into sex. After licking my lips at her smooth back, sharp shoulder blades, rounded shoulders, and silky brunette hair, my mouth fell open. "I hope you don't mind me saying this, Martha. The pill is fine for not getting pregnant, but it doesn't stop diseases."

Martha grinned over her shoulder. "You poor, poor thing. You're as shy as you can be."

I buttoned my shirt. "I'm sorry, but I'm not looking for a one-night stand. We can go dancing if you still want to, but I'm not doing this."

She took a plastic bag of what looked like cigarette tobacco from her purse. Next came wrapping papers. She rolled a cigarette, lit it, and took a long drag. "This will loosen you up, Seth baby. If you've never done it smoking weed, you've never done it."

The sun had almost lowered below the horizon. The glowing tip of the joint, which is what my Vietnam buddies called it, brightened. Martha placed it between my lips and said to give it a try. I'll admit to being tempted. A partially dressed woman with the background of the sound at the end of a sunset would do that to most any guy. Fortunately for me, or unfortunately, depending on your point of view, I remembered how Mindy had gotten pregnant by taking advantage of me so long ago. Sure, Martha couldn't get pregnant, but that didn't help matters any. I wanted love instead of lust, and all Jeff's sister wanted was lust.

But boy did she look good.

No, I didn't cave to the crave. Yes, she got mad. No, I didn't have to walk home. Yes, she drove me. I said I wouldn't tell her brother if she wouldn't. She said she wouldn't mind except for the part where she'd be too embarrassed to admit that all her womanly wiles hadn't worked on me. Before I climbed from the Corvette, she pecked my cheek and said she was going to the casino, adding that she'd tell Jeff and Ellie I wasn't her type. I thanked her for wanting me and left to get Talia. Of course, my little pearl was upset about leaving so soon, but I reminded her that she'd get to play with J.J. in the morning, when I went fishing.

No, Martha wasn't one of those womanly category five hurricanes of my life, but she wasn't far from it. If anything, I'd rate her a strong category two. Thinking about her later, with how she tempted me, I would've rated her a category three if her morals kept her from sleeping with someone before she hardly knew more about him than his name. As far as I was concerned, the so-called sexual revolution she mentioned was just an excuse to not commit to a loving relationship with a guy. Sure, everyone doesn't have to get married and have a family, but to me, casual sex lacked the connection to true love, and that was one of the saddest thoughts I've ever had.

Back home again, Talia and I settled down to watch *The Andy Griffith Show.* She never said so, but I thought she had a crush on Opie. For myself, I had a crush on Barbara Eden from

I Dream of Jeannie, which hit the airwaves two years ago, in 1965. The day she showed up in Mayberry to be a manicurist, not only did her cute smile and sexy curves knock the socks off of all the men there, they knocked my socks off too.

Along with Martha's proposition, thinking about Jeannie made me realize how much I missed a woman in my life. Sure, the memory of making love with Alma would stay with me forever, and that meant I wanted a love like we had, not the lust I considered having with Martha. At least I was still young and, according to Jeff's sister, "hot," so it wasn't too late to use my manly wiles to start dating again after my long layoff from my disastrous ending with Mindy.

Talia's laughter brought me out of my thoughts. On the TV, Barney Fife, Andy Griffith's hilarious deputy, was wearing a wedding dress to distract a character named Ernest T. Bass while the real bride got married. As we both laughed, the phone rang at my elbow, on one of the end tables beside the sofa. When I answered it, Dad asked if Talia was nearby, because he had something to tell me that might upset her. Wondering what it was, I told Talia I was going to talk to Dad on the deck while she watched more of Barney and Andy.

On the deck, with the sliding glass doors closed as tightly as possible without damaging the phone cord, I pressed the handset to my ear. "Ok, Dad, what's this about?"

"Son, it's two things, and one of them will break your heart like it has mine. I got home from a church meeting a few minutes ago and …"

Dad coughed a hard sob, and the only thing I could imagine was something was wrong with Grandpa Callahan. "Dad?" I asked, trying not to sob myself. "Is it Grandpa? Did something happen to him?"

"I found him on the sofa, Son. It looks like he was watching Andy Griffith and passed away."

My knees weakened. I leaned against the house to steady myself. "I'm sorry, Dad. Do you want me to come over?"

"No, Son. I need you to talk to Talia. I'm sitting at the table, opening the mail until the undertaker gets here. I just read a letter from a man saying he's Morris's attorney. Morris passed away two weeks ago. I know we expected it, but it's still a shock. I'm sure the news will break Talia's heart."

"Good Lord," I mumbled. "She just lost both of her grandpas. This will be tough to tell her, Dad."

"I know, Son, I know. You're a good father. I know you'll find the words." Dad paused. "I hear a car outside. It should be the undertaker. I've got to make some calls after he leaves. I'll let you know about the visitation and the funeral."

After Dad ended the call, tears filled my eyes. I hardly knew my mom's dad, but I knew Grandpa Callahan well. I couldn't begin to number my memories of him, but I'd spend the next few days trying. Now I had to share this same feeling with Talia, and I wasn't sure how to do it.

Back on the sofa again, I waited until Andy Griffith ended before I got up to turn the TV off. On the sofa again, I faced Talia. "Sweetheart, remember how your Grandpa Morris is sick?"

She nodded. "Very sick, Daddy. Saba said he would be with Mommy and Lia and Savta soon."

"How do you feel about that?" I asked, wanting to know how upset she'd be when I told her the news.

Her darks eyes lowered. "I was sad when Mommy and Lia and Savta died." She looked back up at me. "But they're in Heaven, so I shouldn't be sad, right?"

"That's right." I cleared emotion from my throat. "My daddy just called. He got a letter that said your saba is now with all the people he loves."

"Oh. That's why you talked to him outside."

I nodded. "There's something else. My daddy said he just got home from church. My saba is now with all the people he loves."

"You mean—" Talia's voice broke. Tears filled her eyes.

Then she wiped them away and shook her head violently. "We should be happy, Daddy. We can remember everything we did with our sabas until we see them again one day."

"That's true," I said, my heart filling with gratitude for my wonderful daughter.

She hugged my neck and asked if I was all right. I said I was because I loved her so much. She kissed my cheek. "Like I love you so much, Daddy." She sat again, quiet for a moment. "Can we go see my far away family some time?"

"Far away family" was what she called her loved ones in Israel. I'd thought about doing the same thing, especially to visit Alma's grave, but traveling so far would be too expensive. Then again, if my job of taking tourists to see the horses earned enough money, Talia, Dad, and I might be able to do it sooner than later.

Talia yawned. "Can you read to me in bed?"

"Sure. Go brush your teeth. We can get baths in the morning."

As the bathroom door closed, Dad called again. "Son, I stopped reading the letter from Morris's attorney when I called you. In case you were wondering for Talia's sake, he spent most of his savings on his cancer treatments. Both the house and rental have to be sold to take care of the rest."

"That's okay, Dad. My new job should handle everything I need to take care of her. Do you know anything about Grandpa Callahan's will?"

"He left me the house. I'll leave it to you, of course, when I pass on. He had a little savings, but not much. I don't mind either. If I had to choose between money and all the fine memories I have of him and mom, I'll take the memories every time. I just wanted to let you know."

After Dad ended the call by saying he needed to phone his brothers and sisters, I went to the sliding glass doors to look at the stars flickering over the sound. When I was a kid, Mom used to say each star was the soul of someone's loved one, now passed on. The thought calmed me. Sadly, though, because it'd been so long since she left Dad and me, I wondered if one of those stars could be her.

Behind me, the patter of bare feet came closer. Talia wrapped her slender fingers around my thumb. "It's okay, Daddy. My saba and your saba are in Heaven now."

She wore a white nightgown with lace at the collar. If ever there was an angel on earth, my sweet daughter was one. She led me to her room. I tucked her in and settled down beside her. In the glow of the lamp illuminating us and the book, I started to read. Before I finished the first paragraph, she was asleep. I kissed her forehead and turned the lamp off.

At the sliding glass doors again, I studied the stars. What was my destiny? I loved being a dad, and despite my date with Martha, who turned out to want one thing and one thing only from me, I still believed I'd find the right woman one day. I was sure to meet plenty of women during the horse tours, but I preferred someone like Ellie, a local who appreciated Kitty Hawk and the Outer Banks for their beauty instead of simply a tourist location.

I shoved that mess out of my mind. My family had just suffered the death of a fine man. That was important now, not horses, women, or tourists.

Unfortunately, as I climbed into bed and tried to fall asleep, the female part of my life's equation, or rather, the fact that a female who loved Talia and I like Alma had was missing from my life's equation, weighed on my heart as if Death were grinding its heal into it. *Who are you to think you deserve happiness, Seth Callahan? You're just a bum fisherman with dreams of the impossible. No woman will ever love a single father. You might as well forget that mess and give up on love.*

In the darkness, I told Death exactly what it could do with those lies. Unlike Mindy and Martha, there were women in the world who would love Talia and me. It was just a matter of her finding me or me finding her, and I'd keep my eyes peeled for every chance I got. As far as I knew, we might even find each other on one of my coming horse tours.

Chapter 21

It's strange how a person can oversleep and still be exhausted. Lying in bed, wondering if I have the strength to get up and write, I glare again at the alarm clock on my nightstand. How could my ragged old self have slept twelve hours and feel this bad? Six or seven have been plenty for years. Maybe it's my body's way of saying my time is running out. Then again, maybe my brain needed a breather after the great lunch Liz and I shared yesterday.

I dress and go to the kitchen to check the weather. The gray clouds and dreary rain shove aside any ideas of spending more time with Liz. Too bad. A walk on the beach would've been perfect for gathering my thoughts about the next chapter in this story.

I make coffee and scrambled eggs, toast and bacon. Yeah, yeah, I'm supposed to watch my cholesterol. How about you watch me eat this bacon. Like I glared at the alarm clock and glared at the rain, I glare at my pill bottles. Yeah, yeah, I take my stupid pills anyway. I'd give anything if my wife were across the table waggling her finger at me, saying I better take my pills or I wouldn't get lucky tonight. I crunch another piece of bacon. Maybe it'll clog my heart and send me on my way to see her.

"Seth," her ghost says, "you know better than to act like that. You've still got children and grandchildren who love you every bit as much as I love you. Now be good for me and make the best of your day. You can start by working on that next chapter."

I look at the laptop on the coffee table. "You're right, sweetheart. I'm sorry."

Feeling chastised, I throw the rest of the bacon in the trash and have more coffee while I wash dishes. Through the window over the sink, I can see Jack's kitchen window. He and Louise are at the sink. He's washing and she's drying. My wife and I did the same thing. Something so simple, yet I'd give anything if she were here now, handing me something to wash or dry, commenting on one of the kids' report cards, suggesting a walk along the sound after supper, or sitting in our rocking chairs on the pier. It's strange how the years go by, stranger still how we met.

Instead of drying my few dishes, I leave them and the frying pan in the strainer. What does it matter when it's just me in this lonely old house, where I hear her whispers in the night, where I smell her perfume on her pillow, where I open the closet and slip between her dresses and nightgowns to feel her arms wrap around me.

The laptop taunts me. Yep, I need to get to work. With more coffee on the table, I bring the laptop over. Seconds later I'm typing away, too immersed to hear the rain tapping on the windows.

I haven't thought about Grandpa's funeral in years. Unlike today, sunshine filled the cemetery with August warmth as mourners dressed in black gathered there. Like Dad and me, Grandpa loved the outdoors and his solitude, so he'd left a note to Dad for a short service outside instead of inside the church. That way, so he said in the note, people could get back to the business of living instead of the business of dying.

At the head of the grave, Dad opened his bible. He studied it for a minute, heaved a huge breath, and closed it again. To his right, Helen's eyes asked what he was doing. I felt the same.

He'd worked hard on Grandpa's eulogy, and it seemed he was abandoning it.

His nostrils flared, and I knew he was taking in the aroma of fresh air. He looked at the sky, so blue it might take your breath. His head turned left to right, likely to admire the crooked limbs on the crooked live oak trees scattered about the cemetery. Finally, he faced the crowd, including his siblings circling the grave. "On behalf of Seth and myself, thank you all for coming. Your kind words since my father died have comforted us, but it's still one of the hardest blows we've been forced to take." He glanced at the bible still held at his waist. "My father wasn't what you'd call a regular church goer. Regardless of that, he was a believer. I knew this because of our many talks on the subject, as well as his belief in love. Like most married couples, he and my mother had their ups and downs. I even witnessed a few fusses, as he called them, when I was a boy. Most of them happened at the end of a hard day of him fishing and my mother running the general store until he joined her. They never failed, though, usually before supper, to sit at the kitchen table and remind each other that they should've talked instead of fussing. 'God made men and women to partner in life,' he always told me. 'Come good, bad, or in between, always take time to listen to each other, and you'll have a fine life together.'"

Murmurs and nods of agreement spread throughout the mourners. Outer Banks dwellers know how important it is to work together, not only in marriage but in our challenging existence on the slender strip of sand we call home.

A few paces to my right, Jeff held a squirming J.J. On his other side, Ellie smiled at Jeff with a look of pure love, and it saddened me to think I was stupid enough to not find her in Elizebeth City before she found Jeff.

Dad looked around the crowd, eventually stopping at me. "Love can be a fleeting thing. We do our best to hold onto it and we lose it anyway. My father said when that happens, it's best to let it go."

Grandpa must've given Dad that advice when Mom left us so long ago, and now Dad was sharing it with me concerning all my lost loves. Yes, Ellie, Alma, and Mindy were dreams gone out with the tide, but I regretted Alma the most. I had no doubt of how happy we could've been together, raising Talia and any other kids we would've had.

Dad ended the service with the Lord's Prayer, Grandpa's favorite, and again thanked everyone for coming. People started leaving for the church fellowship hall, where a meal was waiting. With Talia's small hand in mine, I joined Dad at the head of the grave. Grandpa's oak coffin waited to be lowered. We moved to the shade of one of the many live oak trees to let the funeral home workers do their job. Helen came with us. Ellie told Jeff to go ahead and eat, that she would be along soon. Talia looked up at me. "Can I go, Daddy? I'm hungry." I sent her to catch up with Jeff, knowing he'd help her with her food like the great dad he was.

Sensing a reason for Ellie to stay, I asked her if anything was wrong.

"You didn't see her, did you?" Ellie's tone was critical.

"See who?" I asked.

"Mindy," Helen said, her tone as critical as Ellie's.

"I'm glad she came," Dad said. "She didn't have to do that."

"Did you see her?" Helen asked.

"I was busy," Dad said, doing a good job at keeping any sarcasm from his voice.

Ellie twisted her lips into a frown. "I'm glad you didn't see her, Seth. She was with some guy. Word has it that they're engaged, and she can't wait to start a family."

I glared at Ellie. "Did I hear you right? After she broke up with me because of Alma, now she wants a family?"

"Be glad you didn't marry her," Dad said. "You couldn't have counted on a thing she said."

I said nothing. All this time I'd blamed Mindy not wanting

kids for our breakup. It was either that or she never cared for me to start with. If that were true, maybe the real reason we broke up was that something was wrong with me. Maybe I really was a bum. Maybe, despite my new job of taking tourists to see the wild Spanish horses soon, a bum was all I'd ever be. If not for Talia, that's exactly how I'd feel, like a doggone bum who was good for nothing but fishing.

"Enough of talking about Mindy," Ellie said to no one in particular. "Would you believe Martha met someone at the casino and is head over heels in love already? She's already talking about starting a family."

I fought back a string of curses. After Martha practically threw herself at me that night, wasn't I good enough to marry? Was I scum? Did I smell like fish? Was I ugly? I had all my hair. I had all my teeth. I wasn't stupid. Since all of that was true, why were women running away from me like I had the freaking plague or something?

Dad said we should go eat. He, Helen, and Ellie left, and I followed along behind them like a whipped dog. I'd just give up on love and concentrate on raising my daughter. Nothing was more important than that, although earning a good living with my new job so she could go to college was a close second.

There isn't much more to say about the meal. The best part was Mindy and her boyfriend didn't attend it. Thank goodness for that. After aborting my baby and kicking me aside because of Talia, I wouldn't have been able to stomach her.

Possibly noticing my mood, Ellie didn't mention Martha again. On our trip to the dessert table, she said she was sorry for mentioning her after I heard about Mindy. I said I was okay, but Ellie wasn't having it. "I can tell it bothers you, Seth Callahan. We've known each other since we were kids, remember?"

I placed a slice of pecan pie on a saucer. "I guess I'm not meant to fall in love again. Alma might've been the only girl for me." I took a plastic fork from a box. "Maybe I should just give up and be done with it."

Ellie elbowed me. "Hush all that mess. You might be trying too hard. Just go out on dates without thinking of them as someone you might marry. You do deserve some fun as hard as you work." She spooned banana pudding into a saucer. "I'm sure some of the ladies on your horse tours would like to go out for a little fun while they're in the area."

"Not too much fun," I said, remembering Martha's attitude about the sexual revolution, made possible for her by those birth control pills she'd lied to get.

Ellie returned to Jeff and J.J. I returned to Talia, sitting beside her across from them. Dad was off speaking to some of the other folks.

Ellie might have a point about having fun. Unfortunately for me, I believed Talia needed a mom in her life, so it was hard to not consider that if I went out with anyone.

With that thought still in mind on a Saturday morning two weeks later, on Labor Day weekend, I drove to Corolla to meet my first group of horse seeking tourists. Dad, thinking it would be good for marketing, had bought me a cowboy hat. I didn't like the thing, but he, as a partner in our business, demanded I wear it. He'd also decided that I should meet my customers near the red brick tower of the Currituck Lighthouse. I couldn't argue that, as it would be easy for customers to spot.

When I parked nearby, men, women, and children started climbing from their vehicles and gathering in front of the Suburban. Most wore sunglasses. Most carried cameras. Two men and one woman carried binoculars. Everyone studied me expectantly.

"See there," a boy of about ten said to a girl of about eight. "I told you he's a cowboy." Beside them, their dad I assumed, raised his hand. "Do we get to ride the horses?"

"I hope so," a woman to his left said. "I've always wanted to ride a horse."

Some of the other customers shook their heads, and I didn't

blame them. My ad clearly stated the horses were wild. I removed my hat and pressed it to my chest. "Thank you all for coming. As far as riding the horses, they're wild and dangerous. For your safety and theirs, we're here to look and not touch, all right?"

"What a gyp," the boy said.

Let's go to the beach," his sister said.

"Let's go shopping," the man's wife said.

"I'd rather go fishing," he said.

I tried not to frown as those four customers climbed into their car and left, taking my fee with them.

"Don't worry about them," a middle-aged platinum blonde with a clipped northern accent said. "They're just idiots who can't read a simple ad." She raised scarlet fingernails to her sunglasses and inserted them into her hair. "My, my, aren't you quite the cowboy?" Her blue eyes sparkled with interest.

I asked everyone to board the Suburban, adding how I'd take the fee while they did.

The blonde went to the end of the short line and asked if she could sit beside me. Although I'd heard of older women flirting with younger guys, I'd never experienced it. It made me feel kind of good about myself. Maybe there was hope for me after all.

The tour went well. The woman turned out to be nice, saying she needed to bring her kids next time. Her smile distracted me. Between that and being careful to not get stuck in patches of soft sand, I couldn't tell my customers much about the horses or answer many of their questions. At the end of the tour, most thanked me, while a few said they would've enjoyed it better if I could've told them more.

Without any flirting, the five remaining tours went the same. Two twenty-somethings did look me up and down like they wanted me for supper, but I let it go. Being grateful for the money I'd made, plus a few nice tips, tended to help me ignore that stuff.

Being a minister, the one thing Dad didn't like about my new business was my missing church. I told him that was the price of success, but I could go when things wound down in the winter. It helped when I showed him the cash from that Sunday. Scratching his head, he eyed the cash and then me. "If you keep making that kind of money, Talia can go to medical school. It'll be nice to have a doctor in the family."

Wondering if my success had anything to do with the cowboy hat, I bought a pair of western boots and a wide belt with a fancy buckle. Two weeks later, when the next kid asked if I was a cowboy, I hooked my thumbs in my blue jeans pockets and tilted my head to one side. "Why, little partner, I shore am a cowboy. Whatcha think about that?"

The kid, a boy of about ten who reminded me of the main character in the Dennis the Menace cartoon, with a cowlick and a cap gun in a holster hanging from his belt, scowled. "You ain't no cowboy. It's *pardner,* not partner."

The joys of being an entrepreneur.

October business maintained a brisk rate, but it started dropping off in November. Some days with no customers sent me fishing. Some days I had two. Some days I had one. On the weekend after Thanksgiving, Saturday was packed and Sunday wasn't, likely from customers heading home in time to start work on Monday.

After the middle-aged woman and the two younger ones eyeing me like they wanted me for supper, I did work up the nerve to ask a few ladies out. Being the honest cowboy I am, I made sure to tell them I was the proud dad of a four-year old daughter.

The responses went something like this.

"What's your wife think of you asking other women out?"

"I don't mind if your wife doesn't mind."

"You have got to be kidding."

"Look, baby, a date's fine, but you can forget me being a mommy."

Then there was the brief but pithy, "You what?"

Needless to say, I gave up on that idea. The possibility of finding love on one of my tours was the same as Christmas coming in July. Like the cowlicked cap-gun kid would say, "Pardner, that ain't happening."

Speaking of Christmas, weekend tours between it and Thanksgiving dropped off the proverbial cliff. At least it gave me more time with Talia and more Sundays in church. Then, out of the blue, I got a letter from a customer who wanted a tour on the Saturday after New Years Day. The person even wanted to pay a hundred dollars instead of fifty. He or she didn't give a name, but I didn't care. I had no intention of turning down a paid tour for twice the money.

I pause my pecking on the laptop to check the time in the screen's right-hand corner. No wonder my stomach had been growling. Six o'clock had come and gone, and it was almost seven. I'd been happily writing away for over five hours without realizing it.

I get up from the chair, and my left knee pops. The right knee doesn't because it was replaced three years ago. My back aches. My arthritic fingers curl like fishhooks. How I could've typed all that time, I'll never know. At least that's something to be grateful for as my body deteriorates before my eyes.

Everything considered, so says my doctor, I'm in decent shape. When Talia comes, she worries over me like an old mother hen. "Take your meds, Dad. Walk every day, Dad. Use that watch I gave you for your last birthday that tells your heart rate, Dad. You've got to keep it high to get any benefit from exercise."

My daughter the doctor. It's a good thing she isn't local. I'd live forever, and who wants to do that? Not me, that's for sure.

At the sink, I rinse the dregs from my coffee mug. At the open refrigerator door, I consider supper. At a restaurant up the road, I enjoy a fried seafood platter, making sure to take my pills when I get home. So what if I wash them down with beer?

So what if I pour two fingers of Jack Daniels? So what if I sip it on the pier in my chair until the sun slides below the horizon?

I wonder what Liz is doing but choose not to bother her. I wonder what Jack is doing but choose not to bother him. I wonder what my kids and grandkids and great-grandkids are doing but choose not to bother them.

Inside again, I refill my glass and lie on the sofa. With the TV on, I find one of the Andy Griffith rerun channels. Yeah, I'm unapologetically nostalgic, what of it? That's what happens when the direction of a person's life is no longer known because the person you love isn't around to show you the way anymore.

More Jack Daniels. More Andy Griffith. More bad attitude. Yeah, I'm a curmudgeon who knows better and refuses to do better. What am I talking about? I'm doing better because I'm writing the story my wife insisted I write. She sure knew what she was doing when she demanded that.

I turn out the lights. In the bathroom, I brush and floss. In the bedroom, I undress, set the alarm clock for eight, and pull the covers up to my chin. Like myself, our story is winding down, so I'll get up bright and early like the good boy my wife and Talia want me to be and write again.

Chapter 22

I wake at six, not because I want to get up and write, but because I almost wet the durn bed. Don't laugh. Age gets us all in the end.

Dressed and in the kitchen, where my smart phone is on the table by the laptop, I find a text from Sarah, my daughter who came along after Talia. She asks how I'm doing, ending with, "I love you, Daddy."

Like her mother, she's a bit more emotional than Talia, so we haven't told her about me writing this story. I don't mean emotional in a bad way. She just tends to experience emotions stronger than my other kids. There's a reason for that, and we've talked about it. I'll get to it eventually. Right now I want to keep my train of thought concerning this chapter. A lot is going to happen, and I want everything I write to be as accurate as possible.

As I wrote earlier, a customer wanted to see the horses the Saturday after New Years Day. Ellie had some things to do, so Dad came over to stay with Talia. Of course I left them watching Bugs Bunny outwitting Elmer Fudd, the Roadrunner outwitting Wile E. Coyote, and Foghorn Leghorn outwitting his hound dog counterpart. I chuckled at those cartoon characters from the kitchen before I left, making a scrambled egg and bacon sandwich to eat on the road. Evidenced by the wind whipping the sound into whitecaps and Dad's heavy coat when he came in, the day was typical for January on the Outer Banks, cold and raw and made bearable by the Thermos of coffee I took to the Suburban.

If there's a time of the year you could describe the area as abandoned, midwinter is it. That was much more obvious in 1968 than in 2024. Except for a few hardcore fisherman pulling into pier parking lots, a family out to get groceries, or a waterfowl hunter trailering a flat-bottomed skiff in from an early hunt, few vehicles were on the road on a frigid Saturday morning. Given that, there wasn't much to see on my drive to Corolla.

When I neared the town of Duck, as I chewed the last bite of my sandwich and washed it down with lukewarm coffee, a curious sight in my rear-view mirror caught my eye. What the heck was a taxi cab doing out here on a January morning? In fact, searching back through my memory, I didn't recall ever seeing a taxi out here in the summer, much less in the winter. Live and learn, I guess. Stranger still, the taxi followed me all the way to the red-brick tower of the Currituck Lighthouse and parked beside me.

In the back seat, a young guy with straight hair to the collar of his jean jacket handed money to the driver. Then he climbed out, the wind whipping the thin jacket around his narrow waist. Something seemed off, and I didn't figure it out until he hurried to the Suburban and opened the door. "You live on the Outer Banks," he said with a feminine, southern accent. "Why are you wearing that stupid cowboy hat?"

I liked her voice, a silky, sultry tone. "The hat's a marketing thing," I said, touching the brim. "You know, for the horses."

She climbed in and shut the door. "No. You mean it's a marketing things for customers like me."

The taxi left. Her breath clouded the passenger door window as she watched the yellow Dodge drive away before facing me again. "You're Seth, right? If you are, turn the heat up before I freeze to death. The heat in that stupid taxi didn't reach the back seat." I did as she asked. She took a crumpled wad of cash from one of her jeans pockets and offered it to me. "Fifty bucks, right?"

I was tempted to cock an eyebrow at her. She wasn't much shorter than me. Except for the brown roots in the part in the center of her head, her hair was blonde. The cut was sort of ragged, as if she'd done it herself. A few freckles splotched her straight nose. No lipstick colored her full lips above a well-defined chin, and no makeup added depth to her high cheekbones. Not to criticize her looks, but her best feature was her huge brown eyes, a shade lighter than Alma's eyes.

She took my hand from the steering wheel and slapped the cash into it. "Can we leave or not? I've got places to go and stuff to see and things to do."

I shoved the cash into my pocket, ignoring how she'd paid me fifty dollars instead of one hundred. "You know my name," I said. "Can I know yours?"

Her brown eyes narrowed. "Look, buster, I'm not here for a social call."

By "social call," I assumed she meant for a date. "Hey, just being neighborly. If you don't want to tell me your name, so be it."

"It's Roz," she huffed.

I backed the Suburban away from its view of the lighthouse and headed toward the main road. "Is Roz short for something?"

Her chin jutted out. "In case you haven't noticed, nothing on me is short."

I silently agreed. When she'd unfolded herself from the taxi, I'd noticed she was all arms and legs. "Is your family on vacation in the middle of winter? It's usually nothing out here but fishermen then."

"It's just me, Mr. Nosy."

I ignored her sarcasm. "That taxi left. How're you getting back to wherever you came from?"

She sniffed. "I smell bacon and coffee. I didn't know you fed your customers." She looked toward the back seats. "Where's it at?"

Her eyes darted back and forth like a hungry shark's. If she'd gotten so thin from not eating, no wonder she was asking about food. I nodded toward the empty Thermos beside me. "Sorry about that. What you smell is what's left of my breakfast."

She snatched the Thermos up and took the top off, poked her freckled nose inside and sniffed loudly. "Oh, what I wouldn't give for a cup of coffee." She raised the Thermos over her open mouth until a single drop dotted her tongue.

I felt sorry for her, so I suggested a hole-in-the wall diner that had a fine breakfast menu. Instead of taking me up on my offer, she capped the Thermos, set it back beside me, and faced the passenger door window. The way her money had been crumpled gave me an idea. "You know," I said, hoping she was listening, "that sandwich I had wasn't enough. If you're not in a hurry to see the horses, I could use something else."

She didn't face me. "Whatever."

The diner was just up ahead to the left. "Is that a yes?"

"Whatever."

I flipped my signal and turned in. After parking beside a rusted 4x4 that had seen many a mile on the beach, I opened my door. "Aren't you coming? They've got great coffee."

She pulled a few crumpled bills from her pocket, counted them while blinking furiously, and joined me inside.

I led her to a corner table beside a window overlooking the sound. When a waitress came, I ordered pancakes, country ham, bacon, hash brown potatoes, grits, and scrambled eggs. Ignoring the menu, Roz ordered black coffee. The waitress said the food would be right up and left. Roz's eyes cut toward me. "You're gonna eat all that?"

"I'll save some for lunch." I nodded toward the window. "The wind sure is up today."

Roz's nostrils flared. Unless I was mistaken, the combined smells of the strongest aromas coming from the kitchen—coffee, bacon, and salt-cured country ham—were making her mouth water, and when she licked her lips at all the plates my breakfast came in, I was sure of it.

The waitress left and returned with our coffee. "Sorry I didn't bring it before. I was making a fresh pot. Sugar and cream?"

"Please," I said, and she hurried away.

Roz sipped her coffee. "My Dad's coffee is better." She sipped again, the steam rising against her cheeks. "Not bad, though."

As I'd hoped, the eggs were in the plate with the bacon and ham; the pancakes were in their own plate; and the hash browns and grits were in their own bowls. I put half of everything in the pancake plate and shoved it toward Roz. "Have some of that if you want. I won't need any lunch after I eat all this stuff."

Sipping coffee, Roz lowered the cup. "I'm no charity case, buster."

I crunched bacon, poured syrup over the melting butter on the pancakes, and cut a bite of ham. "Suit yourself. The waitress will just throw it out."

When the waitress returned with cream and sugar, she asked about the food I'd set aside. Before I could tell her to throw it out, Roz pulled it over. "We're sharing. Is that all right?"

"Sure, hon, we don't charge for that here. Y'all enjoy."

I nudged the syrup toward Roz. "Since you're not a charity case, you can pay half the bill."

Roz forked a triangle of pancake and shoved it in her mouth. Done with that bite, she cut a piece of ham. "In your dreams, buster."

"The name is Seth, remember?"

She chewed and swallowed the ham. "Is there a Mrs. Seth,

Seth? I don't see a wedding ring."

"Is that a come on?"

"You're not my type."

She wasn't my type either, but I didn't say so. I spooned grits, followed with more coffee, and ended with more pancake. "As you saw on my Suburban, I'm from Kitty Hawk."

Roz licked syrup from her lips. "And that's my opening to tell you where I'm from, right?"

"Only if you want to," I said, hoping she would. "You can't be more than seventeen. It's kind of odd for someone that young to take a taxi all the way to Corolla in the middle of the winter."

"Because my parents would worry."

"Exactly."

"You need glasses. I'm twenty, in my second year of college at the University of Tex—"

She stopped in the middle of what could only be "Texas," and I offered an easy smile. "If you're from Texas, you're a long way from home."

"Whatever."

"What're you studying in college?" I asked, adding sugar and cream to my coffee. "I went straight to work after high school. I never could figure out what I wanted to do."

Roz crunched bacon. "I'm going to be a large animal veterinarian."

"And you came all the way here from Texas to see horses," I said, knowing I sounded critical. "Aren't there enough horses in Texas to see?" I added more syrup to my pancakes.

"Not horses like the ones in Corolla." She jabbed her fork at me. "Being an expert on them, I thought you knew that."

I knew a fair amount about the horses, but I doubted if I knew everything. Curious about them, I asked Roz, who was eating scrambled eggs like they were her favorite food in the whole world, how our horses were different from other horses.

"Really?" she asked, pausing the rise and fall of her fork.

"You're a tour operator, and you don't even know that?"

Sipping coffee, I lowered the cup. "Enlighten me, Roz. Then I'll know what I might not know."

She set her fork down. "For starters, they're not as big. Anyone can see that. They're also shorter from head to tail and only weigh between 600 and 800 pounds."

"Anyone can see that too," I said. "What else?"

Roz's chin dropped. "Isn't that enough?"

"Not to me," I said, wondering what else she knew about them. "I think the most interesting part is their origin," I continued. "They either came here from a shipwreck or a failed Spanish colonization attempt. You have to admit, that's pretty cool." I forked another piece of ham. "Being from Texas, how do you know so much about our horses?"

"One of my professors mentioned them."

"And they're so interesting that you traveled all the way from Texas in a taxi to see them?"

"I traveled by bus. Then I took that taxi from Elizabeth City."

I downed the ham. "Still, it's a weird thing to do." I waved a hand over the table. "Are you done? We can head out to the beach if you are."

Refilling coffee cups, the waitress came over. "I'll get y'all a to-go box. Be right back."

Roz dumped my leftover food onto her plate, and I wondered if she hoped it would last all the way back to Texas. That and how she'd counted her cash created a stream of questions without answers.

The waitress returned. I paid her while Roz filled the to-go box. She looked up with a nice smile. "Sorry for being such a pain. I appreciate the food."

Although Roz was smiling at me, the waitress must've thought it was for her. "You're not a pain, darlin'. Why say that?"

Roz tipped her head toward me. "I meant Seth."

The waitress took us in. "Y'all having a lover's spat? You're too cute a couple for that."

Roz's lips tightened until she burst out laughing. "Me and him? You've got to be kidding."

I almost strangled on my last swallow of coffee. The waitress gave me a napkin. "Wipe you're chin and show this sweet young thing a nice time on the beach. I heard y'all talking about it." She faced Roz. "He's got a hot bod. Send him back to me if you kick him to the curb."

As the waitress left, Roz stood with the to-go box. "You heard the lady, Mr. Hot Bod. Show this sweet young thing a good time on the beach."

In the Suburban again, I wondered how Roz was here when college was in session. Along with why she'd come all the way from Texas, plus how she seemed almost starved to death from her lack of cash, plus how she might not be able to afford another taxi to Elizabeth City and the bus fare back to Texas, none of it made any sense.

We continued along Highway 12. Some days you'd see horses in town, some days not. I hoped they were on the beach. Seeing them there, sometimes playing in the surf, sometimes watching the waves roll in, sometimes trotting along the dunes, gave customers the biggest thrills.

At the turn going onto the beach, I stopped the Suburban to lock the front hubs into four-wheel-drive. Before I got back inside, the wind blowing off the Atlantic sent my cowboy hat into the highway. Through the open driver's side door, I could clearly hear Roz's laughter as I chased my hat across the pavement. Thankfully, it hung on a low live oak limb. Clutching it in my hands, I hurried back to the Suburban and slammed the door.

Now giggling, Roz grinned at me. "That wind blew your hair all over, cowboy." She leaned close to finger my hair behind my ears. "There you go. Now you can put that hat back on."

I did so, eyeing the roaring surf. "I doubt if the horses will be out today. What do you think about tomorrow?"

Roz looked at the waves. The crests, each white with foam, ducked their chins like old bearded fishermen until they crashed onto the beach. "It's so wild and free here. I like Texas, but this is amazing."

Her voice, soft and low, appealed to me. Alma had sounded like this, and the memories rushed in, almost drowning me as if I were in the undertow of those waves curling and crashing to the beach. I touched Roz's slender fingers on the seat beside her. "If you'd rather go tomorrow, I'll give you half your money back." I didn't say the rest. *And then you'll have money for food on your way back to Texas.*

She pressed her forehead against the passenger door window. "That's nice, but ..."

I patted her hand. "But you don't have a place to stay, and can't afford a hotel, right?"

She shook her head. Her chest rose and fell with three huge breaths. "You're so nice," she said, not facing me. "I've made a mess of my life, and I don't know what to do about it."

"Welcome to my world," I said, meaning it. "I've had my ups and downs. Still, as you Texans say, I get back in the saddle."

Roz was still facing the ocean. I gave her arm a little tug. "Whatever it is, I'm sure you can handle it."

She finally faced me. "I wish they made guys like you in Texas."

That statement meant she was having guy problems. I patted her hand again. "Since you have such a high opinion of me, I know where you can get a room for the night, and it won't cost you a dime."

Those brown eyes narrowed. "Yeah, right. Breakfast in bed comes with it too, I bet. You men are all alike."

I showed her my palms. "Look, I really am a nice guy. I'm just offering you a room. If you don't want it, fine."

"Where is it?"

"Like the logo on my Suburban says, in Kitty Hawk."

"Does the door lock?"

"Absolutely. If that's not enough, you can sleep with a butcher knife under your pillow."

Roz's chin dropped again. "I don't know."

Although she was thinking about it, I decided to add a little more information. "My place has a great view of the sound. The sunsets from the deck and the dock are amazing. If that and the butcher knife isn't enough, you can put my shotgun under your pillow. I use it for ducks and geese, but it'll work on Kitty Hawk cowboys too."

My humor made her share the hint of a smile. "Are you a good cook? You said you aren't married."

"My daugh—" I didn't finish my sentence about Talia because I wasn't sure I could trust Roz around her. Sure, she seemed nice enough, but with all the drugs and alcohol infesting college campuses these days, a dad couldn't be too sure.

Roz studied me. "What were you going to say?"

"I was going to say my dog likes my cooking, but he died a while back. I used to fish for a living, so I know seafood. That means I'm a good cook." I paused, knowing I needed to ask Ellie if Talia could stay with her tonight. Tomorrow, with any luck, I'd take Roz to see the horses. If she were ready to head back to Texas and needed money for the trip, I'd offer it. Then my life could get back to normal.

Chapter 23

As I type those last lines at the kitchen table, someone bangs on the sliding glass doors, and that someone is Jack. "Hey, Seth," his muffled voice says. "Let's go to Jennette's and drown some bait." Wearing a floppy hat, a white T-shirt, and green shorts, he raises a tackle box. "I got a new cooler for beer."

I get up and unlock the doors. He comes in and sets the tackle box on the table. "See?" he asks, opening it. "It's made to look like a tackle box, but it's really a cooler. See how much ice it holds?"

As anyone who knows the Jennette's Pier of 2024 knows, alcohol isn't permitted there. I dig down in the ice, pull out a bottle of water, and show it to Jack. "Does this look like beer?"

"Hey, I can always pretend," he says, taking the water from me. "How about it? It's nice out, and you need a break from all that writing."

I assume he got that from Liz. Opposite the sliding glass doors, sunshine glints off the rippled water of the sound. I shut the laptop and slap a ball cap on my head. "Why not? Let me grab my tackle. I'll meet you at your pickup."

At the pier, we pay our fees and walk across the gray boards. Jack pulls a folding wagon with our stuff in it. On the beach to the left and right, families enjoy the water and sand. Yes, despite my age, a few skimpy bikinis catch my eye. The first time I saw my wife in a bikini, I was tempted to howl at the moon. Well, the moon wasn't out in the afternoon, but you know what I mean.

We set up at the second porch, where two overhangs offer shade on both sides of the pier. With our lines in the water, we watch the rod tips for the telltale twitch of a fish biting. We sip water and crunch granola bars Jack brought. Louise likes to make sure he gets his fiber.

Such a simple thing, fiber. Sometimes it's funny, sometimes it's not. Sometimes, like now, despite my friend's generosity and our view of the gorgeous aquamarine swells rolling toward the beach, I'd give anything if my wife were here to make sure I get mine.

Wait a minute. I thought it was February, when Liz and me went out for lunch. Jack wouldn't take me fishing in February. It isn't warm in February. Shapely young ladies don't wear bikinis in February. Buff guys don't wear Speedos and surf in February. I check my digital watch. June? How did I lose three whole months?

Jack eyes me. "You all right, Seth? You got a weird look on that ugly mug of yours."

Jack wants Hollywood to remake *Grumpy Old Men* and *Grumpier Old Men*. Instead of setting those movies in Minnesota, he wants them set on the Outer Banks. His idea has merit, except for the part where he plays Walter Matthau and I play John Lemmon. In my opinion, he's more like Burgess Meredith. I'm not a bad John Lemmon, though, especially since my hair has gone white.

I tell Jack I'm just concentrating on seeing if my rod tip twitches or not. He nods and returns to doing the same thing.

The thought of losing three months frustrates me. Then again, with all the writing I've been doing, maybe that time slipped by like the time Roz stayed with me slipped by. At my age, anything's possible.

When I was young, I never thought about growing old. Even when Grandpa and Dad died, I didn't give it any thought. Sure, I gave love plenty of thought, and I'm glad I did. Some folks will disagree, but to me, life without love sort of drags on, day after day. Now I'm alone except for distant family and nearby friends, and I have to keep telling myself that's enough to keep getting up in the morning.

If you're one of my grandkids reading this, all the material stuff in the world isn't worth the love of a great spouse. If you don't believe me, try seeing how warm a smart phone keeps you in bed at night and let me know how that turns out. The same goes for fancy clothes and floofy hairdos and expensive vehicles. Like my old Suburban, all that stuff will be in the junkyard one day, not worth the time it took to think it was so great. I know, I know, that stuff will impress your friends. Well, let an old man whose greatest treasure was the love of a good woman tell you something — impressing your friends doesn't make them friends. The ones who stand by you through thick and thin, like my dad and grandpa and wife did, are what makes them your friends.

Yep, Talia says I still have anger issues because of Mom leaving Dad and me. I guess I do, but only when I remember how bad it made us feel. Sure, she had her reasons. Whatever they were, though, considering how she did it, they weren't good enough. I'll put it this way — with how she left without so much as a goodbye to her only son, if she could've had an abortion, would she have done that to me?

If she had, and if Dad had found out, I know it would've broken his heart like Mindy broke mine. Yep, when I think about what Mindy did to my son or daughter, I've got anger issues about that too.

I press a fingertip to my wrist. My pulse says my heart is about to beat out of my chest. I press a palm to my chest. Its rapid rise and fall says my lungs are about to explode into a trillion fragments of pink cells.

Yes, I've got a right to feel this way. When I would wake from one of my rare nightmares about it, my wife never failed to calm me down. Lord in Heaven, how I pray she were with me to do that now.

June. Imagine that. Well, at least I've written all that time. At almost 80,000 words, I did pretty darned good.

Jack and I check our hooks. Each is bare. We bait up, cast them out, and return to our bench.

The afternoon passes slowly. On the beach, kids squeal. Above us, laughing gulls laugh. Behind us, tourists and folks going fishing pass by, evidenced by their shoes clomping on the boards.

Jack's rod tip twitches. He reels in an empty hook. After glaring at it, he pretends he's Walter Matthau. "My old nag and one of her girlfriends went shopping up in Corolla and Duck. Let's go to my place and get drunk. I need to break the seal on a bottle of Crown Royal."

I wave Jack's idea off. "No thanks. I need to finish the chapter I'm working on."

"Is it helping?"

"I think so," I lie. "I came out here with you, didn't I?"

Jack hooks the hook to his rod and leans it against the pier railing. "You really loved her, didn't you?"

"More than life itself, Jack. More than life itself."

Jack's mouth twitches. That happens when he's wondering something. "You wouldn't do anything stupid to be with her, would you?"

I pat my pal's shoulder. "And leave you without a fishing buddy?"

His mouth stops twitching. "My thoughts exactly. Let me get you home so you can finish that chapter."

When I get out of Jack's pickup, I thank him for Jennette's. After storing my tackle, I climb up the steps to the deck and go inside. A trip to the bathroom rids me of the water. I come back to the laptop. Instead of writing inside, I take it to the pier and settle down in the rocking chair beside my wife's rocking chair. Like when I started this story, I nudge her chair. It rocks a few times and stops. I take that as a signal to get my rear in gear, so I press my fingertips to the keys.

On the way home from the diner, Roz didn't say much. She did ask again if I was married, and I said again that I wasn't. She did ask why that was when I was young and kind of, sort of, maybe a little bit, handsome. Her freckles and cheek bones weren't bad. She was also tanned, and I liked that. Maybe she lived on a farm with horses, seeing as how she liked them so much. I liked her full lips because they reminded me of Alma's lips. All in all, concerning looks, I suppose my opinion of hers matched her opinion of mine.

When a new person drops into your life, especially one you're kind of, sort of, maybe a little bit, attracted to, you should be careful. Yeah, because of my past with women, I knew I was vulnerable. This meant I'd have to make sure Roz didn't harpoon me with some sob story about why she'd come all the way here from Texas, especially when it might have something to do with a guy. Who wants to get involved in a mess like that? Not yours truly, not by a long shot.

At my place, Roz asked for the bathroom. I started to call Ellie about Talia staying overnight but didn't because Roz might hear me. Then, like in the TV show *I Love Lucy*, I might have some "'splainin'" to do about having a daughter without a wife. Yeah, I'm nostalgic about 1960's TV, but most folks my age are.

Breakfast at the diner and the drive back had taken close to two hours. I'd met Roz at nine, so it was now eleven. When she came from the bathroom, she opened the to-go box she'd left on the kitchen table and started picking at her food. "You want some of this?" she asked while chewing ham.

"I'm good," I said, feeling the wheels of an idea turning in my head. "If we're having seafood tonight, I'll buy some while you eat. What do you like? I like broiled flounder, shrimp, and scallops, with fries and slaw on the side."

She stopped eating to look at me like I'd lost my mind.

"Broiled? Why not live a little and have fried?"

"Why not?" I said, taking my keys from my pocket. I pointed at the sofa and TV. "Make yourself at home. I'm heading to the seafood market."

I hurried to the Suburban and drove to Ellie's. Jeff opened the door. "Hey, Seth. Did your one customer enjoy the horses?" Ellie, J.J., and Talia were working on coloring books at the kitchen table. Jeff returned to a kitchen counter, where he was making peanut butter and jelly sandwiches, presumably for lunch.

I sat across from Ellie. How to handle this without making her curious? I touched Ellie's hand. "Would you mind if Talia stayed overnight? I've kinda got a date."

Ellie stopped coloring. "'Kinda?' You don't know if you have a date or not?"

"Fine with me," Jeff said.

"Me too, Daddy," Talia said, taking a crayon from a box.

As I got up from the table, Ellie got up and gave J.J. to Jeff. "Let me run over and pack some of Talia's clothes. You men would forget your noses if they weren't in the middle of your faces."

The wheels of an idea turned in my head again. "I'll run you over in the Suburban so you don't have to walk. Let's go."

Safely within the privacy of the Suburban, I faced Ellie. "Look, this isn't what it sounds like, but I'm going to have someone stay over tonight, and it's a woman."

"What woman, Seth? I didn't know you were seeing anyone, let alone sleeping with them."

"She's my customer. She came all the way from Texas to see the horses, but the weather was too rough. You saw how windy it was this morning."

"Why can't she stay in a hotel?"

"She doesn't have the money."

"Why can't she stay in her car?"

"She came on a bus to Elizabeth City and took a taxi to

Corolla." I took a breath. "I'll take her to see the horses in the morning and that'll be that."

Ellie blinked once, blinked once more, and blinked again. "If she doesn't have enough money for a hotel room, how'll she get back to Texas?"

I was expecting this. "I'll give her the money, that's how. I don't know her well enough to let her be around Talia tonight, okay? It's just one night."

"Are you attracted to her?"

Ellie knew my record with women, so I was expecting this too. "She's tall and skinny and bony. You know, like you when you tried to seduce me that time."

"Don't remind me," Ellie said. "I was also young and dumb." She sighed. "We'll keep Talia, but you better be telling the truth about this woman. The last thing you need is another bad relationship."

I agreed and drove back home. After parking, I slapped my hand over my eyes. "Look, Ellie, I don't want her to know I've got a daughter. I'm supposed to be getting seafood for supper. That was my excuse for going out so I could ask you if Talia could stay overnight."

Ellie crossed her arms. "Take me with you. When we get back, you can pack Talia a bag and drop me off at home."

Ellie's suggestion was great, but not great enough. "I can't keep going in and out. She'll get suspicious."

"That's what happens when you can't keep your lies straight, Seth Callahan. Take me with you. When we come back, say you're taking the trash out and give me Talia's bag."

"Won't Jeff get worried when you're gone so long?"

"Not one bit. I'll tell him everything when we're alone." Ellie shook her head. "Unlike you and this so-called customer of yours, my husband and I don't keep secrets."

Long story short, Ellie's plan worked. When I got back with the seafood, Roz was asleep on the sofa. I packed Talia's bag and took it to Ellie, who said she'd walk back home so I could get back inside and tend to my so-called customer. Of course, each word dripped with sarcasm, and I understood. Even I knew my behavior over this woman was completely out of character, and I had no idea why.

At the sink, I rinsed the shrimp, shelled and deveined them, then rinsed them again before putting them in the fridge. The flounder was already filleted, and the scallops had been removed from the shells. In the fridge they went. I took oil and cornmeal for frying from a cabinet. After all that, I cut french fries with the peeling on for that perfect earthy flavor, rinsed them and put them in a bowl with water to keep them from turning dark. Into the fridge they went.

About to grate a cabbage, I went to the living room to ask Roz what kind of dressing Texans liked on their slaw. Some folks like it more vinegary than sweet, so you never know.

On the sofa, Roz lay on her side, curled in a ball as if she were cold. Her jacket lay across her middle. I went to my room for a blanket and returned to cover her from chin to toe. Sitting on the coffee table, I wondered about this stranger who had fallen into my life out of nowhere.

She wore a baggy, gray sweatshirt, which practically swallowed her thin frame past her waist. Just below her left ear, a small tattoo of horseshoe reflected her love of horses on her slender neck. Several strands of oily, blonde hair hung over her eyes. One sniff told me she'd come all the way from Texas without a shower. Who was she? What happened in Texas to make her come all the way here without money to get back? Who were her parents? Why was some guy giving her grief? Most college kids, I thought, would have a car, so why didn't she? Done with my questions, I decided on my recipe for slaw, not too sweet, not too vinegary, and stored it in the fridge until whenever Roz woke.

While I waited, I straightened Talia's room and closed the door again, glad Roz hadn't been able to look inside. When I went back to the kitchen, Roz was standing by the sliding glass doors. She turned at my footfalls. "You were right. This is a great view." As I joined her, she faced the sound again. "I'd love to wake up to this every morning." She looked at me. "Like you said, I bet the sunsets are amazing."

"I like sunsets from the pier," I said, gesturing toward it. "You get to hear the waves lapping against the pilings and in the marsh."

Roz paused. Several seconds passed. "Does your daughter like them? I saw her pink toothbrush and your wife's hairbrush in the bathroom. I'd leave if you didn't owe me a horse tour. Where's your wife and daughter? Oh, and I don't like being lied to."

Yeah, I'd forgotten about Talia's pink toothbrush. Score one for Roz. I told her it was a long story about my daughter, adding how her mom passed away a few years after Talia was born. I didn't see any need to mention that I wasn't married to Alma. I also added how I didn't know my guest very well, so Talia was staying with her sitter overnight.

"A concerned dad, I like that," Roz said. "Sorry about the lying thing. You say her name is Talia? That's pretty."

I liked how Roz recognized the value of a concerned dad. Maybe she had a concerned dad back in Texas, worried about her like I'd be if I were him.

Still looking outside, Roz faced me. "I could use a shower before supper. Do you mind?"

"Not at all. If you don't want to put your dirty clothes back on, you can wear something of mine while I wash and dry yours."

"Not a bad idea, thanks. Where do you keep your linens?"

I turned Roz toward the hall and pointed. "The bathroom's down the hall. Give me your clothes after you undress. I'll bring the linens and a pair of jeans and a shirt." I grinned to let her know I was joking. "I doubt if you want to wear a pair of my underwear."

Roz returned the grin. "Not bad. The Kitty Hawk Cowboy's

a good dad with a sense of humor. What other secrets are you hiding?"

"Nothing, except how great a seafood cook I am." I gave her a little push in the small of her back toward the hall. "Go ahead. I'll be there in a minute."

Roz did as I asked. Since she seemed to like sweatshirts, I went to my room for one of mine, a pair of jeans, and a pair of socks. At the linen closet across from the bathroom, I added a towel and a washcloth to my load and tapped on the bathroom door. She opened it a crack. Her slender hand shoved her clothes at me. "So, you're a gentleman too. Most guys would've barged in to see me naked."

I take her clothes and pile my load onto her long arm, which extends into the hallway like a gull's wing. Just how many guys have tried to see her naked? Well, she's in college, so she probably dates. That doesn't mean she sleeps around. As hard a time as she gave me when we met, I doubt it.

Writing this, I realize I've let my past invade my present. I shouldn't be surprised. After everything that happened from this point forward, it makes sense.

Roz closed the door. "I'll need a belt. In case you haven't noticed, you're a lot bigger than me."

I get one from my room and hang it on the door knob. The shower is running. I stop typing. There I go again, slipping into the present.

Let's try this again.

I *got* one from my room and *hung* it on the doorknob. The shower *was* running. "The belt's on the doorknob," I said loudly.

"Thanks!"

Feeling strangely unneeded, I left for the kitchen and made coffee. Feeling cool, not strangely because it was January, I turned the thermostat up. At the picture window behind the sofa, from the warm air blowing from the vent in the floor, the curtain fluttered.

Yeah, I was bored. Since September, Saturdays were for horse tours. If I had no tours, Saturdays were for Talia. Now, with a stranger in my own home and no tours and no Talia, I didn't know what to do with myself. I'd bought groceries Thursday. I'd washed clothes and vacuumed Friday. I'd totaled my horse tour receipts for my 1967 tax year Wednesday, and found I had quite the income for the last four months. I was glad. It would easily hold Talia and me until the season ramped up in May.

Down the hall, the bathroom door clicked open. Sock feet thudded toward me. Roz stopped at the kitchen table, hair shiny and damp. She pointed at her clothes on the table. "Where's your washer and dryer?"

As loose as my clothes fit her, she looked like someone about to die from starvation. Those huge, brown eyes were bright, though, the question about the washer and dryer still in them. "Sorry about that," I said, picking her clothes up. "I'll wash them now."

She took them from me. "Let's pretend we're married. "Now, dear, as we well know, it's your sweetie's job to do the laundry."

"Right," I said sarcastically. "And each and every feminist in America is cringing."

"I don't mind traditional marriage roles," Roz said. "It's the fact that some couples refuse to compromise on them that's a problem. There's nothing wrong with men doing women things and women doing men things. It's about whatever works for that couple." She raised the pile of clothes in her arms. "Are you gonna tell me where the washer is, or do I use the kitchen sink?"

I enjoyed Roz's sense of humor, a bit dry like my own. "On the left, down the hall past the bathroom."

"Great. I'll have some of that coffee I smell when I come back."

I poured her a cup and sat it by mine on the table.

Something about them said we were a couple. Something about that told me I was an idiot. Sure, I was curious about her, but she'd be gone after her tour tomorrow, and that would be that.

The washer cranked up. Roz's sock feet thumped in the hall and to my side. She sat and sipped coffee. "I love coffee. I also love the view through your sliding glass doors. How long have you lived here?"

I sat beside her. "All of my life. My dad moved to Manteo to minister the Methodist church there. My grandpa died last year, so Dad's staying in his house."

"A minister, huh? What's your mom do?"

I did not like the turn of this conversation. "She's not in the picture."

Roz sipped more coffee. "That's all I get? Did she die? Did they divorce? I'm sure she didn't just vanish into thin air."

Anger heated my cheeks. "Why not? After all, you didn't tell me much more than that about your boyfriend."

"That's personal," Roz said, frustration filling her voice.

"So's my mom," I said, equally frustrated.

"Huh, aren't we a pair?" Roz asked, eyeing me curiously. Skeletons in our closets out the wazoo." She sipped coffee again. "I'll tell you about one of my skeletons if you tell me about one of yours. My mom's a pain, and my dad died last summer. I met the wrong guy and let him talk me into doing stuff like dyeing my hair and getting a tattoo. Talk about stupid."

Not ready to let any of my skeletons out of their closet, I sipped coffee.

Roz cleared her throat. "Hey, it's your turn, cowboy."

Aware that she'd mentioned three skeletons instead of one, I mentioned only one. "My mom left my dad and me when I was only nine. We think her mom helped her. Dad was a great husband. She didn't like living here, or him being a fisherman. We haven't heard from her in almost twenty years. How's that for a freaking skeleton?"

Roz's full lips formed an O. "Whoa, that's one heck of a skeleton. By your red cheeks and the tone of your voice, she's a sore subject, right?"

"You have no idea."

"Sure, I do. My mom's a pain, remember? To her, the lawyer that she is, a career is everything. I'm an only child, if that gives you a hint. Dad wanted more kids but she didn't. After I was born, she actually started sleeping in another room, and it broke Dad's heart." Roz slipped her thin arm around my shoulders. "I'm sure it broke your dad's heart when your mom left, didn't it?"

The sincerity in her voice struck me as genuine. "It did. He was a young guy back then, and he never remarried. He didn't even divorce her when he could have. I think he's always hoped she'd come back."

"Aw, that's sad and romantic at the same time. My guy isn't the least bit romantic. Why I haven't ditched him by now, I don't know."

Roz took her arm from my shoulders, and I missed it immediately. How long had it been since I'd been touched with real affection instead of fake like from Mindy? The last I'd heard about her, she was married and pregnant. What the heck was wrong with me? I could've given her the same thing, and she hadn't even given me a chance.

Out over the sound, dark clouds gathered. Minutes later, fine snow sifted down into the gray water.

Roz took her coffee to the sliding glass doors. "We never get snow in Texas."

I didn't know whether to go to her or to stay at the table. She seemed confident, but the fact that she let her boyfriend talk her into dyeing her hair and getting a tattoo didn't reflect confidence. Maybe she'd come to the Outer Banks to make a serious life decision, and the seriousness of the subject had made her see the error of doing what other people said instead of doing what was right for her.

Finally, her voice broke the quiet. "Tell me about Talia's mom. Were you married long? Oh, how old is Talia? She must be young—you know, for you to not want her to be around a stranger overnight."

"She turned four last August."

"I bet she's sweet as can be. Does she look like you?"

"She's the spitting image of her mom." I warmed my coffee and joined Roz. The snow was thickening. Huge flakes were sticking to the deck. "If this keeps up, you might have to wait for your tour."

I can't help it. My past returns to my present.

Roz takes the coffee cup from me. She sets both on the table and comes back. "Would you mind if we held each other? I've got a feeling that we've needed a good hug for a long time."

I don't answer. She slips her arms around my waist, raises on tiptoe, and presses her cheek to mine. I respond by drawing her close. She's warm and firm, and smells clean from the shower. My mouth waters with the need to kiss her, and I know that would be a mistake. I'm not the least bit attracted to her, so why am I having these feelings? It can't be the fact that I haven't felt this way since Alma, can it?

Roz's lips brush my ear. "I understand why you don't want me around your daughter," she whispers. "I look like a bum, and my two-toned hair is weird. My story about coming here from Texas is pretty lame, but I'm still a good person. I'd love to meet her if you'll let me. Maybe she can come on my tour tomorrow."

I pull away enough to look outside. "If that snow keeps falling, no one's going anywhere tomorrow."

"Like that's a bad thing." Roz lowers her head until her forehead presses against my chest. Her shoulders shudder with a sob. Her knees give way and I catch her. She sobs again and again, crying like I did in bed when mom left. Something very wrong has happened to her, and I want to know what it is so I can help her. Yes, I believe she's a good person. Yes, I believe she's sincere with everything she's told me. Yes, I believe I'm having feelings for her that I shouldn't have, and I don't know what to do about them.

Still crying, Roz runs to the bathroom and slams the door. I haven't told her where she can sleep yet. If I had, I'm sure she would bury her face into the pillow and cry like I did when Mom left.

My chest is wet from her tears. My cheeks are wet from my tears. The pain from losing Mom and Alma, including the heartache from losing my unborn child because of Mindy, is as real as Roz's pain. Had I known I would eventually suffer from her choices, I might've kicked her out into the snow. Yes, that's a shocker to anyone reading this. Like they say, that's just the tip of the iceberg.

I close the laptop. I'm sitting at the kitchen table. Night has swallowed the sound. Lights sparkle on the horizon. People on the North Carolina mainland are living their lives like I did so long ago.

Supper is a tuna salad sandwich and coffee. I choke my meds down. I turn the TV on and don't watch it. I go to bed and don't sleep. Lying there in the darkness, I try to see my hand above my face. I can't.

Is this how it feels to be dead, to be in your coffin in the ground?

I hope my wife knew what she was doing when she said I should write my story to ease the pain of losing her. If not, I have no idea how it will end.

Chapter 24

After Roz ran to the bathroom, I put on a coat and my cowboy hat and stood on the deck, hoping the frigid air and the snow falling all around me would clear my head. Fat chance. I stood there until the snow covered my cowboy boots. Then I went back inside, hung my hat on a rack by the sliding glass doors, and stomped the snow off my boots on the mat. I didn't see Roz, so I walked down the hall. Light shown beneath the bathroom door, but I didn't hear crying. I went to Dad's old room, down and across the hall from Talia's room, and made the bed with fresh sheets, adding a quilt for the cold night to come. In the hall again, I realized the washer had stopped. With the clothes tumbling in the dryer, I tapped on the bathroom door. "If you want to lie down, your room is down the hall to the left."

The commode flushed. She said nothing. I went to the kitchen. She must've heard my footfalls leave the bathroom. Minutes later, I heard hers go down the hall, followed by the soft click of Dad's door closing. I understood. Everyone needs to be alone now and then.

I emptied our coffee cups and rinsed them. It was almost 4:30, evidenced by my empty stomach and twilight darkening the world. Might as well get the shrimp, flounder, and scallops frying. The fries could wait. Who likes warm instead of hot fries? Not me.

I set the fryer up on the stove and added oil. Dad and I installed a vent fan over the stove a few years back because we got tired of oil smell all over the house. I took our seafood from the fridge, spread it out on a platter, and dried it with paper towels. With a bowl of milk to wet the seafood, and the corn meal mix in a plastic bag to shake the seafood in, I was ready to cook.

The vent fan did okay, but the smell of frying seafood would still drift around the house. Knowing this, I started cooking, hoping the aromas would draw Roz from her room.

When I had the golden brown shrimp on a platter covered with paper towels, Roz's footfalls thumped in the hall. She came to the shrimp, eyes red, cheeks scarlet. As if she hadn't shed a single tear, she popped a shrimp into her mouth, chewed and swallowed. "Got any tartar sauce?"

I told her it was in the fridge, and started frying the scallops. "Can you drain that bowl of french fries in the sink and towel them off? They pop a lot if I fry them wet."

Roz did as I asked, then took the slaw to the table and came back. "Sorry about my stupid crying."

Checking the scallops, I glanced at her. "People need to cry sometimes. It's not stupid."

She took the tartar sauce to the table and came back to pop another shrimp into her mouth. I ate one too, enjoying its crunchy crust. "Not bad," I said. "I like broiled better. You taste whatever seafood you're eating instead of the crust."

"I guess," Roz said, looking in the fridge.

"There's beer in the bottom if you want it," I said. "I have one once in a while. I'm not much of a drinker."

"I've done my share at frat parties," Roz said. "I'll have tea, if that's what the brown stuff in a pitcher is."

I told her it was. The scallops looked ready, as golden brown as the shrimp. I added them beside the shrimp to drain, dipped the flounder fillets in milk, shook them in corn meal, and lowered them into the hot oil.

Roz poured tea, asked if I wanted any, and filled another glass after I said I did. I asked her to cut a lemon for it, which she did.

Next came the fries, cooked to the same golden brown as everything else. As much as I loved broiled seafood, I still looked forward to fried. We took everything to the table, added plates and forks, and settled into the two chairs facing the sound. Roz offered me her right hand. "How do you feel about a blessing?"

I took her hand. "My dad's a minister, remember?"

"Oh, yeah. Mind if I do the honors?"

I bowed my head. Roz did the same and closed her eyes.

"Where to start? Well, God, it's been quite a day. Please tell Dad I'm doing okay, despite Mom being a pain and my personal life being shot. Let him know I met a decent guy who seems to be a good cook like he was. I even got him to fry me some seafood like he used to do. It's nice to know there are still some good people in the world. I guess that's all for now. Please bless this food, amen." Roz released my hand. "I haven't done that since Dad died. I sure miss him."

"I miss my grandpa," I said, adding fries to my plate.

Roz went to the fridge and came back with ketchup. She filled her plate with portions of everything, and drizzled ketchup on her fries. "Wow, this is gonna be good. I'm about to starve."

I've known people who could really eat, but Roz could really eat. She'd go after the shrimp like they were trying to dart away, followed by a scallop or three and a bite of flounder. Slaw and fries came next, sometimes in that order, sometimes not, sometimes with ketchup on the fries and tartar on the seafood, sometimes not. The way my huge shirt and jeans hung on her thin body made her look like a starving hobo. Her hair, oily before the shower, looked full and soft, and I found myself wondering what she'd look like if it were all brown and hanging to her shoulders like Alma's did. It also had a little wave in it, unlike Alma's straight hair.

About to eat a fry, Roz stopped. "Why are you staring at me like that?"

I offered a friendly smile. "You said I seemed to be a good cook like your dad. The way you're eating, you should upgrade that to a fantastic cook."

"Whatever. Stop watching me. It makes me nervous."

I like watching you hovered on the tip of my tongue, which made no sense when Roz was anything but my type. Maybe it was that slight splash of freckles across her nose, like stars splashed across the sky over the sound on a freezing winter night, as your breath puffed twin clouds of white from your nose.

Taking a chance on personal conversation, I asked about her guy problem, and her eyes narrowed. "I'm not going there, okay? That subject is strictly off limits."

"No problem," I said. "I was just making conversation."

"Make some about your wife. How did you meet?"

Since I'd told Roz my wife had died, I thought I'd get away with not telling her anything else. Now, though, as she studied me for a reaction, I might as well get it over with. Regardless, I'd rather do that after supper, maybe with coffee on the sofa. When I told Roz this, she silently returned to her plate, so I silently returned to mine.

Our little spat hadn't hurt her appetite any. By the time I finished my food, she'd finished hers, filled her plate again, and had eaten half of that food.

Done, I asked if she was going to have enough. She said she was, after raking the rest of the shrimp into her plate. I stored the leftovers in the fridge and started washing dishes. While I did, Roz slowed her eating pace, possibly to taste it instead of wolfing it down. The fryer hadn't cooled, so I left it on the stove to clean later. Leaving the dishes in the strainer to dry, I made coffee. Roz finished eating, washed her things, and left them in the strainer with mine. I poured us coffee and took it to the table in front of the sofa. Roz took the hint and joined me there. Mug in hand, she tucked her narrow feet in my huge socks beneath her and faced me. "I apologize for bugging you about your wife after what I said about my boyfriend. Just thinking about him gets on my last nerve. You don't have to tell me about her if you don't want to."

I admired Roz's willingness to apologize. In my experience, it takes a person with a fine character to do that. My past mistakes don't say much for *my* character, but I learned early on to realize when I'm wrong. After all, doing that helped me be a better person.

Because of Roz's openness, I felt like being open about Alma. I started with the trip to Israel, filled in the middle with our time on the beach, and ended with our last night together.

"Oh, so that's how Talia came along," Roz said. "Did it bother your dad or her parents that you weren't married? Mom is totally against having kids without being married."

I hated this next part, which was Morris bringing Talia here because Alma and her sister and mom died from a terrorist attack, along with him eventually dying of cancer. When I told Roz, her narrow chin fell toward her chest like a curling wave fell toward the beach.

After a moment, she raised her head to give me a serious look. "And you took on the role of a single dad without even questioning it. That sounds like something my dad would've done." Roz paused for coffee. "I told you I'm an only child and my mom's a lawyer. At a family reunion one time, I overheard her telling her sister that she didn't mean to have me. Then she went on to say I ruined her career. I was twelve or thirteen, old enough to know what she meant and young enough to let her break my heart. At home that night, all I could think about was how her and Dad's choice to have unprotected sex brought me, an innocent bystander, into the world. The nerve of her telling her sister I'd ruined her career when it didn't. Three months after I was born, she ran right back to college, leaving Dad to take care of me alone."

Roz returned to her coffee while I returned to a single thought—thank God her mom hadn't aborted her like Mindy had aborted my son or daughter. My men's intuition—yes, we have that too—said this stranger on my sofa was a good and decent person, and she would do well in life regardless of its beginning.

Silence, or possibly regret, filled the space between us. For myself, the silence was because I didn't know where Roz stood with her boyfriend, and the regret was because I wanted the time to get to know her better and couldn't. She'd be gone tomorrow, and, as I'd been telling myself, that would be that.

If you haven't figured it out by now, I'm a hopeless romantic. A fireplace would've been great that evening—the smell of oak alight, the crackle of it burning, the pop of a knot bursting, flames smoldering to embers, two people discussing their pasts and their futures, both bathed in flickering hues of red and gold as the warmth grew between them. Not long after our wedding, my wife and I talked about having a contractor install a fireplace in our bedroom. She said the romantic mood would lead to kids coming sooner than later, which it certainly did.

As if she were in deep thought, Roz was running the tip of her index finger along the rim of the coffee mug. She wore nail polish, chipped as if she'd been chewing her nails from worry. She stopped and faced me. "You're about the right age. Did you go to Vietnam?"

I wondered if she was one of those people who spit on Vietnam vets and called them "baby killers." My men's intuition said she wasn't, so I touched my left shoulder. "I was stationed on a patrol boat in the Mekong Delta. A sniper hit me with a million dollar bullet right here."

Roz winced. "At least you made it back alive. A lot of guys can't say that. Some of the protestors at school make me sick. They blame America instead of the communists who started all this mess."

I told Roz the causes of the war were complicated. "Regardless," I added, "a country should be allowed to determine its own government, not another country. No matter how you cut it, war is insane."

Like the bullet that had drilled itself through my shoulder, a vision of Minh and Trang in their pitiful little hut drilled itself into my brain. In January, the North Vietnamese and Viet Cong had hit South Vietnam with a massive, coordinated attack. If Minh and Trang were alive, it would be a miracle.

My shoulder bothered me from time to time, but not enough to show. Evidenced by my vision of Minh and Trang, I still had some mental injuries. Thank God they rarely bothered me either. I wish I could say the same for the veterans who came back with PTSD.

Roz asked if I wanted more coffee, and I said I did. She refilled the mugs. On the sofa again, she tucked her feet beneath her like she had earlier. "When I passed the sliding glass doors, I saw the snow had stopped. I'm not sure if I'm glad or not."

Sipping coffee, I lowered the mug. "Because?"

"Because I haven't felt this peaceful in a long time." She looked away and back. "So far you seem like a great guy. Why hasn't some woman snatched you up?"

I laughed. "Wait a minute. I bought you breakfast, cooked you a fine seafood supper, opened up to you about my past, and I just seem like a great guy?"

Roz poked my chest. "Oh, hush. We did just meet, you know. I need more proof than your cooking skills."

Her smile surprised me. Bright and toothy, it transformed an ordinary face into one I could easily get used to. Ellie and I used to tease in our younger years, and I enjoyed it. We were kids, though, so it wasn't the same as now, with Roz and me. For myself, both then and now, humor between an adult man and a woman adds a spark to the conversation. Mindy wasn't much for humor. Alma tended toward the analytical, maybe because of Morris's background in history. Dad often said Helen's humor was what drew them together, and I understood what he meant.

Hoping my smile was as welcome to Roz as hers was to me, I beamed it at her. "How are your cooking skills? Can you boil water without melting the pot?"

She poked me again. "Maybe you'll find out one day, Mr. Kitty Hawk Cowboy. This cowgirl might take a notion to visit all the way from Texas when you least expect it."

As the word "it" dropped from Roz's lips, her animated expression fell, and I felt the same way. We knew when she was gone, she'd never come back, and with the snow having stopped, that would happen a lot sooner than later.

I tried to resuscitate our dying discussion with a question about her studies, but she yawned and said she was ready for bed. She did ask what time I got up, so that was something. When I told her late instead of early because she was my only customer, she nodded and faded down the darkened hall.

I washed our coffee mugs and the percolator, took her clothes from the dryer and went to her door to tap on it. "I'll leave your clothes by the door. If you want to brush your teeth, there's a new toothbrush in the right hand drawer below the bathroom sink." She said nothing, so I went to my room to sit on the bed. A moment later, I heard her footfalls go to the bathroom, eventually returning to Dad's bedroom. I felt like a fool for thinking it, but I wished she would open my door and ask if we could hold each other all night because she was as lonely as I was.

Yeah. What an idiotic thing for a loser like me to think.

Chapter 25

I had a hard time falling asleep with a stranger in my house. Well, maybe it wasn't that. Maybe it was because I didn't want Roz to leave after I showed her the horses. I must've slept. If not, the smell of bell peppers cooking and coffee brewing wouldn't have startled me awake. Blinking sleepily, I rolled over to check my alarm clock and saw it was 7:30. I also saw sunshine through my curtains, so those clouds that had brought that brief snowstorm had cleared.

I got dressed. While shaving, I wondered why Roz was cooking bell peppers. The coffee made sense for breakfast, but bell peppers didn't. Roz tapped the door. "Good morning, cowboy. In case you couldn't tell by the smell, I'm making omelets."

The bell peppers made sense now. "Talia loves omelets."

"Oh, so that's why you keep the stuff for making them in the fridge."

"Except the bacon," I said, shaving under my nose. "I was going to get that today."

"We'll do without," Roz said. "I found the flour. I was going to make biscuits, but I used all the eggs."

I grinned at my reflection. We sounded like an old married couple talking about a grocery list. "I'll be out in a minute."

"Good. The cheese is just about melted."

As Roz's footfalls thumped away, I rinsed the leftover

shaving cream from my face. With my hair combed, I found Roz setting two mugs of steaming coffee by two steaming omelets. Not only were the yellow edges bulging with red bell pepper slices, they were bulging with sliced mushrooms, diced onions, and melted cheese. I liked milk and sugar in my morning coffee. After getting both, I pulled Roz's chair out. "The least I can do for you after you made this fine breakfast is to help you with your chair, cowgirl."

Looking over her shoulder at me, Roz shared a grin. "Why, thank you, kind sir. You're quite the gentleman, aren't you?"

I sat beside her. "Only around strangers I'm trying to impress with my manners." I offered my palm to Roz. "Since you said the blessing last night, I'll say it this morning if you plop your hand in mine." Roz did as I asked, so I bowed my head. "Dear Lord, thank you for the snow last night. It sure was pretty while it fell. Thank you for my new friend. If her omelets taste as good as they smell, they might be as good as mine."

Roz squeezed my hand. "They're better, cowboy."

I squeezed back. "We'll see in a minute, cowgirl. Also, Lord, be with Roz during whatever struggles she's going through, and see her back to Texas safe and sound. Amen."

Roz released my hand. "I see you're in a hurry to get rid of me."

Slicing a bite of omelet, I didn't face her. "That's your plan, right? Go back and deal with whatever's going on." I ate the bite, as delicious as mine, and chased it with coffee. "College is in session. Did you get some kind of leave?"

"I don't see where that's any of your business," Roz said, a hint of anger in her voice.

"I welcomed you into my home," I said, a hint suspicion in my voice. "As far as I know, you could be an ax murderer."

Roz slammed her fork to the table. "Fine. I just up and left college without an explanation. I'm only going to be gone a few days."

"Look, Roz, you came all the way out here without enough money for the bus fare back to Texas. Make that make sense."

That pointed chin, whose cuteness was growing on me, lowered. "I can't make it make sense. Dad taught me to think things through. After he died, that ability sort of abandoned me."

Beyond the sliding glass doors, beyond the patches of snow brightening the frostbitten grass, beyond the two rocking chairs, a pair of gulls lands on the pier. Like a card player, they shuffle their white wings into place, and my past slips back into my present. When you love someone as much as my wife and I loved each other, time blurs back and forth with thousands upon thousands of memories, each a treasure to tuck away into the recesses of your mind, held there to visit over and over again. This includes the good and the not so good, because a great marriage is all those things and more, made precious as the love grows between you while the years press forward like the tides.

Remembering Roz's statement about abandonment, the memory of a wife leaving her husband and son so long ago brings tears to my eyes. I hate that memory. Each time I recall it, I try not to hate Mom, but when someone you love and trust does to you what she did to Dad and me, the anger and resentment carves itself into the bloody muscle of your heart. My wife and I discussed it over the years. She even suggested I see a shrink — my word, not hers — to come to terms with my feelings. Fortunately, though it might not sound like it, her love and patience eventually healed Mom's bloody cuts crisscrossing my heart.

I've stopped typing. No gulls are on the pier. The rocking chairs tip back and forth with the breeze blowing the marsh. It's time to return to my past.

"Well," Roz continued, "since your mom left you and your dad, I'm sure you know how it feels to be abandoned." She sipped coffee. "Dad's death really messed me up." She touched the brown roots above her blonde hair, then the tattoo below her ear. "I told you how I let my boyfriend talk me into this stuff. Talk about stupid."

I agreed but didn't say so. Like the old gospel song, *I Saw the Light*, Roz had seen the light about her boyfriend, a positive in anyone's book.

A huge sigh swelled Roz's chest, barely visible beneath the baggy sweatshirt of hers that she now wore instead of mine. It made sense. Like she'd said, she was leaving today, so she was wearing her clothes again. "You know," she said, "I haven't talked to anyone about my personal life like I've talked to you."

Her eyes lowered. Could she be searching for any significance to the connection we'd made in less than twenty-four hours? Although I hoped so, what good would it do when she was leaving after she saw the horses?

My chest rose and fell also, but with only a slight sigh. "I'm surprised at how much I've told you about my life," I admitted. "I don't usually take to strangers like this."

Roz offered her hand. "Well, cowboy, we need to fix that. I'm Roz Miller. I hail from a minuscule dot on the map called McDade, Texas. Nice to meetcha," she drawled.

I enjoyed her exaggerated drawl. As I took her hand, I exaggerated my own drawl. "Wayul, little lady, it's nice ta meetcha back. Are you in town fer long? If you are, maybe we could take a long walk on the beach and look for sea shells. Whatcha think 'bout that?"

Roz sputtered laughter. When she had it under control, she hugged my neck, kissed my cheek, and pulled away. "You, Seth Callahan, have made me laugh more than anyone since my dad died. I hope you know how special that is."

Those ragged brown bangs fell across her eyebrows. I fingered them back and palmed her cheek. "You, Roz Miller, are a fine person. I hope you know how special you are too."

Our eyes met. She pressed her hand to mine. I leaned forward, hoping she wanted to kiss me as much as I wanted to kiss her. Her lips parted. I parted mine. Adrenaline tingled into my bloodstream. Had I finally found the woman of my dreams, who would love me as much as I would love her?

Roz answered my question by taking my hand from her cheek. "I can't, Seth," she whispered. "The last thing I need is another complication in my life."

After everything she'd told me, I knew she was right. I said I understood, and added how we should eat our cooling breakfast and get to Corolla. Little did I know, like I wrote earlier, this was the beginning of the end between us. Roz had roared into my life like the next category five hurricane she would eventually be. If I'd known that, I might've refunded her money, called her a taxi, and sent her back to Texas.

Done with our meals, we quickly washed and dried the dishes, perhaps sensing the need to end our time together before we caused each other anymore pain then we'd already experienced.

As I put the last dish away, someone knocked on the sliding glass doors, and that someone was Ellie, with Talia at her side. "Open the door, Daddy! It's cold out here!"

Without a doubt, Ellie's curiosity about my guest had gotten the better of her, and she'd braved the frigid morning to make sure I wasn't about to rush into a relationship like the disaster I had with Mindy. I liked to think I wasn't that stupid. Well, maybe I was half stupid. After all, despite the baggage in Roz's life, which I'd be forced to deal with if our relationship took its natural course, I'd just tried to kiss her. Yeah, I was stupid, idiotic, and just plain dumb.

I opened the doors and closed them behind Ellie, who nodded at Roz. "I'm Ellie, an old friend of Seth's. Nice to meet you."

"We grew up together," I clarified to Roz. "She keeps Talia when I work."

Standing in the entrance to the hall, Roz darted her gaze between Ellie and me. Unless I missed my guess, she'd focused on Ellie's left hand for a fraction of a second. Then she verified my guess for me. "Your ring says you're married. I guess you and Seth never dated."

Ellie admitted to having a crush on me in our teens, "and that was it," she added. "I'm happily married to a great guy."

Talia tugged Ellie's hand. "Don't forget J.J."

"J.J.?" Roz asked.

"For Jeff junior," I said. "Jeff is Ellie's husband's name."

"Sounds like a happy marriage," Roz said. "I'm all for happy marriages." She came to Talia and knelt beside her. "My goodness, aren't you pretty. Your dad says you look like your mom."

"I do." Talia brushed her dark bangs from her eyes. "I've got a picture, wanna see?" Without waiting for an answer, Talia ran down the hall to her room and ran back to hand Roz a framed photo of Alma that Morris had given her.

Roz, still kneeling, took the picture. "I see, I see." She returned the picture and stood. "Your daddy is taking me to see the horses. Wouldn't you like to come?"

Talia faced me. "Can I, even if you're working?"

I couldn't deny the sweet, plaintive tone in her voice. "I don't see why not."

"In that case," Ellie said icily, "you need to come with me to get her suitcase."

Yeah, I was in trouble. Halfway between her house and mine, my old crush whirled to grab my arm. "I could smell bell peppers and coffee. You made her the omelets Talia likes so much, didn't you?"

"Well, we had to eat. Besides, Roz got up early and made them, not me."

"Right. I bet you needed to regain your strength after a night in bed together."

"That's a bet you'd lose, Ellie." To lower the temperature of our argument, I tried a different angle. "Look, she's a nice person who's going through a hard time. She'll see the horses and head home, okay?"

"I don't like her around Talia."

I snorted laughter. "You brought Talia home, remember? Did you think about that?"

Ellie shook her head. "You, Seth Callahan, are impossible." She pulled me toward her house, went inside, and came back to shove Talia's suitcase into my arms. "Go. Git. Now."

I winked. "I love it when your southern drawl comes out." Grinning to myself, I hurried back home, shivering without a coat in the cold air. The sun, though, was melting the last few patches of sparkling snow.

Inside, Talia had left her coat on the sofa, where both she and Roz were giggling. I left the suitcase by the washer and returned to the living room. "Do I get to know what y'all are giggling about?"

"Roz told me her real name, Daddy. I like it a lot."

"I told your cutie pie daughter why I stayed last night," Roz said. "She's glad because you need a girlfriend and she needs a mommy."

I crossed my arms. "Why do I have the feeling that wasn't what you two were really giggling about?"

"It wasn't, Daddy. I asked Roz if she heard you snoring like an old bear. She said she sure did."

Ignoring their humor, I asked Talia if she'd eaten breakfast at Ellie's. When she said yes, I told the two gigglers to put their coats on if they wanted to see the horses.

Taking advantage of the Suburban's huge bench seats, Talia sat between Roz and me in the front. In case you didn't know it, vehicle safety seats for kids weren't a thing in 1968. Thank goodness they are in 2024.

As I turned left onto the road, I asked Roz what her real name was.

"No, Daddy," Talia said. "It's a secret for us girls."

Roz offered Talia one of her curled pinkies. "That's right, pinkie swear."

Talia hooked her curled pinkie with Roz's. "See, Daddy? That's what a pinkie swear is."

"I see that. Roz has all kinds of secrets, doesn't she?"

"Don't be a spoil sport," Roz said.

"That's right, Daddy. Don't spoil our sports."

That finally got a chuckle out of me. What had I gotten myself into, both with Roz and her suggestion for Talia to see the horses with us?

Thankfully, quiet descended into the Suburban. After so little sleep, I wasn't in the mood for a bunch of girlish conversation. I just kept my eyes ahead and my mind clear. No, that was a lie. I kept regretting how Roz would leave in a few hours.

Minutes later, Roz pointed out the passenger window. "There's a dog. Let's play cow poke."

Talia's plaintive voice came from beside me. "Why would we poke a dog if it's called cow poke?"

"It's a game," Roz said. "You count all the four-legged animals on your side of the road. The person who gets the most wins."

"Wins what?" Talia asked.

"Wins the game, I guess," I said. "It's too bad we have more two legged sea gulls than four legged sea gulls. As far as cows, forget that."

From the corner of my eye, I caught Roz's grin. "Talia," she said, "your daddy is just an old poop. Is he any fun at all?"

Talia nodded. "He's a good belly blower. That's fun."

"Really?" Roz asked, playfully adding a doubtful tone to her voice. "Do you think he would blow on my belly if I asked him to?"

Talia turned her questioning expression toward me. "Daddy, if Roz asks, will you blow on her belly?"

I clicked the signal and took a right, almost missing the turn for Duck. "Tell Roz she's too old for belly blowing."

Talia poked my thigh. "Roz is right. You're just an old

poop."

I said nothing. It was hard for me to talk when I was imagining my lips pressed against the soft, silky skin of a feminine stomach.

Roz pointed out the window again. "There's a cat. That's two for me."

"That's not fair," Talia said. "I can't see."

Roz patted the seat. "Get up on your knees so you can see. Then we'll gang up on your old poop daddy."

By the time I steered the Suburban onto the beach north of Corolla, the cow poke count was zero for me and five for team Talia and Roz. Naturally, Talia squealed with delight at having won against her old poop daddy. I was both surprised and disappointed at how well she and Roz were getting along. For one thing, it made me see exactly how much Talia would like having a mommy in her life. For another, it made me see exactly how much I'd like having a girlfriend — well, a wife — in my life. For the final thing, as I'd kept reminding myself, Roz would soon be nothing more than a memory on its way to Texas.

To our right, the lead pelican in a line of pelicans glided down the face of a building swell. Almost on its tailfeathers, the next pelican followed, then the next and the next, so on and so forth. When the lead pelican approached another swell, it flapped upward to clear it, and the remaining pelicans did the same, forming a rising and falling roller coaster of long beaks and brown feathers that skimmed within inches of the aquamarine Atlantic.

Some people don't need other people to be happy in life. Unlike them, I was a human pelican, traveling the Outer Banks in need of a fellow pelican who would help me over the swells of our existence. Maybe it was something in my DNA. Maybe it was because Mom had ripped mine and Dad's hearts apart when she left, and I thought I could heal them by having an intact family of my own. Whatever the reason, I couldn't deny how I wanted a love like Alma and I had shared during our short time together. Where that love would come from, I had no idea.

Roz's low murmur broke the silence. "I love pelicans. They glide up and over those waves by breaking the wind for each other. They're amazing." Grinning, she nudged Talia with her elbow. "We could always play pelican poke. Then we'd have lots more things to count."

Talia climbed into Roz's lap. "Now I can see better. I like the sanderlings. Their skinny legs look like their knees are on backwards." She leaned back against Roz's chest. Roz wrapped her arms around her and touched her chin to Talia's head.

No, this scene wasn't lost on me, and the tears stinging my eyes proved it. What single dad doesn't want his child to feel that safe and secure in the arms of a woman offering both like Roz was offering? This was what I prayed for on many a night for Dad and me when Mom left. Now, after nearly twenty years, I prayed for it for Talia and me.

Although the sun shined brightly, no horses were on the beach, possibly because of the cold. The same went for fisherman on the deserted strip of sand stretching to the horizon. After a few miles, I steered the Suburban through a cut in the dunes and along a sandy path, toward a watering hole tucked amongst a grove of those crooked-limbed live oaks.

Talia sat up in Roz's lap and peeked over the dashboard. "Those old poop horses are hiding in the woods, aren't they, Daddy?"

"I would too," Roz said. "They don't have a heater like we do."

For the next hour, I drove sandy paths, followed shadowed tunnels within the evergreen live oaks, and visited both marsh and water holes. Finally, I parked with a view of the sound and left the engine running for the heat. "I'm sorry, Roz. Like Talia said, the horses are old poops today."

"That's okay," she said. "Stuff happens."

I took my wallet out and offered her the fee. "Here's your refund." I didn't say the rest, which was how I knew the horses preferred a certain thicket on days like this, and I'd avoided it so she could get back to Texas to handle her problems.

Roz shoved the money back. "No way, cowboy. It's not your fault you couldn't find the horses. Besides, you burned a lot of gas looking for them."

Her sense of fairness added yet another reason to admire her on the long list of reasons to admire her. Still, my unsaid question hung between us. *How will you get back home if you don't have the money?*

Roz touched her chin to Talia's head again. "Sweetie, I need to talk to your dad outside a minute."

Taking the hint, Talia slid from Roz's lap to the seat. "Okay. I'll stay where it's warm."

Roz and I closed the doors. Not knowing how this conversation would go, I went to the back of the Suburban, where Talia couldn't see us.

Roz met me there, crossing her arms over her narrow chest. "Look, I'll save you the trouble. I know horses like thickets on days like this. That means you're trying to be nice by giving me my money back."

"You need the money to get home. The last place you want to be stranded is on the Outer Banks in the winter."

"What I need is a job so I can earn the money. I'm not taking handouts, cowboy."

Yet another reason to admire her. "It's like a western ghost town out here now," I said. "You saw that on the way up here. We passed maybe five vehicles."

Roz's lips twisted back and forth. "Well ..."

"Come on, Roz, you need the money and I'm offering." I took the cash from my wallet again. "Just take it and get home, okay?"

Her lips stopped twisting. "You could hire me. I'll write a

script about the history of the horses, and you can learn it for your next tours. It'll make them a lot more interesting."

Her thin jacket wasn't doing its job, and she started shivering. I unzipped my coat and opened it. "Here you go. Just another friendly hug to get you warm."

As Roz wrapped her arms around me, I closed the coat over her back. It took more than a minute before she stopped shivering. Regardless, neither one of us wanted to let go.

She lay her head on my shoulder. "Why don't they make guys like you in Texas, Seth? You're about the sweetest man I've known except for my dad."

Despite the intimate moment, I chuckled. "What happened to me being an old poop who snores?"

She pressed herself into me, snuggled her cheek against mine. "I was teasing, and you know it."

Roz was thin in my arms, all boney and angular. It felt like I was holding a scarecrow without stuffing. Still, I hadn't been this happy since Alma. I had a decision to make. I could either drive her to Elizabeth City and force the money on her at the bus station, or I could accept her job offer.

I rubbed a circle between her shoulder blades. "How long will it take you to write that script? I'll be paying you by the hour, so it better not take more than a month."

Roz laughed, all sultry and low in her throat. "Imagine that, the Kitty Hawk Cowboy is a big spender. What if I take room and board for a month and 100 dollars cash on the old barrel head when the script is done? Is it a deal?"

I pulled away to agree, but as soon as my mouth opened to tell her, she kissed me and danced around in a circle, yelling, "Woo-hoo! I done caught me a genuine cowboy for a month, and I get paid for the privilege at the same time!"

What can a guy do but laugh at something like that?

So I did.

Chapter 26

I should've known Ellie wouldn't stop aggravating me about Roz. I got it. She cared about Talia and me. That's why the phone was ringing as soon as Roz, Talia, and I entered the sliding glass doors. Since I'd unlocked them, I was able to get to the phone before Talia did. "Hello?"

Ellie usually answered with a perky, "Hi, Seth," before adding the reason for the call. Not this time. This time she knew I'd recognize her voice, so what I got was, "Did you bring Roz home? Don't tell me you brought Roz home. If you brought Roz home, I'll git Tom involved, durn it all."

This time I didn't grin at her southern drawl. I stretched the handset line as far as it would go outside and closed the sliding doors on it. "Leave Dad out of this," I said, trying to keep my voice low so Roz and Talia wouldn't hear. "It's none of his business like it's none of your business."

"It's both our businesses, Seth Callahan. We care about you and Talia. The last thing you need is some skank in your life."

"Skank?" I asked, astonished at her judgmental tone. "I remember when you stripped naked and tried to get me to fool around by the sound."

Ellie showed me her palm. "Don't use my past against me. I was young and stupid."

"Oh, yeah," I said, ready with the perfect comeback. "What's your excuse now, skank?"

That last sentence had the desired effect. Yep, you got it. Ellie hung up on me. I *did* have to laugh at that. Once she got to know Roz over the next month, she'd get over being mad at me.

I went inside and cradled the phone. Talia was at the table with a glass of milk. Looking through the kitchen cabinets, Roz opened another one. "There it is." She took peanut butter and jelly to the table, poured herself a glass of milk, got a knife from a drawer, and took that and a loaf of bread to the table. "Us girls are hungry, Daddy. Want one?"

I said no. She made the sandwiches and gave Talia hers. "Be right back, sweetie. I need to ask your daddy something." At the hall entrance, she crooked her finger for me to follow. We ended up in Dad's room, now her room for a month, and she closed the door. "Your walls are thin as paper. Who's a skank?"

Not wanting her to think ill of Ellie, I had to lie. "Nobody's a skank. Ellie said she saw a skunk and was warning me about it."

"Don't lie to me, Seth." Roz crossed her arms. "I clearly heard you say skank."

I didn't care to share my past with Mindy and complicate our situation even more. "Well, that's not what you heard."

Roz uncrossed her arms. "Whatever." She paused. "How do we explain my staying here to Talia? While you were on the phone, she asked me if I was your girlfriend. Not only that, I don't want your Dad or your neighbors to think we're living together. I'm sure I'll meet him before I leave."

Yet another reason to admire Roz—she cared about what people thought of me. I wasn't sure what Dad would think of Roz, let alone her staying here for a month. She wasn't, as Ellie had said, a skank. Still, her blonde hair with brunette roots, especially with the way it'd been wacked off at the nape of her neck, sort of gave her a skanky look. That and her scarecrow figure beneath that baggy sweatshirt and ill-fitting jeans didn't help any.

"Yeah," I told her, "I'm sure he'll come around. Even if he doesn't, I see him at church."

Roz asked if I went every Sunday. When I said I did, she tapped her lips with a fingertip. "Mom never went, but Dad and I did. I could buy a dress and go with you as someone you just met, but that would confuse Talia."

Each doubt I was having about Roz continued to fade away. She might look sort of skanky, but her caring about Talia's feelings was another positive in her favor. I told her Talia and I would go to church, and I'd ask her to not mention our guest, making sure she knew it wasn't lying to do that."

Roz's chest rose and fell with a slow, steady breath. She started to touch my hand but stopped at the last moment. "You're a great dad, Seth. I admire that a lot." She touched her sweatshirt. "I guess you've wondered why I wear this baggy thing. It's my Dad's. I wore it on this trip because I wanted to feel like he was with me."

She blinked until tears rolled down her cheeks. "I miss him so much," she said, her expression twisting with grief. She covered her face. "I'm such an idiot."

Not knowing what I should do, even though I knew what I wanted to do, I waited while her shoulders heaved with heavy sobs. She stumbled toward me. I took her in my arms and rubbed her back. "Hey, you're no more an idiot than anyone else. The main thing is what we learn from being an idiot, you know?"

She nodded. Her narrow chin rubbed my shoulder. "That's what Dad used to say." She pulled away enough to look into my eyes and cup my cheek with her palm. Her thumb rubbed a small circle there. "I wish …"

"I wish too, Roz, but you've got a boyfriend."

Roz lowered her hand from my cheek. "I know, and I've got to go back to deal with him. Besides, you don't know me. We just met yesterday, and rushing into a relationship is stupid. That's what happened with my boyfriend, the jerk."

I stated the obvious. "If he's a jerk, and you don't get along with your mom, stay here. We'll take it slow and see how it goes."

Roz whirled away. "I can't. I've got to go back and deal with the mess I've made." She faced me again. "Please, Seth, don't ask me that or mention my mom or boyfriend again. Let's just enjoy our month together and let that be the end of it."

I asked the obvious. "If we, as you say, enjoy our month together, you know what might happen."

"No," she said firmly. "If we grow close that way, it'll hurt both of us worse when I leave." She came to me again, her warm palm to my cheek. "Believe me, I'd like to stay. I left because I finally realized my boyfriend made me feel like a nothing. You don't make me feel like nothing. You make me feel like I'm important to you, and so does Talia. Both of you give me hope."

I shared a soft smile. "Well, by the end of our month together, I hope you have all the hope you need to get your life back on track by kicking that sorry boyfriend of yours to the curb." I went to the door. "We better check on Talia before she ruins her appetite for supper. That child is crazy about a peanut butter and jelly sandwich."

When my hand touched the doorknob, Roz grabbed my arm. "What do we tell her about me staying here?"

"The truth," I said, positive of my choice. "You're a good friend from Texas. You're writing a script about the horses for my tours. You don't have a place to stay, so you're staying here. If my dad shows up, that's what we'll tell him too."

Roz thought for a moment. "But he's not Talia. He'll wonder why I don't have a place to stay, or how I came all the way here almost broke."

"Look, Roz, Dad's not like that. He wouldn't ask you anything personal out of respect for you. Regardless of that, like any good dad would, he'd ask me in private."

After a smile, Roz said, "Your dad sounds like a good guy.

I think I like him already." Her smile changed to a frown. "But what will you tell him?"

I raked my hand through my hair. "Give me a break. I haven't thought of that."

Talia knocked on the door. "I need more milk. My peanut butter is glued in my mouth."

Rushing by me to open the door, Roz giggled. "Okay, little cowgirl, let's unglue that peanut butter."

At the kitchen table, I save the Word document and close the laptop. It's been a month since Jack and I went to Jennette's. June is gone and July is here. On the sound, zigzagging Jet Skis roar by, sending rooster tails of white water high in the air behind them. Further out, a boat pulls a parasail. On the pier, the summer breeze gently sways the two rocking chairs back and forth.

The month with Roz went better than expected. She finished the script in a week. When I gave it my approval, she shoved her open palm at me. "Fork up, cowboy."

"Nope," I said, shaking my head. "Our deal was for a month, and you darn well know it."

On the sofa, watching Saturday cartoons, Talia looked at us, standing by the kitchen table. "That's right, cowgirl. You darn well know it."

Roz stuck her tongue out at both of us. "You old poops, I'm not going anywhere right now. I just want to get paid, that's all."

"Good," Talia said. "You promised to stay a month. Daddy will spank you if you don't."

I grabbed Roz from behind and dug my fingers into her ribs. "I'd rather the tickle monster got her."

Roz squealed and slapped at my hands. "Stop that before I wet my jeans!"

I picked her up, carried her squirming self to the sofa, and sat with her in my lap. Talia piled on top of us and tickled both of us. As all of us laughed, we rolled into the floor, fingers still digging into each other's ribs until we gave out of breath.

"All right, all right," I said, "that's enough."

Roz jumped up. "Durn, I wet my durn jeans, durn it."

I admired her use of "durn" instead of anything else she could've said around Talia. She took off for the bathroom. I got her a pair of my jeans and knocked on the door. "I'm hanging a pair of my jeans on the doorknob, Miss Wet Drawers."

Roz growled. "You just wait, cowboy. I'll get you back before I leave."

I laughed. "Promises, promises."

The following Saturday, right out of the wild blue yonder, Dad showed up about an hour before supper. When he came in, he went to the kitchen table. Thank goodness Roz was in her room, editing the script. At the table, Talia was choosing a crayon for a coloring book. "Hi, Grandpa. Wanna help me color?"

Dad looked at me. "Where's the food you're supposed to take to Ellie's cookout? She said to help you carry it over."

I started to rake my hand through my hair when I'd rather pull it out. No doubt Ellie had told Dad about Roz, and this was her way of having Dad see if she was a skank or not.

Dad sat at the table. "Call Ellie and see what's up. Maybe she gave me the wrong date."

The phone rang. It was Ellie. "I saw your dad drive by. Are you gonna bring the food or what?"

"There's no picnic and you know it, Ellie." I didn't say skank, but I sure wanted to.

"Well, imagine that. Now you have to introduce Tom to Roz. Put that in your skank pipe and smoke it."

Like before, Ellie hung up on me. I cradled the phone and faced Dad. "I think we both know why you're here."

"Ellie and I care about you, Son. Let me take you, Talia, and your guest out to dinner. I'd like to get to know her."

"Yay!" Talia squealed. "Can we get pizza?"

Because I thought Dad would like Roz once he got to know

her, I honestly thought it was a good idea. Unfortunately, she didn't have anything decent to wear out to dinner. Then an idea hit me. I told Dad I'd be right back and went to knock on Roz's door. "Can I come in?"

It's open."

She was lying on the bed on her stomach, feet up, ankles crossed, the script beneath her face, a pencil in hand. "Did I hear my little cowgirl squeal something about pizza?"

At the closet door, I opened it, reached into the back, and took out a red skirt, a white sweater, and a pair of red sandals. Mom must've missed this stuff in the back of the closet when she abandoned us, and Dad left it when he moved to Manteo. I showed everything to Roz. "My dad wants to take us out to eat. I thought you might like to wear this."

"From one of your old girlfriends after a roll in the hay? No way."

I told her how Mom left the clothes. Roz got up and pressed the hangers to herself. "They're a little big." She lay the clothes on the bed. "How did your dad find out about me?"

"Well ..." I said, drawing it out because I didn't know what she'd think. "Ellie told him about you. She's afraid we'll have some kind of relationship, and you'll break my heart." I dropped to the bed. "Someone did that before. She and Dad worry about it happening again."

Roz sat beside me. "I get it. She doesn't like my looks. Is that it?"

"That's not it, Roz. She doesn't know you like I know you."

"Fine," Roz said, rolling her eyes. She got up and unbuttoned her jeans. "Get out of here unless you want to see me naked. I'm gonna show your dad exactly who I am and how great a girlfriend I can be."

In the kitchen, Dad was helping Talia color. I told him Roz would be out soon. As I sat beside him, a thought hit me like a huge wave to the back of my head. Roz and I had agreed to tell Dad that she was just a friend. She must've forgotten, since she said she was going to show him how great a girlfriend she could be, especially a girlfriend who was living with me and his granddaughter. Not good. Not good at all.

I said I needed to spruce up for supper and hurried down the hall. When I knocked, Roz opened the door and turned around. "Not bad, huh, cowboy?"

Red lipstick matched the skirt and the shoes. A hint of makeup hid most of her freckles. Mascara highlighted her brown eyes perfectly. She grinned. "Your bugging eyes say I look good enough to hop on a horse and ride off into the sunset with."

"You look amazing," I said, meaning every word of it.

"I found some of your mom's makeup in a drawer. Are you ready to go?"

I closed the door. "You can't be my girlfriend. We have to stick to the truth about the script and you not having a place to stay. If you're my girlfriend, it looks like you're living with me for the sake of just living with me. Dad won't like that."

A cute pout pursed Roz's red lips. "Isn't that a shame, and I was gonna give you a big kiss to show your dad how much I care."

To say the least, Roz charmed Dad's socks off during supper. To say the most, by the time he left for home, he believed our story about the script and her not having a place to stay, adding how he always knew his son had a huge heart.

Now to convince Ellie of that.

A week later, I called and asked if she could keep Talia while I took a couple on a tour. Of course, she asked why my skank couldn't watch Talia. Of course also, I said my skank had a headache. When Ellie said to bring Talia over, my plan fell into place. "Talia wants to stay here," I said. "Jeff's off, so can't he stay home with J.J.?"

"He could," Ellie replied. "Or I could bring J.J. with me."

"Sounds great," I said. "Y'all can watch cartoons."

"Will the skank stay in her room with her headache?"

"Come on, Ellie, I can't make her do that."

Needless to say, though I'll say it anyway, when I got back from the fake tour, Roz had charmed Ellie like she had charmed Dad. Everyone was sprawled out in the floor with popcorn while Wile. E. Coyote was hatching up another plan to get the Roadrunner.

The only person who looked up as I came in was Ellie. She hopped up and led me to the deck. "Roz told me everything. She's great, and she's great with Talia. It's a shame she has to leave. I'd love to have her as a friend."

As people often say, life was good.

Then came Roz's last night here. Talia had been wanting to see the Disney movie *The Jungle Book.* Since it came out last year, I should've taken her but hadn't. When I mentioned it to Ellie, she said she'd be glad to take her, following with a sleepover at her house. Ellie and Roz had been spending more time together, so I wondered if Ellie had matchmaking on her mind. To be honest, I had matchmaking on my mind too.

That afternoon, before Ellie came for Talia, Roz sat her down on the sofa to say goodbye. In the kitchen with my gut churning, I had an idea how it would go, and I was right.

As soon as Talia realized what was happening, she threw her arms around Roz's neck and began to cry. "Why can't you stay, Roz? It's not fair."

I swallowed, but the hard knot in my throat wouldn't go down.

Roz patted Talia's back. "I know it isn't fair, sweetie, but I need to get back to college. I told you how I want to be a doctor for animals, so you know how important it is to me."

Talia pulled away, eyes red, tears streaming. "But you never saw our horses yet."

"Well, that's true," Roz said, adding an understanding smile. "Maybe I'll come back one day to see them. If I do, I'll make sure to stop by to see you and your old poop dad, okay?"

Satisfied, Talia bobbed her head. "Okay."

Bugs Bunny came on. Roz came to the kitchen for a handful of tissues from a box on the counter. "This is a lot harder than I thought it'd be."

I could see that in her wet eyes. I took a tissue from her and stuck it in my shirt pocket. "I know what you mean."

Blinking furiously, Roz went to Talia and dried her cheeks. "There. How about a smile from one cowgirl to another?"

Roz really knew how to get a grin out of my daughter. Then they hugged, whispered something in each other's ears, and hooked pinkies, making some pinkie swear about who knew what.

A few hours later, Ellie was hugging Roz on the deck with Talia watching, a little suitcase beside her on the gray boards. In no time at all, Ellie considered Roz to be her best friend, and she hated to see her go as much as Talia and I did. Dad, who'd stopped by last night to say goodbye, felt the same, telling her to come back for a free horse tour anytime.

As Ellie and Talia left, Roz came in. "Durn," she said, wiping her eyes. "This goodbye stuff is rough."

I took her hand. "That's why I've got something special planned for our goodbye." I led her down the hall and to her bedroom, where I asked her to sit on the bed.

"You have lost your mind, cowboy. We're not doing that and you know it."

I took the red skirt, white sweater, and red sandals from the closet and lay them beside her. "Get dressed, cowgirl. I want to take you out to supper. We won't ever see each other again. Talia and I have enjoyed your company, so I want to take you someplace special."

Her narrow chin fell toward her chest. "Seth, I …"

The tears in her eyes filled me with sympathy. "Hey, stop those tears. You'll go back home and tell your boyfriend to take a hike. Then you'll go back to college and learn to be a great veterinarian."

"I wish it were that easy," she said, upsetting me with how

sad she sounded.

I rubbed her shoulder. "Come on, cowgirl, you need to have faith in yourself. You're a strong, intelligent woman. I've seen it. Dad's seen it. Ellie's seen it. Jeff's seen it. Talia's seen it. You'll have a great life."

She ran her fingertips along the skirt. "A great life like you have despite your mom leaving you."

I tried to smile but couldn't. "Never mind me. You'll find a great guy who'll love you. As far as women are concerned, all the ones I've cared about have left me."

Sniffling and wiping her eyes with the heels of her hands, Roz got up from the bed. At the door, she waved me out. "Get your behind to your room. You're not dressed to go out either. Let me get that stuff on so I can see where you're taking me."

I'd been planning this for a week. I put two old coats of mine and Dad's and a quilt in the Suburban. Yesterday, while out for groceries, I'd gotten everything else ready. I didn't know if Roz had ever done this. I had, so I thought she'd like it. In my room, I dressed in nice slacks, a Sunday shirt, and loafers without socks, another part of my plan, and waited for Roz at her door. "Hey, if you're putting on makeup and lipstick, I think you look great without it."

She snatched the door open and pointed at her face. "Now you tell me." She pursed her lips, red with lipstick. "I don't like this stuff much either. It's okay once in a while."

I waved her down the hall. "After you, cowgirl."

I ignored my coat. When she started putting her thin one on, I said she wouldn't need it. She slapped her hands to her hips. "It's the first of March on the windy Outer Banks. Are you nuts?"

"It's breezy, not windy. It'll lay soon."

Rolling her eyes, Roz returned the coat to the rack. "Whatever. I won't freeze walking to a restaurant."

In the Suburban, I headed to a seafood restaurant for my take-out order. My watch said 7:20, and they were supposed to have it ready at 7:30.

Roz shoved my arm. "Did you make a reservation? I hope it isn't a fancy place. This cowgirl and fancy don't mix."

"You'll like our dining room," I said, giving her a sly grin. "We'll have it all to ourselves."

Those red lips twisted back and forth. "This cowgirl and romance don't mix either."

I gave a turn signal and parked at the restaurant. "How do you like the restaurant's name?"

Roz leaned forward to look out the windshield. "*The Sea Horse* is a cute name." She opened the passenger door.

"Nope," I said. "I made a call-out order. Be right back."

As I got out, Roz closed her door, frowning. "Why didn't you just cook like you did that day we met? This is a lot of trouble."

About to close my door, I stopped. "Aren't you worth it?"

"You're darned right I'm worth it. Git your fanny in there. I'm hungry."

When I returned with a large paper bag, Roz looked puzzled. "I don't get it. Why are we dressed up for a take-out order?"

"Patience, cowgirl, patience." I set the bag between us and cranked the Suburban.

Roz unfolded the bag and peeked inside. "It smells like seafood, but not fried." She closed the bag. "Is it broiled? You know I like fried."

I turned onto the road and headed south. "Trying something new is good for a person."

"Where are we going? This isn't the way home."

I almost said her way home, as much as I hated it, was west. Instead, I told her to be patient again, that everything was planned. She rolled those big brown eyes at me but said nothing.

I continued down Highway 12. A few miles later, we crossed the arching and curving span of the Bonner Bridge, which crossed Oregon Inlet. When it reached its highest point, Roz craned her neck while looking left and right. "Oh, wow, what a view."

Ahead of us, the slender strip of sand to the left of the road, and the wide marsh to the right, looked as if it could be blown away by a hurricane any minute, but it had been here for centuries.

"This is an amazing place," Roz said. "It's almost like another planet."

A few miles after the bridge, I pulled into a small parking area. "How do you feel about eating on the beach? I've got two coats if we get cold."

Roz touched my hand on the steering wheel. "You're trying to get me to stay, aren't you?"

"No," I said, lying to myself. "I know you've got to leave. I just want to make your last night special." I aimed a thumb toward the back. "If you carry the food and the quilt, I'll carry our coats and the cooler with our drinks." After opening the door and leaving my shoes in the Suburban's floor, I told Roz to do the same thing with her sandals, because barefoot is always best for the beach, even when it's cool.

Carrying everything, we climbed up the sandy path that led toward a slight depression in the dunes. Low brush flanked the path, so I told Roz to watch for sandspurs, little round balls filled with hooked stickers that hurt like the dickens when one gets embedded in the sole of your foot. At the crest of the dunes, sea oat stalks swayed in the breeze. The sound of waves crashing and the cries of gulls grew louder with each step.

Ahead of me, Roz stopped at the top of the rise. The breeze off the Atlantic stirred her hair and skirt. Her chest rose and fell with a deep breath. "Wow, smell that salt air."

Beside her, I pointed out to the ocean and to the left. "See that smokestack sticking out of the water? That's the wreck of the *Oriental*. It didn't have much time with the ocean. It was built in Philadelphia in 1861, and ran aground in 1862." I didn't say the rest: *like we didn't have much time with each other after we met.*

A gust blew off the ocean. Roz wrapped her bare arms around herself. "How do you know about it? It's pretty remote out here."

"When Mom left, Dad would take me surf fishing here. I think he did it to get us out of the house and away from our memories." I adjusted my grip on the cooler. "The sun will set soon. I've planned something that'll warm us up and help us see while we eat."

As we eased down the dune, the cooling sand shifted beneath our feet, causing us to slide with each step. I led Roz to a pile of driftwood I'd gathered and left near the dune. "I hope you like bonfires. After a long afternoon of surf fishing, Dad and I used to stay out here. We'd cook our catch, roast marshmallows, and watch the stars come out. Those are some of my best memories of him."

We put everything down. I helped Roz spread the quilt. She got out the food and drinks while I lit the driftwood. When I joined her on the quilt, she took my hand and said, "Since I said the blessing for our first supper together, I'll do the same for our last supper together."

She closed her eyes and bowed her head.

"Well, God, where to start, right? It's been a great month with Seth and Talia. I also enjoyed getting to know Tom and Ellie and her family, and I know I'll miss them." Roz's voice caught. "I'll miss Seth a lot. He's a very special guy. If I could drag him and Talia back to Texas, I would. I know that's impossible, though. He loves Kitty Hawk as much as I've come to love it, and I'll have a hard time leaving tomorrow. Please bless this food and bless Seth. I hope a special woman comes into his life one day. He and Talia sure deserve one. Amen."

I released Roz's hand. We said nothing as we ate, the fire warming us despite the cooling breeze. I was glad Roz said she would miss everyone. Once she'd been back in Texas a while,

I hoped she'd miss us enough to come back to Kitty Hawk.

Done with our food, we fed the paper bag and the cardboard to-go boxes to the flames. A log shifted, sending a shower of sparks into the darkening sky. They reminded me of that smattering of freckles across Roz's nose and cheeks. What I wouldn't give to kiss her there, to say how cute I thought they were, to say how, because of all the tender moments I'd witnessed between her and Talia, I had fallen in love with her.

Twilight gave way to night. I leaned back on my elbows to gaze at the stars. After a moment or two, Roz did the same. "Thank you for this, Seth. I'll never forget it."

There we were, two people lying on a quilt on an Outer Banks beach, illuminated by the flickering flames, our heads tilted back to watch those trillions of stars winking down from the black of night, the fire crackling nearby, its heat warming us.

Roz shivered. I offered the coat and she declined. I rolled onto my side. As natural of breathing, she slid close to spoon me, then took my hand and pulled it between her breasts, where I could feel the steady thrum of her heart. I nuzzled her hair, sweet with the floral shampoo she used. She pressed into me, resting her head on my other arm, and pulled that hand to her lips for a kiss.

If she cared about me this much, why wouldn't she say something? I shoved that question out of my head. Give her time. Maybe she'd admit to loving me before bed, or after breakfast, or before we said goodbye, for what would likely be forever.

One after another, as they'd done for billions of years, grinding stone and shell into the very sand beneath us, the breakers continued to crash to the beach, followed by the swish of surf and its murmuring whisper as each dying wave returned to its watery home.

The dying flames allowed darkness to overtake us. Before I made a fool of myself by telling Roz I loved her, I said we should go because of her long day tomorrow. Not having a shovel, I used my hands to bury the fire with sand. Like Roz and me, those blackened lengths of driftwood would never flair with warmth again.

The drive back home passed silently. My night in bed passed sleeplessly. Feeling as if my eyes were filled with sand, I dressed and shuffled to the kitchen to make Roz our last breakfast together—and stopped to stare at a sheet of paper on the table. A step closer helped me recognize it. Another step closer made me want to burn it. Like I've said, she was going to be another category five hurricane, and not in a good way.

The paper was my horse tour script and nothing else. Her leaving in the middle of the night had sort of passed my mind, but I thought she cared enough to say goodbye, or to at least write a goodbye note. She'd done neither, and it pissed me off.

I made coffee. One cup cleared the cobwebs of sleep. Another made me look at things differently. She was an adult. This was her choice. One of the reasons I loved her was her intelligence. If she thought leaving me like this was the right thing to do, so be it. It was a clean break. Down and dirty. No holds barred. She was gone, and I'd be an idiot to go out in the Suburban to look for her. Time to man up and get on with life.

Besides, I had a daughter to take care of.

Chapter 27

It's 2024. I haven't written anything since June. Almost two months have passed, and October is on the horizon. Liz took me out to lunch twice. Jack took me fishing three times. Talia, Sarah, and my other kids have called to check on me every week or so. "Did you take your meds, Dad? Are you walking like Mom wanted you to? Have you written much? I hope Mom was right about it, and you don't miss her so much. You know she wants you to be happy, like you'd want her to be happy if you were her."

I dutifully say I'm doing all that stuff. Anything less would make them worry, and I don't want them to worry.

When I'm not writing, lunching, fishing or otherwise engaged, such as watching *The Andy Griffith Show* and *The Bugs Bunny Show* reruns, I sit in my rocking chair on the pier and rest my hand on the armrest of my wife's rocking chair. I'd give anything if I could do that again, except with her hand in mine.

You see, when Roz left, she broke my heart and shattered my soul. I stopped attending church, stopped fishing for fun, stopped laughing at Andy, Barney, and Bugs. Basically, except for horse tours, and for taking care of Talia like a good dad should, I stopped living.

Of course, Ellie and Dad said I needed to get out of whatever rut I was in, but it took until June, three months after Roz left, for the lightbulb to go off over their heads.

For Ellie, it happened when Talia and I met her, J.J., and Jeff on a walk by the sound. We made small talk for a few minutes about the weather, and how busy I was with tour customers, things like that. A little while after Talia and I got back home, Ellie called on the phone. "Seth, ever since Roz left, you don't look the least bit happy, and I just figured out why. You fell in love with her."

Although Talia was in her room, I kept my voice down. "Right, Ellie," I said, using my most sarcastic tone. "You said it yourself. I fall for every skank that comes along."

"Oh, hush, Seth. Roz isn't a skank and you know it. Tell the truth, don't you love her?"

I said nothing. Roz was gone, so what I felt didn't matter anymore.

"I hear you breathing," Ellie said. "I saw how great you two were together. I've never seen two people smile so much at each other. She's wonderful with Talia. You should give her a call. Maybe she loves you too."

I told Ellie I didn't have her number. "Anyway," I continued, "she wouldn't have left if she loved me."

"Roz isn't your mom, Seth Callahan." Ellie huffed a hard breath. "Durn it, you need to get over that mess like Tom did."

I rubbed my eyes. A person does that when they lose sleep because of a broken heart. I told Ellie I'd think about everything she'd said and cradled the receiver.

The next day, a Saturday, Dad came by to ask when I would come back to church, especially for Talia's sake. He could lay the guilt on when he wanted to.

It was a scorching afternoon. I'd come back from a heavy tour day, and I was sitting on the steps of the deck with three cans of ice cold beer. I heard Dad's vehicle engine at the front of the house. Since I didn't know it was his vehicle, I didn't worry about the three beers. He might not say anything about one, but he would about three.

When he rounded the corner, I was guzzling the last swallow from the first can, and I knew he'd caught me in the act. Thank goodness Talia was still with Ellie, or he would've given me a lot more grief about the beers.

Setting a shoe on the bottom step, Dad looked up at me, shaking his head. "I hope my granddaughter is still at Ellie's. I'd hate for her to see how her dad's become an alcoholic over losing Roz."

Feeling ornery, I crunched the can and threw it over my shoulder to the deck, where it clanked along the boards until it stopped. "I had a lot of customers today, Dad. Don't I have the right to a beer? One guy asked me to take his picture with him petting a stallion. One woman asked if she could buy one of the foals. A kid shot his cap pistol, and I had to get the heck away from a mare that didn't like the noise."

Dad crossed his arms. "One beer is fine after a hard day. Three, like I just said, means you're in love with Roz."

I popped the top on the second beer. "Right. Ellie told me that same story yesterday."

Dad came up to sit beside me. "Son, this is me talking. I just wish I'd have realized it earlier. When I saw those three beers, I remembered how great you and Roz got along. I remember how much she and Talia liked each other too. I'm sure that has something to do with your feelings for her. Why don't you give her a call?"

I swallowed beer. "I don't have her number."

"Okay, but you know she lives in McDade, Texas. Maybe you can get the number by calling information." Dad raised a finger. "No, forget that. The best thing is to go there. Don't be an idiot like me and not try to get her back."

After swallowing more beer, I smirked. "Oh, you're in love

with her too? Why don't you drive out there like you didn't drive somewhere to get mom and bring her back."

Dad popped the top on the third beer. "You know doggone well what I meant." He tipped the can and licked his lips. "Look, you can take my new pickup. I'll handle your customers while you're gone. You owe it to yourself to try. Like I said, don't be an idiot like me."

There was no need to remind Dad that he didn't know where Mom was so long ago. If he'd known, like I know now about Roz, he'd have gone for sure. I agreed to his proposal. He went home for a suitcase of clean clothes and came back. By then I'd brought Talia home. Of course, Ellie was tickled pink at the news, almost as much as Talia was. "I'm glad, Daddy. Roz needs to be here with us. You smiled a lot more then."

I couldn't argue that. What I could argue was how Roz had made her choice to leave, so the odds of her admitting she loved me, much less that she would come home with me, were practically zero.

Dad cooked hot dogs and fries while I packed a suitcase. To get an early start, I filled his pickup, a 1968 Chevrolet C10 painted sky blue, with gas, and bought a United States map. The next morning, after kissing my sleeping daughter goodbye, I headed west. Lookout, McDade, Texas, and Roz Miller, Seth Callahan, also known as The Kitty Hawk Cowboy, was on his way.

Yeah, despite my doubts, I was feeling positive. After all, maybe Roz wanted to finish college before she came back to Kitty Hawk. I'd find out soon enough.

Having never been off the Outer Banks except to Elizabeth City, and to there by boat, driving across the country would've been more interesting if Roz wasn't filling my thoughts. If things didn't work out between us, I'd give up on women for good. Instead, I'd concentrate on raising Talia to have the best life possible.

Towns and cities came and went. I drove until my eyes would hardly stay open. Roadside pull-offs offered a nap. A few towns offered hotels and restaurants for a decent night's sleep and a meal. Like I said, I'd offer more detail, but all I could think about was bringing Roz home.

A flat tire on the outskirts of Baton Rouge, Louisiana, almost startled me into an oncoming car. A Cajun meal of shrimp gumbo made me ask for the recipe. The waiter folded his arms and remarked, "Is you crazy, boy? Dat's a killin' offense 'round hee-ah."

And I thought Ellie's accent was amusing.

In Houston, Texas, two bowls of chili went down spicy but delicious. When I asked the waitress for the recipe, she winked and leaned near my ear to whisper, "Big man like you, I'll write it out if you come back to my place after my shift ends."

Needless to say, I declined her offer.

Then came McDade. I arrived at three in the morning, worn out to the soles of my feet. That's what driving over 1500 miles in two days will do for you—blurry eyes, aching back, hip bones feeling like they're poking through your behind. I parked in front of the post office, figuring someone there might know the Miller family, and lay on my side on the Chevrolet's bench seat to get some sleep. When I woke, I realized I stunk because I hadn't showered since I left home. I checked into a hotel, showered and changed clothes. By then I was ready for breakfast at a diner across the street.

It's amazing what a good meal will do for your attitude. I considered asking around for places to rent horses. Roz would think it hilarious if I showed up in the saddle to ride her away into the sunset.

Opting for my original plan, I entered the post office and approached the clerk, an old guy with a handlebar moustache, reading glasses perched on the end of his nose, and something I'd never seen, a bow tie. I thought the bow tie meant he'd be easy to get along with. I thought wrong. When I asked if he knew any Millers in the area, he angled his head upward and squinted at me through the glasses. "Yup," he said, like a genuine cowboy would say.

I was tempted to squint back, but didn't want to create a confrontation. "I'm looking for a Roz Miller. Can you tell me where she lives?"

He aimed an arthritic thumb, its base joint swollen, toward the west. "Out yonder. Won't do you any good to go. Word has it that she's off to Austin for a wedding dress."

Like on May 12, 1942, when a German U-boat sank the HMT *Bedfordshire* off of Ocracoke Island, my re-broken heart sank into the watery grave of my re-shattered soul. "Wedding dress?" I asked. "As in Roz is getting married?"

The clerk's moustache twitched. "Never seen you round these parts. What's yer business with Rosaline?"

I paused, trying to think of something to satisfy him. "I'm a cousin from Houston, come for a visit. That's all."

"Oh. She never mentioned any cousins. Well, most people got cousins." The clerk paused, eyes narrowed as if he were thinking hard. "You call her Roz?"

I nodded. "Yes, sir, I do"

The clerk's eyes returned to their relaxed squint. "Her pap, God rest his soul, called her Rose, so I can see how some might call her Roz. Christian name is Rosaline."

The more this information sank in, the more I was sure the woman getting married was Roz. I remembered her and Talia making a pinkie swear about her real name, so Rosaline must be it. I could call home and make sure, but I didn't see the need.

Back in the Chevrolet, I considered my choices. For one, since Roz had apparently made up with her boyfriend, I'd be an idiot to interfere. For two, her decision to marry him meant she didn't love me. For three, I cranked the Chevrolet, checked out of the hotel, filled the tank with gas, and pointed the hood east, toward Kitty Hawk.

Having left the pier and the rocking chairs to write, I lean back from the laptop on the kitchen table to read those last paragraphs. Satisfied, I make coffee and a tuna salad sandwich for supper, place both on a tray and return to the pier and my rocking chair.

Done with the sandwich, I sip the cooling coffee.

Throughout our lives, my wife and I did this very thing on many a darkening afternoon, as twilight settled over the sound and the noise of the day quieted. We especially liked the fall, when the cooling air nipped at our noses. We liked it even better in November, our breaths pluming, our coffee steaming, the sunset laying a scarlet ribbon far to the west, over the distant blur of the North Carolina mainland. We'd sip and hold hands. Sometimes we'd talk about our day. Sometimes we'd talk about phone calls from children and grandchildren. Sometimes, more often than not, words weren't necessary. Just the clasp of our hands, the warmth growing between them, was all we needed to share our love.

Time slips by. Wavelets kiss the pier pilings. The marsh whispers her name. September becomes October. October becomes November. I've turned seventy-nine, and can't remember if my family visited to celebrate. Or have I already written about me turning seventy-nine?

It's strange how some people live to be a hundred or more. They keep their right mind. They drive. They aren't forced into a nursing home from Alzheimer's. Then there's folks like my wife and myself. Cancer took her at age— Wait a minute. How old was she when I found her in the hospital bed at the foot of our bed, her chest as still as my leg that's gone to sleep?

How long will the years drag by for me? Liz is a great friend, but I'm not interested in romance. Jack is a great friend, but even fishing can get boring after a while. I don't want to be one of those people who live to be a hundred, or even ninety, and I sometimes hope I don't make it to eighty. Then I remember my family, so I take my meds and walk and do the things I need to do to keep my ragged old body going.

Thanksgiving comes. The house is filled with family. Talia and Sarah run everyone out of the kitchen. The aromas of their mom's recipes soon fill the air. Turkey with oyster stuffing. Glazed ham. Broiled flounder. Fried shrimp and oysters. Of course we have side dishes, but all of the above is what makes my mouth water as if my tongue is the beach and my spit is the tide.

Before I know it, after kisses and hugs goodbye, the house is empty again. I get out the laptop and take it to the kitchen table. The end is in sight, and I'm not sure how I feel about it.

Unlike when I drove to McDade, I took my time going home to Kitty Hawk. Knowing Dad, Talia, and Ellie would wonder how things were going with Roz—well, Rosaline—I called with cryptic messages that things went as I expected, and I was headed east. They were glad. They were happy. I was neither.

Yeah, things fell apart when I told them the truth. None of them could understand it, but they hoped Roz would be happy in her marriage.

A few days later, as Talia and I were watching cartoons from the sofa, she patted my hand and snuggled close. "It's okay, Daddy. You still got me."

I kissed the top of her head. "That's right, little cowgirl."

Giggling, she looked up at me. "Roz said I could tell you her real name. Do you want to know what it is?"

I'll admit that I hadn't asked because I hoped I was wrong about Roz getting married. At Talia's offer, an ember of hope kindled inside my shattered soul. "Sure, honey, what's Roz's real name?"

"Guess."

"Do I get a hint?"

"Horses."

Confused, I turned sideways on the sofa to face Talia. "How so?"

"Her name came from a horse. Her daddy gave it to her. She said it came from Germany."

Thank goodness for Dad. On one of our trips to see the horses after Mom left, he said our ancestors on his side of the family came from Germany, and his great-great grandmother was named Rosaline, which means "soft horse." No wonder Roz's dad had named her that, since she loved horses so much.

Unfortunately, the clarification of Roz to Rosaline confirmed her marriage, so I finally had to give up on her coming back.

That night, depressed over everything, I took a six pack of beer to my room and drank myself into a stupor. The next night, I stared at a fresh six pack from the grocery, and managed to leave it in the refrigerator. The night after that, I took it to my room. Over the next year, more often than not, the beer stayed in the fridge. I think that was because Talia started kindergarten, and my subconscious kept me sober for her.

The horse tours became monotonous. I did what I had to do to earn a living, both for me and for Talia, plus for her college savings. My success grew. I bought another Suburban and hired a driver. Sure, my bank account was bulging at the seams, but as we've often heard, money isn't the key to happiness.

1970 followed. Talia entered the first grade. Despite Dad's relationship with Helen, he refused to divorce Mom, so Helen moved near her family in Idaho. I couldn't understand his faith in a woman who had hurt us so deeply, and I didn't until July 4th weekend.

Both Suburbans were booked with tours that Saturday. Because of demand, much to Dad's dismay, I started working on Sunday. This left me little quality time with Talia, so I understood Dad's concern, including my not going to church.

Anyway, on my last tour of that Saturday, customers were paying me while boarding the Suburban, which, as usual, was parked with a full view of the Currituck Lighthouse's red brick form. The line ended. Three seats were left. From toward the lighthouse, a woman of about Dad's age, with a little girl who couldn't have been much more than a year old in her arms, came to the Suburban. "So, you're this Kitty Hawk cowboy I've been hearing so much about."

I touched the brim of my cowboy hat. "Yes, ma'am, that's me. Is anyone with you? I've got three seats left."

She gestured toward the lighthouse. "Someone else is coming. We were admiring that beautiful, old lighthouse." She peeked inside the Suburban. "Is it alright if my granddaughter sits in my lap? I imagine the beach can make for a rough ride."

I said that'd be fine. She paid me and climbed in. Along the same path the woman had just used, a much younger woman hurried toward me, and I was immediately struck by how much she resembled Roz.

There were some differences, though. Her hair was solid brunette instead of blond with brunette roots. It fell to just below her shoulders instead of ending in a ragged cut at the nape of her neck. Beyond those differences, she leaned toward medium sized instead of skinny like Roz. As she neared, the hem of a yellow sundress flaring about her calves, the splash of freckles on her nose, along with her brown eyes the color of chocolate, made my breath hitch in my throat. She wasn't some facsimile of Roz. Not only was this Rosaline, she and her husband had a daughter, and she was here with her mom.

If I look back through everything I've written, I bet I couldn't find the word "dumbfounded" more than a few times, and that's how I felt. Sure, I was glad she was happy and well, and she was definitely happy and well. In fact, she was glowing, and that glow made her stunning, at least in my eyes.

Mrs. Miller got out of the Suburban and returned the fee. "We've changed our mind, haven't we Rosaline?"

Nodding, Roz faced me. "Hey there, cowboy. Long time no see." She poked my stomach. "I see you put a little weight on."

She was right. That's what too much beer does for a guy.

Mrs. Miller placed her granddaughter in Roz's arms. "I'll

take a stroll while you two talk."

Anger and hurt boiled inside my chest. I knew I shouldn't have felt that way, but I couldn't help it. Despite that, I asked Roz how she was doing and if she'd finished college, polite talk to avoid blowing my stack.

Her daughter twisted her head around to watch Grandma walk toward the lighthouse. With brunette curls, a button nose, and a creamy complexion, I'm sure Roz looked just like her at that age. One pudgy hand gripped the left sleeve of the yellow sundress. The other hand gripped the right sleeve. Regret from not knowing Talia at this age tightened my throat. Sure, children at any age are a blessing, but there was something about this little girl's innocence that filled my soul with sweetness.

"Do you want to hold her?" Roz asked. "You can if you want." She placed her daughter in my arms. The delicate eyelashes fluttered. The fine brows formed a miniscule V. She patted my cheek with a pudgy hand, and Roz laughed. "Well durn. The first time her daddy held her, she threw up on him."

Good for her, I didn't say. I gave the little girl back. "I need to tend to my customers. I'm glad you're doing okay."

Roz touched my arm. "Can we get together later? I need to explain why—"

"No need," I said, cutting her off. "You're doing well. That's what matters."

When I turned to leave, she grabbed my arm. "Please, Seth. It's important."

More than anything, I wanted to pluck her hand from my arm, but something in her pleading expression made me think, *You idiot, the woman you love cares enough to want to explain why she left in the middle of the night. What's wrong with hearing what she has to say?*

I gently pulled away. "When and where?"

She pointed toward a shiny, two-door Cadillac, gold with a black vinyl top and chrome bumpers. "That's Mom's. A lawyer can afford a car like that. I'll pick you up at eight. Maybe Ellie can keep Talia."

Knowing my customers were getting tired of waiting, I agreed.

"Great," Roz said, beaming a smile. "See you at eight."

Needless to say, I kept my mouth shut during the tour. That saying about being mad enough to boil an egg on your forehead didn't cut it for me. I could've char-grilled a side of beef on my forehead in ten seconds flat.

I sit back from the laptop. Like I said, Roz, Rosaline, whatever, had roared into my life as a full blown category five hurricane. Worse than that, she'd turn into a category six that night.

After the tour, I was tempted to take Talia over to Ellie right away. Then I could get rip roaring drunk before Roz came. If I did that, my tongue would be loose enough to cuss a blue streak at her when she tried to explain how it was okay to rip my heart out and spit on it by coming here all happily married.

Yeah, it sounds like I've held a grudge all these years when I haven't. It's just that those memories are as real as if they'd just happened, even to the point of making me take a break from writing.

Christmas with my family was a repeat of Thanksgiving. This time, though, prime rib and oyster stew replaced the turkey and ham. My appetite had been off from writing the part about Roz wanting to talk to me, but it sure came back for Talia's prime rib and Sarah's oyster stew.

After the meal, when we all sprawled out in the living room, pretending to watch TV while our food settled, eyelids drooping sleepily, Talia and Sarah were at the table with my laptop. I didn't mind them reading the story. After all, to me, it was more for my family after I was gone than for me while I was still kicking around Kitty Hawk. I knew they'd sniffle during my wife's prologue. It made me ball like a durn baby.

James and Daniel, my sons-in-law, snore softly, each

leaning against the sofa's armrests with their heads back. Tom and Seth Jr., my sons, lie in the floor with everyone's kids and grandkids scattered about, reminding me of several hound dogs piled under Grandpa's porch. On the deck, Tom and Seth's wives, Lisa and Jennifer, both wearing coats for the December cold, are watching the sound.

As the old saying goes, life is good. As I say, it would be a lot better if we weren't missing my wife, their mom, their grandma, and their great-grandma.

I'm in the middle of the sofa, trying to keep from falling asleep, when Talia and Sarah come over to kiss my cheeks. "The first chapters are great , Dad," Talia says.

"Just perfect," Sarah says. "We can't wait until you finish it."

Their praise wakes everyone. Coats are donned. Leftovers are taken. I wave goodbye from the deck. They wave back.

And … of course … I'm alone again.

I don't fault them for their lives. Good parents raise good kids so they have good lives, jobs, and families of their own. Anyway, that's what my wife used to say, and I agree.

January, February, and March pass by. My birthday comes on a month I can't remember at the moment. I do remember how eighty, over two years of being without my wife, felt. It wasn't much different than I've felt before then unless, and this is entirely possible, I'm fooling myself.

June comes, the same month as when Roz, her mom, and her daughter arrived to turn my world upside down. Yeah, I know that's not much of a description of how it felt, and I can't think of a better one to describe what Roz told me that night either.

I'll wait until July to write again. This old lovesick fool needs to get his head on straight to finish this story.

Chapter 28

It's August first. After breakfast, my meds, and a morning walk while it was cool, I sit at the kitchen table and open the laptop, hopefully for the last time.

When I got home from my last tour after seeing Roz, I called Ellie about keeping Talia. She said sure, bring her over, which I did. At home again, I took a shower to wash a full day of June perspiration from my body, dressed in jeans and a T-shirt and made a peanut butter and jelly sandwich. After a hard week of work, Talia and I usually went out for supper on Saturday. If I could ditch Roz in time, I'd still do that, no doubt adding a few beers to my meal because Talia would eat with Ellie.

With my keys in my pocket, I went to the pier to wait. In 1970, things were changing on the Outer Banks. It was common knowledge that Andy Griffith was a character in the Lost Colony play in 1947. As the success of *The Andy Griffith Show*, which hit the airways in 1960, grew, he shared his time between Hollywood and Manteo. Then Don Knotts left the show in 1965, much to the dismay of many viewers, and Andy followed in 1968. One thing's for sure, Andy loved Manteo enough to live there much of the time. More evidence of this is how he was often seen at Basnight's Lone Cedar Restaurant on the Manteo causeway, as well as at Owen's Restaurant in Nags Head. Although my wife and I enjoyed eating at both restaurants, we never saw him there. It's probably a good thing. As much as I loved his show, I might've been tempted to tell him that, and it was common knowledge that he preferred his privacy. I understand. Being the old curmudgeon I am now, I prefer my privacy too.

Another change, of course, was the growth of tourism, evidenced by the increase in hotels and restaurants, not to mention boats on the sound. I didn't mind the soft putter of a fishing skiff passing, but I'd eventually mind the roaring whine of Jet Skis ruining my solitude.

I checked my watch. Roz was a few minutes late. With any luck, she wouldn't show up. No sooner than that thought entered my mind, the sound of a car engine came from the road in front of the house. The engine turned off. A car door slammed. Roz rounded the corner of the house and joined me on the pier, where she turned a circle. "I hope you didn't mind me borrowing your mom's red skirt, white sweater, and red sandals when I left."

Her matter of fact tone aggravated me. "After two years, I call it stealing."

"Did you miss them?"

"No."

"Then hush." She faced the sound. "I sure missed this view." Wavelets lapped against the pilings. Roz faced me. "Believe it or not, I missed you and Talia too."

I could believe she missed Talia. As far as me, since she was happily married, nope. "What did you want to talk about?"

"Not here," she said, leaving me.

Tempted to go inside and lock the door, I followed her to the Cadillac instead. Minutes later we were headed south on Highway 12. When we reached the intersection to continue south toward Oregon Inlet, or west toward Manteo, she continued toward Oregon Inlet. She said nothing, possibly because she knew I was upset, possibly because she was trying get her lies straight in her head, possibly because she knew I was on the verge of not caring.

We passed the Bodie Island Lighthouse to our right. Scrub pines and twisted live oaks led to marsh waving in the soft breeze. The day was dying. If I was lucky, my love for Roz would die also. A man can't take loving a woman who had acted like she wanted him before marrying someone else. Like a filleted flounder, it guts a fellow.

When we reached the top of the Bonner Bridge's arch, I figured she was taking me to the wreck of the *Oriental*, where we'd lain in each other's arms by a bonfire, and where I'd realized I'd fallen in love with her. No doubt about it, Roz's fillet knife was razor sharp and ready.

She parked at the same pull off and faced me. "I'm sure you're upset, and I don't blame you. I brought you here because our time together was the best of my life, and I ruined it when I left."

She got out. I didn't. The trunk popped open, then closed. She opened my door, a folded quilt across her arm. "Are you coming?"

Every time I look back at all the life-changing decisions I've made, this one is the most important. I could either stay in that Cadillac and not hear what she wanted to say, or I could face it and see what happened.

My regrets are few. Among them, losing my child because Mindy didn't see the value in him or her hurts the most. Yes, you'd think my biggest regret was losing Mom. I had no control over that, nor did I have any control over Mindy sleeping with me while I was stoned on marijuana. Let me put it this way: part of why losing my child is my biggest regret is because, being the father, I should've had some control over whether or not my child would live or die, and I had absolutely none.

The next biggest regret was Minh and Trang. I had no control over that situation either. Still, knowing they would likely die—if they weren't dead already at the hands of the North Vietnamese or the Viet Cong—would live inside my skull for the rest of my days, waking me with occasional nightmares that would have my wife comforting me by saying there was nothing I could've done.

Saying all that, I knew the list of my regrets would grow if I didn't hear Roz out.

I followed her up the sandy path. At the top of the dune, the salty breath of the Atlantic blew into our faces. She took her sandals off. I took my shoes off. Barefooted, we slid down the dune and onto the beach.

Roz's wavy brunette hair fluttered around her shoulders. As she started walking north, she fingered a loose curl behind her ear.

Toward the east, over the swells rising on the ocean, the sky was darkening. On the rise of sand above the surf, a flock of sanderlings scurried up and down, alternately chasing the blanket of white foam and running from it, their pencil thin beaks probing the wet sand like miniature jack hammers.

Roz squealed. I looked from the sanderlings in time to see her sidestepping a huge ghost crab, the red skirt flaring about her knees.

Despite my apprehension, I couldn't help smiling.

Yes, I loved her humor, but I also loved her appearance. Before, when she was as skinny as an unstuffed scarecrow, I hadn't been attracted to her very much. Now, the scarecrow had enough stuffing to fill out the skirt and sweater, and it was all I could do to not wonder how she'd look undressed. Tall and still slender, with just enough curves to make her feminine, she drew me like bait drew fish to a hook.

Up ahead, a pile of driftwood caught my attention. Roz spread the quilt and knelt to light the wood. I just stood there, fear and intrigue fighting within me, a battle of wills I'd never experienced.

The wood smoked. The flames grew. Roz tucked her feet beneath her. I felt like an idiot, so I sat cross legged a few feet away from her, afraid more of her than of the flames, sure I was about to get burned by her again.

The sky continued to darken. A single star glittered into view, followed by another and another. A larger than average wave crashed, its roiling white death a ghost in the night.

Roz shifted around to face me, the fire yellowing her profile. "I'm sorry I left like I did. You deserved better. Talia deserved better. I knew y'all cared about me, and I did it anyway, like the coward I was."

A stick of wood popped. Sparks flared. Roz watched them rise into the night sky until their light faded.

"I was really messed up, Seth. My boyfriend and my mom were telling me to do stuff I wasn't sure about. Well, I was sure about veterinary school because dad was a vet. That made my choices a lot harder."

The serious tone in her soft voice made me believe her. "What kind of choices?" I asked, hoping I sounded as sincere as she did.

She looked away for several seconds before returning to me. "One choice was the hardest. I left because I was still considering it, and you would've hated me for it."

She picked at a loose thread in the quilt, a sign of either fear, hesitation, or both. "I know about Mindy. Ellie told me."

Mindy was the last topic I wanted to discuss. "That tide has gone out to sea, Roz."

"Not all of it," she said, her voice just above a whisper. "I know about the abortion. I know it broke your heart. When Ellie told me, I knew you'd hate me. That's why I had to leave."

For ten beats of my heart, confusion filled my mind. Then clarity cleared it. "Wait a minute. You came here because you were pregnant, and needed time to think because you were considering an abortion?"

Roz nodded. "I'm not the least bit proud of it." She'd stopped nodding with her head down, her hair hiding her face. She raised it to me again. "On the way home, I kept thinking about you and Talia. You're a great dad, and you made me think my boyfriend could be a great dad if he had the chance."

"Right. So you—"

"That's not all," Roz interrupted. "I came out here to get away from him and Mom because they were aggravating me about the abortion. She said my education was more important. Since abortion is illegal, she said she had connections to help with it. My boyfriend said he didn't want a kid. He said I should use those connections. Like I said, I hoped I could change their minds. When I told Mom I was going to have the baby, she fussed and fumed and finally took it in stride. When my daughter was born, Mom cried and cried. I just knew she was disappointed in me. I told her I was sorry I let her down. She said she was sorry for telling me to get the abortion, because it would've been wrong to end the life of someone as precious as her granddaughter."

Roz fingered tears. "That made me hope my boyfriend would feel the same. He watched her in my arms in the hospital for a long time. Then he said he reckoned we better get married."

Roz's story pretty much verified what the post office clerk told me. "So," I said, shrugging, "things worked out. Your mom loves her granddaughter. Your marriage is great. What about veterinary school?"

"Mom's paying for daycare while I go to college. My degree so far isn't enough to be a vet, but I can be an assistant. I'm trying to decide if I should go back to college or go to work." Roz paused, picking at the quilt again.

I digested everything she'd said, and one question was left. "Okay, your life is great. Why did you come here? Since y'all didn't take the tour, it wasn't to see the horses."

Another piece of wood shifted in the fire, sending a shower of sparks skyward. Waves continued to crash. A breeze tousled Roz's hair as she raised her eyes to me. Here it came. She wanted me to forgive her for what she'd done to Talia and me. Then she could go back to Texas with a clear conscience and shove us out of her heart forever.

"Seth, I hurt you, and I'm sorry. Can you forgive me?" She reached for my hand. "I need to know, okay? It's the most important thing in my life to know how you feel about me and all of this mess."

I let her take my hand. She pressed it to her heart. My anger faded. If you love someone, you know when it's time to let them go. "I forgive you, Roz. All I've ever wanted is for you to be happy. If your husband does that, he's a lucky man."

She shook her head. The firelight illuminated tears filling her eyes. "You don't understand. Your love for Talia changed my life. Before I met you, I might've had the abortion. After I met you, I saw what the love of a good man is." With her other hand, she wiped tears. "I didn't get married because I knew it wouldn't work. When I told my boyfriend, he just shrugged and asked if he still had to pay child support. I said no. All I wanted was for him to give up his rights to our daughter. He couldn't sign the papers quick enough. After that, I attended college until I had the baby, and went back until I had my current degree. Then I asked Mom to come here." Roz smiled, teeth gleaming in the firelight. "She was like, 'it's about time you suggested it. All I hear is Seth this, Talia that. I've got to meet the man who made such a difference in my daughter's life, and in my life.'"

While Roz told me all of that, I'd been taking it in, trying to figure out why she was here. After all, she could've called instead of coming all the way from Texas. Then the proverbial lightbulb went off over my head.

"Wait a minute," I said, daring to hope my guess was right. "You didn't get married. Now you and your Mom came all the way here because you say Talia and I changed your lives. "Does that mean what I think it means?"

Nodding, Roz raised my hand to her lips, kissed my knuckles and lowered it. "It does. I love you, Seth. I haven't stopped thinking about you for a single minute since I left. No matter where I was or what I was doing, I couldn't wait to get back and tell you." She kissed my knuckles again, and pressed my hand to her heart. "Unless I miss my guess, cowboy, you love me too, right?"

Forgive an old man for crying at such an important part in this story. I take my fingertips from the laptop keys and snatch a handful of tissues from the box on the table, where I'd put it because I knew I'd need them. It takes two more handfuls before I stop sobbing enough to dry my eyes.

Ever since I started writing this story, I've thought long and hard about how I'd describe my feelings when Roz said she loved me, and no words—not a single one—will do them justice.

What I can write is this, and I'm now adding it to the Word document.

Roz and I spent most of our lives searching for the one person who would love us like we loved each other, and we never would've found each other if not for our daughters, who were never planned for by their parents.

In case you haven't figured it out, Roz's daughter—now my adopted daughter—is named Sarah.

Another thing you might not have figured out, because there aren't enough hints in our story, is our first son's name is Seth Jr., and our second son's name is Tom, named after Dad.

If you really need a description of how happy I was when Roz said she loved me, I jumped up from the quilt, stripped down to my boxers, and ran toward the Atlantic, yelling as loud as I could, "She loves me, Dad! She really loves me!"

Running after me and laughing, Roz caught up before I reached the surf. "Are you crazy, cowboy? You can't go swimming in March."

I grabbed her for a kiss. "I'm only crazy for you, cowgirl," and dove into the frigid water.

Sure, I was happy, but I needed that cold water to keep me from wanting to start a family right then and there instead of waiting for our honeymoon.

Hey, I never claimed to be perfect, just human.

Here are some details you'd like to know.

After that night, Roz admitted to using that name after her Dad died. You see, he called her Rosaline for serious times, but mostly he called her Rose, and she couldn't stand her boyfriend calling her Rose. By the way, her mom hated the name Roz. I don't blame her. I love Rose a lot better myself. As you might guess, our lives — like our love — bloomed.

Mrs. Miller surprised me twice. The first, which came after Rose and I shared the news of our coming wedding, was to kiss my cheek, demand I call her Mom, and jokingly add how she'd sue my pants off if I hurt her daughter. The second was to buy a place on Manteo so she could be near Rose, Sarah, and her new extended family.

Talia, of course, wasn't a surprise. To borrow two words from Jane Austen's *Pride and Prejudice*, she was "incandescently happy," especially because she was getting a little sister.

Dad and Ellie were so happy that they immediately planned a cookout for the next afternoon. After the meal of seafood, both broiled and fried, and all the fixings, he congratulated the bride and groom to be, adding, "I happen to know the pastor of a fine church on Manteo. I'm sure he would be interested in performing the ceremony."

Beside me on the deck, holding my hand, Rose raised a single eyebrow at me before facing Dad. "That's a good idea, Tom, except I want a wedding on the beach." She squeezed my hand. "And Seth and I know the perfect spot."

That's how, on the following Saturday morning, just after sunrise, Rose and I and all of our loved ones met not far from the ashes of a very certain, very specific bonfire, within sight of the wreck of the *Oriental*.

She wore a flowing white gown and a matching veil. I wore a white shirt with the tail out and dark slacks. During our kiss, after I'd draped the veil down her back, the breeze billowed both it and her gown, and I took it as a blessing from Mom, wherever she was.

Life wasn't only good, it was great. I'd come to terms with my past. Now it was time for a future with Rose and our two daughters.

I sit back in the chair. I have more to write, but I need a break.

I ease down the steps from the deck to the yard and amble my tired self to my rocking chair on the pier. With my right hand on the arm of Rose's chair, I watch the sound and listen to the waves whispering in the marsh.

Our kids spent many happy years here. While Rose and I were younger, we swam and water skied with them. When we grew older, we still swam, but we traded water skiing for fishing. Driftwood fires near the pier roasted hot dogs and marshmallows. Hurricanes came and went, but the house, huge and rambling now from the extra rooms built for our family, never failed us. Arguments were few. Hugs were many. High school graduations ended and college started. Marriages began. Grandchildren came. Rose and I were truly blessed.

Dad adored his grandchildren and great-grandchildren. Mrs. Miller—Mom, I mean—did too. As they aged, they became good friends. Whether they were ever more than friends, Rose and I didn't ask. We were happy that they were happy. What more can a person hope for?

I face the chair beside mine, and imagine Rose smiling at me. "Well, cowboy, you've almost finished your story, haven't you? I've been watching over your shoulder. I was hoping for a spicy sex scene or two from our honeymoon. You did the right thing, though, leaving them out. Anyone who reads your story might get embarrassed at how we drove down to the wreck of the *Oriental* each night after supper, spreading a quilt and spending the night there for an entire week, while Mom,

Ellie, and Tom took turns keeping Talia and Sarah."

It might sound a little conceited, but Rose and I considered ourselves to be the perfect couple. The most important reason for this was how we always admitted when we were wrong. Regardless of that fact, in the case of calling my story my story, she refused to agree that it was our story because her life wasn't as varied as mine. With trips to Israel and South Vietnam under my belt, including all the category five women in my life, she had a point.

Dad, bless his sweet heart, passed away in his sleep at the age of eighty-four, just a few months shy of his eighty-fifth birthday. Mrs. Miller had already left us a few years before.

When Rose and I were going through their things, we recognized a pair of Dad's pajamas at her mom's house, and one of her mom's nightgowns at his house, solving the mystery of if they were more than friends. We grinned like maniacs, before we laughed like lunatics, before we cried at how they found love in their later years.

After reading that last paragraph, Jack might say, "See there, Seth, you might live as long as your old man. Why not see if you can leave your PJs at Liz's and see if Liz can leave her nighty at your place? It's worth a shot, right?"

"No, Jack," I'd have to tell him. "When you find your soulmate like I found mine, casual sex just isn't worth the effort."

I take my hand from the arm of Rose's chair, shuffle to the end of the pier, and look into the gray depths of the sound. The ends of my shoes hang off the edges of the gray boards. How easy it would be to shift my weight and fall in. I can't do it, though. When I join her in Heaven, she'd waggle a finger at me and say, "Now, Seth Callahan, you know better than that. I wanted you to write your story to ease the pain of losing me, not to make you drown your silly self." Then, like Jack, she'll point toward Liz's house. "Git your behind in there to Liz. She can comfort you like my mom comforted your dad. Is that clear to your hardheaded cowboy self?"

In all honesty, I'd rather find comfort in the memories of mine and Rose's lives together than in the arms of another woman, so there's only one thing to do.

Like in my youth, when I fished from my skiff, I place my right foot behind me and open my hands wide. In my fingers, their knuckles swollen with arthritis, I grip a throw net. With as much strength as my old body can muster, I snap my hips around and sling the net toward the sound. It opens into a large circle. The weights lining the edges splash. I let them touch bottom before I pull the line to close the circle and bring the net in.

You're wondering if I caught mine and Rose's memories of nearly fifty-five years together, aren't you? Well, this old man is about to bust with happiness at the answer.

I go inside and finish writing my story. Then I go back to my rocking chair and rest my hand on the arm of Rose's chair. The sun will set soon, and I can't wait to see it.

One more thing before I go. Like I told Rose whenever she called me her hero, "Life is full of heroes, but the best heroes save each other."

Thank you, cowgirl, for coming back to me so long ago. As you well know, you were my hero just as much as I was yours.

Chapter 29

I don't know how to say this, so I'll just say it. This is Talia. Sarah and I— Hold on while I get something to wipe my eyes.

This is Sarah. Talia's looking for another box of tissues. I just emptied the box on the kitchen table at Dad's house. We're finishing his story that Mom wanted him to write so badly. Okay, Talia's back.

Whew, I'm a mess. Well, everyone, we wanted to make sure we wrote what happened so you'd believe it. To tell the truth, Sarah and I are having a hard time believing it ourselves, even though we have proof from Liz and Jack.

To start with, we've been up all night, reading Dad's story, hoping we'd get a clue as to what happened. To end with, Liz and Jack called me yesterday morning. Then I called Sarah, and we got here as quick as we could. Yes, y'all know Dad passed away yesterday because we left you texts and emails, but you don't know how he died and where.

This is Sarah again. Talia had to go to the deck to get some air. By the time we got here, the Dare County Coroner's Office had picked Dad up. Lucky for us, Liz had taken a picture of Dad before they took him away.

Okay, Talia's back. I better get some air myself.

Yes, this is Talia again. When Liz woke yesterday morning, she saw Dad in his rocking chair on the pier. She thought it was strange because she saw him there yesterday, right before sunset. An hour later he was still there. Thinking he'd gotten up early to enjoy the view and had fallen asleep, she took a picture of him with her phone to tease him with. When she touched his hand to wake him, it was ice cold. She called 911, and ran for Jack and his wife. When they came, Jack called Sarah and me.

The picture is hard to explain, but after reading Dad's story, Sarah and I have what we think is a reasonable explanation. Sure, farfetched but reasonable, considering how much Mom and Dad loved each other.

"Ouch!" Sarah just smacked my hand. "What'd you do that for?"

"Move over so I can tell you. It's not how much Mom and Dad loved each other. It's how much they love each other. They're in Heaven, and that rose proves it. Now git back over here and type."

Talia again. Don't you love it when Mom's Texas accent spills over into Sarah's North Carolina accent, like with that "git?" She's slapping my arm again and telling me to type. I better get on with it.

Oh, I forgot something important. Liz said yesterday, before she saw Dad in his rocking chair, he was out on the end of the pier, swinging his arms like he was throwing an imaginary net. After he pulled it in, he was smiling big enough for her to see from her kitchen window. Then he went inside for a few minutes and came back out, to sit in his rocking chair and put his hand on the arm of Mom's rocking chair.

I know the part about throwing the net sounds strange, but something even stranger is coming.

When Liz took the photo, Dad's right hand was on the arm of Mom's chair, and his other hand was in his lap. When she looked at the photo, both of his hands were in his lap, and he was holding a fresh rose cupped in his palms. It startled her so badly that she dropped her phone in the sand. After she brushed it off, she looked at Dad, and he still held that fresh rose in his hands.

Sarah and I don't know what everyone will think of Liz's story about the rose, but she, Jack, Jack's wife, and Sarah and I think it's a sign that Mom and Dad are together again. In fact, Liz took the rose before the coroner's office took Dad, and it's now in a vase, right here on the kitchen table.

Now, let's discuss why the coroner came after the EMTs verified his death.

Although Dad was eighty, he was in good health. He took his meds, walked regularly, and saw his doctor on time every time. Since that's the case, his death was unexpected, so the coroner wants to verify the cause. Sarah and I think it's ridiculous, and we've already called the coroner to tell him to leave Dad alone, for the simple reason that we think Dad willed himself to be with Mom.

We hope y'all believe it too, because we don't know of any other explanation. After all, when Dad spread Mom's ashes at the end of the pier, he also dropped a single, huge, long-stemmed red rose in the water after, and it's exactly like the rose he was holding in the photo Liz took.

Yes, it's hard to believe he threw an imaginary net and caught a rose that lay with Mom's ashes for more than two years—a rose that hadn't aged one bit, much less moved with the tides or storms—especially after the rose didn't appear until Liz took the photo.

Well, as the saying goes, it is what it is, and what's important is Dad and Mom are together again.

Sarah wants to add something. I'll give her the laptop.

Sarah here. I'm so glad Mom got Dad to write this story. Over the years he's mentioned the Kitty Hawk of his past—walking with Ellie as kids along sandy trails through live oak woods to the Up the Road school, attending the methodist church in the area called Down the Road, visiting the general store for the mail and the latest news, various hurricanes that ravaged the Outer Banks, including the powerful nor'easter of 1962, known as the Ash Wednesday Storm. Those things are parts of his past I'll always treasure, things that will never, ever, as long as the Outer Banks exists, return.

Talia here again. Y'all know about Dad's horse tour business and how successful it was. Mom did consider going back to college to become a veterinarian. Dad was all for it. Instead, she believed her true calling was to raise her family, so she could instill the same ideals in them as those she and Dad valued.

When Dad sold his business and retired in the spring of 2011, he and Mom celebrated with a trip to Israel to visit Alma's grave. Of course I joined them. Although the memories of my birth mom were hazy, I thanked her for having me, touching my fingertips to her headstone while I did. I then did the same thing at the headstones of Aunt Lia, Grandma Rachel, and Grandpa Morris.

On a sadder note, while we were there, Hamas attacked Israel several times. One such attack was even carried out on a school bus, when a Hamas terrorist fired an anti-tank missile into it, injuring the driver and killing a young boy. Following that attack, Hamas continued firing rockets into Israel.

That night, after the attacks ended, I tried to imagine Mom, Lia, and Grandma out for a fun day of shopping in Tel Aviv, only to have it end when a bomb exploded near them. As soon as the screams and blood and the wailing of sirens become real, I open my eyes to end that horrible scene. They're at peace now, so I'll choose to be at peace myself. I just pray for the Palestinians and the Israelis to eventually be brave enough to choose peace for the future instead of hatred for the past, or the deaths on both sides will continue.

Okay, enough of that. It's time to finish Dad's story.

I want to say how proud his family is of him for his service in Vietnam. Like with choosing to raise me as a single dad, he chose to support the country he loved. Like him, I wonder if

Minh and Trang survived. Also like him, I doubt if they did.

What else is there to say about a man who means so much to so many? Maybe Sarah and I will wait until after the funeral to finish his story. We found the paperwork for his pre-planned service, along with his instructions to us for the gathering of family and friends. No doubt, as he used to say, "It'll be a hoot."

Chapter 30

This is Talia again.

It's a week later on a Saturday afternoon at five o'clock. The late August sun is beaming down. Dad's family is gathered along the pier. We're fairly comfortable because he said we could wear casual clothes instead of dressy. Friends trail out into the yard. Many wear shorts. Some wear slacks. Some wear dresses and skirts. A very few wear shoes. In the yard below the deck, a caterer is cooking fried and broiled seafood. Tossed salad, coleslaw, and fries are the sides. Iced tea with lemon is the beverage. Homemade strawberry ice cream is the dessert.

The minister of the methodist church in Manteo stands with us. I'm holding Dad's urn. Sarah holds two roses. I nod at the minister to start the brief service. Its theme is to treasure two very special things—life and love.

"Without the lives of Talia and Sarah," the minister says after a few opening lines, "love might not have found Seth and Rose," and everyone nods in agreement.

He continues with humorous stories about Dad growing up in Kitty Hawk when so few people lived here, how Grandpa Tom named Dad's business The Kitty Hawk Cowboy, and of his walks to the Down the Road school with Ellie. At Dad's suggestion, the minister doesn't mention Lucille, Tom's wife and Dad's mom. Dad and Grandpa forgave her a long time ago, so it's best to let old wounds stay healed.

After the minister offers a final prayer, Sarah and I step to the end of the pier. Despite Dad's wish for a celebration instead of a somber occasion, several sobs come from the crowd.

I kneel, remove the lid from the urn, and gently pour Dad's ashes into the water. Sarah kneels beside me, and gives me one of the roses. We kiss them, tell Mom and Dad thank you for everything, add that we love them, and drop the roses into the water.

I stand with the lidded urn. Sarah stands and we hug. We aren't sisters by blood, but we're sisters in every way that counts, especially since we could just as easily not be here if our moms had made different decisions.

We release each other and take in our family—brothers, husbands, children, grandchildren, all joined by the common thread of life, as well as love for each other, and from Mom and Dad. I can't imagine our families not being here, and I don't care to try.

Ellie, a lovely woman with a cane and white hair, comes to us with hesitant steps. She lost Jeff a few years ago. J.J. and his family couldn't make it. Her daughter, Alison, born when J.J. was five, has an arm looped around one of Ellie's arms to help her. Tears fill Ellie's eyes. We hug. Sarah and I thank her for being friends with Dad all those years ago. Ellie says her childhood in Kitty Hawk was all the better because of Dad.

Jack and his wife, Louise, come over. He's wiping his eyes with a handkerchief. In honor of Dad, a Jennette's Pier ballcap is perched on his head. He shoves the handkerchief in his short's pocket and manages a smile. "You know, Talia, I loved that old fart. I never told him, and I hope he knows it."

"We both did," Louise says. "We sure will miss him."

Behind Jack, waiting in the growing line, Liz pokes his shoulder. "Seth was a sweetheart, Jack. The only old fart in this neighborhood is you." While Jack grins, Louise and Liz laugh.

When Liz and I hug, she bursts out crying. Sarah and I take turns comforting her, adding how much we appreciate her being such a fine companion to Dad. We also promise to print copies of The Kitty Hawk Cowboy for her and Jack.

Waiting in line, my family greets more guests who've come to remember Mom and Dad. I wonder if Mindy ever regretted her decision to end the lives of not one, but two babies, when something as simple as a condom would've prevented their conception. Still, since she did marry and have a family, I like to believe she came to terms with her choices, because love can have that effect on a person. As a doctor, though, I know some abortions are medically necessary. As a woman, though, I try to put myself in her place. As a daughter, a sister, a mother, and a grandmother, though, I have a hard time doing that. After all, Sarah and I might not have been spared in this day and time, and we wouldn't have seen our family tree bloom like the rose Dad's imaginary net caught before he left us.

The line dwindles. The minister says the blessing. Supper is served. The crowd eats at several tables we rented for the day.

When Sarah and I finish, we stroll arm in arm to the end of the pier. Mom and Dad's rocking chairs were moved for the service. We'll make sure they're returned later.

Sarah heaves a huge sigh. "Dad did a good job planning this. Everything was perfect."

"How about the rose he caught?" I ask. "Do we leave it in the vase on the kitchen table to see how long it lives?"

"I don't know," Sarah says, offering a slight smile. "We're in our sixties, so we might not live that long."

Our childhood seats us on the edge of the pier. We hang our bare feet off and swing them back and forth, a ritual passed on to our families like Mom and Dad passed it on to us.

The sky above us is darkening. Like dad wrote, the sunset is laying a scarlet ribbon far to the west, over the distant blur of the North Carolina mainland. The sound reflects it back at us.

Dad left his four kids the house. When Sarah and I asked if it should be sold, we were immediately greeted with a chorus of, "Are you kidding? Where will everyone go for Thanksgiving and Christmas and vacations?"

Sarah then suggested that she and I and our husbands, since we'll retire soon, live here, where we would welcome everyone anytime they wanted. As anyone can imagine, the suggestion passed with a hearty approval.

Behind us, the crowd is breaking up. Families and neighbors are going home, hopefully with treasured memories of Mom and Dad to bring them a laugh and a smile when they're needed.

The fading red ribbon transforms to deep purple, leaving the yellow glow of the sun beneath the horizon. Along the edges of the pier, the LED lights Dad installed a few years ago come on. A breeze ripples the water beneath mine and Sarah's feet, and she pats my hand in my lap. "I wonder if they can see us down here?"

I bump her shoulder with mine. "If they can, they're happy that we're happy."

"Exactly," my sister says, nodding.

As if Mom and Dad agree with our conversation, the two roses we dropped into the water earlier, which slowly sank to the bottom, rise slowly to the top. They float there for a moment, two blooms to remind us of how life, like love, is a miracle, never to be taken for granted.

Then, as Sarah and I smile at Mom and Dad's final message to us, their miracles, the roses slowly sink once more.

About the Author

J. Willis Sanders lives in southern Virginia, with his wife and several stringed, musical instruments.

With over twenty books completed and more on the way, he enjoys crafting intriguing characters with equally intriguing conflicts to overcome.

His first idea for a novel, The Coincidence of Hope, is a ghostly World War II era historical that takes place mostly in the Midwestern United States, which utilizes some little-known facts about German POW camps there at the time. It's the first of a three-book series, in which characters from the first continue their lives.

Although he loves history, he has written several contemporary novels as well, and some include interesting paranormal twists, both with and without religious themes.

He also loves the Outer Banks of North Carolina, and he has written several novels within different time frames based on the area, what he calls his Outer Banks of North Carolina Series.

For his Amish novels, some, such as his Amish Holiday Series, have inspirational messages, while some, such as the Eliza Gray and Clara Engelman Series, tend toward romance.

For another inspirational novel, readers may enjoy The Essence of Emmaline Strong. In it, the main character, an accomplished musician on the same instruments as the author, must struggle to regain her faith after a series of personal tragedies.

Other hobbies include reading (of course), vegetable gardening, playing music with friends, and songwriting, some of which are in a few of his novels.

To follow his work, search the internet with "J. Willis Sanders" on Amazon and Facebook. To visit his website, search with "J. Willis Sanders Wix."

Readers: to help those considering a purchase, please leave a review on Amazon.com, Goodreads.com, or wherever you bought this book.
They help authors more than you may realize.

www.ingramcontent.com/pod-product-compliance
Lightning Source LLC
Chambersburg PA
CBHW060647190726

48289CB00002B/309